Books by John C. Tibbetts
The Furies of Marjorie Bowen
The Gothic Imagination
The Gothic Worlds of Peter Straub
Schumann: A Chorus of Voices
Peter Weir: Interviews
The American Theatrical Film
Dvorak in America
Composers in the Movies
All My Loving: The Films of Tony Palmer
Those Who Made It
Introduction to the Photoplay

with James M. Welsh
The Cinema of Tony Richardson
Douglas Fairbanks and the American Century
The Encyclopedia of Novels into Film
The Encyclopedia of Stage Plays into Film

with William A. Everett and Michael Saffle
Performing Music History

The Devil Snar'd

Novels, Appreciations, and Appendices

Illustration for the novel "Five Winds."

MARJORIE BOWEN

The Devil Snar'd
Novels, Appreciations, and Appendices

Selected and Edited by John C. Tibbetts

Hippocampus Press

New York

Contents

This book is gratefully dedicated to Sharon Eden without whose stewardship of the Estate of Gabrielle Long (Marjorie Bowen) this book would not have been possible.

Young Marjorie Bowen

Introduction:
"Ill-Suppressed Furies and
Half-Hidden Fears"

"You, signor, have contrived to draw the starry veil, the rosy canopy,
so completely over your own existence that your life is entirely artificial, would you not sometimes care to see things in the common
light of truth?"

—Marjorie Bowen[1]

Celebrated in her lifetime, but clouded in relative obscurity since
her death in 1952, Marjorie Bowen has at least never lacked for
the admiration of littérateurs, past and present. Noted scholar
and anthologist Edward Wagenknecht has called her "a literary
phenomenon" whose talent "remains dazzling" and whose work
recalls, by turns, Virginia Woolf, E. T. A. Hoffmann, and
Franz Kafka: "Many writers have surpassed her in this area or
that, but who else ever did so many different things so well?
. . . and she had few equals and no superiors as a creator of atmosphere."[2] Jessica Amanda Salmonson, herself an acclaimed
author and editor of fantasy and the supernatural, has argued: "I
declare her supernatural romances not merely among the best
ever composed, but more than that, they deliver evidence that
even at our lowest and meanest, there is something of merit and

---

1. "A Trip to Verona," *Bagatelle* (New York: Dodd, Mead, 1931), 282.
2. Edward Wagenknecht, "Marjorie Bowen," in *Seven Masters of Supernatural Fiction* (Westport, CT: Greenwood Press, 1991), 180.

beauty in the transience and suffering of human existence."[3] S. T. Joshi, a noted historian of the weird tale, applauds her "fusion of the historical tale and the supernatural."[4] And in his recent assessment of weird fiction by women, including Elizabeth Gaskell, Vernon Lee, and Edith Wharton, Pulitzer Prize–winning critic Michael Dirda declares Bowen the finest British woman writer of the uncanny of the last century.[5]

While a measure of fame has at least managed to cling to Bowen's weird short stories over the years—a selection of which appears in my previous compilation, *The Grey Chamber* (Hippocampus Press, 2022)—this volume contains representations from a vast body of work that has yet to receive its proper measure: the novels. The pageant of history was Bowen's great subject. Historical settings and characters, from the Middle Ages to the Victorian era, provided not just the backdrop but the color and dramatic intensity of most of her novels, as they did in her short stories, biographies, and social commentaries. Although she began her career (and celebrity) as a historical romancer with *The Viper of Milan* in 1916, quickly followed by a succession of books about her favorite historical figure, William of Orange (see the excerpts included in these pages), she went on to a second career, as it were, with many book-length fictions that displayed her mastery of the Tale of Terror, while investing them with their own historical backdrops.

Included in this volume are excerpts from several of the novels. Here we find the fine pagan frenzy of the forces that over-

---

3. Jessica Amanda Salmonson, ed., *Twilight* (Ashcroft, BC: Ash-Tree Press, 1998), xix.

4 S. T. Joshi, *Unutterable Horror: A History of Supernatural Fiction* (2012; New York: Hippocampus Press, 2014), 2.431.

5 Michael Dirda, "Ghostly Women," *Weekly Standard* (6 March 2017): 38–41.

whelm the monastery in *The Haunted Vintage;* the gruesome details of the ritual horrors that the Comte de St. Germain unleashes in his séances in *The Courtly Charlatan;* the presumption to the papal throne by the Antichrist in *Black Magic;* the ghostly possession of a family lineage in *"Five Winds";* the heartbreaking chronicle of the slave uprisings in nineteenth-century Jamaica in *The Golden Violet;* the sinister conspiracies of the cabal of female poisoners that seeks to topple the Court of Louis XIV in *The Poisoners;* the stark, pungent melodrama of warring city-states in *The Viper of Milan;* the swashbuckling exploits of her favorite historical character, William of Orange. Standing apart from the above is her autobiographical novel, *Stinging Nettles,* an account of the horrors she endured during the last days of her confinement with her terminally ill husband in Italy during the Great War.

Of special interest in this volume is the inclusion of Bowen's short novel *The Devil Snar'd,* published in 1932 under her pseudonym of "George R. Preedy." Long out of print and very scarce, it is a grim tale of haunted houses, a haunted book, and a possessed writer (Bowen herself?). It deserves the wider audience it has been denied all these years.

Also included are a number of appreciations of Bowen by associates, friends, and family members, which provide both professional and intimate views of the writer. These include Graham Greene, who remembers the decisive influence Bowen's early work had on his determination to become a writer; Rebecca West, who shares her sympathies with Bowen's private struggles; Edward Wagenknecht, who remembers his friendship with her and his own efforts to promote her work in America; novelist Sally Benson, who writes of the work of the pseudonymous "Joseph Shearing"; Lieutenant-General F. de Bas, who praises Bowen's expertise in her military histories; novelist Michael Sadleir, who examines Bowen's "Tales of Terror"; and Hilary Long, who shares loving memories of a son about his mother.

Finally, there are three appendices. The first documents the letters (1938–52) between Marjorie Bowen, family members, and her American editors, Edward Wagenknecht of Boston University and August Derleth of Arkham House. The second examines the literary and biographical links between Bowen and Mary Shelley. And the third is a bibliographical checklist.

Through the many years that I have immersed myself in the life and work of this remarkable writer, I have come to feel rather like a ghost myself, haunting the House of Bowen. I imagine it is a fine, rambling eighteenth-century mansion, rearing up against a clouded moon. Rain falls on the crumbling stone. Over the door is the sign of Scorpio. The windows disclose a riot of writhing midnight plants and noxiously blooming flowers. The walls are hung with medieval tapestries, maps of military campaigns, and ancient portraits of laughing cavaliers and frowning queens. Many rooms are filled with curiosities: here is a complement of armor and swords; there, a library of ancient sorceries; and behind another door, an altar to a misshapen pagan god. Flickering lights and sulfurous fumes emanate from a small laboratory hidden under the stairs. And down in the cellar footsteps shuffle and drag. But the stairway is treacherous, and what lurks at the bottom is a mystery I dread to know.

Finally, I make no apology for the enthusiasm, respect, and affection I have come to feel for the tumultuous life, indomitable character, and incredibly varied body of work of this remarkable woman. She matches the estimation that Michael Dirda once wrote about a contemporary of Bowen, Arthur Machen: If not an "important writer, here is someone who is even better—a

writer who inspires deep affection and devotion" in her readers.[6]
At the same time, I am fully aware of the warning G. K. Chesterton issues to enthusiasts like me: "The moment we begin to believe a thing ourselves, that moment we begin easily to overstate it; and the moment our souls become serious, our words become a little wild."[7] Forgive me, then, for my own enthusiasms; you are invited to test them against your own.

Sharon and Mike Eden, of the Gabrielle Long (Marjorie Bowen) Estate

6. Michael Dirda, "Rending the Veil," *New York Review of Books* (28 May 2020): 43.

7. G. K. Chesterton, *Charles Dickens: A Critical Study* (New York: Dodd Mead), 19.

ACKNOWLEDGMENTS

Above all, I wish to thank Sharon Eden and the Estate of Gabrielle Long for permissions to quote from the many writings cited in this book. Ms. Eden has been a constant resource, always responsive to my many questions and unfailingly generous in sharing materials and enthusiasms. This association has proven to be an exceptionally happy experiences in preparing this book. My thanks also to S. T. Joshi, Derrick Hussey, Jordan Smith, and David E. Schultz of Hippocampus Press for their support and guidance. And my appreciation to Moira Fitzgerald of the Beinecke Rare Book and Manuscript Library at Yale University for access to the Marjorie Bowen Papers; Alex Rankin of the Mugar Library at Boston University for access to the correspondence between Gabriel Long (Marjorie Bowen) and Edward Wagenknecht; and Lee Grady of the Wisconsin Historical Society for access to letters from Marjorie Bowen to August Derleth. Thanks to Nicholas Diak and Michelle Brittany, who invited me to speak about Marjorie Bowen at the Ann Radcliffe Academic Conference, held in Providence, Rhode Island, as part of the 2018 StokerCon. My gratitude goes also to Jessica Amanda Salmonson, who shared with me her views on Bowen. Many friends and colleagues who have read and commented on portions of the manuscript, include Michael Dirda, T. E. D. Klein, Jon Lellenberg, Sunni Brock, William F. Nolan, Caleb Carr, Harry Haskell, Dan Nastali, and Professors Baerbel Goebel-Stolz, Rodney Hill, Brian Faucette, Joshua Wille. My colleagues in the Department of Film and Media Studies at the University of Kansas have been very supportive, and I want to acknowledge my Chair in the Department of Film and Media Studies, Professor Michael Baskett, and Professors Matt Jacobson, Kevin Willmott (congratulations on your Oscar!), Catherine Preston, Brian Faucette, Josh and Stephanie Wille. My Department Executive

Secretary, Karla Conrad, and University Administrative Assistant, Ms. Pam LeRow ably assisted me in the preparation and formatting of the manuscript. I hope I have not exhausted the patience of personal friends who gave of their time to read portions of the manuscript, including Professors Baerbel Goebel Stolz of Coventry University and Cindy Miller of Emerson College. And, of course, my love and thanks to the Muse and Enchanter of my life, Mary Lou Pagano, whose wise counsel, patience, and encouragement have seen me through more than a few doubts, hesitations, and obstacles encountered along the way

All that said, any errors in the book are mine alone.

John C. Tibbetts at the Mugar Library, Boston University

Nightcap and Plume *(1945), a dramatization of the life of King Gustav III of Sweden, is among her most colorful and rigorously researched historical novels.*

Prologue

It may be protested that these characters and their stories are to the last degree artificial, mere puppets adorned with tinsel; but to those who understand them they have the essence of accomplished, successful humanity, disappointed (as always) in its final achievement. They are worldlings defying their own negation; they are creatures who pile up games and trifles at higher cost with fiercer greed, the more they realize their own futility; the men taste the brittleness of success, the women the limits of beauty; all, men and women, pursue each other in vain hoping to clasp the long-lost, the perfect lover, and always embrace delusion. They desperately carry the elements of carnival, music, players, clowns, dwarfs, fine clothes and furniture. They discuss philosophy (that cloudy disguise of lack of faith), they bandy terms, but they believe in nothing save their own secret and endless disappointment. The writer who has evoked them despairs of rendering them as they appear to his "inner eye," but has not lacked earnestness in the attempt.

—*Bagatelle*

Marjorie Bowen

21

Part One: Selections from the Novels

"I thought that their spirits were about me like pictures depicted in primary colours, and the thought that they had once lived was enough to fill me with subdued satisfaction."

—Marjorie Bowen

Marjorie Bowen was best known in her lifetime as, in the estimation of her contemporary, the novelist Hugh Walpole, "the greatest historical novelist England has produced in a generation."[1] Her breakout success, *The Viper of Milan,* a sensational melodrama of feudal Italy, was written in her teens and launched a succession of dramatic studies and biographies of historical figures such as Oliver Cromwell, John Wesley, William of Orange, King Gustav II of Sweden, Charlotte Corday, William Hogarth, and Mary Queen of Scots, as well as broader subjects such as witchcraft in the Elizabethan age, the plague in Restoration England, and the rise of religious sects in the nineteenth century. Even the series of her "true-crime" novels were richly detailed reconstructions of the periods and contexts involved. Respected by her peers, she was an invited member of the respected Royal Society of Literature, the Royal Historical Society, and a Diplomée and Honorary Fellow of kindred societies in the Netherlands.

---

1. Quoted in Edward Wagenknecht, "Bowen, Preedy, Shearing & Co.: A Note in Memory and a Check List," *Boston University Studies in English* 3 (Autumn 1957): 182.

Ironically, readers today know little about these works, since they have been subsequently eclipsed by the remarkable group of weird short stories that have become her chief claim to fame. It is the contention of more than one commentator that a resurgence of popular and critical interest in the novels is long overdue.

History, no matter what the period and the characters involved, was avowedly a personal passion for her, an escape from her prosaic surroundings, inflected broadly with her own idiosyncratic tastes and her painterly love of color. "When we speak of a Victorian atmosphere," she explained, "an eighteenth-century atmosphere, a Spanish atmosphere, don't we mean something quite peculiar to ourselves? . . . Pile up the facts as you like, they remain dead until we give them a breath from our individual life." It is the writer's "personality"—the tastes, feelings, and prejudices—that illuminates the atmosphere ("Through the Eyes of an Author").

Thus, the handful of historical novels excerpted here reveal much about Marjorie Bowen herself—her lifelong devotion to the tapestry of medieval history in *The Viper of Milan;* her avowed admiration for her great hero, William, Prince of Orange, in *Defender of the Faith;* her fascination with magicians and alchemists, like the Comte de St. Germain in *The Courtly Charlatan,* "Pope Joan" in *Black Magic,* and Dr. John Dee, astrologer to Queen Elizabeth in *I Dwelt in High Places* (see the essay elsewhere in this book); her preoccupation with the notorious poisoners of history, like the cabal of poisoners in the Court of Louis XIV in *The Poisoners;* and her impassioned protest at the exploitation of slaves in early nineteenth-century Jamaica in *The Golden Violet.*

Although three additional novels included here—*The Haunted Vintage,* "Five Winds," and *The Devil Snar'd*—are free-form fantasies that display her mastery of the Tale of the Terror, they too owe much to their richly detailed historical backdrops. The last is considered separately in its entirety elsewhere in this book.

Finally, *Stinging Nettles* is a rarity among her novels, a contemporary, semi-autobiographical account of Bowen's struggles to nurse her terminally ill husband in Italy during the First World War, while maintaining her career as a professional writer.

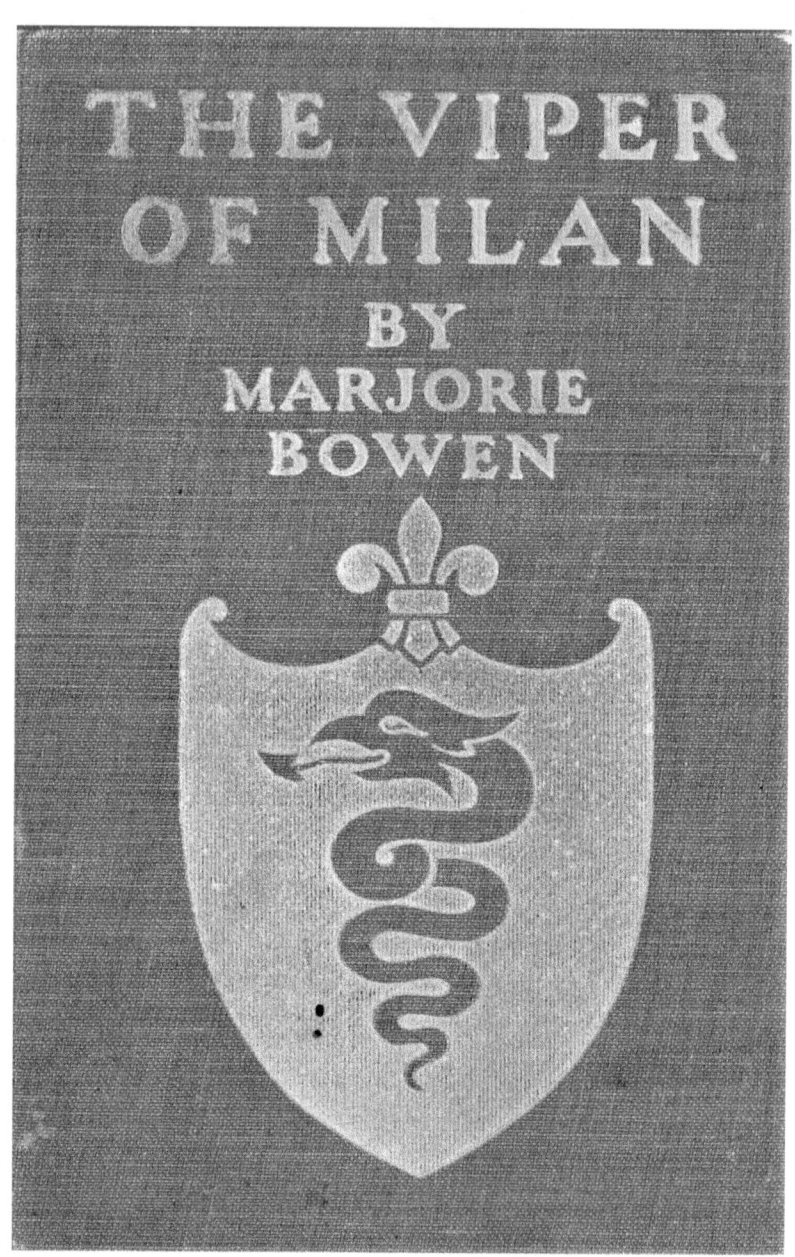

The Viper of Milan, *first edition cover*

The Viper of Milan

London: Alston Rivers, 1906.

> "[Mastino] was riding in a nightmare. He only knew [his wife] was
> dead; he also knew he was riding to find Visconti—nothing more."

Marjorie Bowen's debut novel, begun in her mid-teens and published in 1906 when she was twenty-one, astonished readers and
critics alike. Hailed as the work of a "precocious author" and admired by Graham Greene, who pronounced it a major influence
on his own writing career [see Greene's essay in the "Appreciations" section], *The Viper of Milan* has remained one of Bowen's
most celebrated achievements.

The setting is Lombardy, northern Italy, 1360. An ongoing
war for territory and power sets the villainous Gian Galeazzo Visconti, Duke of Milan, the last of the Visconti line, against the
swashbuckling noble, Mastino Orazio della Scala, Duke of Verona. And over it all waves the Visconti banner, a green figure
against a silver field. As the story begins, Mastino's city of Verona
has been sacked and burned. His wife has been captured by the
conquering Visconti and imprisoned in a tower in Milan. Now,
Mastino is on the road, in rags, disguised as the wanderer "Fran-
cisco," seeking revenge and the recovery of his wife and lands. He
gathers his armies to launch a powerful assault against Visconti.
But in the end, he is thwarted by treachery on the part of his allies
and a vulnerability and weakness in his own nature. So desperate
is he to recover his wife Isotta that he enters into an unholy bar-
gain with Visconti: she will be spared and Mastino can live out
his life back in his beloved Verona if he will cede his armies, his
lands and towns—Verona, Ferrara, Novara, Mantua—to Viscon-

ti. But at the last minute, during the exchange, Visconti poisons her. Mastino, who in the meantime has admitted his treachery to his captains and his armies, is left dishonored and his wife dead. Subsequently, his desperate attempt to murder Visconti fails.

In this excerpt from the penultimate chapter of the book, Mastino rides for revenge against Visconti. He dies, a hero irrevocably stained and humiliated, his armies and allies betrayed and fallen. Visconti, too, will later die, betrayed by his own secretary, Giannotto. Neither the nobility of love nor the machinations of evil can prevail against either man. Only a desolate sense of loss and futility remains.

For hours had Mastino Della Scala ridden with his wife against his breast, riding always toward Novara; and now he had ridden suddenly into a wild red glare that lit the sky.

Mastino's thoughts were centered on one thing—Visconti. There was no reflection in them; neither the past nor present had meaning. He was riding in a nightmare. He only knew he carried his wife Isotta, and that she was dead; he also knew he was riding to find Visconti—nothing more.

The red glare rose into the sky in pointed flames.

"'Tis a burning city," said Mastino; but the words had no meaning.

That blinding flare, though still a mile away, lit up the great posterns of a gate near by, and a long wall adjoining was glowering red in it, the trails of the flowers showing like blood as they hung over it, spectral and strange. It was a noble's summer palace, lit by Novara burning yonder.

Mastino stopped his horse, that needed no checking, worn out by that wild ride, and gazed before him at the flames, and slowly something of reasoning power returned. He had ridden to meet Visconti, and Visconti was here. He knew it—either of God or devil—knew it surely; and he rode his horse on slowly, with the double burden, through the unguarded gates, and came to a flight of steps unguarded too, leading up to a wide balcony, overlooked by high, open, lighted windows. Here was the place—unguarded. Here was Visconti, and the soul of Mastino suddenly blazed into a white heat that for a moment blinded him.

Then he dismounted, and laid Isotta down, speaking the while to his horse. The glow from the burning city wrapped them both and made the fair dead face rosy. The tempest was over, and only a soft rain fell, ceasing gradually. Mastino found a sheltered spot beneath the bushes, and with a pitiful gentleness laid Isotta down and drew the hood about her head.

"I will come back," he murmured, kissing her. Then he turned to the steps with his naked dagger in his hand. He wore no armor; he was bare-headed—he gave it no thought. He was here to slay Visconti. That was God's fact.

Along the steps, a soldier came lazily, and Mastino sprang on him and strangled him before he could cry out, bearing the body noiselessly to the ground. Then, listening, he heard from within the palace a laugh and a voice—Visconti's. Della Scala looked around. How was he to get to him? He must feel Visconti's blood run warm over his hands, and quickly.

"Hot it blazes! The soldiers will have poor spoil," said Visconti. "But we will build another town, de Lana: we are rich enough."

"Outside the walls just now we found a ghastly thing," said a second voice: "a human hand grasping tight a knot of scarlet ribbons—just the hand, a beautiful hand."

"Your tales sicken me—I have always hated horrors," said Visconti.

Mastino crept along and found a door.

"I will get in here," he said within himself; and then within himself he laughed for it was opened.

The tapestry within was moved aside, and there was a glimpse of a white sleeve and a delicate, ringed hand. The next moment the curtain was torn, in a giant's grip, from its fastening, and Mastino, trampling it under him, was upon them—in his madness staying to reckon on no odds.

Where was Visconti? Not far, for he himself, with his own hand, had opened the door.

But from the red glare outside, the blaze within blinded Della Scala. He looked round him for Visconti. Then a voice screamed: "Keep him off!" and suddenly his eyes met the Duke's, and he strode forward. It seemed almost done. Visconti, in wild fear, fell back before that terrible face, staggering against the wall, his hand fumbling for his dagger, and the men in the room scattered to right and left, as before an apparition.

"Gentlemen!" shrieked Visconti, "you are ten to one: stop him! A fortune for the one who slays him!"

But Mastino had him in his grip—almost: another moment—

But Visconti fell, and crouched along the wall, those reaching hands above him; and a dozen swords leaped out: the soldiers flocked in from the ante-room: there was a wild confusion.

"Slay him!" shrieked Visconti. But from Della Scala, as they closed on him, came a yell that froze the marrow.

Ten to one! They needed to be. The place began to run with blood.

"Gian Visconti! Gian Visconti!"

Visconti rose by the wall again. "Kill him!" he gasped. "Kill him!" and cowered away. He was not sure if that face or that figure, struggling ever toward him, could be killed; that they were earthly, or that that was the voice of a man that, with no sound of the human left in it, called his name.

"Let them kill him!" screamed Visconti.

But de Lana did not move, he did not look round; neither did Visconti.

"Visconti! Visconti!" gasped the voice. . . . "Ah! . . ." There was a great scuffling of feet, the dragging of a heavy body, and Mastino, an inert mass upon the soldiers' arms, was forced back upon the balcony.

They let him fall there, and one heard him moan. He was bleeding from twenty wounds. They left him and closed the door.

Visconti looked round fearfully.

"Is he gone?" he said.

The great candelabra had been overturned and the room was in a semi-gloom, broken only by the dim candles in their sconces and the fitful flare from the city.

No one answered Visconti. The men drew breath in silence and looked at their wounds. How he had fought! A horror fell upon them.

"Is he dead?" asked Visconti, shaking like a leaf.

"There were fifteen men to kill him," said de Lana, and he wiped some blood from his hand with a shiver.

No one else broke the silence, all stood still as if spellbound; it was a horrible, horrible thing, and they drew back from the door—afraid.

"Hush!—what was that?"

Visconti leaned forward fearfully.

"What was it?"

The sound of someone on the balcony. Visconti's face went livid.

"He is alive—"

A horrid shudder ran through them all. De Lana strove to speak and could not.

"The door is not fastened," whispered Visconti, hoarsely. "Fasten the door—some one!"

But no one moved, no one dared, for superstitious horror.

Something fell back from the door, then the sound of something that dragged itself against it painfully, then a rattle at the unbolted door.

"He is not dead!" half screamed Visconti. "A town to the man who will go out and slay him!"

No one moved.

"A half-dead man!" cried the Duke, "and no one will end his misery?"

They dared not.

"Hark! he will have the door open. De Lana, I command you—" He pointed with a shaking hand, but de Lana only shook his head.

"There has too much been done already," he said, shudderingly.

The Duke looked round wildly.

"A town, a fortune to the one who will have compassion"; and with a shrug and a grimace, a rough soldier stepped forward, his drawn sword in his hand, and opening the door, pushed something back before him and went out.

Gian breathed heavily listening, but the next second the soldier was in the room again, with altered face, and the door ajar behind him.

"I cannot," he gasped—"it's blind, struggling—it—does not look like a man—I—"

"Shut the door!" yelled Visconti, and then fell back against de Lana, shaking, for a livid face appeared, with dim eyes and a bare throat streaked with blood. For one moment the ghastly apparition showed there, then fell into the dark again.

There was a sickening pause. Visconti spoke first, looking around.

"Are we fools or women?—he came to murder me, and he is slain—what is there in that? Go and see *now* if he be dead."

Some one went, fearfully.

"He lies very still, my lord; he is dead—"

The trembling pages had brought more lights, and light was life to Visconti. He came forward and looked, a little nearer, on the figure in the doorway, but very slowly, with de Lana between.

Mastino lay out straight, in a sudden up-flare from the burning city, his arm flung over his face.

"He was a giant," whispered Visconti, fearfully. "And how dark!—I do not remember him so dark—"

He looked over de Lana's shoulder at him.

The soldiers peered behind him. That man was Mastino della Scala once!—it was strange even to their cold hearts.

He was dead—*dead!* Visconti's fear, the superstitious fear of the righteous, God-sent vengeance, turned to a savage joy; still he was afraid, still afraid.

He touched the body with the point of his gold shoe.

"Throw him into the garden," he said to the soldiers, showing his teeth.

Giannotto and de Lana exchanged a curious glance; the solder set his lips.

"Are you all traitors or cowards, that you do not heed me?" cried Visconti, in a fury. "Throw, thrust, kick this thing into the garden—let him lie there till the morning."

"My lord," said de Lana, with a dangerous look in his eyes, "he was a Prince and a Scaliger!"

"He was my enemy—scorn for scorn! Throw Mastino de Scala from the balcony—or—"

And a half a dozen men came forward and lifted the prostrate body.

"Haste," said Visconti, his eyes on de Lana. "Throw him out of my sight."

"Let them carry him down the steps, my lord," cried de Lana.

But Visconti turned on him, his face and hair glowing in the light of the flames from Novara, his face fiendish.

"They shall do as I bid or hang from the nearest tree! Now haste!" he said again, as if he feared the dead might yet arise.

They carried the body to the edge of the steps and pushed it over, crashing dully down the foliage that half overspread the marble.

Visconti stepped to the parapet and looked over.

"He said something as he fell," he whispered to himself. "I heard him—but he must be dead now.—"

He turned back into the room, breathing more freely.

"Now close the door again," he said, and watched while it was done.

Black Magic

London: Allston Rivers, 1909.

"Whatsoever I am, I perish on the heights, but I do not descend from them."

Citing *Black Magic* as one of the "100 Best Fantasy Books," editors Cawthorn and Moorcock write: "Lightning forks and flickers about the characters as they act out their complex loves and hatreds . . . It is a hectic, high-key world, into which black diabolism fits without incongruity."[1] And in her preface, Marjorie Bowen declares: "In the following narrative the author has endeavoured to catch the spirit of such an atmosphere, and of times when these things were, and when belief in the supernatural and visions swayed the lives and destinies of many."

Black Magic is a gender-bending story about two practitioners of the Satanic arts whose machinations threaten to topple the papal seat and bring the world to the brink of apocalypse. Epic in scope, written in heavily perfumed prose, fraught with Bowen's penchant for atmosphere and scene, it features the most extravagant characters and situations this side of the Gothic novel it most resembles, Matthew Gregory Lewis's *The Monk* (1796). The story is based on the ninth-century legends of a female pope, Pope Joan, who reigned for a few years disguised as a man. Her true identity was only revealed when her pregnancy was discovered. After her death, by accident or murder, the Vatican mandated that future popes would be male. Most modern scholars

---

1. James Cawthorn and Michael Moorcock, *Fantasy: The 100 Best Books* (New York: Carroll & Graf, 1988), 55–56.

dismiss Pope Joan as a medieval legend. See Donna Woolfolk Cross, *Pope Joan* (New York: Crown, 1996).

The legend provides Marjorie Bowen an unusual love story of magic and eroticism between Dirk Renswoude, an avid student of black magic, and Theirry of Dendermonde, his more feckless companion in the black arts. Their relationship is contentious throughout and is fraught with hints of a barely repressed homosexuality. During the course of their many adventures, Theirry realizes he is not as committed to Satanism as Dirk, and he breaks off their relationship. When next they meet, in Rome, Dirk has assumed the title of Cardinal Caprarola with ambitions to become Pope Michael II; and Theirry has returned a penitent bent on absolution for his sins.

In this first of four excerpts from the concluding chapters, we find Theirry arriving in the apartments of Cardinal Caprarola. He doesn't realize at first that the cardinal is none other than his estranged companion of old, Dirk Renswoude. Moreover, he soon will discover that the love he and Dirk have shared in the past is not, as has been hinted, homosexual in nature; rather, he begins to suspect that Dirk is a woman who has managed to hide her identity and heterosexual passion during all their years together. "He" will soon reign as Michael II (but in reality as the first female Pope). As they converse, the city is convulsing under a lowering storm, tortured by the advent of the plague, and haunted by ghosts and devils.

"*In nomine Patris, et Filii, et Spiritus Sancti;* I give you greeting," said the Cardinal in a low grave voice; he crossed to the ivory chair and seated himself.

Theirry lifted his head and looked eagerly at the man who he hoped would be his saviour.

The Cardinal was young, of the middle height, of a full but elegant person and conveying an impression of slightness and delicacy, though he was in reality neither small nor fragile. His face was pale, by this light only dimly to be seen; he wore a robe of vivid pink and violet silk that spread about the step on which his chair was placed; his hands were very beautiful, and ornamented with a variety of costly rings; on his head was a black skull-cap, and outside it his hair showed, thick, curling and of a chestnut-red colour; his foot, very small and well shaped, encased in a gold slipper, showed beneath his gown.

He caught hold of the ivory arms of his seat and looked straight at Theirry with intense, dark eyes.

"On what matters did you wish to speak with me?" he asked.

Theirry could not find words, a choking sense of horror, of something dreadful and blasphemous beyond all words clutched at his heart . . . he stared at the young Cardinal . . . he must be going mad . . .

"The air—the incense makes me giddy, holy father," he murmured.

The Cardinal touched a bell that stood by the sand clock, and motioned to Theirry to rise.

A beautiful boy in a white tunic answered the summons.

"Extinguish the incense," said the Cardinal, "and open the window, Gian . . . it is very hot, a storm gathers, does it not?"

The youth drew apart the painted curtains and unlatched the window; as the cooler air was wafted into the close chamber Theirry breathed more freely.

"The stars are all hidden, your Eminence," said Gian, looking at the night. "Certainly, it is a storm."

He raised the brazier, shook out the incense, leaving it smouldering greyly, went on one knee to the Cardinal, then withdrew backwards.

As the door closed behind him Luigi Caprarola turned to the man standing humbly before him. "Now can you speak?" he said gravely.

Theirry flushed.

"Scarcely have I the heart . . . your Eminence abashes me, I have a sickening tale to relate . . . hearing of you I thought, this holy man can give me peace, and I came half across the world to lay my troubles at your feet; but now, sir, now—I fear to speak, indeed, am scarce able, unreal and hideous it seems in this place."

"In brief, sir," said the Cardinal, "ye have changed your mind—I think ye were ever of a changeful disposition, Theirry of Dendermonde."

"How does your Eminence know that of me is, alas! true."

"I see it in your face," answered the Cardinal, "and something else I see—you are, and long have been, unhappy."

"It is my great unhappiness that has brought me before your Eminence."

Luigi Caprarola rested his elbow on the ivory chair arm and his cheek on his palm; the pale, dim light was full on his face; because of something powerful and intense that shone in his eyes Theirry did not care to look at him.

"Weary of sin and afraid of Heaven ye have come to seek absolution of me," said the Cardinal.

"Yea, if it might be granted me, if by any penitence I might obtain pardon."

Then Theirry, whose gaze was fixed on the ground as he spoke, had an extraordinary vivid impression that the Cardinal was laughing; he looked up quickly, only to behold Luigi Caprarola calm and grave.

A peal of thunder sounded, and the echoes hovered in the chamber.

"The confession must come before the absolution," said the Cardinal. "Tell me, my son, what troubles you."

Theirry shuddered.

"It involves others than myself . . ."

"The seal of the confession is sacred, and I will ask for no names. Theirry of Dendermonde, kneel here and confess."

He pointed to the ivory footstool close to his raised seat; Theirry came and humbly knelt.

The curtains fluttered in the hot wind, a flash of lightning darted in between them and mingled with the luminous colour cast by the faint lamps.

The Cardinal took up the gold book and laid it on his knee, his pink silk sleeve almost touched Theirry's lips . . . his garments gave out a strange and beautiful perfume. "Tell me of these sins of thine," he said, half under his breath.

"I must go far back," answered the penitent in a trembling voice, "for your Eminence to understand my sins—they had small beginnings."

He paused and fixed his gaze on the Cardinal's long fair fingers resting across the gold cover of the breviary.

"I was born in Dendermonde," he said at length. "My father was a clerk who taught me his learning. When he died I came to Courtrai. I was eighteen, ambitious and clever beyond other scholars of my age. I wished above everything to go to one of the colleges . . ."

He gave a hot sigh, as if he could still recall the passionate throb of that early desire.

"To gain a living I taught the arts I was acquainted with, among others I gave lessons in music to the daughter of a great lord in Courtrai . . . in this manner I came to know her brother, who was a young knight of lusty desires."

The Cardinal was listening intently; his breathing seemed hardly to stir his robe; the hand on the gilt and turkis cover was very still.

Theirry wiped his damp forehead, and continued—

"He was, as I, restless and impatient with Courtrai . . . but, unlike me, he was innocent, for I,"—he moistened his lips—"I about this time began to practise—black magic."

The thunder rolled sombrely yet triumphantly round the seven hills, and the first rain dashed against the window.

"Black magic," repeated the Cardinal, "go on."

"I read forbidden books that I found in an old library in the house of a Jew whose son I taught—I tried to work spells, to raise spirits; I was very desperate to better myself, I wished to become as Alcuin, as Saint Jerome—nay, as Zerdusht himself, but I was not skilful enough. I could do little or nothing . . ."

The Cardinal moved slightly; Theirry, in an agony of old bitter memories, torn between horror and ease at uttering these things at last, continued in a low desperate voice—

"The young knight I have spoken of was in love with a mighty lady who came through Courtrai, he wished to follow her to Frankfort, she had given him hopes that she would find him service there—he asked me to bear him company, and I was glad to go. On the journey he told me of his marriage to the daughter of a neighbouring lord—and—though that is no matter here—he knew not if she were alive or dead, but he knew of the place where she had last been known of, and we went thither—it was in the old, half-deserted town of Antwerp . . ."

"And the young knight hoped to find she was dead," interrupted the Cardinal. "Was she, I wonder?"

"All the world thought so. It is a strange story, not for my telling; we found the house, and there we met a youth, who told us of the maid's death and showed us her grave . . ."

The thunder, coming nearer, shook the palace, and Theirry hid his face in his hands. "What of this youth?" asked the Cardinal softly, "tell me of him."

"He ruined me—by night he came to me and told of his studies—black magic! black magic! . . . cast spells and raised a devil . . . in a mirror he showed me visions, I swore with him faithful friendship . . . he ruined my soul—he sold some of the goods in the house, and we went together to Basle College."

"Ye make him out your evil angel," said the Cardinal. "Who was he?"

"I know not; he was high-born, I think, dainty in ways and pleasant to look upon; my faltering soul was caught by his wiles, for he spoke of great rewards; I know not who he was, man or demon . . . I think he loved me."

There was a little silence in the chamber, then the Cardinal spoke.

"Loved you?—what makes you think he loved you?"

"Certes, he said so, and acted so . . . we went to Basle College—then, I also thought I loved him . . . he was the only thing in the world I had ever spoken to of my hopes, my desires . . . we continued our experiments . . . our researches were blasphemous, horrible, he was ever more skilful than I . . . then one day I met a lady, and then I knew myself hideous, but that very night I was drawn into the toils again . . . we cast a spell over another student—we were discovered and fled the college."

A flash of lightning pierced the blue gloom like a sword rending silk; Theirry winced and shuddered as the thunder crashed overhead.

"Does your tale end here?" demanded the Cardinal.

"Alas! alas! no; I fell from worse sin to worse sin—we were poor, we met a monk, robbed him of God His moneys, and left him for dead . . . we came to Frankfort and lived in the house of an Egyptian hag, and I began to loathe the youth because the lady was ever in my thoughts, and he hated the lady bitterly because of this; he tempted me to do murder for gain, and I refused for her sake." Theirry's voice became hot and passionate. "Then I found that he was tempting her—my saint! but I had no fear that she would fall, and while she spurned him I thought I could also, ay, and I did . . . but she proved no stronger—she loved her steward, and bid him slay his wife: 'You staked on her virtue,' the Devil cried to me, 'and you've lost! lost!'"

The sobs thickened his voice, and the bitter tears gathered in his beautiful eyes.

"I was the youth's prey again, but now I hated him for his victory . . . we came back to Frankfort, and he was sweet and soft to me, while I was thinking how I might injure him as he had injured me . . . I dwelt on that picture of—her—dishonoured and undone, and I hated him, so waited my chance, and the night we reached the city I betrayed him for what he was, betrayed him to whom I had sworn friendship . . . Well, half the town came howling through the snow to seize him, but we were too late, we found a flaming house . . . it burnt to ashes, he with it . . . I had had my revenge, but it brought me no peace. I left the West and went to the East, to India, Persia, to Greece, I avoided both God and the Devil, I dreaded Hell and dared not hope for Heaven, I tried to forget but could not, I tried to repent but could not. Good and evil strove for me, until the Lord had pity . . . I heard of you, and I have come to Rome to cast myself at your feet, to ask your aid to help throw myself on God His mercy."

He rose with his hands clasped on his breast and his wild eyes fixed on the white face of Luigi Caprarola; thunder and lightning together were rending the hot air; Theirry's gorgeous dress glimmered in gold and purple, his face was flushed and exalted.

"God wins, I think, this time," he said in an unsteady voice. "I have confessed my sins, I will do penance for them, and die at least in peace—God and the angels win!"

The Cardinal rose; with one hand he held to the back of the

ivory chair, with the other he clasped the golden book to his breast; the light shining on his red hair showed it in filmy brightness against the wall of ebony and mother-of-pearl; his face and lips were very pale above the vivid hue of his robe, his eyes, large and dark, stared at Theirry.

Again the lightning flashed between the two, and seemed to sink into the floor at the Cardinal's feet.

He lifted his head proudly and listened to the following mighty roll; when the echoes had quivered again into hot stillness he spoke.

"The Devil and his legions win, I think," he said. "At least they have served Dirk Renswoude well."

Theirry fell back, and back, until he crouched against the gleaming wall.

"Cardinal Caprarola!" he cried fearfully. "Cardinal Caprarola, speak to me! even here I hear the fiends jibe!"

The Cardinal stepped from the ebony dais, his stiff robes making a rustling as he walked; he laughed.

"Have I learned a mien so holy my old comrade knows me not? Have I changed so, I who was dainty and pleasant to look upon, your friend and your bane?"

He paused in the centre of the room; the open window, the dark beyond it, the waving curtains, the fierce lightning made a terrific background for his haughty figure.

But Theirry moaned and whispered in his throat. "Look at me," commanded the Cardinal, "look at me well, you who betrayed me, am I not he who gilded a devil one August afternoon in a certain town in Flanders?"

Theirry drew himself up and pressed his clenched hands to his temples.

"Betrayed!" he shrieked. "It is I who am betrayed. I sought God, and have been delivered unto the Devil!"

The thunder crashed so that his words were lost in the great noise of it, the blue and forked lightning darted between them.

"You know me now?" asked the Cardinal.

Theirry slipped to his knees, crying like a child.

"Where is God? where is God?"

The Cardinal smiled.

"He is not here," he answered, "nor in any place where I have been."

An awful stillness fell after the crash of thunder; Theirry hid his face, cowering like a man who feels his back bared to the lash.

"Cannot you look at me?" asked the Cardinal in a half-mournful scorn; "after all these years am I to meet you—thus? At my feet!"

Theirry sprang up, his features mask-like in their unnatural distortion and lifeless hue.

"You do well to taunt me," he answered, "for I am an accursed fool, I have been seeking for what does not exist—God!—ay, now I know that there is no God and no Heaven, therefore what matter for my soul . . . what matter for any of it since the Devil owns us all!"

The storm was renewed with the ending of his speech, and he saw through the open window the vineyards and gardens of the Janiculum Hill blue for many seconds beneath the black sky.

"Your soul!" cried the Cardinal, as before. "Always have you thought too much, and not enough, of that; you served too many masters and not one faithfully; had you been a stronger man you had stayed with your fallen saint, not spurned her, and then avenged her by my betrayal."

He crossed to the window and closed it, the while the lightning picked him out in a fierce flash, and waited until the after-crash had rocked to silence, his eyes all the while not leaving the shrinking, horror-stricken figure of Theirry.

"Well, it is all a long while ago," he said. "And I and you have changed."

"How did you escape that night?" asked Theirry hoarsely; hardly could he believe that this man was Dirk Renswoude, yet his straining eyes traced in the altered older face the once famil-iar features.

As the Cardinal moved slowly across the gleaming chamber Theirry marked with a horrible fascination the likeness of the haughty priest to the poor student in black magic.

The straight dark hair was now curled, bleached and stained a deep red colour, after the manner of the women of the East; eyes and brows were the same as they had ever been, the first as bright and keen, the last as straight and heavy; his clear skin showed less pallor, his mouth seemed fuller and more firmly set, the upper lip heavily shaded with a dark down, the chin less prominent, but the line of the jaw was as strong and clear as ever; a handsomer face than it had been, a remarkable face, with an ex-pression composed and imperious, with eyes to tremble before.

"I thought you burnt," faltered Theirry.

"The master I serve is powerful," smiled the Cardinal. "He saved me then and set me where I am now, the greatest man in Rome—so great a man that did you wish a second time to be-tray me you might shout the truth in the streets and find no one to believe you."

The lightning darted in vain at the closed window, and the thunder rolled more faintly in the distance.

"Betray you!" cried Theirry, wild-eyed. "No, I bow the knee to the greatest thing I have met, and kiss your hand, your Emi-nence!"

The Cardinal turned and looked at him over his shoulder.

"I never broke my vows," he said softly, "the vows of comradeship I made to you; just now you said you thought I loved you, then, I mean, in the old days . . ."—he paused and his delicate hand crept over his heart—"well, I . . . loved you . . . and it ruined me, as the devils promised. Last night I was warned that you would come to-day and that you would be my bane . . . well, I do not care since you are come, for, sir, I love you still."

"Dirk!" cried Theirry.

The Cardinal gazed on him with ardent eyes.

"Do you suppose it matters to me that you are weak, foolish, or that you betrayed me? You are the one thing in all the world I care for . . . Love! what was your love when you left her at Sebastian's feet?—had she been my lady I had stayed and laughed at all of it . . ."

"It is not the Devil who has taught you to be so faithful," said Theirry.

For the first time a look of trouble, almost of despair, came into the Cardinal's eyes; he turned his head away.

"You shame me," continued Theirry; "I have no constancy in me; thinking of my own soul, almost have I forgotten Jacobea of Martzburg—and yet—"

"And yet you loved her."

"Maybe I did—it is long ago."

A bitter little smile curved the Cardinal's lips.

"Is that the way men care for women?" he said. "Certes, not in that manner had I wooed and remembered, had I been a—a—lover."

"Strange that we, meeting here like this, should talk of love!" cried Theirry, his heart heaving, his eyes dilating, "strange that I, driven round the world by fear of God, that I, coming here to one of God's own saints, should find myself in the Devil's net again; come, he has done much for you, what will he do for me?"

The Cardinal smiled sadly.

"Neither God nor Devil will do anything for you, for you are not single-hearted, neither constant to good nor evil; but I—will risk everything to serve your desires."

Theirry laughed.

"Heaven has cast the world away and we are mad! You, you famous as a holy man—did you murder the young Blaise? I will back to India, to the East, and die an idol-worshipper. See yonder crucifix, it hangs upon your walls, but the Christ does not rise to smite you; you handle the Holy Mysteries in the Church and no angel slays you on the altar steps—-let me away from Rome!"

He turned to the gilt door, but the Cardinal caught his sleeve.

"Stay," he said, "stay, and all I promised you in the old days shall come true—do you doubt me? Look about you, see what I have won for myself . . ."

Theirry's beautiful face was flushed and wild. "Nay, let me go . . ."

The last rumble of the thunder crossed their speech.

"Stay, and I will make you Emperor."

"Oh devil!" cried Theirry, "can you do that?"

"We will rule the world between us; yea, I will make you Emperor, if you will stay in Rome and serve me; I will snatch the diadem from Balthasar's head and cast his Empress out as I ever meant to do, and you shall bear the sceptre of the Cæsars, oh, my friend, my friend!"

He held out his right hand as he spoke; Theirry caught it, crushed the fingers in his hot grasp and kissed the brilliant rings; the Cardinal flushed and dropped his lids over sparkling eyes.

"You will stay?" he breathed.

"Yea, my sweet fiend, I am yours, and wholly yours; lo!"

[Months pass. While Rome is assaulted by lowering storms, Theirry, under the spell of Dirk Renswoude, who is now Pope Michael II, has won the crown of Emperor. He returns to Rome in triumph. The Pope promises him riches and power.]

"It is done," [the Pope] said in a low eager voice, "and to-morrow I crown you in St. Peter's church; Theirry, it is done."

"Truly our fortunes are marvelous," answered Theirry, "to-day—when I heard the Princes elect me—an unknown adventurer!—when I heard the mob of Rome shout for me—I thought I had gone mad!"

"It is I who have done this for you," said the Pope softly.

Theirry seemed to shudder in his gorgeous mail.

"Are you afraid of me?" the other asked. "Why do you so seldom look at me?"

Theirry slowly turned his beautiful face.

"I am afraid of my own fortunes—I am not as bold as you," he said fearfully. "You never hesitated to sin."

The Pope moved and his garments sparkled against the gleaming marble wall.

"I do not sin," he smiled. "I am Sin—I do not evil for I am Evil—but you"—his face became grave, almost sad—"you are very human, better had it been for me never to have met you!"

He placed his little hands either side of him on the smooth heads of the basalt lions.

"Theirry—for your sake I have risked everything, for your sake maybe I must leave this strange fair life and go back whence I came—so much I care for you, so dearly have I kept the vows we made in Frankfurt—cannot you meet with the courage the destiny I offer you?"

Theirry hid his face in his hands.

The Pope flushed and a wild light sparkled in his dark eyes.

"Was not your blood warmed by that charge in Tivoli? When knight and horse fell before your spears and your host humbled an Emperor, when Rome rose to greet you and I came to meet you with a kingdom for a gift, did not some fire creep into your veins that might serve to heat you now?"

"A kingdom!" cried Theirry, "the kingdom of Antichrist. The victory was not mine—the cohorts of the Devil galloped beside us and urged us to unholy triumph—Rome is a place of horror, full of witches, ghosts and strange beasts!"

"You said you would be Emperor," answered the Pope. "And I have granted you your wish; if you fail me or betray me now . . . it is over—for both of us."

"Ay, I will be Emperor," he cried feverishly. "Theirry of Dendermonde crowned by the Devil in St. Peter's church—why should I hesitate? I am on the road to hell, to hell . . ."

The Pope fixed ardent eyes on him.

"And if ye fail me, ye shall go there instantly."

[But in a subsequent complex course of events, Theirry does betray the Pope and denounces him as Antichrist. He leads forces against his old friend, who fears his downfall.]

Michael II walked to and fro in his gorgeous cabinet. In the three days since Theirry had fled the city, his power had crumbled like a handful of sand; Rome had turned against him, and every hour men fell away from his cause.

The devils, too, had forsaken him; he could not raise the spirits, the magic fires would not burn . . . all was blank darkness and silence.

Up and down he paced, listening to the mob surging in the Piazza of St. Peter.

The day wore on and the storm grew in violence.

Paolo Orsini came again to him, his face pale.

"Half the Cardinals are fled to Viterbo and those remaining refuse to acknowledge your Holiness."

The Pope smiled.

"I had expected it."

"News comes from a Greek runner that Theirry of Dendermonde is with Balthasar's host—"

"Also, I expected that," said Michael II wildly.

"And they proclaim you," continued Orsini in an agitated manner, "an imposter, one given to evil practices, and by these means incite the people against you; Cardinal Orvieto has led a thousand men across the marshes to the Emperor's army—"

"And Theirry of Dendermonde has denounced me!" said the Pope.

As he spoke one beat for admission on the gilt door.

The secretary opened and there entered an Eastern chamberlain.

"Holiness," he cried fearfully, "the people have set fire to your palace on the Palatine Hill, and Cardinal Colonna, with his brother Octavian, have seized Castel San Angelo for the Emperor, and hold it in defiance of your Grace."

[At last Theirry, at the head of invading forces, arrives at the Papal apartments, determined to learn at last the secret of his old friend's suspected gender identity.]

It was a common thought among the knights that Michael II had escaped; a monk offered to show them the secret passage where his Holiness might be even now. Many went, but Theirry followed the attendants to the gilt door of the ebony cabinet.

They broke the lock and entered, fearfully.

On the floor torn fragments of parchments, a pile of ashes with a ruby ring lying in the midst.

Nothing else.

"His Holiness is in his chamber—we dare not enter."

They had always been afraid of him; even now his name held terror. They tiptoed to the other gilt door; it took them some time to remove the lock.

When at last the door gave and swung open, they shrunk away—but Theirry passed into the chamber.

The somber light of dawn filled it; heavy shadows obscured the rich splendours of golden colours, of gleaming white walls; the men crept after him—it seemed to Theirry as if the world had stopped about them.

On the magnificent purple bed lay the Pope; on his brow the tiara glittered, and on his breast the chasuble; the crozier lay by his side on the samite coverlet, and his feet glittered in their golden shoes. By the crozier was a letter and a jade bottle.

The attendants shrieked and fled.

Theirry crept to the bedside and took up the parchment; his name was over the top; he broke the seal.

He read the fair writing.

"If I be a devil, I go whence I came; if a man I lived as one and die as one; if woman I have known Love, conquered it and by it have been vanquished. Whatsoever I am, I perish on the heights, but I do not descend from them. I have known things in their fulness and will not stay to taste the dregs. So, to you greeting, and not for long, farewell!"

The letter fell from Theirry's hand, fluttered and sank to the floor.

He raised his eyes and saw through the window the meteor, blazing over Rome.

Dead . . .

He looked now at the proud smooth face on the pillow, the gems of the papal crown gleaming above the red locks, the jeweled chasuble sparkling in the strengthening dawn until he was nearly fooled into thinking the bosom heaved beneath.

He was alone.

At least he could know.

The air was like incense sweet and stifling; his blood seemed to beat in his brain with a little foolish sound of melody; a shaft of grey light fell over the splendours of the bed, the roses and dragons, hawks and hounds sewn on the curtain and coverlets. From the Pope's garments rose a subtle and beautiful perfume.

Without, the thunder muttered.

To know—

He lifted the dead Pope's arm; there seemed to be neither weight nor substance under the stiff silk.

He dropped the sleeve; his cold fingers unclasped the heavy chasuble. Underneath lay perfumed samite, white and soft.

An awful sensation crept through his veins; he thought that under these gorgeous vestments was nothing—nothing—ashes.

He did not dare to uncover the bosom that lay, that must lie, under the gleaming samite.

But he must know.

He lifted up the fair crowned head to peer madly into the proud features . . .

It came away in his hands, like crumbling wood that may preserve, till touched, the semblance of the carving . . . so the Pope's head parted from the trunk.

Theirry smiled with horror and stared at what he held.

Then it disappeared, fell into ashes before his eyes, and the tiara rolled on to the floor.

Gone—like an image of smoke.

He sank across the headless thing on the bed.

"Must I *follow* you to know, follow you to hell?" he whispered.

Now he could open the rich garments.

They were empty of all save dust.

The strange, strong perfume was stinging and numbing his brain, his heart; he thought he heard the fiends coming for his soul—at last.

He hid his face in the purple silk robes and felt his blood grow cold.

The room darkened about him, he knew he was being drawn downwards into eternity. He sighed and slipped from the bed on to the floor.

As his last breath hovered on his lips, the meteor vanished, the thunder-clouds rolled away from a fair blue sky, and a glorious sunrise laughed over the city.

Through the Pope's chamber the notes of silver trumpets quivered.

Balthasar's hosts marched triumphantly into Rome.

The Poisoners

London: Hutchison, 1936.

> "When has there been a moment that idle, great ladies have not amused themselves with charms, philtres, and incantations?"

The historical incident that came to be known as the notorious "Affair of the Poisons," during the reign of Louis XIV, involved a series of mysterious poisonings, allegedly led by a cabal of women, a few of whom were highly placed in the Court. There were many trials and many executions. The historical record estimates nearly a hundred and fifty people were executed for the crimes of poisoning, sorcery, infanticide, and blasphemy, while many more suspects fled France. However, the scandals were deliberately hushed up by the Chief of Police, M. de la Reynie, and the king himself.[1]

Published under Marjorie Bowen's pseudonym, "George R. Preedy," *The Poisoners* combines a roaring melodrama of pursuit and capture with a scrupulously researched account of events that begins in 1678 and for the next ten years involves a series of poisonings that reach from the gritty streets of Paris to the Palace of Versailles. Suspicions of alchemy, witchcraft, and grim atrocities of the Black Mass attend these events. Indeed, it is whispered that one of the poisoners guilty of Satanism and infanticide is none other than the king's own mistress, "The Queen of the Left

---

1. For an overview of this story, see Anne Somerset, *The Affair of the Poisons: Murder, Infanticide and Satanism at the Court of Louis XIV* (London: Weidenfeld & Nicolson, 2003). These events at the court of Louis XIV are dramatized in season two of the three-part series, *Versailles* (2015–18), a Franco-Canadian-European-British series currently streaming on Netflix.

Hand," Mme. de Montespan. Her purported motive is to exercise black magic to maintain a hold over the king against his presumptive mistresses.

"The women—always the women!" exclaims de la Reynie, the Paris chief of police. "They are kept so close, they lead unnatural lives, almost like prisoners—they have lively passions and no means of expressing them. And very often their husbands or their fathers are cruel. Well, they take the only weapon to their hand. It seems that we may find it is a weapon that has been used very freely." To which the minister of war adds: "When has there been a moment that idle, great ladies have not amused themselves with charms, philtres and incantations?"

Behind this cabal of women is a shadowy, elusive figure, a "Grand Master," who, with his band of masked accomplices is attempting to undermine the French aristocracy. It is suspected that he has ties to the Pope in Rome. On his trail are M. de la Reynie, his young lieutenant, Desgrez, and a stalwart policeman, la Tulipe. The wild nocturnal chase begins in a low rag and bone shop and ends at the Pont Henri-Quatre bridge, high above the Seine.

In this first of two excerpts, Louis XIV's chief of police discusses with his lieutenant, Desgrez, the problems facing his investigations into the mysterious cabal of poisoners working from the streets of Paris to the high offices of Versailles.

"Understand, Desgrez," said the Chief of Police, M. de la Reynie, "there may not be very much in this. These people are wealthy, idle, licentious—they are indulging in all the intrigues that one must expect about a Court, especially a Court ruled by women. Some low scoundrels, men and women, deal in drugs, charms, abortion, fortune-telling, astrology and the like, and they have induced—we do not yet know the link—these great ones to trade with them. It is possible that some of these people are in this ugly business for mere cynic amusement. It is hard to believe that a man like the Marechal could believe in these crude witchcrafts."

"Can anyone of education believe in this foul rubbish?" asked Desgrez with aversion.

"A large number of people believe anything," replied de la Reynie. "The matter is neither so simple nor so foolish as it seems. The witchcraft of two hundred years ago was a very potent evil—it was a network of secret societies dealing in every kind of abomination, directly opposed to Christianity and encouraging paganism and atheism. It had its network all over Europe and there was hardly a town of any importance without some branch society affiliated to the headquarters, which were probably here in Paris."

"All this is ancient history, is it not?" asked Desgrez. "I frightened them by mentioning the Boulle affair—but surely that kind of thing is stamped out?"

"By no means. We believe that we have broken up this organization, rooted out its members, and, by the most severe punishments, abolished its practices—but a remnant exists here and there, and this remnant is, perhaps, far more powerful than we know. It seems that we have our finger on it here. These people may be mere ignorant imitators, they may know nothing of the secrets of the true black magic cult—they may be mere dabblers in wizardry, but that they practice it there seems little doubt."

"And little doubt that they deal in poisons, Monsieur," said Desgrez. "I heard quite enough last night. They do intend to murder Delmas, they practically admitted that the Duke of Savoy was made away with by means of a shirt washed with arsenic soap. At least, I put so much together from what they said."

M. de la Reynie made a wry grimace. "Here we touch on high matters. . . . It would not be for the honour of the King or for the honour of France to expose a scandal of this magnitude. But we are not defeated yet, we may get these people on some other account."

"Is there no justice in the country?" said Desgrez scornfully. "Is all corruption and intrigue?"

"No," replied the Chief of Police gravely while he twisted his long white quill pen in restless fingers, "and the King is at heart just and generous—he does not know what goes on. M. Colbert is an honest man, and so are many others who hold high offices, but these streams of iniquity flow under the feet of these great ones, who never see how their shoes are being soiled. The King has the greatest horror of these kinds of practices—of Satanism, of witchcraft, of any manner of wizardry . . ."

"I see, Monsieur," replied Desgrez gravely. "The King is an absolute Monarch, but yet he is a man who is ruled by his own passions. Therefore he is in some sense a slave, not a King."

"That is true. For twelve years he has been ruled by Madame de Montespan, whom, as is said, I think he has never loved. She is so imperious, so violent, such an adept at seduction and scenes of temper and fury, he has never been able to free himself from her. . . . I sometimes believe in Black Magic myself, Desgrez, seeing how I have been baffled for so long by these scoundrels. Take care, do not despise them. I have shown you these things in order to warn you. I am myself taking great precautions, my food, my drink, my linen are all carefully supervised. I touch nothing sent by strangers . . ."

"At every turn we are defeated!" exclaimed Desgrez. "I think you for your warning. My wife has given me a charm to wear." He smiled tenderly, shyly. "Some words from St. John, written on virgin parchment, in a silk bag, poor child!"

"Wear it, Desgrez, it can do no harm. And since we believe in God, we must believe in His power to protect us."

[In this second excerpt, the investigation discovers that behind the cabal of poisoners lurks the machinations of "The Grand Master," suspected to be the Marchese Innocenzo Pignata, nephew to His Holiness the Pope, sent to undermine the authority of Louis. De le Reynie, Desgrez, and La Tulipe track him down to a low rag-and-bone shop.]

It was a still, warm night of early spring when the Chief of Police, Desgrez and la Tulipe, in the plain clothes of sober citizens, passed the noble façade of the *Hôtel de Savoie* and made their way through the network of dark, shabby streets at the back of the mansion. They soon reached, close to a miserable wine shop, the dark alley known as the *Impasse de l'Enfer*.

"The three of us should be enough," muttered la Reynie. "The Master and his dwarf may have assistants or accomplices, but we cannot take a large number or we shall rouse suspicion. Let us not delay, as you may be sure these people will be getting out of Paris as soon as possible . . ."

La Tulipe, who looked the humblest of the three, entered this tavern, and after ordering a pint of claret got into conversation with the landlord and asked him where he might find the shop of an old woman who bought disused clothes. His wife was lately dead, and the woman who nursed her had recommended this shop but had forgotten to give him the exact address. By this ruse, la Tulipe discovered that la Voisin's daughter had spoken the truth for once—there was such a rag shop and it was kept by an old woman who was looked upon, according to the wine-shop keeper, with a good deal of awe and suspicion, since she was supposed to be a witch, or at least to have witch-like qualities. She was avoided because she was secretive, morose and vile-tempered. Her shop was often closed for weeks together; she sometimes wandered the country selling ballads or peddling trifles; then again, for long periods, she would be in the shop and appear to do a thriving trade in old clothes, bones and rubbish; she was suspected of selling charms.

When la Tulipe joined the other two men outside in the still, moonless night, he related his information: "This supposed shop is where they keep all their disguises, Monsieur. It is a simple but clever expedient. One can understand that they could here, without the least difficulty, keep every manner of costume, wig, material for making themselves up, as well as different weapons and any other kind of trumpery."

"It is curious," said la Reynie, as they turned down the little dark alley, badly lit by the flickering lamp over the shrine at the corner, picking their way carefully through the filth on the cobbles. "It is strange that this affair that has led us to the very heights of the Royal Court of Versailles should finally bring us to a ragpicker's shop in a slum!"

They found, without much difficulty, the miserable habitation the wine seller had spoken of. The lower windows were stuffed with rags, the upper windows had weather-beaten shutters across them, but the three police officers noted that the door was firmly fastened, and the lock-plates were in good condition. At the side of this door was a low arch that led down a narrow passage—this was in complete darkness.

"That, said la Reynie, "is probably where they enter. They have chosen a very good lair. This is a poor, miserable street, probably inhabited by thieves and gutter scum. Almost any evil activities would be quite unremarked here."

"Monsieur, what are we to do?" asked Desgrez. "We might watch the house all night in vain and see no light anywhere."

"Let us go down the passage," replied la Reynie. "Both of you, have your hands on your weapons. We shall probably take them completely by surprise. As I think I have rounded all the poisoners, I do not believe there will be more than these two, the man who goes by the name of Saint-Richard, and the dwarf who was in the establishment of la Fontanges." He glanced at the filthy-looking shop and added grimly, "No doubt it was here that the poisoned letter was fabricated."

The three went cautiously down the dark, vile-smelling passage that turned abruptly to the right and led them, as they had supposed it would, to back of the rag shop. This looked upon a tall, walled courtyard, in the middle of which was a pump. The scene was illuminated by the light that fell from one of the back windows of the half tumble-down house. La Tulipe, an adept at this sort of work, edged up to this window, and resting his fingers on the sill, peered through the dirty glass.

Returning to the two men who remained in the shadow of the wall, he reported that he had seen within an old woman in full skirt, shawl and high Norman cap, who easily might be the dwarf Grimaldi and a dark young man seated at a table watching a retort in which bubbled some chemicals.

The room was small, wretched, and lined with clothes hanging on pegs or draped on to wooden figures. The only light was a lamp on the table by the stranger; there seemed to be a good deal of magical apparatus about the place.

"We will take," decided M. de la Reynie, "a bold course."

He crossed the yard, went to the back door, and knocked on it loudly with the hilt of his sword. He kept la Tulipe with him and sent Desgrez to return down the passage and wait at the front of the rag shop. Then a commanding voice said:

"Open."

There was another pause, a shuffling sound within the house, a key turning in its lock, and the door was opened by the old woman who, peering out of uncertain light, gazed with dark, twinkling eyes suspiciously at the tall figure of la Reynie. A glass mask covered her ugly features.

A thrill of exultation, not untouched with fear, caused the Chief of Police to clasp his sword tightly. Had he, at last, unexpectedly, almost by chance, come upon the heart of this terrifying mystery? Was this hideous creature, whose glass mask left little room for doubt as to his occupation, perhaps the Master himself?

"I wish to speak to your master," said the Chief of Police. "It is most important. Admit me without delay."

He stepped over the threshold, brushing the old woman aside against the wall of the corridor. At this she turned and clutched his cloak with a surprising strength, but la Tulipe, following quickly, had the creature gripped firmly by the collar of her bodice at the back of the neck.

"You are caught, Grimaldi—Satanic whelp, whatever you call yourself," he said shortly. "Do not give us any trouble!"

But the dwarf, with amazing strength and agility, writhed free from his captor and, shouting out harshly in a strange language, rushed back into the lighted room; the two police officers were on his track in a second. The young man, whom la Tulipe had observed through the window, had risen and was standing by the table. He was of medium height, slender, and attired in dark green. La Reynie, glancing eagerly at his face, was astonished at his blank expression; and for all his professional insensibility, he could not help a chill of distaste when he saw that it was a mask he gazed at. A wax mask, exactly fitting the man's face, was tied over his features by black ribbons fastened across his thick hair; there were small holes at eyes, nose and mouth.

On the table, casting monstrous shadows in the light of the one lamp, stood a chemical apparatus, brazier filled with charcoal, an alembic, some tubes, retorts, phials, moulds, seals and several sheets of paper marked with black wafers and inverted crosses.

"No doubt!" exclaimed la Reynie, advancing while la Tulipe kept the door and struggled with the dwarf, "you are engaged in another attempt to poison me. But your luck is out, Saint-Richard."

The masked young man stood his ground, not only with courage, but with disdain. He folded his hands covered with loose gloves on his breast and replied in tones that whistled horribly through the hole in the wax that had been painted to a doll-like prettiness.

"I am indeed Saint-Richard. You are powerless to harm me. We have been matching wits for a year now and you are as far from learning the truth about me as you ever were."

"Whoever you are, or whoever you pretend to be, I shall soon know—you'll need the help of all the devils of your acquaintance now."

The young man leaned forward and snatched the alembic in which the poisonous essence seethed behind the glass globe.

"Seize him!" exclaimed la Reynie to la Tulipe, reaching out his hand for the lamp. The young man was too quick; he had seized and dashed down the light and, in the moment of confusion of darkness full of stifling fumes, escaped, followed by the dwarf, the Chief of Police and la Tulipe in pursuit.

"Desgrez will catch them!" exclaimed la Reynie, as they gained the street; but even as he spoke he saw the police lieutenant sprawling over the broken step in front of the shuttered rag shop. Desgrez explained ruefully as he scrambled to his feet that the two fugitives had flung themselves on him, caught him unawares, thrown him off his balance and escaped.

"The young man made a pass at me with his dagger but missed." Desgrez, laughing bitterly at himself, showed a bleeding hand.

"Quick, in pursuit, la Tulipe is a swift runner, and you are young," gasped la Reynie. "I shall follow as quickly as I can. They cannot get far. The young is light on his feet—the dwarf won't be, especially impeded by those skirts."

Desgrez, smarting from his humiliation, started off at a quick pace; he found la Tulipe, who was wiry and lean, well able to keep up with him. The slum quarter through which the pursuit took place was deserted, save for a few beggars crouching in doorways and tattered drunkards lurching out of poor wine shops. The moonlight shone full on the street as Desgrez turned out of the dark *impasse,* for the moon had just risen above the dark roofs of Paris. In this silver light he could see before him the two flying figures. The dwarf had discarded his skirt and shawl and now wore nothing but the masculine attire he had had concealed beneath this disguise. "Fools," thought Desgrez, "where do they think they can hide? What is the use of this flight?"

The pursuit had settled into a steady race; all four were conserving their efforts. The moonlight made concealment difficult; they came out on the quay, and Desgrez saw the two dark figures running towards the bridge, the *Pont Henri-Quatre.* The police agents were steadily gaining upon the fugitives. The whole scene, the whole circumstances had to Desgrez, panting along the quay, an air of unreality. He looked up at the sky, clear, full of moonlight, at the dark roofs, towers and *tourelles* of Paris. He looked ahead of him at the silent silver scene, at the arch of the bridge, at those two running figures, bent before the night wind; he spurred his strength another effort—la Tulipe was slightly ahead of him.

Desgrez gained the bridge and began to cross it. He had fallen to a steady pace, not so fast now; the pursuit began to seem hopeless. His temples throbbed and there was a pain in his side. If these two escaped, even now, what irony! And they might escape, in some alley, through some door—and the identity of the man in the waxen mask would remain a mystery.

But la Tulipe was gaining on the two fugitives; his trained agility was telling in the race; he had often had to risk his life on his speed.

A clock chimed, breaking the stillness with startling clangs. A cold wind rose suddenly from the river. Desgrez felt his strength fail him; he paused for a second, grasping the cold parapet of the bridge, drawing his breath in great gasps. He could see the three dark figures ahead, now almost blended into one. Nerving himself to one more effort, Desgrez struggled on.

In the centre of the bridge the dwarf had fallen, broken by fatigue and stumbling in the deep cobbles. He made a clutch at the cloak of his companion, who brutally shook him off. This second's delay was sufficient to give la Tulipe time to overtake his men; with Desgrez panting a few paces behind, he came up to them.

The dwarf had risen; the two police officers seized him; the young man turned aside and began to climb the parapet of the bridge.

"Don't let him escape!" shrieked the dwarf, writing in the strong hands of la Tulipe. "It is right he should suffer, too! . . ."

"He will scarcely escape by falling into the Seine," gasped Desgrez, hastening to the place where the young man clung to the parapet.

"Yes, yes he will!" screamed the dwarf. "He knows how to get away."

Desgrez hurled himself upon the young man, seizing him by the cloak, by the arm, by the leg, fighting with him desperately.

"Don't let him go over!" he shouted to la Tulipe. "Get hold of him, even if you have to let the other go!"

"He shan't escape!" yelled the dwarf. "Let him taste the wheel, the stake!"

"Fool," came the unnatural voice hissing from behind the wax mask, help me now and you shall have your heart's desire."

As he spoke, he snatched his cloak from the grasp of Desgrez and began to lower himself over the side of the parapet. His gloves had been torn off in the struggle and a dark red stone on one of his fingers gleamed dully in the moonlight.

The dwarf in what seemed a frenzy of malice, had seized the young man by the throat, thus causing him to lose his balance. The two toppled together over the bridge with a terrible cry, and the police agents, gazing over the parapet, saw the bodies tightly locked being borne down the rapid current . . .

"Come, la Tulipe," cried Desgrez, "let us go down to the foreshore. The currents may wash them up!"

Panting, frantic, the two police agents hastened off the bridge and ran along the river below the narrow parapet of the embankment. Too late! The bodies, swirled along the muddy yellow river, were already out of sight.

Desgrez found a boat and waterman not many paces from the bridge. He and la Tulipe sprang in and told the astonished man to row them down the river.

"Nothing!" muttered la Tulipe bitterly.

Desgrez, leaning eagerly from the boat and peering into the turgid water, drew out a wax mask to which was attached black strings. As he gazed at the beautifully modelled classic features a sensation of superstitious horror such as he had never known before him; and glancing at the impassive face of la Tulipe, he muttered, "The Grand Master! The Devil himself, I should say!"

With the staring wax mask with its painted, wistful smile in his hand, the long strings dripping water, Desgrez gazed about him. Above was the moon, remote, high, cold; around was the gloomy outline of Paris roof, towers, *tourelles*, black against the silver-filled atmosphere; below the boat in which he sat with the darkling, huddled figures of the boatman and la Tulipe, the powerful river swirled in muddy currents towards the sea.

The police sealed up the rag and bone shop in the *Impasse de l'Enfer*. M. de la Reynie and Charles Desgrez examined the contents of that hideous little house in private. Standing amid the sinister-looking apparatus, the books on magic, the rows of dresses, coats and costumes that hung like shriveled corpses round the wall, the rows of masks that grinned or simpered from their hooks like dead face. La Reynie showed Desgrez a notice in the weekly *Gazette*:

> *The body of the Pope's nephew, Innocenzo Pignata, who disappeared on the eve of his departure for Rome, has been found washed ashore at Saint-Cloud.*

This distinguished person had been a victim of foul play, or an accident, it was supposed. He had been identified only by some curious marks on his body that had been known to his servant, and by the magnificent ruby that he wore on his left hand as a charm against evil, for his face had been entirely eaten by water-rats.

The Haunted Vintage

London: Odhams Press, 1921.

> "Ghosts and nymphs and penates, kobolds and fairies, water spirits and wood spirits, devils and wild hunters had never been exorcised from the banks of the Rhine."

In *The Haunted Vintage,* a Christian monastery and vineyard in Bavaria are under assault. Primal Nature is beating at its doors. A fine pagan frenzy surrounds character and scene at harvest time, revealing "glimpses of the age of the Pagan gods before monk and nun, ghost and demon, robber knight came to dwell on the banks of the Rhine." Edward Wagenknecht has pronounced *The Haunted Vintage* "a masterpiece of atmospheric invocation and concentration; the description of the harvest is a brilliant tour-de-force on both the natural and the supernatural level."[1]

Lally Duchene, on the commission of the local Duke of Nassau, has left behind his old life and the fair Pauline, the woman he loves, to take on the position of commandant of the Eberbach prison and lunatic asylum, where he oversees 250 prisoners and a hundred lunatics. Once a monastery, its aspect disturbs Lally—"How much more fitted for the worship of heathen gods was this building, placed in this rich garden of Nature's fairest fruits, than for the rites of a spiritual religion!" Meanwhile, a hidden, ancient temple is excavated nearby. It is a temple to the god Mithias, an Eastern deity, a god who ruled over the sun and was attended by fire-worshippers. Inside are altars once used for human sacrifices.

---

1. Edward Wagenknecht, *Seven Masters of Supernatural Fiction* (Westport, CT: Greenwood Press, 1991), 156.

In this excerpt from the concluding chapters, 28–32, the principal characters are all here for the harvest—Lally's servant, Luy, a peculiar fellow, whose grotesque features resemble the hideous medieval animal carvings on the old cathedral walls; one of the female prisoners, identified as "Gertruda Gerhart, Dissolute," who is reputed to be a witch who allegedly has lured several of the local citizens into the forest, where they disappeared; the recently arrived Duke, who is soon smitten by Gertruda's charms; and Pauline, whose love for Lally will contend with the evil forces engulfing the area.

The vintage was very early that year—early, that is, for the Rhinegau, where it is sometimes as late as November, and nearly always after the first frost. But this spring and summer had been so fiercely hot that the grapes were ripe to bursting by early September, and the harvest could no longer be delayed. Lally felt in a vague and uneasy fashion as if this harvest was the climax of a great drama, unseen, only half guessed at, in which forces beyond even the comprehension of a mortal were involved. The glorious days seemed heavy with menace; the purple nights heavy with portents . . .

Lally was caught up in the strong wheel of circumstance and sent round and round the routine of days that he began to dread and fear. There seemed no escape and no hope. He would have given much to have got away from the scornful reproach of Pauline's silence, from the spectacle of the Duke's ghastly calm, from the pastor's gloomy hints and fearful suggestion, from the queer, watchful eyes of Luy, and the moans of the maniacs of the pavilions—and the nights, heavy with mysterious portents—of what?

The Riesling grapes had now become of a rose-red colour; the stalks were drying, and some bunches beginning to shrivel and drop to the ground, the harvest could no longer be delayed.

The Haunted Vintage, *cover illustration*

"This year they will be late," said the pastor, and for all Lally's pressing he would not explain himself further.

Then one morning he said:

"They have come."

Lally looked round the white sun-filled refectory. The books and the benches were alike put away, for the children were helping in the harvest and did not come to lessons now; only the big Bible remained on a stand of black oak.

"Who have come? asked Lally impatiently.

"Go to the Steinberg," said the old man, "and you will see them. . . ."

An old vine-dresser, complacently observing the result of his long labours, was also sheltering in the pavilion, and Lally, from sheer weariness of spirit, began to talk to him.

"It will be a magnificent harvest, eh?"

"Yes, Herr Graff, but better if we could have waited for the first frost. Never have I known the harvest before October, but this year the grapes would not have kept a moment longer. They will soon be overripe as it is!"

With a chuckle he added: "I thought that they would be late this year!"

Lally started.

"Who are they?"

"Why, the foreigners who come to help in the vintage."

"Are they foreigners?"

"Well, the come from a long way off and they speak a strange language among themselves," replied the old peasant vaguely, "and they seem to know a good deal about foreign countries."

Lally smiled, with a certain sense of relief.

"They come from another part of Nassau and speak another dialect, I suppose," he said. "Probably they go all over Germany, or do they always come here?"

"Some of them always; they have never missed a year since I can remember. But then, isn't this the best vineyard in Germany—better than Rudesheim or Johannisberg, Morcobrunner or Ellfeld, where they still grow the vine in *stock?*"

"Yes, yes," said Lally impatiently, "but who are these people? And why do they wander about instead of working in their native places like others?"

"I cannot tell you that, Herr Graf. It is enough that they are good workers and can tell you fine tales. There is nothing that they do not know about vines—about the Lieste vineyard, where they grow the Hermitage grape to make the wine that goes into the cellars of the castle of Wartzburg in Franconia, where there are tuns so high one must use a ladder of twenty-four steps to reach the top; and the Champagne, where good King Probus began making wine—the 'stopper jumper' or 'devil's wine.'"

Lally rose, hastily interrupting.

"You talk nonsense, old man; I think that you are doited."

The peasant laughed quietly to himself. Lally thought now that he had a peculiar and unpleasant face.

I will talk with these people myself."

With this Lally left the shade of the pavilion, and, following one of the carriage roads that intersected the vineyard, made his way to the group standing in the narrow shade of the roofed wall.

He was greeted by respectful salutations from all, and the farmer would have stopped his instructions in deference to the commandant of Kloster Eberbach, but Lally bade him proceed, and, leaning against the wall, observed the newcomers. He counted eight of them mingled with the prisoners and the peasants always employed on the farm. They were all so young that the vine-dresser's tale was proved absurd; it was impossible that he could have seen them year after year.

There were six men and two women, all wearing the blue smocks and leather belts of Nassau. The women had the usual white kerchiefs folded over their heads.

Save that they were all more than usual handsome, robust, tall, fair, and fresh-coloured, Lally could see nothing unusual about them. Fine types and a heavy type of animal beauty was not rare among the peasantry of the Rhinegau. This favoured spot, like a bay in the mountain, bounded by the Rhine and the Tannus, and so overflowing with fruitfulness as to have been called the Garden of Bacchus—these were fitting inhabitants of such a country. Lally admired them, yet found something repellant in their size, their strength, and their calm.

He remarked with anger that the girl Gertruda was among them. She was of the same type and bearing, and seemed to be conversing with them in their own dialect.

Lally was vexed that she should have been allowed the privilege of working in the Steinberg, one usually accorded only to those prisoners whose sentences were light and offences slight.

He went over to her, looking an incongruous figure in his uniform, with his sword and powder.

"Do you know these strangers?" he asked her rudely.

"Yes, I know them."

"What district do they come from?"

"All from the Rhinegau, but they have travelled."

He now perceived that two of the men had a shaggy, wild appearance and an aspect serene but ferocious, while the others were youths of a more noble aspect, flushed and handsome.

The women were like Gertruda, heavy-browed, wide-eyed, large limbed, with the animal look Lally had so often noticed among the peasantry who toiled in the earth and were untouched by any breath of any town.

Everyone was now supplied with scissors and knives and little baskets, and to every six labourers was allotted a collector, who carried a quantity of empty baskets. Those vintagers who were new to the work were told to cut out of every branch thick stalks, tendrils, unripe and decayed berries, and to proceed as fast as possible with their labours.

Lally walked beside Gertruda as she stepped between the rows of vines; the other side of her walked one of the young peasant strangers. He and the girl were almost of a height, and their stride swung well together. Lally felt incongruous, alien, but he kept his pace.

The perfume of the grapes, overripe and bursting; the sight of them, rose-red, bunch after bunch on the well pruned vines, from which all superfluous wood and foliage had been cut away; the unshaded azure of the sky, which danced with points of light; this press of people, burnt and coloured by the sun, their healthy flesh scantily covered, the sweet odours of the open air coming from their skin, their hair, their breath—all these things began to affect the senses of Lally. A feeling of giddiness possessed him; purple of fruit and sky, rose of fruit and flesh, gold of hair and sun, all mingled together in a whirl of piercing colour that made him giddy. He had to put his hand to his eyes.

"The sun makes you dizzy," said Gertruda. "If one is not used to it one cannot support the vintage time."

Lally give her a savage look; but he did indeed feel that he must at once leave the vineyard .

As he turned away all the vintagers were laughing together, and it seemed to Lally that they were laughing mockingly at him.

Lally, like everyone else save Pauline, spent his day in the vineyard. It seemed, indeed, impossible to keep away from the place where all life and interest was now concentrating. The excitement over the good harvest was contagious; without doubt the vintage was magnificent. This year there would be no need to make the wine palatable by the addition of sugar or to put chalk into the cask; the wines of the Steinberg would, this autumn, compare with any from Walluf to Lorch, and even probably be better than those from the Rudesheimer Berg and the Johannisberg; nay, better than the best that could be produced from any of the terraces of the whole chain of the Taunus hills.

The *auslere,* or first gathering, had been splendid.

To make the choicest of Cabinet wines—those that were sold in bottles only under the seal of the Prince—the best bunches of grapes were plucked by the vintagers, all faulty fruit removed from them, and delivered to the collectors, who sent over them again before throwing from the baskets into the first press, a small perforated tub which rested on two boards placed across a larger one. In the first tub a young boy stood treading the grapes with bare feet, so that all passed through the holes into the larger cask before.

As there were not sufficient of these presses for the splendid abundance of the harvest, several casks of a different kind were being used in which the women, with bare arms stained to the elbow, beat the grapes to a pulp with heavy pieces of wood.

The grapes, where pulped by hands or feet, were then poured into wooden tubs to the rows of carts that stood waiting on the carriage way harnessed to stout little ponies or to oxen.

Those carts consisted of huge casks on wheels, with a funnel at the top, which were at once driven to the press house. The juice, skins, and stalks were then poured through an opening at the end of the cask into tubs, which were immediately carried to the press reserved for the Cabinet wines.

These men were operating the presses—gently at first, to prevent the overflowing of the abundant juice; afterwards so vigorously that they sweated at their task, and the pure juice, free now from skin and stalk, ran in a thick yellow stream out of the two holes in the press into a small vat beneath, and then directly into pipes that ran into the tuns in the vaults beneath, which had been prepared by washings with hot water and afterwards with sulphur.

Lally tasted this raw wine and found it of a sweet and pleasant flavour; a cloying, over-luscious liquor. Perhaps, he thought, this was the old nectar of the gods. . . .

The rosy, purple stain of the grape was everywhere—on the bare limbs of the vintagers, trodden into the warm earth, on the wall and floors of the press houses, on the casks and carts and baskets, on the late vivid-coloured wild flowers that grew outside the wall of the Steinberg.

Lally didn't see much of Gertruda; she kept with the two women strangers; but in the men he found good companions.

As they worked or as they rested over their meals they told him tales and legends, and gave him accounts of the different vineyards of the world. The youngest and handsomest, a youth whose heavy beauty seemed to increase daily, and who owned the strange name of Gereon (after, he said, the basilica of that name, in which are laid the bones of a hundred saints, slain by order of Diocletian and Maximin), spoke more than the others of the vine and its glory.

He told Lally of the great scorching arid desert, extending from Coquimbo, in Chili, to Payter, in Peru, where were town of Rica and Matilla, whose vineyards, in this rainless land, are irrigated by the melting of the snows on the Cordilleras; of Teneriffe, or Vidonia, in the Canary Islands, from which came the ancient sack; of the luxurious vines that covered the bleak mountains of Maderia; of the coarse, sweet wines of Hungary, Tokay, Meneses, St. Gyorgy, and Oden, the rare wines of Russia, Massandra, Aidanil, and Aloupka, from the Crimea. The vineyards of Sicily, Italy, and Greece were also well known to this young man, and he spoke of the vine-covered islands of the Archipelago as if they were his home. Particularly did he dwell on the luscious taste of *commander* from Cyprus and Napoli de Malvasia, and the beauties of the little Isle of Santorin, green with vines from one end to the other. . . .

The eldest, a heavy-shouldered fellow whose locks were bleached to a fairness that had almost a greenish tint, spoke of the days when there were no cathedrals in Germany, but when the gods were worshipped in grove and thicket. These altars, he added were overthrown by the monks and saints, but they had never been able to entirely destroy the gods themselves nor the myriads of spirits who attended them. Ghosts and nymphs and penates, kobolds and fairies, water spirits and wood spirits, devils and wild hunters had never been exorcised from the banks of the Rhine. Lally, absorbed, listened to tales of the fiery chariot of Main; of the phantom of Nicias Varus at Niers; of the wild hunter and his hell-hounds who haunted the Odenwold and Rodenstein, and his hideous host who possessed the Berstrasse. This man who was called by his companions Hoddeken, which Lally guessed to be a vulgar dialect name, was full of such wild and ghastly stories and of others that Lally dimly remembered to have heard before, such as the river fight of Westhofen, with its prelude; St. George's Day, when the cathedral and palace of Cologne were sacked by the mob, who betook themselves to the bishop's cellars and there were either suffocated by the fumes of the strong wines or drowned by the overflowing of the butts which they had broken open.

[Another] peasant, who was known by his surname of Vatermann, and was of a more gloomy and taciturn character, sometimes told Lally tales of the Rhine, and Undine, the nixie, the water wolf, the Lorelai, and the wonderful halls of pearl and crystal beneath the waters of the Rhine.

He knew also of the romances of the *Nibelungen Lied,* of Siegfried working under Mime, at Xanten, and the marvellous hoard lost forever beneath the waves of the river. In these stories he was joined by the fifth peasant, whom he spoke of as his brother. This was a man of much the same appearance as himself named Ursel, but if he was so called from that village or no Lally could not discover. The last stranger, Willigis, seemed a whimsical fellow, and related many stories—which appeared to give him great delight—of the tricks played by gnomes, goblins, and pixies on human beings.

Lally, listening all day in the wine-scented atmosphere to these tales, thought less and less of Pauline and the Duke; less and less of past or future.

One evening, returning in the hot and purple dusk from the vineyard, he met the pastor, who appeared to be in search of him. . . .

"And you are so simple that you do not understand, Herr Graf? Is it possible?" asked the pastor anxiously. "Cannot you see what is disguised behind these foolish names. Do you not see that you are not dealing with human beings at all?"

Lally laughed loud in the darkness.

"You have indeed lived too long alone with your old books, Herr Sandemann, when you see in these poor peasants evil spirits."

"Did I say evil spirits? Perhaps rather gods."

"What gods?" whispered Lally.

"I dare not name them."

"But I do," said Lally in the same tone. "Bacchus, Mithias, Freia—" He caught himself up with another laugh. "What madness we talk!"

"As well say," returned the pastor, "that the others are Heerwisch, the Kobold, the water-wolf—the Rhine himself, eh? As well say that, Herr Graf?"

"Say what you like," said Lally desperately. "I am not bemused nor enchanted. Your ugly stories do not frighten me—no, not at all! . . ."

These were strange days for Lally; neither the past nor the future seemed to hold any meaning, and the present was like a dream in which emotion is fantastically heightened and action nullified.

He had no more desire to rouse himself from this mood than the drugged man to escape from his drowsy sleep. The only two people who could bring him into touch with reality—Pauline and the Duke—he avoided.

The doctor, Herr Lindpainter, was one of those who came to Eberbach for the harvest. For some time Lally avoided meeting him, but at length they found themselves face to face beneath the hot walls of the Steinberg.

The doctor looked at Lally very queerly and told him bluntly that he appeared ill.

Lally, who had never felt better in his life, laughed . . .

He was conscious that he had neglected his dress of late. His uniform was untidy, his hair unpowdered; he was lean and sunburnt too, he knew, and that something too flamboyant, too coarsely handsome, in his appearance that he had been so careful to subdue at Wiesbaden was now very noticeable. The eyes were too splendid the brows too heavy, the hair too thick—but ill? No, he was not ill.

The doctor asked him if his appointment at Eberbach was a permanent one, and when Lally merely laughed Herr Lindpainter turned away, shaking his head . . .

*   *   *

The merchants, the wine brokers, and most of the vintagers had gone; the presses were empty and the casks full. Only the wood and the leaves remained in the vineyard, and these were brown and dry. Round the press houses and the roofed walls of the Steinberg the murk and dregs lay decaying in the sun, swarmed over by pale wasps and peculiar little flies.

The last handful of grain had been gathered from the fields, the last apple plucked from the orchards. The music of the merry-makers was stilled, for the peasants had turned to other labours of the year; only a few remained to watch the fermenting of the new wine in the cellars.

The harvest was complete.

Only the sunshine remained unchanged, unclouded, undiminished, only taking on daily the deeper hue that paints the luscious tints of autumn. If it had not been for the heavy dews drought might have been feared; as it was the leaves and grass dried before their season. Where the hay had been cut for the second time the fields were like burnt gold, and the woods had taken on fiery and metallic colours—scarlet, crimson, and red yellow.

Only the strange peasants lingered, despite their talk of leaving early in order to go to some other vintage.

They had now no definite work to do. They had taken their fee and accomplished their labours, but they remained at Eberbach as if for their own pleasure. They spent a great deal of their time in the wood; Lally knew that. He was tempted to follow them, but he never did. He had not been into the wood since a day that he did not allow his memory to dwell on.

And he was well assured that the Duke did not leave Eberbach.

These young men still avoided each other, and the woman lived alone in the rooms above the refectory; but on the second day after the departure of the pastor, Lally, with a greater effort of will than he had for some time made, and with this problem of Pauline beating in his heavy head, sought out the Duke in the evening, when the great heat was over.

The Duke was seated at the harpsichord playing over old airs; he had the manner of one waiting. The room was most quiet, as if filled with the very essence of sleep.

The Duke looked completely pale, thinner, too, Lally thought, even ill, yet even more than usually serene and aloof. He smiled at Lally and ceased his playing.

He had put aside the heavy braided coat, and his slender figure was covered to the waist by the thin lawn shirt; only his cravat was loose, leaving his throat bare between the frills. His hair was unpowdered and falling free. He seemed very young—a boy.

He looked at Lally without malice or surprise.

"The splendour of the harvest has fatigued you," he said.

"Do I also look weary?" asked Lally, conscious of some haggard looks.

"There has been almost too much sun, too rich a vintage," replied the Duke. "The whole world seems stained with wine and to smell of ripe fruit. Every night I dream of apples tumbling into bins and grapes crushed into the press."

"You dream of nights?" questioned Lally, leaning over the harpsichord.

"I dream, yes, but it is difficult to know which are the dreams. The woods are so full of curious things."

"The woods!" cried Lally sharply. "But you do not go into the woods; you are here all day. I know that."

"All day," repeated the Duke vaguely.

"And at night you dream—you have just said so."

The Duke's fingers strayed over the keyboard.

"The harvest is over now," continued Lally, with an accent of fear, "and you are free to return to Wiesbaden, Highness."

"The boar," said the Duke, "comes to-night with all his troop."

"The boar!" cried Lally, with wild laughter. "What fairy tale is this?"

"I mean the boar of Eberbach, who persuaded St. Bernard to build this place and who has never left it, hardly for a day, since, save to go into the woods where the gods dwell. They always come for the harvest, and when they go they take someone with them."

Lally laughed again; it had a mournful sound in the quiet chamber.

"You babble, poor youth!" he said.

"Are you afraid?" asked the Duke serenely.

Lally lowered his voice.

"Are not you?"

"Why should I be? It is more wonderful than anything I ever dreamed of."

"It is a dream."

"A dream?"

"A dream."

The Duke sighed. A little breeze rippled in through the open window and faintly stirred the heavy curtains of the massive bed. At the faint stir this made Lally quickly turn his head and gave the corner a fearful glance.

"Listen," he said thickly, "there is Pauline. We must think of Pauline. Herr Sandemann has gone, and she is left to our charge."

"Pauline?" repeated the Duke vaguely. He was different now indeed to the anguished young man of the interview in the press house, whose whole soul had seemed to hang on this one name—Pauline!

"You should have married her," continued Lally heavily, "but now the pastor is not here."

"Has he taken the Bible?" interrupted the Duke, with sudden sharpness.

He leant forward across the harpsichord; the light was beginning to fade, and his sudden animation gave his face a sharp, foxy look.

"What do you know about the Bible?" demanded Lally, moving back.

"Luy told me."

"You have been seeing Luy?"

"Isn't he—"

Lally interrupted.

"You must not talk of it or think of it. Herr Jesus! we must leave Eberbach."

The Duke shivered.

"For me it is too late. I would rather go with them."

"Speak reason—speak words of good omen," cried Lally. "Will you wait to be lured to those places that are neither heaven nor hell nor earth, to wander as the victims of the Willis, the nixie, or the Heerwisch?"

The Duke did not reply; it seemed as if he had not heard Lally's words. The twilight was closing in and it seemed that, after the heat of the day, the chamber was suddenly chill. Lally felt his body relax, his senses dull; only by a great effort, like that by which a man swooning under a drug will keep his senses for a little while by fixing them on some tangible object, did he keep his mind on Pauline—Pauline.

"She is going to be your wife," he said, "your wife."

The Duke repeated "Wife?" as if the word was unfamiliar to him. Lally thought that many of the terms and symbols used by humanity were becoming strange to him now.

"I speak of Pauline," added Lally, but wearily. He felt how useless it all was; also, what a matter of indifference. A great star had appeared in the square of pellucid sky framed by the window. Looking at that like a crystal twinkling with many colours,

Lally felt that nothing mattered.

"Well, good-night," he said.

He glanced towards the bed, now almost obscured by the shadows that began to deepen in the corners. Surely a foot and ankle gleamed, like silver under water, through the transparent shade, as if someone lying carelessly asleep there, had thrust out a delicate limb beneath the folds of the faded damask.

"She is here," whispered Lally, and the Duke looked up with an air of expectancy. The wind blew with a stronger gust, stirring the curtain with a quick movement, and the foot was gone.

"My fancy," muttered Lally, "and the shadows. Good-night, again."

He sighed, hesitated, then, still striving to hold to that tangible image of Pauline, he added:

"Shall we not all go to Wiesbaden to-morrow? Yes, if we are wise."

"There is no such thing as wisdom," answered the Duke. "We are all fools."

And he looked away from Lally and out of the window at the star which seemed to be larger and swinging nearer, like a lamp in a trembling hand, and his face showed a gentle impatience for the other man's presence—indeed, for all the things of this world.

Lally left with a sudden quickening of his pace. He remembered with a curious thrill of panic that it would soon be dark and that he did not want to be out after night had fallen. . . . He looked up at the star, and the sight of it seemed to reassure him. The woods were still just visible against the light violet of the sky. In this dusk their hot and vivid autumn colours were hidden; they appeared dark as when Lally had first seen them and seemed to have again the fantastic shape of a beast crouching to spring into the valley below.

Lally hastened through the cloister garden. The flowers were all fallen and the herbs all plucked. He lingered by the door of the laboratory; it was quiet and very desolate the red roses were withered from the window, and only the bare thorns and dead leaves laced across the casement. The odour of musk, tonqin, and neroli still clung to the threshold.

Lally hurried on his way. As he passed the boar's head he saw that it was hung with a garland of autumn berries. Everything was so still that he paused to listen.

Not a sound from the prisoners, the maniacs, the soldiers; no one seemed abroad.

He went to his room and called for Luy. There was no answer, nor had he really expected one.

He lit the lantern and all the candles that he could find, and then hesitated, peering about the room and down the corridor.

Nothing.

He crossed himself from some long-dormant instinct and left the room, taking with him the lantern.

With a nervous step he hastened to the women's quarters, where Gertruda was imprisoned. The lamps were lit as usual and everything seemed in order.

Of late, Lally had ordered a guard to be set here at night. He saw the man now, prone on the floor, heavily asleep. Lally did not wake him.

Proceeding cautiously down the long corridor, he paused before the door of Gertruda's cell.

It was wide open. He could see the little square of window that just framed the great star.

He looked in; she was not there; the cell was redolent of the scent of rose and grape and lily, and quite empty. It seemed to him that a white bird fluttered somewhere out of the reach of the lantern beams, but he was not sure.

He went back to his room, cautiously, softly; he did not reason or wonder. Feeling deeply drowsy, he went to sleep flung across his bed in his uniform, but he remembered to unbuckle his sword and put the hilt of it near his hand—it was the only cross he had.

Lally woke and lay still, gazing into the darkness. He knew at once that during his sleep everything had changed; that what they had all been waiting for had come.

Just as some dweller on a marshy coast, who daily sees the ocean and knows the peril of it, yet never thinks of it, wakes some night to hear the waves lapping against his window and knows that he is doomed; just as a sick man, lulled by the length of a tedious illness into thinking no more of death, all at once finds the moment come in which he must die; so did Lally, who had long known of the mysteries and awful forces that surrounded him, know that now the hour had come when they were unbound from whatever restraint had held them, and upon him.

Something was pouring into the old building through every window and every door; something was filling it from cellar to roof—something that filled him with panic fear, and yet was alluring him, calling him.

He put his hands to his face and felt the cold sweat there; his soul fumbled for some assistance.

"Christ—Jesus," he said.

He listened.

There were voices everywhere, the sound of feet and hoofs, and winged things continually passed the bed; sometimes so heavily that Lally was shaken, sometimes so lightly that he felt a mere quiver of movement.

And yet there was nothing there; his outer senses knew nothing save darkness and silence. He flung out his hands and circled empty space, though fingertips and sweeping hair touched his face.

He put his feet to the ground, grasped his sword, and called his servant; but he knew quite well that there would be no answer; knew that he should never see Luy again.

They were crowding, pressing all about him; hurrying, they seemed to him; yet as he made his way from the bed to the door nothing impeded him—the room seemed empty.

The corridor was full of them. They had invaded and overwhelmed the whole building; they were in complete possession now, without disguise or subterfuge. Lally moved slowly, grasping his sword, fumbling in the darkness. He wondered why he had been enabled to break the enchantment that held all the others asleep. Without conscious volition he went downstairs and out into the orchard.

There were a few stars abroad, but the night was cloudy and dark—seemed too full of dark yet stifling vapours, like the emanations of a marsh. A low wisp of fire flickered here and there among the orchard trees. "Heerwisch," thought Lally.

A shrill, thin piping, like the voice of a single reed, pierced the darkness; it appeared to come from the direction of the vineyard.

Lally shivered to hear this unearthly note, more ancient than music, more enduring than humanity, that rose and fell with a passionless menace. Lally looked up at the stars; these also seemed far away and unfriendly, and he to be adrift in an alien world.

There were so many of them—in the dry grass, lurking under the stripped trees—that he did not dare proceed, but stood with his back against the building, as if that afforded him some protection.

He thought of the vineyard and the temple near by, and the Duke in his lonely apartment, and Gertruda's cell, with the door standing ajar and the great star looking in through the tiny square of the window.

The piping shrank to a low whimpering, like something tired of waiting for its prey. Lally turned in the direction of the vineyard.

Then he paused, hesitating.

Surely the piping came from the wood, not the vineyard. Wherever it was he must follow it. Was it not a call to the altar of Bacchus or Mithias, where he should once more find Freia and the boar?

The trail of frail light glanced across his path. Lally began to follow it; the Heerwisch would be the guide to where the pipe played.

He went quickly after the dancing globe of frail fire that now kept deliberately in his path. The night was warmer and heavily scented with the perfume of the grape; he felt that they were all urging him on to follow the will o' the wisp.

Then someone caught hold of him, flung arms round his waist and held him still; he knew at once the touch of common humanity.

"Who are you—abroad to-night?" he asked hoarsely.

"Pauline," came the woman's voice, "Pauline."

He had forgotten Pauline; the name sounded unfamiliar; he was annoyed that she prevented his following the will o' the wisp.

"Listen," he said. "I must go up to the woods. Do you understand? The Heerwisch is guiding me."

"I see nothing," she answered quickly, "yet certainly there is something evil abroad to-night. That is why I came to find you."

"Do you not hear the piping?" asked Lally.

"No; there is only an awful stillness."

"Do you not feel them—everywhere, Pauline?"

"Yes, but you will not go with them; you will stay with me."

She put her arms along his shoulders now and drew his head down until his cheek touched hers. This gave him a curious sensation; the light of Heerwisch grew dimmer, and the call of the pipe fainter. The touch of her warm humanity gave him a certain strength. His breathed more freely; the air seemed less oppressive. He could just see the shape and substance of her as she leant against him.

"It is the Duke you should have gone to find," he said.

"I only care for you," replied Pauline; "the only man I could save to-night was my lover. You were once—and never another. That is something between us. There is no love now, I know—"

He interrupted.

"Oh, Pauline, Pauline! What has happened? I think we have all been wicked! Pauline, I am lost now. I must go with them; there is no hope. I think they make a sacrifice in the woods. They will slay me across Freia's knees, and the boar will lap my blood. This will crown the vintage of the gods."

"You are distraught with these strange happenings," said Pauline, and he felt her tears on his face. "Come with me to the little chapel."

But he struggled with her, knowing he must follow the piping and the dancing light. Pauline was strong and held him tightly. His sword fell down between them; Lally felt weak and faint; he was conscious that something—an animal—was leaping up at him, snapping at his hand, at his throat; that the red eyes of Luy were looking at him out of the visage of a boar; that the white form of Gertruda, showing at the flowing open of the Madonna's blue robe, was before him, and that she beckoned him with star wreathed head—and yet, all the while, he knew that the human woman held him fast.

A great wind blew, and he lost sense of time and space; a vast eternity, in which a lifetime seemed but a twinkling, enveloped him. He felt his feet on the edge of plumbless abysses, measureless skies above him. Nothing mattered but sleep.

He was thus far on the paths that humanity dreads to even dream of when the woman, who must have surely loved him, stayed his steps, so that he became conscious, though with agony, of her fleshly presence, of her hard grip of him and her tears, and so with deep pangs of spirit shuddered back to the earth, and found himself standing there with her in the withered orchard beneath the broken clouds that showed the stars.

And nothing had happened.

There was only Pauline, weeping to be comforted, a woman, poor creature after all.

"They have gone," said Lally.

They said no more, for both were very weary. He led her to the refectory through a world that began to glimmer with the soft fires of the dawn, and though neither had thought much of these things before, they spent the short time till daylight in the Lutheran chapel, where the Baroness already kept vigil on her knees.

With the stir of life in Eberbach came the news both expected. The strange vintagers had gone, and the girl Gertruda, and Luy—and the Duke.

This last the searchers found, but not a life, and scarcely in human shape. His fate was clear; he had ventured into the forest after dusk and been slain and mangled by a wild boar. Lally saw that the poor remains were honoured by burial beside that other Prince of Nassau in the cathedral church, but he dare say no Christian rites over the grave. Shaken free of these poor bones and flesh, the young man wandered in some region of which it was best not to think.

It was certain that he would return for the next vintage in the train of the old gods, following Freia and Luy the boar—nay, it was likely that he was here now, somewhere, and would never again leave Eberbach. But Lally and Pauline returned to the world, loving each other at last in a kind and human fashion.

The Golden Violet

London: Heinemann, 1936.

> "She belonged to the tropic night, to the rich, strange Island, to those tangled excitements."

"[Joseph] Shearing" has given us a new quality of exquisite shivering," enthuses Sinclair Lewis of *The Golden Violet*, "of sophisticated naivete, of dried rose-leaves soaked with blood."[1]

The story takes place against the violent backdrop of a slave rebellion in Jamaica in the British West Indies, presumably based on the eleven-day Jamaican Slave Revolt of 1831–32. Inspired by the abolitionist movement in London and abetted by many missionaries, tens of thousands of slaves rebelled against the harsh conditions of the sugar cane plantation owners and the Jamaican government. Recruited to help suppress the rebellion were the Jamaican Maroons of Accompong Town, i.e., blacks descended from Africans who had escaped from slavery and had established free communities in the mountainous interior. Once suppressed, the rebels were slaughtered in great numbers by the government and the plantocracy. In 1833 British parliament passed the abolition of slavery.

Angelica Cowley, a successful novelist, has come to Jamaica as the wife of a plantation owner, Thomas Thicknesse. Suffering from the tropical climate and appalled at the simmering racial unrest among the slaves, whom she regards as "base, wretched chattels," she quickly regrets an "enslavement" of her own—her marriage.

---

1. Sinclair Lewis, "Preface" to *The Golden Violet* (New York: The Reader's Club, 1943), 6.

Only her growing attraction to a nearby plantation owner, John Seba Gordon, brings her solace and comfort. Thus, while her husband indulges in adultery with a "half-caste" woman, or what was known then as a "mulatto," Angel herself draws closer to Gordon.

The following excerpts are from Chapters 4 and 7. In the first, Angelica makes her way alone through the wild, luxuriant landscape to John Gordon's house. Their conversation reveals her naïveté about brewing unrest on the Island, her growing attraction to him, and Gordon's own cautious tiptoeing around what she does not yet know—that he is a mulatto.

Angel sighed. She was exhausted and she tried to stop her thoughts—she could not endure to wonder if [John Gordon] would be pleased to see her and to give her a welcome, to wonder if he would know her again, if he had some explanation to offer for his unfulfilled promise and neglect. She tried to distract herself by listening to that concert which had scarcely ceased since she had left her home, the cooing of the doves, the waving of the canes one against the other above the buzz of the unseen insects in the wayside flowers.

A few moments elapsed and she saw John Gordon coming towards her; she saw him hasten his steps, and she felt as she had felt when she had seen him before in the church in Spanish Town, the satisfaction and the pain of his comeliness.

She had indeed no fault to find with his welcome. He received her with amazement and all the chivalrous surprise, with all the tender respect that she had hoped for. He seemed amazed, overwhelmed, gratified. His manner had the same tender courtesy that she had noted with such greedy thankfulness before. Her joy made her sincere. As her hand rested in his, she said:

"You did not come to see me, so I have come to see you."

As he did not immediately answer this reproach, she added:

"Do you know my husband?"

The Golden Violet, *cover illustration*

"I have seen him, yes, but not very often. You know that he has been away for a long while at a time from the Island?"

"But you are neighbors and the place is so lonely, and I have never heard him mention you."

"It often happens like that, I suppose. . . . I have been occupied with this war with the Maroons and the slave rising, and not so very much on my estate. You will find it slightly neglected."

"My husband thinks that ours is neglected, too. I don't know what they should be like. The negroes are filthy creatures, are they not?"

"You dislike them?"

"Oh, yes. Don't you?"

"You're not happy then, at Venables. But let us come in out of the sun. Will you come into my house? You see," he smiled, "I know the rules and what should be done, but I have no wife, nor mother, nor sister."

That roused her curiosity, which was always avid about this man . . . She had a great and almost overwhelming desire to be frank with him, to confess everything to him, all her confusions and her complexities. Now she was with him, she realized how much she needed a friend, companionship, someone in whom to confide. Her need became passionate, she trembled with the desire for it, as a starving man will tremble with the desire for food or water . . . A dozen questions concerning this man pricked her mind. Why had he been content to live in Jamaica? How had he obtained his education? He had an air of finer breeding than any man she had met.

"Why weren't you at the Governor's dinner?" she asked sharply.

"I do not like those formal, official occasions. I had seen the Governor that morning about the Maroons. You see, Mrs. Thicknesse, I have been His Excellency's emissary to the chief of the Maroons. I have been able to do him some service."

"Yes, he said he believed in you and that you were a fine man. He seemed to admire you."

"Where is Mr. Thicknesse now?"

"He has gone away for two or three days and left me alone with all those negro servants. Don't you think that's hateful?"

"You mustn't be afraid of them, you know. You should make friends with them. It is quite easy to get their devotion."

"It is? I hate them anyway; don't let us talk of them. I'm never going near their village, their chapel or their hospital again. I used to feel so sorry for them, but I don't now, not even when one of them gets beaten. I think that some of my husband's overseers are harsh men, but I don't feel sorry about it."

Her head sank back into the soft, yellow cushions and she stared at the window. Across the light lattice she could see the shape of leaves, firm, hard, and as green as jade. On a table near were some of his drawings of birds, neat, careful—the nightingale, the banana quit, the joggerhead.

"I'm talking nonsense," she said with her finger to her lips. "I don't really know what I'm saying. Now, tell me something about yourself. I suppose I mustn't stay long. Tell me." She sat up pleading like a child asking for a fairy story.

"Why, there's really nothing to tell you, Mrs. Thicknesse. I was born and bred on the Island I inherited this estate. I think I understand the slaves and the Maroons—that's an ugly English word—Cimeroons, it should be. When there was trouble, I offered my services to Sir William Hayes and went up into the mountains to the Cockpits for him with some of the soldiers. That's all. There's really been nothing else in my life."

"Do you live here alone?"

"Yes, my parents are dead, and I have neither brothers nor sisters."

"Nor any other relations in the whole Island? Are you a member of the Assembly? You don't go to Spanish Town or Kingston in the winter? Are you a head magistrate like my husband or in the Militia?"

"None of those," he smiled, "except the last. We all have to be, you know, between the ages of eighteen and sixty."

"How much do the slaves cost? Where do you buy them? Who are the overseers? What are the likely profits on sugar, on rum, and on the cotton?"

Mr. Gordon laughed.

"I might buy a negro, a healthy male, for about eighty pounds. A planter is forced to keep an overseer, who is generally a white man, for the first hundred slaves, and after that another free man for every seventy. The free blacks are worse off than the slaves—they live in laziness and misery. Their poverty is extreme, as there is no work for them to do in the Island. The slaves are better off. Yet I do what I can for the emancipation of the slaves. Most of the clergymen work for that, too."

"And who are these Maroons, these desperate, wild savages against whom you distinguished yourself?" Angel wished to avoid the tedious subject of the slaves.

"They mostly live in the Johnny Crow hills, and are hunters of the wild boar," he answered, amused at her curiosity. "They have their own settlements and towns—Accompony Town, Charles Town. They speak to one another with horns, from which they obtain a great variety of notes. It is pleasing and amusing to hear them echoing through the hills, when one is riding in a lonely part. There are not more than three thousand of them. Now there is nothing to be afraid of—they are poor creatures, who ask for nothing but to be allowed to live in peace. Escaped slaves and some of the free blacks join them now and then—the Coromantees and the Cottawoods. But does this mean anything to you? You are quite safe, I assure you, on Venables Penn."

"I suppose so; I never think about it. What was that skull on a stick that I passed on the way here?"

"It was that of a man who was executed for murder. It was put there as a warning. Did it frighten you?"

"Why do slaves rise and rebel if they're well and happy?"

"Some of them are cruelly treated," replied Gordon quietly. "A bad master has power of life and death over his negroes. Although there are laws against it, it is still possible for these wretched creatures to suffer the utmost pain and misery. Besides, slavery—the fact that they can be bought and sold—" He broke off. "And why are you questioning me on these subjects? I don't believe you really care."

"No, I don't," said Angel. "It was just something to speak to you about. But I do feel a vague curiosity, too. Yes, and a horror."

"I came back from Government Penn yesterday," said Mr. Gordon irrelevantly. "I had been to see Sir William. He thinks there is going to be some more trouble. There has been a little marauding round Moor Town and Charles Town. He wishes to introduce the Spanish chasseurs. They come over here from Cuba with their dogs and they hunt the Maroons in the mountains and in the interior where the white people and even our negroes cannot get."

"Hunt them with dogs!" exclaimed Angel.

"Yes, they are well-trained and very fierce, and their masters are very hardy. They have exterminated the native Indians in Cuba. They live on vegetables and a little salt."

"And they go on hunting, then," said Angel.

"Yes." Mr. Gordon smiled. He rose and leaned against the window so that the shadow of the lattice bars and of the large leaves spread across his handsome face. "Each of them has three

large dogs, which are always kept muzzled and roped. They have
with them other little dogs, 'finders' of keen scent that smell out
the tracks of the Maroons. These chasseurs are armed with a little knife—which is razor sharp—and nothing else. They are honest, hardy and desperate, most temperate men who seldom fail of
their prey. They are paid," he added, looking at Angel, "two
hundred dollars for a three months' hunt."

"It sounds horrible," said Angel. "I hope none of them come
my way."

"You will probably see them if they are imported again into
the Island. They are tall, lean men, wearing a check cotton shirt
open to show a crucifix on their bare chests, with a wide pair of
trousers; they have straw hats made of morass thatch. Their one
diversion when they are off duty is to smoke a segar. They wear
odd boots of untanned leather, 'porco zopatos'—these are the
legs of newly-killed hogs, into which they thrust their feet, letting the hide dry on their own flesh. Of course," added Mr.
Gordon in a toneless voice, "they are white men and Chris-
tians—and so they are well paid and respected."

"Why don't you want them brought into the Island? What
had you to say to the Governor?" asked Angel, sensing his reserve, his pain; she glanced at his drawings, the sight of them
filled her with profound tenderness. "It is necessary and cruel to
hunt these poor wretches out in that manner. They can be treated with. I was successful once. This trouble would not have occurred again if the white men had kept their word. I told all this
to Sir William Hayes, and he agreed with me—but he is not all-
powerful in the Island. A twice-conquered country! What do the
English care about anything save money—trade!"

Angel lay still on the silk cushions; the heat was over her like
a veil. She was perfectly contented in this man's company—let

him talk of what he would. She clasped her hands behind her fair hair, feeling beautifully at ease. . . .

"Will you come some day," he said after a second's pause, "and see my estate, and how my slaves live? There is a doctor here and a Wesleyan minister—both are white men. We do what we can. I should like you to see for yourself the result. . . ."

They stood side by side in silence for a moment; she was sure that he liked her, admired her. That tender regard he turned on her could not be for every woman whom he met. Every woman!—how was it that he was not wedded or betrothed? There must be some marriageable girls in the Island—he had no air of a misanthrope or a hermit. . . .

She picked up her hat and the buttercup-coloured parasol. He did not ask her to stay longer and they left the shadowed room, passed down the stone steps that led from the verandah into the garden, full of nodding bells and stars pendent from delicate boughs. When they reached the gate a party of negroes was going past, returning to their work; they were singing a chant with an odd kind of rhythm, which they emphasized by waving their hands up and down. Angel could catch some of the words, which seemed to her very odd.

> *Take him to de gully*
> *Take him to de gully*
> *But bringee back de frock and de board.*
> *Oh, Massa, Massa! Me no deadee yet*
> *Take him to de gully,*
> *Take him to de gully,*
> *Carry him along!*

"What is it they sing?" she asked.

"They call that 'The Tale of the Frock and the Board.' Don't ask what it means. It refers to some cruel deeds that were done here once."

"But I'd like to know, I must know all I possibly can. I've got to get things straight, you see."

"Will it help you to know about cruelty?" He looked at her quickly. Well, there was an owner here who used to grudge the time and money that a sick slave cost, so when he saw that one of these poor wretches was incurable, he used to have him taken out to a gully and thrown down it to die. And the slaves who were commanded to do this were always told to bring home the frock that this man wore and the board on which he had been lying."

"That must be long ago," said Angel. "People don't do things like that now, do they?"

"I don't know. Sick slaves are a nuisance and an expense, and these people think it kinder to find means of allowing them to die."

As he opened the gate for her, she asked impulsively: "Tell me, you must have something you hold by, living like this, and not believing, I think in any of it. I mean, you don't like it, do you, having slaves, the way people behave in the Island? Then, those books you read—yet you've never been to Europe . . ."

"One is born into a world one did not make, that one does not like. What you want, and what life offers, do not fit together. Well, then, there is nothing for it but to try to get as little unpleasantness as possible out of a condition of things that one finds, perhaps, odious . . . These people have their fancies— 'neger tricks' and 'nancy stories,' as they call them."

She did not answer; she was impressed by the feeling that this man who seemed so gentle, even soft, was absolutely fearless, and she realized, in a baffled fashion, how rare was this quality of serene courage. She refused his escort across his estate and went slowly on her way. Through the hot air drifted the plaintive rhythm:

> *Take him to de gully*
> *Take him to de gully . . .*

[In this second excerpt, from Chapter 7, Angel's furtive, increasingly intimate affair with John Gordon is torn apart when it is revealed that his mother was a mulatto, making him a "quadroon with black blood," who has no civil rights, no vote, and strictly limited property rights. How basely he had deceived her, she rages. He is nothing more than "an ape or beast," like the rest of the slaves. "I understand these people," he responds patiently. "In a way they are my people. To you, no doubt, they are filthy, bestial, fit only for contempt, but I know differently." Then, despairing, he adds: "If you had felt that it made no difference—if you had not really cared at all that I was—a dirty nigger—what a love ours would have been!"

Meanwhile, conditions on the Island are growing perilous for the whites. A slave uprising threatens to overrun some of the plantations, including that of Angel's husband, who is now joining the Militia against the rebels in the Blue Mountains. Gordon himself, under a mandate from the governor, is also taking to the hills to try to negotiate with the rebels. Aware of the danger Gordon faces, Angel looks deep within herself, recovers her love for him, and prepares to follow him. She is transformed: "She, Angel Cowley [Thicknesse], an adulteress who had taken as a paramour a coloured man; but England and those people who would think of her thus were too far away. She belonged to the tropic night, to the rich, strange Island, to these tangled excitements."

Upon learning Gordon has been arrested by the militia, Angel determines to go to him and plead for his life with the governor. She forms a strange alliance with the mulatto slave girl, Luna, her husband's mistress, who claims to know the encampment where Gordon is being held. They set forth with only the uncertain light of the tropical night to guide them. What they discover sets her mind for the climactic vengeful fury she will subsequently wreak against her husband.]

Without speaking, the two women crept along the grove of anatta trees to the shadow of the boiler-house; the flowers and leaves were changed by the starlight into dim hues of blue, violet and purple. Here and there a white blossom showed an unnatural pallid purity.

Angel thought: "What is this errand I am going on? Perhaps all this girl has told me is false, how do I know? Perhaps all I have ever heard of her is a lie, too. What is it that I have in common with her? Why do I like and trust her?—we're all females, slaves, helpless."

"We ought to be there by the dawn, at Sinclair, I mean," said Luna. "You mustn't mind what you see," she added in a whisper as they passed by the rustling sugar-canes, which, unattended and entangled, swayed in the night breeze.

"What do you mean—what I see?"

"Sambo said there would be killing. There was a bloody battle, you know. Some of the white clergymen, besides Mr. Fremantle, took the side of the slaves—and some of Mr. Gordon's people came up and fought for him. I expect they will begin hanging them as soon as it's light—the prisoners, I mean . . ."

They way took them past the mausoleum, which lay in the clear purple shadows of the palm trees.

"I just stop," sighed Angel. "I can't walk so fast, I have a pain in my side." She stared at the dark face so close to her own, hollowed and fine, like a shell washed by many tides. "Tell me, have you ever met John Gordon by a limestone pool?"

"Yes, and in many other places. There is no one like him, none."

"How cool you are! I don't believe you have a soul. You loved him and let him go—like that."

"Luna is a slave. Luna is not born for happiness."

"Who was your father' father?"

"I don't know. I had a black mammie. She was Massa Thicknesse's slave, and so I was born a slave, too . . ."

They hurried on through the crossing shadows. They had to

pass the field of dodder, the dry and twisted plant which lay spread like a silver net in the still night. A nightingale was singing in the dark boughs of a tall black tree. The women moved quickly, the mulatto always a few steps in advance, and drawing, as it were, the white woman after her. They passed the spot on which the murderer's skull had been stuck until the night of the hurricane wind. Amid the wayside ferns curled black and yellow snakes, like those which when she had first come to the Island so frightened her. She regarded them now with indifference. She was envious of everything peaceful in the tranquil night, the sleeping birds, the insects folded away in the blossoms, the reptiles slipping through the ferns, envious of any creature, however humble, who was not bewildered and foolish Angel Thicknesse.

"Will he ever forgive me for what I said to him by the pool? Will he ever care for me again? . . ."

This walk through the night seemed endless; as if she were suffering some fantastic punishment, to wander for ever in this strange starlight, with this dark guide. They turned on to a path unfamiliar to her; half-unconsciously mindful of her husband's warning, she had never gone far in the Island, only along that familiar road which led to the limestone pool and a cedar tree, and the confines of the Gordon estate.

"What shall I do" she asked stupidly, "when I reach the village? I suppose they still will be in bed. I will go to my husband, and what shall I say? He doesn't love me or respect me."

"I don't know what you'll do," said Luna, still moving lightly, briskly ahead. "You'll be a white woman amongst white people."

"I don't think that I can say anything they'll listen to. I shall have to go to the Governor. He can't prevent my doing that."

She tried to imagine what she would make a heroine of a novel do under these circumstances, but her thoughts fell to pieces.

Luna left the road, still holding Angel's hand, and guided her through a heavy grove of dense and massive mangoes. Trailing creepers caught at their clothes and thick ferns impeded their feet as they made their way swiftly; they heard the distant croaking of frogs and the call of owls overhead. Bats, dark as the trees from which they flew, were for an instant silvered by the clear air, then disappeared into shadow again.

"It must be nearly six o'clock," thought Angel. "It will soon be light."

She braced herself against that sudden dawn, which would mean a dreadful day.

"We have nearly reached the bridge," whispered Luna. "You can hear the water falling over the rocks."

Neither of them spoke, but each, as if urged on by some inner and secret fear, hastened her pace with every step. The stars were setting. Angel did not know if the universal brightness, which began to glimmer on the vivid and brilliant flowers, was that of day or night. They reached a slight rocky eminence from which they could look down on the savannah or pasture-land which stretched either side of the Rio Cobre. The water fell in veils down the face of the stone cliffs to join the pool that spread into the river.

This landscape seemed new to Angel; it had an unearthly look and gave her a sense of panic; yet she remembered she had passed that way many times when driving to and from Spanish Town.

"Do you see," whispered the slave, coming to a sudden halt, "down there, the bridge?" She fell on her knees, parted the clusters of fern and gazed below.

Angel looked over her shoulder. There was the single-arch bridge spanning the river. By the side of it grew bushes of African rose. Suspended from the centre was an object hanging heavily at the end of a rope fastened to a coping-stone.

"It is a man," said Luna. "They've hanged a man over the

bridge. I remember when they did that before."

Angel stood gazing at the unnatural-looking landscape clear in the odd half-tone of the colourless light, which in a second became brilliant day. A fresh breeze was blowing from the lofty peaks of the Blue Mountains. Angel turned her head to catch the wind on her face and remembered how she had seen the mighty mountain fifty miles away on the ocean—and here she was standing with its breezes on her face. She turned to look at the bridge, now clearly visible in the rarefied air.

A man, the slave said, a man hanging there; she could see patches of white and light brown—yes, that might be shirt, cravat, kerseymere trousers, that patch of dark might be a man's bent head, the hair falling over the face.

"Do you dare to go and see?" asked the mulatto.

Angel nodded. The two women scrambled down the cliff among the ferns, the water-breaks, the broken stones, the tufts of flowers and on the pasture-land along the side of the winding river, which was edged by sorrel, reeds, sedges and water buttercups.

"It's a scarecrow," muttered Angel, "or a dummy. Something someone has been making a joke with—see the shadow—see how all is reflected in the water."

Luna did not reply. Angel continued:

"They don't use scarecrows in this country, do they?"

The figure was clear now in every detail—a man in shirt and trousers, with his hands bound and yet thrust into his pockets, with his feet hanging down pointing towards the water, with his head sunk on his breast and twisted unnaturally sideways, with his black hair stirring in the lovely morning air.

"Too late," sighed the slave. She gripped Angel's hand and held her in her place on the bank of the river, below the fine veils of falling water that wetted their dresses and hair with delicate spray.

"I will go to the Governor," whispered Angel. "I will go to

Sir William Hayes."

"Don't speak, you don't know who's near." She pressed close to the white woman, whispering in her ear. "They've had their will—it's no use to be weak or foolish—I knew they'd hang him."

"Hang him?" said Angel, leaning weakly on the other woman. "Hang some negro, some rebel?"

"John Gordon. That's John Gordon dangling from the bridge. See all the blood on his left shirt-sleeve where he was shot? His clothes are torn, too. There's no need to go any nearer."

Angel sank on her knees on the thick fresh plants by the edge of the waterfall. The odd landscape seemed to circle round that pendant figure as if it were the center of a wheel of garish colour. Then she bent down on the damp ferns, hiding her face in the rough leaves, thinking only of her beautiful love which was now over and which perhaps had never existed. The mulatto pulled her up, using simple and direct energy. Angel saw the girl's face grey and hollow beneath the thick black hair.

"Nothing can be done now. We must go back. Afterwards we can think what to do . . . Perhaps I can help you, perhaps I can tell you what to do."

The two women looked at each other in the long shadow of the boughs waving overhead. Angel saw with horror that Luna's face had changed; it had curved into an expression of implacable hatred and despair, such as Angel remembered seeing once on a mask of the Medusa. Perhaps, she thought, this is how I look.

"You must go back," said the mulatto, "and pretend that you have seen nothing. That is the way women have to work—tricks and pretense."

"Yes, woman and slaves. What are you thinking, what are you going to suggest?"

"I shall think. He suffered much, as someone else will have to suffer too."

The Courtly Charlatan

London: Herbert Jenkins, 1942.

> ". . . you come here tonight, looking at me with eager expectancy, hoping that I will tell you of some miracle."

The Courtly Charlatan [as by "George R. Preedy"] is a semi-fictional account of the notorious, enigmatic magician/alchemist/storyteller, the Comte de St. Germain (1712–1784), and his exploits at the court of Louis XV, where he found favor with Madame de Pompadour and became the unofficial "advisor" to the king. Included are accounts of the infernal practices of other historical magicians, such as Albertus Magnus, Roger Bacon, and Paracelsus. St. Germain himself maintains an essential ambivalence about his practices, frequently disavowing their supernatural aspect with a wink. His birth and background—not to mention his sorceries—are suitably obscure, although there seems to be at least one allegation accepted by many that he is the son of Prince Francis II Rákóczi of Transylvania.

Among the many storytellers who have since followed Bowen's example in chronicling St. Germain's exploits are Chelsea Quinn Yarbro and Diana Gabaldon.

In this excerpt from the chapter entitled "A Magician in the Age of Reason," St. Germain has arrived at a time when "the foul fogs of boredom" are demanding diversions and entertainments. At a time when religious skepticism is at its height, the practice of magic enlists ready believers. "What is it you desire?" St. Germain asks as he prepares to preside at one of the many séances held by controversial Jansenists. "You can pursue all the caprices that enter your mind. Philosophy, art, science, are all at your service, yet you come here tonight, looking at me with eager expectancy, hoping that I will tell you of some miracle."

The stage is set for the sensational events—both sacred and profane—that follow.

The meeting was held in a handsome apartment that was hung with crimson damask, lit by thick candles in massive brass sticks, and the heroine of the occasion was a young lace-maker, who was voluntarily offering herself to be crucified. It had lately become difficult to convey ready-made crosses into private houses, therefore in order to avoid all trouble a plank had been laid upon the floor with four large nails beside it.

The girl lay down upon the board, and the masked master of the house, now to most of those present, however, as an ex-councillor of Parliament, drove with a large hammer, according to the evidence of the senses of these men, heavy nails through her hands.

The company then fell on their knees and appeared to fall into an ecstasy of prayer, while the girl on the plank, using the whimpering voice of an infant, moaned, "Father Elijah, where are you? Do you say that I am a very naughty little girl? Oh, you are right, my little papa! But I shall behave myself better! Only teach me what I ought to do and I shall obey."

After she had been babbling in this manner for a little while she stuck out her tongue and the man still standing over her declared that she was demanding to have her speech loosened. He, therefore, delicately using a cloth and a razor, made three snicks in the form of a cross in the girl's tongue, catching the blood in a small basin; and the little childish voice was heard again as the girl began to prophesy, the while her tongue bled profusely.

Another member of the company came forward with a note-book and seemed to be writing down what the girl said, but M. de Lacondamine, at least, could not hear anything but absurdities, although he listened as keenly as he could, his trumpet in his ear. For half an hour the little lace-maker continued her rambling prophecies, which, M. de Nesle whispered contemptuously to von Gleichen, were more obscure than those of *"Nostradamus Mysterium Tremendum,"* he mocked.

Then the Councillor appeared to thrust a needle repeatedly into the girl's arm and thrashed her severely with a heavy stick. She seemed to enjoy this torture and insisted upon being even more sternly punished and "prophesied" with a babble of fluent nonsense.

When, however, she was raised from the plank, there was no sign of wounds or disorder on her dainty person; she drew on her white silk stockings striped with pink, her high-heeled shoes, and smiled at the company.

Baron von Gleichen whispered to M. de Lacondamine that this performance was a piece of obvious fraud, practised for the benefit of any fools who might be present, and M. de Nesle sneered openly at this stupid display.

Suddenly, however, the character of the ceremony changed; St. Germain came forward and muttered what everyone present was forced to regard as a powerful charm. They believed, before their dazed senses entirely left them, that they heard him use some sentences from the Gospel of St. John, so tremendously potent in magic, and able, when recited to expel devils. He then brought from his bosom a paper of yellow skin, on which were written characters in scarlet ink, the candles began to burn straightly with a tall flame, bluish at the tips, and the spell was over the company. A sensation of ineffable sweetness possessed them, they felt as if all their desires were gratified, without even knowing what these desires were; casting off their masks and cloaks, they revealed themselves as distracted men and women who, under various pitiful pretenses, either of scepticism or credulity, were searching for release from pain, delusion and disappointment. Each one of them, from those who had come to mock, to those who had come eager to be deceived, now felt that he was possessed of his chimera and holding it in a close embrace.

The sombre and commonplace room dissolved into vast perspectives, where sharp mountains of dazzling height faded into endless vistas of changing light; the most gentle yet inspiring melodies filled the air and whispered to each listener in the tones of those he most loved or desired. Dim and entrancing glimpses of some celestial bliss soothed these people and their past lives became to them but confused symbols of realities now, at length to be revealed to them.

A serene desire for humble adoration made them bend low on the ground; the figure of the stranger took on the likeness of a God, remote, holy, capable of arousing sentiments of faith, trust and love. Who, or what, stood before them?

Lacondamine and de Nesle were as overwhelmed as the simple-minded women who had come in the hope of seeing a crude miracle; the little lace-maker who had been the central figure in a pitiful display, was now filled by an ebullition of genuine piety. All felt themselves transformed as they gazed (a fascination would not permit them to look aside) at the tremendous yet impalpable figure that shone above and before these endless chains of precipice and ravine, these glittering distances of shifting light.

Then this vision seemed to be rent, as if a gauzy fabric had been torn in twain, and through this tear a bewildering darkness, peopled by writhing forms yet darker, showed.

The company began to shudder, to rave, to tremble into transports and frenzies, a dreadful terror possessed them, with spasms of fear and struggles of horror they sank down, rose up, tore their clothes, shouted and shrieked.

Infernal figures strode about the chamber that had now shrunk to the usual size, the heavenly vistas were scrolled away like a dropcloth in the theatre, and now appeared to be a cheat; what had been sublime became puerile when it was not demoniacal.

They all vanished in a flash of lurid glare that was like an agony and a crowd of disordered people, with dishevelled attire, found themselves shuddering and gasping before the stately figure of the man who called himself M. de St. Germain, who was standing by the plank of wood surveying his victims with a quizzical glance. A tall apparition faintly outlined in a greenish light hovered behind him and was recognized by the elder members of the company as the late Regent.

"Hallucination," muttered M. de Lacondamine feebly. "I am not convinced of anything beyond that I have been deluded."

"Delusions," gasped M. de Nesle. "Yes, I too admit no more than that."

Everything now appeared normal; M. de St. Germain, who was flicking a speck of blue powder from the back of his hand, no longer had an infernal companion; the shamed and exhausted men and women, again self-conscious, hastily replaced their masks and cloaks in a pathetic attempt at self-concealment.

M. de St. Germain glanced at the two sceptics who, though still shaken, were more loudly protesting their utter incredulity.

"Hallucination, delusions," he repeated. "Can you inform me what they are?"

Defender of the Faith:
A Chronicle of William of Orange

London: Methuen, 1911.

> "No man but the Prince of Orange would have dared the attack, and no man but the Duc de Luxembourg would have rallied so soon to meet it."

No historical figure earned Marjorie Bowen's respect and enthusiasm more than William of Orange. His titles were various—Prince of Orange, Stadtholder of Holland, and, from 1689 to his death in 1702, King William III of England, Ireland, and Scotland.

Bowen saw in William a complex character and occasionally a man of action, rooted in a time of turmoil in the last third of the seventeenth century in the relations among England, the Netherlands, and France. "Extravagantly maligned and hated by some," she writes in a lengthy, fair-minded, and solidly researched essay that appears in *World's Wonder*, "extravagantly lauded by others, misunderstood by many, by others merely tolerated, amid a turmoil of stress of business, politics and war, with neither rest nor pleasure, did William III, constant to his own deals, pass the thirteen years of his reign." Here were the very qualities she was disposed to admire, and to which she remained loyal all her life: "[William] was deeply attached to his hereditary Faith and cherished a keen sense of personal honour . . . Added to this were a tenacity of purpose, an indomitable fortitude, and a stern resolution that have seldom been equaled . . . and a courage that nothing could shake."[1]

And she may have responded to him in a more personal way. Having always regarded herself as an "outsider" in her family and in life in general, perhaps she felt an affinity, bordering on identity, with the view held by William's contemporaries that he was a "foreigner," an outsider sitting on the throne of England. She notes this in her full-length scholarly study, *William, Prince of Orange*, about his early years, 1650–73: "He was not English," she writes tartly, "he did not attempt to disguise disappointment and an aloof disdain for much that was English." This attitude was, from first to last, unpardoned; his great services could not take the place of good fellowship; his wide policies could not excuse his scorn for insular absorption in local disputes; he never wholly succeeded, till on his death, in uniting the English in one common front against a common foe."[2] Moreover, she was in sympathy with William's sensitivity and support of the arts (particularly his love of paintings) and his great love for gardening.

Bowen's "William of Orange" trilogy—*I Will Maintain, Defender of the Faith*, and *God and the King* (all first published in the years 1910–12)—is a major achievement in her lifelong devotion to historical subjects. The first book takes up William's early years leading up to the Dutch resistance to the French in 1672, when he became Stadtholder. The second, *Defender of the Faith*, is concerned with his marriage to his cousin, the English princess Mary, and his victory over Louis XIV in the Battle of St. Denis. The third in the trilogy, *God and the King*, depicts William's invasion of England, his assumption, with Mary, to the Crown, the Battle of Namur, his ultimate victory over the forces of Louis XIV, the death of the Queen, and William's demise in 1702.

---

1. Marjorie Bowen, *World's Wonder* (London: Hutchinson, 1937), 112.
2. Marjorie Bowen, *William, Prince of Orange* (London: John Lane/ The Bodley Head, 1928), xv.

This excerpt, from *Defender of the Faith*, Chapter 7, begins in the year 1678. The first phases of the struggle between Louis XIV and William of Orange had come to a conclusion with the Peace of Nymuegen. To William, however, this was but a momentary truce. His protest came in the form of an attack with his 45,000 troops against Marshall Luxembourg's French forces near the village of St. Denis. Both William and Luxumbourg are portrayed as gallant soldiers, united in their chivalry and mutual respect. Events begin in the camp of Luxembourg.[3]

Monsieur de Luxembourg and his officers were waiting in the village of St. Denis for official confirmation of their victory. They amused themselves by picturing the extreme discomfiture of the Prince of Orange at the miserable ending of his strenuous opposition to a conclusion of the war; the uselessness of the marriage that had been considered such a stroke at the time of its accomplishment; his failure to secure the English alliance and the general triumph of the arms and arts of his most Christian Majesty, who was now great indeed, in the eyes of his subjects of an almost superhuman dazzle.

The rejoicing at the peace was the greater because William of Orange was the one man in Europe whom King Louis feared (lesser opponents, such as my Lord Danby, now in the Tower of London, the power of France, soon swept aside), and under the scorn expressed for the servant of a republic who had dared to set himself against the might of the greatest nation in the world was the secret vexation that this young man alone had prevented the United Provinces being added to the conquests of France; and brilliant as the peace might be for them, of the country they had undertaken so light-heartedly to conquer they had not suc-

---

3. Francois Henri de Montmorency-Bouteville, Duke of Piney-Luxembourg (1628–1695) was a Marshal of France under Louis XIV and contended against William of Orange in several campaigns.

ceeded in retaining a single acre; so though they magnified their triumph after the manner of their nation, the wisest of them admitted to themselves that the greatest glory lay on the side, not of the victorious Louis, but of the defeated Prince of Orange.

Monsieur de Luxembourg had burnt the village of St. Denis and put the inhabitants to the sword some months before; his gorgeous camp was spread among the ruins of orchards and cornfields, farm-houses and humbler dwellings, and strangely in the midst of it rose the dumb stark church with blank windows and broken doors. The moon was now high in the heavens and of a great luminous brightness. The officers who had been at the supper given by Monsieur de Luxembourg had returned to their quarters, save one young captain of cavalry, the Marquis de Croissy, a relation of the general.

The tent of Monsieur de Luxembourg was large and splendid; the canvas hung with velvet and stamped leather, the floor spread with carpets from Persia and the new factories as Aubusson, lamps of silver, crystal, gilt, and bronze were skilfully hung to the polished tent-poles and cast a soft shaded lustre. At the back was a rich, violet satin curtain, before which was a couch covered with a fine tiger-skin and a scarf of Eastern embroidery. On a low carved chest were guns, swords, gauntlets, and all the appointments of war. A long table covered with a lace cloth, painted glasses, gold plate, agate-handled forks, silver-gilt knives, baskets of fruit, bottles of wine and bowls of white and yellow roses. A great Venetian mirror with a frame of pale-hued glass flowers hung by scarlet silk cords from the roof-pole and reflected dimly the glittering table. A box of books stood by the entrance, where the flap was lifted up to court the hesitating breeze, and Terence in gilt and leather, a volume of French comedies and a bundle of the latest pamphlets from Amsterdam lay scattered on the carpet. By a small table near this entrance sat a man on a folding chair of pierced steel-work with a leather seat; on the table was a glass of iced sherbet, a table watch in rock crystal and a tiny monkey asleep on a white satin cushion. The man wore a flowing dressing-gown of red damask, black silk breeches, scarlet stockings and slippers of white watered silk, laced with silver. He was hunchbacked, but this was largely concealed, as he sat, by the heavy curls of his fair peruke. His face was nearly colourless, his eyes pale and very steady, his hands white, small, and fine; in his long lace cravat was a large brooch of jewels. He held a book in his hand and alternately read a sentence and sipped his sherbet, which he was proud of securing in this barbarous wilderness, as he considered the Low Countries. He was Francois Henri de Montmorency, Duc de Luxembourg, peer and marshal of France.

Monsieur de Luxembourg looked up. "You are very doleful tonight," he remarked.

"Doleful, Monsieur!" The young man turned quickly as if he was startled. The moonlight was full over his habit of pale lemon-coloured silk and his black hair; it gave him a ghostly look.

"Yes, I thought so."

De Croissy smiled, though faintly. "On the contrary, I should feel very joyful tonight since the war is at an end at last," he answered.

Monsieur de Luxembourg laid down his book. "Are you so glad of that?" he asked.

"Well, you know, Monsieur, that I am, for one thing, tired of being exiled from Paris."

"Yet one soon becomes weary of Paris," remarked the Duke dryly.

"And besides," added De Croissy lightly, "there was the prediction of the wise woman . . ."

"Your wise woman!" smiled Monsieur de Luxembourg, stroking the monkey.

"I hear she is more the mode than ever," returned the young man.

"No doubt she will continue to be the fashion, even when she is being burnt on the Place de la Grève. What did she tell you? That you would be slain in this war, was it not?"

"Yes," said De Croissy, "and that would be very unpleasant."

"Well, you cannot be slain in this war," answered the Duke, "because, as you know, the peace was signed three days ago."

"Which is the reason, Monsieur, why I am so lighthearted."

Monsieur de Luxembourg glanced at him curiously. "What is the matter with you, De Croissy?" he asked abruptly.

Again the Marquis gave him that startled look. "What do you mean, Monsieur le Duc?" he asked unsteadily.

The general sipped his sherbet and surveyed him over the glass. "You seem to me," he said quietly, "to look very strange."

Monsieur de Croissy laughed. "I will spare you my company—I am dull tonight." He crossed over to the table, poured out some wine and drank it. The light eyes of Monsieur de Luxembourg watched the noble, slender figure in the rich setting. . . . He came a step forward into the tent and again looked round with an air of startled suspension, as of a sensitive creature alarmed by some distant and ominous sound.

"Get to your quarters, De Croissy," said Monsieur de Luxembourg. "I have a great mind to sleep if you have not—ring for my gentleman."

But the young officer seemed reluctant to depart; he laughed uneasily and sank down on the tiger-skin couch. "I am glad the peace is signed," he said.

The Duke answered grimly. "I am not—for if it had not been I should have taken Mons."

"Ah, Duke, you think of nothing but glory—I think . . ." He broke off and looked sharply round.

"What is the matter?" cried Monsieur de Luxembourg impatiently.

The Marquis rose, trembling violently. "I do not know," he muttered, "it must be the moon. I never saw the moon so bright—it is shining behind that church like an evil dream."

"You have the fever," said the Duke quietly, "you had really better, my friend, go to bed." He touched the bell beside him and a black page with a bronze collar appeared from behind the violet curtain.

"Fetch my surgeon," said Monsieur de Luxembourg. The boy slipped away noiselessly. Monsieur de Croissy appeared not to hear; he stood in an expectant attitude.

"What is going to happen?" he murmured. "I feel . . ."

Monsieur de Luxembourg closed his book. "What?" he asked.

"As if some one was coming for me . . ."

"My faith, De Croissy," said the Duke anxiously, "you are certainly ill with the cursed Dutch fever." He rose slowly from his chair and at that moment the surgeon and the page entered from behind the curtain. They saw a curious scene: the soft shaded light of the rich lamps falling on the glittering table; the fluttering wine-coloured shadows concealing the roof and corners of the tent, the looped-up entrance showing the vivid moonlight and the stark outline of the ruined church without; the dwarfish, hunched figure of Monsieur de Luxembourg in his flowing dressing-gown, and the tall young man gleaming in pale satin, powdered with gold, holding his hand to his heart and gazing before him as if he saw some disembodied terror, the black hair about his brow and shoulders intensifying the unnatural whiteness of his face.

Monsieur de Luxembourg laid his hand on the arm of the Marquis. He turned slowly at the touch. "My dear De Croissy," he said, "let my surgeon cup you . . ."

On the soft and utter silence broke a fierce sound that caused the Duke to stop his speech and swing round with a violent ejaculation. It was repeated, threatening, louder; the crystal lamps shook and the glasses on the table danced.

"Cannon!" cried Monsieur de Croissy on a deep breath. "I knew it." He pulled a crucifix out of his breast and kissed it violently.

"Cannon!" exclaimed Monsieur de Luxembourg. He seized the frightened page by the ear and cast him against the curtain. "Get my clothes—armour . . ."

A breathless officer of the Black Musketeers burst in with a drawn sword. "Monsieur le Duc," he gasped, "the Prince of Orange is attacking us—his artillery is on the heights—by the woods."

Monsieur de Luxembourg flew into a violent passion. "Fools! Dolts!" he cried as he snatched off his dressing-gown and kicked his slippers across the tent. "Is this the first you knew of it? Where were the outposts? I'll have some of you broken for this. Are you all blind and deaf?" He stamped passionately. "To arms, I say—get all these sluggards to arms—get to your troop, De Croissy . . ."

That young man, now perfectly calm, stooped and kissed the Duke's hand. "Good-bye, Monsieur," he said.

Monsieur de Luxembourg did not notice the words. "No delays!" he shouted. His gentlemen were busy about him and as he spoke he struggled into his coat and was buckled into his cuirass. "This is a trick! He would fall on us while we rest under faith of a treaty, this little Prince—which is a move I was not prepared for!" His tent was filling up with the officers of his staff and he nodded to them curtly as he sat down to draw on his boots.

The cannon sounded again and again. The Duke, booted,

sprang up and shook his fist in the direction of the sound. "You think you have me this time," he said, "but that remains to be seen." Strapping on his sword he turned to his officers, who were loud in anger against the Prince of Orange, who must know, they said, that the peace was signed.

"Gentlemen!" cried the Duke, "I admire him for it—and if this move of his breaks off this same paltry peace I shall not be sorry." His horse was at the door of his tent and he mounted and was riding along his hastily summoned ranks a few moments after the first alarm.

It was said afterwards that no man but the Prince of Orange would have dared the attack and no man but the Duc de Luxembourg would have rallied so soon to meet it. The French battalions had to form in face of the Dutch shots, cannon-balls and bombs that dropped into their midst from the shelter of the slightly rising woods where the Prince had his artillery, and many a man dropped as he rode up to take his place. But the ranks of France were not easily discomposed, and before the moon had paled before the hot August dawn, Monsieur de Luxembourg had recovered from the surprise and disposed his infantry in order of battle about the hastily constructed earthwork round the encampment; the cavalry rode up the incline, and succeeded, in spite of many losses, in spiking several of the Dutch guns; upon which the Prince sent out a regiment of Spanish horsemen which, skirting St. Denis, fell on the right flank of the French.

The infantry were ready to receive them; the first rank knelt, the second leant over their shoulders, and the third stood erect. All being armed with pikes, fusees, and bayonets they represented a front impossible to break, as the fire of the fusees maddened the horses and sent them charging backwards into the ranks behind them and so broke the advance into confusion.

The Prince, coming up to the scene with the Dutch regiments, perceived the disorder occasioned by the firm array of the French foot and dismounted his cavalry, who, advancing to the attack with pike and musket, succeeded in breaking the French line.

Monsieur de Luxembourg, having his attention drawn to this, rode up from the centre of the battle, where a confused fight was raging round the French entrenchments, and made a fierce effort to rally his men, who were being rapidly driven off the battle-field under the onslaught of the Spanish and Dutch. Thus, it happened that in the very first hours of the battle these two commanders came near enough to distinguish each other through the smoke of canon and musket, the pale glare of fire, the flare of the rising sun reflected from cuirass, sword, and bayonet.

Monsieur de Luxembourg had withdrawn his men a little within the shelter of their entrenchments and was riding along the front of them with his sword unsheathed, when, in a slow clearing of the smoke, he perceived an officer galloping before the Dutch lines and pausing to give commands to his troops. They were but divided by a few trenches and palisades and it needed not his perspective glass to tell Monsieur de Luxembourg that he beheld the Prince of Orange. He knew him by his blue ribbon and more certainly by that instinct the great have for one another.

At the same moment the Prince saw him and instantly lifted his hat, smiling. Monsieur de Luxembourg uncovered and bowed with an answering laugh. The two bodies of troops rallied and fell upon each other in a fierce disordered combat. The French, who had not sufficient time to form in order of battle fell back before the impetuous charge of the Dutch, which threw them into confusion; they gave way and were pursued into their own entrenchments.

Meanwhile, in the centre and right of the battle they had not broken their ranks and it was the allied army that was being re-pulsed. On news being brought of this, the Prince flew to encourage his troops, but though he again and again led them to the charge the Frenchmen held their ground. By now Monsieur de Luxembourg had brought up his artillery, disposed it to advantage and turned it on the enemy. The sun was high and swooningly hot; the metal belfry of the church shone like molten gold above the dun smoke. There was no breeze to stir the leaves of the beeches in the little wood where the Dutch gunners worked. Here and there a trail of fire licked along the parched grass or caught the roof of some dismantled cottage on the outskirts of the fighting. With undaunted persistency and energy each side maintained their own without obtaining any advantage. It was the most bloody, obstinate and furious battle of the war.

Time after time the cuirassiers and musketeers of France charged the ranks of the allies; time after time the shock was met without flinching and a steady fire of shot emptied saddles and thinned ranks. The Prince led now this regiment and now that, dismounted to encourage the infantry and exposed himself with a reckless ardour that called forth the protests of his officers. He gave his usual answer that he did not risk his life needlessly out of mere foolhardiness, but on due consideration to encourage his comparatively unpractised troops against the veteran arms of France.

By midday he had had two horses killed under him and mounting a third steed, led a detachment of the Spanish cavalry right against the now slightly wavering centre of the enemy. The violent shock of their onslaught brought them into the midst of the French ranks, which fell to right and left before them; and the Prince brought his men into the centre of Monsieur de Luxembourg's body-guard. He rose in his stirrups to shout to those behind when a French officer clapped a pistol to the forehead of his horse, and at the same instant another knocked him out of the saddle with the butt-end of his musket. The Prince sank to the ground, the horse reared and fell; the Spanish troops broke unto disorder. A hand-to-hand fight followed round the Prince, who was actually under the hoofs of the maddened horses and in danger of being bruised to death. Two of his men dismounted and dragged him with difficulty out of the press. He was borne backwards, hatless, with a broken sword, the fire of the French so hot upon him that the balls struck down those about him and carried away the end of the pistol at his waist, even passing through the skirts of his coat. It was believed by all near that he was doomed; but he stopped the first riderless horse that passed him, flung himself into the saddle, grasped one of the swords offered him, waved it aloft, his arm streaming with blood, and again led his men against the French, who this time began to reel back and stagger under the vigorous onslaught; routed squadrons pressed back on those behind them and the invincible Luxembourg cursed heartily, after his fashion when enraged. He began to be in want of powder; he was losing men heavily and he had just been told that a reserve of a thousand that were coming up from the outskirts of the fight had been met and put to confusion by the Dutch.

Engagement followed engagement throughout the stifling August day; neither would give way and neither could gain a definite advantage. Monsieur de Luxembourg was the better general as the Prince was the finer man, and he put the whole force of his genius into resisting the attack, as the Prince put the whole strength of his courage and resolve into leading it. There was a generation between them in years and experience. The French general had served under Condé and Turenne; the Dutch commander had been his own master, but the ardour of youth and high aims supplied the deficiency. Luxembourg made no headway against the dauntless young Stadtholder, whose troops had never been heartened by a victory and had none of the glory of prestige which was such a power to the French.

"Five Winds"

London: Hodder & Stoughton, 1927.

> "He held in his arms a beast form now, with hoofs beneath the purple robe and horns above a furry mask with sharp fangs."

Historian and critic Edward Wagenknecht describes *"Five Winds"* as "a wild saturnalia" and a "study of the confusion created between what really happens and what exists only within the mind of the hero, Denis Burgoyne."[1]

Denis Burgoyne is the last of the Burgoyne line. Abjuring his training as an architect, he is now living a relatively idle life. He has just inherited from his late uncle a fortune and the ancient "Five Winds" estate in the Westmorland valley of Mosedale. Its foundations are a thousand years old and had formerly rested on Pagan ground. Its curious name refers to a legendary "fifth wind," a demonic gale blowing no good, quite apart from the "four winds" of Greek mythology. Burgoyne's lawyer tells him the mansion is virtually unsaleable, that any buyer surely must level it to the ground. Part of the mansion's backstory includes a former inhabitant, Eleanor Engayne, a woman so wicked who, on her deathbed, swore it was useless to bury her in holy ground since she would rise before the Resurrection, reincarnated under a number of names.

As the malignant female agency that targets Burgoyne, Eleanor belongs to the gallery of (dis)honorable women that extends from the Hebrew mythology of Lilith to Euripides' Medea, Shakespeare's Lady Macbeth, Racine's Phedra, Keat's "La Belle

---

1. Edward Wagenknecht, *Seven Masters of Supernatural Fiction* (Westport, CT: Greenwood Press, 199), 156.

Dame Sans Merci," Arthur Machen's Helen Vaughan, and Peter
Straub's Eva Galli, etc.

In the following scene from Chapter 23, Burgoyne slips on
his finger a ring that purportedly was once worn by Eleanor. Immediately, he tries to take it off, but can't. He settles back on his bed,
gazes out the window at the stars in the wintry night sky, and dreams
. . . Eleanor comes to him, and what transpires is one of Bowen's
most erotic scenes, by turns seductive and monstrous, fraught with
necrophilia. It will prove not to be the end of his terrors.

The heavy, harsh curtains that smelt of dust were drawn back
from the darkness that hid the valley. Where Burgoyne lay in his
sombre bed he could see the stars in the midnight sky, flashing
and paling faintly in cold bluish radiance.

If he had not been aware of this starry space where the window was, the dusty smell of the curtains, he would have thought
that he was in a dream, for the darkness about him did not seem
the darkness of his chamber, but an interplay of thick shadows
crowding closely round his bed.

He stretched himself his full length and touched the smooth
mahogany bottom of the bed. That, at least, was solid and definite. He did not use the word "real" in this connection, for reality had long ceased to mean material objects to Burgoyne. He felt
for the ring on his hand. That was solid too, heavy on his finger,
tight to the flesh.

He sighed. A lassitude that was scarcely like the drowsiness
of sleep overcame him. Without moving, he struggled against
this as if he was aware that he was yielding his spirit to the same
powerful and ruthless influence of which he was afraid.

Yet this sense of weakness was delicious too; he felt absolved
from the body, he became unconscious even of the bed beneath
him, only aware of the ring on his finger that he had been holding; he was no longer conscious of lying down, of sitting or

standing, but merely of existing in a dark space that palpitated with shapes of a denser darkness. He relinquished all effort to resist the languor into which he was sinking.

"I am dreaming now," he tried to tell himself, and it was if he set his face towards the corridors of oblivion, peopled by world upon world which men called buried. It was a sweet, strange limbo to which he descended in this dream.

The last thing he knew was that touch of the ring that clasped his finger and that he held with his other hand; but this hard substance ceased to be a ring and became a handle or latch that he grasped in the darkness.

Drowsily he wondered why he no longer saw the stars; these were blotted out. The curtains must be drawn across the window.

Then he forgot stars and windows. He was standing, and there was that cold latch or knob in his hand.

He pressed this, and a door gently opened before him, admitting a glow of mellow light, which fell like a bloom on the darkness, revealing nothing, as if it fell on drifting cloud.

Never before had he known such a thrill of delicious expectancy as that with which he softly pushed that door wider; every emotion of delight that he had ever experienced was but a faint hint of this delight.

The door gave smoothly to his touch, and he entered a room that was familiar to him, but which he had no remembrance of having seen before. He had known of it, but he had not seen it. As he crossed the threshold the door closed behind him without a sound.

It was a long room, and he could see no definite end to the walls. There were two curtained windows, and two hanging lamps that gave the soft, dim light that merged so soon into the soft, dim shadows.

In an alcove opposite the windows long drapery was looped

back from a noble and stately bed, the furniture of which had a precious jewelled gleam.

All was unsubstantial, but Burgoyne felt it to be—felt rather than saw it to be—a brocaded, opulent chamber full of golden fantasy and a melting, voluptuous perfume which exhaled from bouquets of unearthly blooms which dropped from vases of clouded crystal, set on a table that seemed evolved from the shape of ivory dragons. There appeared to be fiery jewels also, tumbling from ornate caskets and slim glasses, through which the light slipped in long lines of blue and green. But Burgoyne was not aware of any detail, only of the shadowy sumptuousness of the vague apartment.

Seated between the table and the bed was the likeness of a woman, very tall, with a slim neck and long arms, whose delicate head was crowned by a monstrous tower-like diadem, which glittered through wreaths and wreaths of pearls. The locks richly braided beneath were of the hue of these pearls, so pale, with a pink silver lustre, and the woman's narrow eyes were pale also, with the pallor of refined, pure gold. The head that wore this light and airy but terrific coronal was small and small featured. Between the pendant ringlets the cheeks, the straight mouth, the straight nose, and those grave eyes showed like the slip of the new moon between piled-up boughs of majestic trees.

Her graceful limbs rose, as far as Burgoyne could discover, from a robe of hyacinth darkness and colour, but when he tried to look at her with eager closeness her outline became cloudy, and even the background of the chamber paled and seemed to shift into dissolving shapes.

He knew this woman well, her wisdom and her seduction, those pearl-hued tresses, those silver eyes, the mighty crown from which curled horns like the horns of the new moon, the purple sombre robe that vanished beneath the coils of the ivory dragons, and the long arms and hands now resting on the surface of the table.

He looked steadily at the grave face under the prodigious casque. She steadily regarded him with that empty stare which is more awful than any expression of horror.

The dim light fluctuated like the pulsing of waves and flowed over and round this crowned, immobile figure which Burgoyne regarded earnestly.

She seemed to grow in grandeur till she towered above him on a vast throne, and he cowered below, catching at the corner of her robe, and still her face was the same, gazing into his face, though now her horned diadem was among the stars which again sparkled in the gloomy darkness.

Burgoyne felt that he was being dawn into infinity; the robe that he grasped seemed to float in space, the grand countenance that looked at him became the countenance of the universe, the diadem was the hills, the horns the moon, the slim, silver limbs were the rivers, the dark garment was woven of flowers, the silver eyes were the planets; he was being swept through space into nothingness.

Then he moved, became in that movement conscious of his body, and touched a hard surface.

The mellow light gathered round him again; there were the two shrouded windows, the two hanging lamps, the rich, dim, encompassing, vague walls, the ivory table scattered with half-seen gems.

What he touched was one of the pillars of the sumptuous bed, from which hung brocade draperies. He was seated on the step of this bed, and the woman was beside him. She now appeared of his own stature and of a human likeness: her diadem was but knots of pearls and two glittering horns; she smiled, and her arms, which he could see and not feel, were round his neck;

the serenity of this clear, narrow face seemed to him divine, the light of the silver eyes more wonderful than the light of the skies, and again he had the swooning sensation of embracing and being embraced by the power and beauty of the universe, air, water, orbs and flame.

He kissed her straight lips; it was as if he had laid his mouth to empty air. He put his head on her lap, and it was as if he had rested it on the warm earth. Her hands passed to and fro his forehead, and it was as if a wind blow over him with gentle yet chill persistence.

He looked up and she was there, an immense and sombre sadness that overwhelmed all the richness of her own allure. She held him and, though her face did not change, he knew that she was hideously exultant; she held him and he could not leave her embraces; she was chilling him with the cold beams from her narrow eyes, and yet it was a voluptuous delight to be so held and so chilled.

The wind was increasing, it was blowing all about him, above and beneath, a steady wind, blowing out the long curtains of the bed like mournful flags; and the sound of this wind was like the sound of pipes playing ghostly music.

The bed curtains blew together, enclosing him with the woman shape, yet there was a pale radiance which revealed to him what he held, what held him, a beast form now, with hoofs beneath the purple robe and horns from above a furry mask with sharp fangs. And then a tattered skeleton, mere rags of flesh, still horned and hooved. And then a woman, uncrowned, unadorned, who drew him down, away, into a pit, a long corridor—space.

He made an effort to escape that gave him a pang of sheer agony; the wind was beating him persistently, and down the noise of the wind he heard himself saying:

"This is a dream, I must wake!"

He leapt through the curtains of the bed into the room.

It was silent, empty; the wind had fallen to a little moaning; he could see nothing very clearly, but he knew that he was surrounded by splendour.

The dark curtains had fallen together over the bed; she was sleeping there, and he hesitated as to whether he should look at her again or escape.

"I may never come back," he pondered, "and I had better look at her while I can."

He drew the curtains and saw what he had hoped to see.

She lay asleep, scarcely pressing the golden pillow, her hands delicately folded across her white breast, her silver hair delicately folded across her white brow, her narrow eyes closed, her straight features unchanged in sleep.

A veil of pearls hung over her neck and bosom and through her smooth locks the wind ran without disturbing those pale tresses.

As Burgoyne stared at her in the rich shadows of the bed he saw that she was not asleep, but that a line of light gleamed under her lashes; she was looking at him, and then he noticed that one of her hands was slowly moving towards him, falling from her slim bosom and creeping along the pillow to catch hold of him. He was afraid that if she moved she would throw off the coverlet that concealed her limbs and show her deformity, and he dropped the shadowy curtain on her false repose and her creeping hand, and hurried across the room in which the light was burning now with a tawny dimness.

"I must wake up," he heard his own voice saying; "I must wake up!"

Again the effort was anguish, a wrenching pain: phantoms impeded his progress, pale men with his own face, and miserable women with the face of Kitty Lovell, who crowded thickly about him, shadows interlacing shadows, all dead and lost and damned. But he fought through them blindly, as one lost in mist fights through mist, and he found the chamber door and grasped the handle.

He was in his own room looking at himself lying in the bed, with his feet pressed against the mahogany end-board, and his right hand over the left that wore the blue ring.

He saw his own face, colourless and troubled, and the heavy slackness of his own figure deeply asleep: then he saw this supine figure move and give a cry, and then he was one with it, sitting up in bed and staring at the long space of the window where the stars were fading in the ineffable loveliness of the dawn, and the valley was just visible, wreathed in exquisite, azure vapours.

He felt his spirit flow back into his body. A dream, nothing but a dream.

His first sensation was one of supreme isolation; he felt lost, in an alien world: it was with bitter pain that he realised that he was chained to this little fraction of time called to-day, that he had returned to the pretty monotony of material existence. He strained his ears for the sound of the wind that had held the melody of pipes, but all was still; the calm of the early morning was unruffled by the faintest breeze.

A dream, nothing but a dream.

And a dream not without horror, a dream from which he had tried to escape, but that very horror was seductive, that dread and terror alluring; there was a voluptuous zest in thinking of that feminine shape, half-horned beast, half-crowned goddess, the vileness fascinated as much as the beauty.

The fresh world unfolded before his window was stale beside that dream.

He knew who she was, and how he had come to dream of

her; the mutilated plinth by the tarn had once been her likeness; the figure on his ring, immensely crowned, was her image again, and the pale, faint face of the portrait above his desk was someone's poor attempt to snatch her likeness—to put her likeness into human features.

"And I may never dream that dream again," he thought bitterly.

He dressed wearily; he was heart-sick and lonely; the thought of the day before him, of all days to follow, days perhaps without dreams, was a burden. He went into the other room and looked at the portrait above the desk.

"Why was she called Eleanor Engayne?" he asked himself idly.

As well that as another; she had a thousand names.

He turned away from the canvas, weary of his longing, weary of his dream, that he had rejected and fled from, and might never find again.

Why did one always struggle back at the climax of a dream, evade the highest delight, the deepest terror?

There were the tall, dusty volumes of *Punch,* of the *Illustrated London News,* and between them the slender volume labelled *Fantasmagoriana—Fantasmagoriana*—that and nothing more. Burgoyne thought of the chance sentence that had met his eye when he had opened those covers: *"A man profoundly moved may, not infrequently, see what is not there."* Well, the greatest cynic of them all had never explained dreams, and without this explanation all other were fantasy themselves and useless.

The early sunlight, strengthening into colour, washed across the portrait—those few feet of canvas that someone had turned into some resemblance of his dream to haunt other men.

The birds began to sing without in the withering tree-tops, the sun crept into the valley. Burgoyne thought with loathing of the long, dull day that was now slowly beginning.

Marjorie Bowen, mature

Stinging Nettles

London and Melbourne: Ward, Lock & Co., 1923.

"What was the use of talking of freedom for women, when the sheer fact of your sex tripped you up every time?"

Stinging Nettles, the most overtly autobiographical of Marjorie Bowen's novels, is a harrowing, even painful account of a young woman's travails while nursing her husband's fatal tuberculosis as she struggles to provide an income for them both. The year is 1914 on the eve of the outbreak of the Great War. Lucie Uden has just buried her first-born and has been summoned by her husband, Pio Simonetti, a Sicilian, to leave London and join him in his native Italy. She intends to bring him back to London, but he refuses and insists on her remaining with him in Italy. Any love between them has long since vanished and been replaced only by her sense of duty and his demands for the income she, as a writer, can provide them.

The historical reality behind *Stinging Nettles* has been documented in Bowen's memoir, *The Debate Continues.* It is clear that the writer/journalist "Lucie" is Marjorie Bowen herself and that the sickly "Pio" is her first husband, Zefferino Emilio Costanza, whom she had met and married in London. Although *Stinging Nettles* dramatizes events and alters the names of the participants, the story remains substantially the same. Highly emotional and sometimes startlingly confessional, it remains one of Bowen's most powerful novels. These excerpts, from early in the novel, begin with Lucie's departure from London and arrival in Turin to meet her husband. She is shocked at Pio's sickly appearance and fears she is "saddled" with a dying man. She faces the challenges

133

of maintaining her personal and professional life as a wife, as a professional writer, and as a woman in the face of daunting circumstances.

On a bitter, iron-grey morning in February, a nervous, tired, rather shabby young woman was among the passengers on the boat-train from Charing Cross. She was now no longer to be considered as Lucie Uden, the quite well-known designer and illustrator and story-writer, but Signora Lucia Simonetti, Italian subject, returning to her country and her husband. She was aware of the ugliness of her clothes, yet she was used to clothes both ugly and cheap . . .

Long discomfort of railway travelling, a dash across a city looking alien, more travelling in a rocking, tearing train, sleeping huddled up with a green shade drawn over the electric light, waking to hear the "clink, clink" of axes, testing the wheels, throat and nose dry from steam heating, blasts of damp, cutting air when you opened the window, waking cramped, touzled [sic], dirty, "tidying" yourself as best you could, pitched into the restaurant car to drink bitter coffee and eat re-heated rolls in common with people as soiled, as absorbed, as queer as you felt yourself, pitched back to your seat to stare out of the window at rain, rain, across the fields of France, heavy, with headache and stiff with cramp, sick of the commonplace yet grotesque folk among whom you had spent so many hours, clutching your money, your ticket, your passport—so into Italy, so into the station, cavernous, iron, dirt, vile smells of Turin.

Lucie climbed out of the train, a fellow passenger handed down her two valises, she stood with them at her feet, staring down the length of the huge covered station; on the roof the rain drummed steadily.

She could not see her husband.

The train roared away.

Lucie felt isolated, ready to cry.

Then, she saw him coming down towards her, leaning on a stick.

Lucie recognized him by the heavy blue overcoat he wore and the long, thick Jaeger scarf wound round his throat; both garments were familiar to her; his face she would hardly have known.

She felt shaken by nervous embarrassment; the man was like a stranger; she tried to force herself to seem natural.

"I hope we are not late—have you been waiting long?"

"I thought you would have come sooner," he said, and kissed her without a smile. "I have been waiting here two days."

His voice was queer, rasping and yet fluting; he looked so terribly ill that her frightened gaze turned from his face; he leant heavily on his stick as if he really needed support.

"Where are the papers for your luggage?"

"I have only these."

"Why?" his face expressed instant annoyance.

"I thought we would go back at once," said Lucie. "You got my letter?"

"Yes. But I'm not going back. Your climate kills me."

A porter had her valises now and they were walking out of the station.

"I think you ought to come back," said Lucie wearily. "Please do, Pio."

"Of course I shall not come, *Dio Cristo!* I should never have been allowed to come alone—I have suffered from it."

"You said you were so much better."

"I am, much better. But still I am not quite well. I want a little care, good food and peace—what I never get in these hotels."

"Where are you staying?" asked Lucie.

"Opposite." His breath whistled in gasps, he was walking at a crawl. "The big hotel. Tomorrow we will go to Viareggio."

"Viareggio?"

"I have taken a house there, where we can be quiet—the doctor said—I was to have sea air."

They stood under the entrance of the station, the rain poured down steadily; streets, buildings, sky, looked mud-coloured; a sharp wind from the Alps drove the rain, using it as a weapon to slash and drive at houses and people.

"I hate this place," said Pio.

Slowly they crossed the wet piazza, followed by the porter, and passed the glass doors of the hotel and into the lift. Porter and liftman looked at him anxiously; he seemed absorbed in some secret trouble and not to notice anything.

Lucie, acutely self-conscious, saw the glances and shivered.

There were more glances from the servant Marianna as Pio asked her to see that tea was brought up to their room.

"He is very ill," thought Lucie, and she was horribly afraid.

When he had first written to her that he was ill, she had had the swift thought—"if he dies, I shall be really free." Now she was as frightened as if she had greatly loved him; shocked as well as frightened, for she had ceased to think seriously of the question of his health; he had always been ailing and sickly; but now surely he was in the grip of something fatal.

Still wearing his heavy overcoat and muffler and holding his light grey felt hat on his knee, he sat silent, staring in front of him.

Lucie had not expected any display of affection or gratitude, she was used to his acceptance of her utmost with no hint of acknowledgment; but he had remained, according to his nature, "in love" with her, and her presence had never before failed to evoke from him a certain emotion of pleasure and excitement.

But now he was utterly listless.

Lucie sat by the window; she felt giddy, as if she was still in the rushing train, stiff and constrained as if she was still crushed in a narrow space with a crowd of strangers, bewildered and aching in all her faculties and limbs . . . She knew now, beyond any shadow of doubt, that she cared nothing for him, was not even interested in him; this sudden sight of him, this realization of his ill-health, had effectively killed any sparks of sentiment she might have been endeavouring to cherish; she loathed sickness and this man's malady repelled her absolutely; she did not feel dislike or contempt, only indifference for the man and horror for the disease.

As she looked back into the past, she felt a blushing amazement that she had ever been able to cheat herself into taking this man for any semblance of Love. . . .

Lucie reminded herself that she lived in an age of feminine "emancipation"; there was hardly any length of freedom to which women might not go; she was able to earn her own living, and there was not only no one with any authority over her, but no one who had any right whatsoever to offer her advice . . . Since she was sixteen she had earned rather more than her own keep and everything she knew she had taught herself, with hardly any encouragement. Why, therefore, did she not cut herself free from Pio and live her own life free from emotional entanglements—really, her *own* life at last?

There were so many things she would have liked to do that she had never been able to dream of doing—yet things that were quite in her power to do, if she could only have stood upright, given herself room to move. What was the use of talking of freedom for women, when the sheer fact of your sex tripped you every time?

Lucie always came back to that.

You weren't free, you simply couldn't be free, when all the instincts of your nature—instincts how strong, how terrible!—

were driving you to find a mate, and the only way for you to secure this mate was marriage, an institution but ill adapted for the independent woman. And what was the use of freedom if you weren't trained to use it?—if, from generations of enclosed women, you had inherited the wish to be enclosed and protected—if you hated to stand alone and be free—simply made a mess of it, if you tried.

And this without being a fool or a clinging, sentimental coquette—but a creature intelligent enough to know yourself.

Intelligent enough to know that you, as a woman, because you were a woman, never could be really free, because of your nerves, and your emotions, and your physical weaknesses, your lack of mental stability, your desperate need of love.

[The couple relocates to the Villa Calvini, in an area outside of Lucca. Lucie is informed she must not refer to Pio's illness as anything more than "heart trouble," lest those fearing the contagion of consumption would avoid the house.]

The days were just bearable; you pretended, then, that things weren't so bad; there was always the desperate hope that the doctor, or some one might come; there was a sort of show of order and decency, method and punctuality that helped; there was a secret feeling that at the very worst you could run out and fly down those two miles to the village and see some human, kindly face.

But the long, wintry nights—ah, they were hell opened.

The day began with [the maid's] journey to the piazza. . . . Lucie would then have her own breakfast and perform the long, laborious toilet of the invalid; few were the days when he would remain in bed. Then there was his room to do, as he would never have the maid near it, and his stove to keep replenished, his medicine and food to prepare and bring up. Then perhaps she would have just time to write a letter or so before he wished to be put back into bed where he would take the midday meal. Lucie had hers at a little table at the foot of his bed, since he could not endure her out of his sight. When this was over, and he had been made comfortable and the room tidied again and the stove filled, she could count on about two hours while he slept.

In this interval she wrote her articles and drew her designs, always using the table at the foot of the bed. When he woke there was more medicine to prepare, patent food to make, "tea" to be carried upstairs, everything to be "tidied" once more, any odd job of mending or washing to be done till it was the moment to bring up his supper, and have her own, facing him in that ghastly mockery of intimacy . . .

The whole house was incredibly dark, damp, and chill; great patches of wet and mildew showed on every wall, and the tiled floors were perpetually oozing. In the kitchen was the usual Italian arrangement—three little receptacles to burn charcoal in for cooking and no oven; in the *salotto* as a ghastly-looking anthracite stove, and in Pio's room was a more amenable and smaller affair that burnt wood. There was no other heating arrangement whatever; the place was wired for electric light, but there were no fittings. Water had to be fetched from the well in the front-garden. There was no telephone available nearer than Forte dei Marmi, and the doctor seemed to live up the mountains, and could only be reached by letter.

When Lucie had thoroughly realized all these conditions, she felt, even more than at first, that the situation was absolutely grotesque, and that she could not be shut up in this alien place away from any glimmer of help or even sympathy, watching the progresses of a loathsome disease, preparing for a ghastly death-bed, and all that appertained. She had not the strength of either mind or of body needful for such a task, nor was she supported

by any inner flame of fervor, of love or devotion; she did not
even believe in the prolonging, by skill or labour, the last stages
of incurable maladies.

She was actuated by nothing but a sense of duty.

And there was always the money question; she *must* go on
with her sketches and her articles, or they would come to disas-
ter. There were no resources for any of them beyond her own
work . . .

A few days later the doctor came. The clatter of the outer
bell woke her from her first snatch of sleep, and Marianna
rushed upstairs with a shawl over her head, shouting, *"Il dottore!
Il dottore!"* Hope leapt up in her anxious heart. Pio had been
awakened also, and she hurried in to him, quickly to "arrange"
him and light the big lamp.

There was not time for her to dress, and she hardly gave this
a thought as her long, high, camel-cloth dressing-gown was as
decorous as a monk's robe, and round her plaited hair she had
twisted her dun-coloured veil, to protect herself from the bitter
draughts.

She ran quickly downstairs, hoping for a few words with the
doctor before he saw his patient, rehearsing in Italian what she
must say to him, how she must represent the desperate urgency
of her case.

Marianna had run out to unlock the large *cancello,* the gate
on to the road, and Lucie's trembling fingers were trying to light
the dining-room lamp when she heard voices in the kitchen.

Lucie looked at [the doctor] with incredulous dismay. He
was short, stout, bald, with a rough black beard, glasses, broken
black teeth, and dirty complexion, one arm bandaged and in a
sling. His clothes were cheap and tawdry.

"Ah," he said with a coarse peasant accent, "this is the time
of night to call—and catch the ladies in their chemises!"

Lucie then saw that he had been drinking; she tried to collect herself to put forward her tale.

"Doctor, I've been very much wanting to see you—"

Pio's bell clanked furiously. Marianna, cheerfully blaspheming, dragged the doctor to the door . . . Lucie dully blew up the fire and put on coffee, broke eggs into the frying-pan, and got out bread and sugar.

The servant came back and Lucie went upstairs to her own room and lit the candle. Her little travelling watch showed her that it was nearly two o'clock.

The door was half-open into her husband's bedroom; she could hear his peevish tones and the doctor's deeper voice— petulant lamenting and jovial reassurance.

Lucie sat on the bed and waited.

Presently Pio also became more cheerful under the doctor's reassurances. Glasses clink, there was a smell of spirit. They were drinking together.

The doctor spoke about his bandaged arm—poisoned during an operation, he said; he made a joke about it—a horrible joke.

Lucie's teeth chattered. Neither of them mentioned her; they began to tell each other vulgar stories about some women they both knew.

Lucie with a trembling heart appeared in the doorway. Pio introduced her, with a queer flash of pride:

"Bella bionda," smiled the doctor without rising.

"He finds me much better," said Pio; "he says I shall be cured before I leave here."

"I'm glad," answered Lucie.

She looked at the doctor, and something in her bearing made the man rise and take his leave with many pleasantries for the patient, whom he called *"Don Pio."* He left the room and Lucie followed him downstairs. He turned into the kitchen where there was light, even a little warmth. Marianna slept with her head on the table.

"Doctor," said Lucie, "what is the state of my husband's health?"

He looked at her curiously.

"Better. Much better—your nursing has done wonders."

"But—it is incurable?"

"Ah, that—yes!"

"Then—how long?"

He shrugged. "Four—five—six months."

"Can he travel?"

"No, he nearly killed himself going to Turin."

"But I can't stay here—like this. You must see how impossible it is—"

He grimaced. "I can suggest nothing."

He was scrawling prescriptions in a dirty notebook.

"It is not right that I should be left her with him," continued Lucie. "It is very lonely and he is often violent—I have no authority over him; he does things that I know are wrong—he drinks too much—even brandy when he has a fever."

Pio's bell clanged.

"I can't go," said Lucie incoherently. "Marianna, run upstairs and tell him so; get him to sleep too—keep him quiet. Is there any doctor nearer?"

"None."

"How often can you come?"

"Every fortnight, three weeks, month—I can do nothing— nothing at all!"

"Is there anyone who would come to help me nurse?"

"No one would come to nurse tuberculosis, it is so infectious."

The doctor took a hasty leave. Pio rang for the third time.

Lucie went to the bottom of the stairs and called up: "I am coming in a moment—please don't ring again."

She could not face him just yet. She had to have a moment in which to recover from her bitter disillusion, her miserable humiliation. She was, it seemed, quite abandoned; there was no one who had the slightest interest in her—and now it wasn't a question of weeks but months. How could she go on? How could she?

[A new element is introduced into Lucie's situation as Pio's condition approaches madness.]

Lucie roused, suddenly and completely.

Her room was full of stormy moonlight, and there was a glow from the night-light in the other room. Her husband was peering at her through the crack of the door.

She saw this instantly and lay perfectly still. Slowly he rounded the door and came into the room; he was still in his dressing-gown and carried a revolver. Lucie felt her heart leap and knew that she was afraid.

No longer did he appear grotesque or farcical, but horrible as the horrors of some long outgrown, childish nightmare. His long black hair clung damp to his wet forehead, his lids were drawn up so that the whites showed above the eyeballs, and his lips were curled back from the glistening teeth.

Never had Lucie guessed that a human face could look so fearful; she saw she was face to face with madness—with *possession*. It was no sane human soul that looked out at her from that distorted countenance; his whole gaunt figure seemed to be rigid and lambent with the furious energy of some evil power.

Never before had she feared him. For all her nervous timidity, she was no physical coward, but sheer terror held her for a second as this awful figure advanced on her with the revolver;

she knew he meant to murder her, and she did not want to die that way.

A light chair stood by her bed. She thought, "I will seize that and knock his arm up." As she turned to grasp it, he turned away and walked to the window and stood there, looking out and muttering. She saw the moonlight on the metal muzzle and on the ghastly face. She lay still.

He began talking about a dog that was outside, and that he was going to shoot. He opened the window and looked out. Lucie waited for the shot. But he did not fire. Muttering to himself, he reeled back to his bed.

When Lucie crept after him, she found him in a deep insensibility.

But the revolver was hidden.

[Months pass, doctor visits are intermittent at best, and Lucie doggedly keeps washing the linens and Pio's room against infection. His health further deteriorates. Help will soon come in the person of a kindly doctor who has heard about Lucie's situation. And soon, after Pio's demise, his presence will become a positive and important part of her future. But for now, Lucie faces an existential crisis . . .]

To what possible purpose was it all being prolonged? What was the sense of this martyrdom? What object was there in this painful sacrifice, this anguish of service to an abhorrent disease, in itself the fruits of ignorance, folly and vice?

Lucie believed in no faith that could help her to an answer; she could not even believe in any Power directing it all, any Intelligence directing human destinies. It seemed to that things just happened, as the wind freshened from the sear or died away, as the stars shone or were veiled by clouds . . .

Nothing could express the indifference of it all to this sick man and to herself; her miseries would never be compensated anywhere, what she had suffered, never rewarded. The sunlight mocked at her penitential days, the pure air that flowed in through her open window reproached her for the monstrous futility of the vile tasks that filled her wasted hours.

She knew that she could never be the same after this; everything seemed petty and meaningless to her now, save this kind of inner life she led, where she tried to find some guidance through the maze of her material experiences.

She began to see the gibbering shapes the sick man saw, to tread with him the dark paths opened through the delirium of fever, heat and alcohol, to feel time and space vanishing into the chaotic realm of unchecked delusion, phantasmagoria and vision.

Part Two: Complete Novel

Family guilts and an aura of the supernatural haunt this cruel and complex dissection of a troubled marriage. Mutual suspicions and recriminations lead to fatal consequences. At the heart of the story is a crude woodcut—"a curious, clumsy carving of a grotesque fiend with medieval horns and tail pursuing a thin creature in grave-clothes who turned at bay and, with an expression of the utmost horror, cast a net over the enemy, who writhed in astonished helplessness." Grace and Philip Fielding are those figures, confronting each other in a "dance of death," which ends tragically when the prey becomes the predator. It's a question of which is which—and when. The true nature of the ghosts that haunt them both is encapsulated in a remark by one of the characters: "It's the devil in ourselves we've got to snare."

The horror of this kind of ghostly narrative, writes Virginia Woolf, "comes from the force with which it makes us realize the power that our minds possess for such excursions into the darkness; when certain lights sink or certain barriers are lowered, the ghosts of the mind, untracked desires, indistinct intimations, are seen to be a large company."[1] Moreover, as a piece of metafiction, it features a story-within-a-story, which acts at times as a parallel, commentary, and stimulus to the larger narrative. Grace and Philip are thus authors and critics of their own story.

The Devil Snar'd has a curious history. For reasons unknown,

---

1. Virginia Woolf, *Granite & Rainbow* (New York: Harcourt Brace Jovanovich, 1958), 61–64.

Marjorie Bowen wrote it under her pseudonym of "George R. Preedy," a name she usually reserved for historical novels, such as *General Crack, The Poisoners,* and *Nightcap and Plume,* and the short story collection *Bagatelle.* It first appeared in 1932 in a small paperback edition from Ernest Benn as No. 13 in a series of "New Ninepenny Novels." A year later it reappeared in a hardcover edition, *Dr. Chaos and The Devil Snar'd.* Neither edition has ever been reprinted and they are very scarce today. This is lamentable, inasmuch as *The Devil Snar'd* in particular is one of Bowen's best ghostly narratives. It is a special privilege to bring it to new generations of readers.

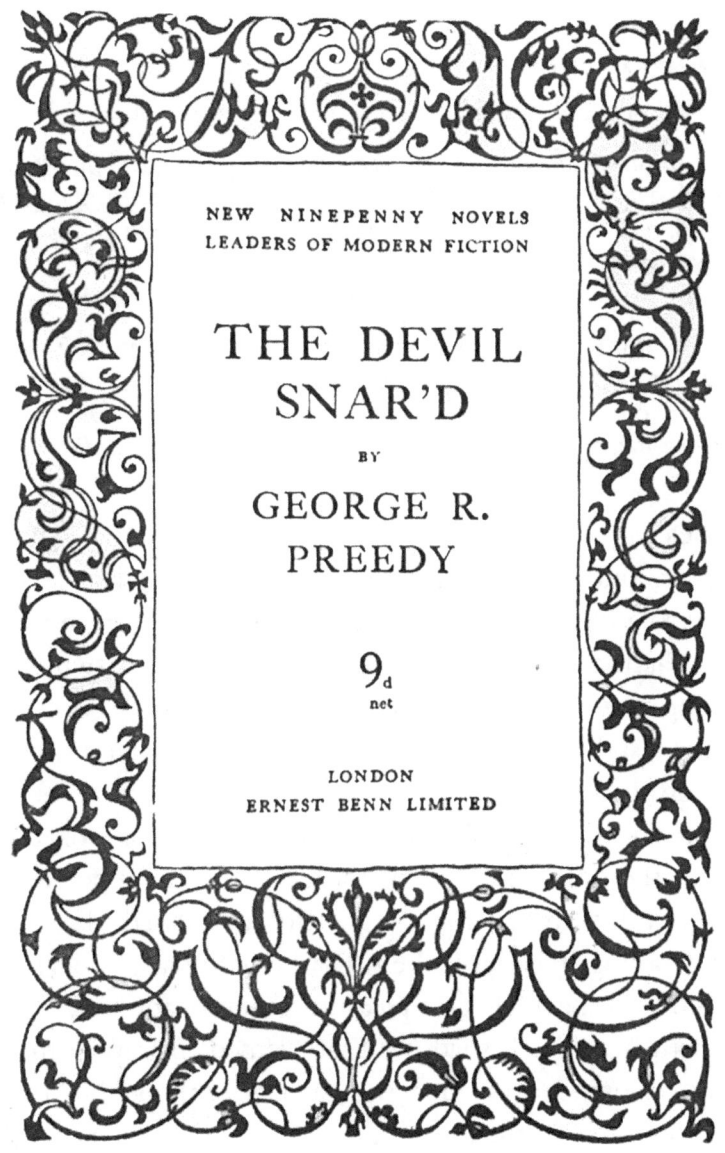

NEW NINEPENNY NOVELS
LEADERS OF MODERN FICTION

THE DEVIL
SNAR'D

BY

GEORGE R.
PREEDY

9_d
net

LONDON
ERNEST BENN LIMITED

The Devil Snar'd, *first edition paper cover*

The Devil Snar'd

London: Ernest Benn, 1932.

It must be admitted that these cases are very perplexing. We might, indeed, get rid of them by denying them, but the instances are too numerous, and the phenomenon has been too well known in all ages to be set aside so easily.

Mrs. Catherine Crowe, The Night-Side of Nature.

We must next remember, that this earthly body we inhabit is more or less a mask, by means of which we conceal from each other those thoughts which, if constantly exposed, would unfit us for living in community; but when we die, this mask falls away and the truth shows nakedly.

Ibid.

Mrs. Fielding knew from the first that this was a frightful journey to an unknown destination, though her ticket was from London to a Northumberland station. She looked from the train window at the strange landscape over which the twilight was darkening down and saw a solitary swan on a black pool; for the first time a sight of this beautiful bird seemed to her a presage of some fearful event.

"For which of us?" she said half aloud; and she looked at her husband, the only occupant of the carriage. He appeared to be asleep, but his stern, unrelaxed attitude showed that he was merely feigning in order to be rid of her company; it was a long while since he had felt any pleasure or even any ease in being alone with her. Thick shadows that seemed to leap in from the gloomy countryside invaded the carriage, but neither of them roused to switch on the light.

Mrs. Fielding tried to struggle with her abominable thoughts; this effort left her as exhausted as if she had undertaken some difficult physical strain; her head was lolling with fatigue against the stiff cushions as she thought fiercely to herself: "I am only tired and depressed. Of course, we are going to be happy again—now, or never—"

Her senses ached into a half-delirium; a travesty of a child-hood game came into her mind; her fingers plucked at the travelling-rug over her knees as if she pulled the petals of a monstrous daisy from the yellow heart: "Now or never—now or never—"

The words beat into the rhythm of the wheels and throb of the engine that was bearing her North—towards Medlar's Farm.

*　*　*

As they drove from the small, lonely station, Grace Fielding had been preparing herself to give an enthusiastic welcome to the house that her husband seemed, in advance, infatuated with; it was desperately necessary that she should please him. But when they arrived she was too tired to do more than smile assent at the arrangements the housekeeper had made.

Besides, her husband never asked her opinion.

"A beautiful view, ma'am," said the housekeeper, holding the curtain apart for a moment to show the Northumberland hills and dales receding into the twilight, and she named several famous places, quite unknown to Mrs. Fielding, that could be seen from this room if the day were fair.

"A queer old house," smiled the traveller faintly. She was exhausted by the long emotional strain she had undergone, by the re-action of a sudden and dubious victory.

"Very old, ma'am, parts of it. Norsemen built some of it, they say. But the west wing isn't above two hundred years old. Mrs. Holmes wasn't sure, ma'am, if you'd want the whole house, or some shut up, being only two of you? I did my best, but the orders was rather vague."

"Yes, I haven't been very well; I had to leave everything to my husband—you know—"

"Ah yes, the gentlemen don't think of such things—do them? But now you're here, perhaps you'd say, ma'am."

Mrs. Fielding tried to clear her head, to recall practical affairs; it had mattered nothing to her what was or where was the house that her husband had taken; all that had concerned her was that they should go away, at once, anywhere, together. All she knew was that he had told her he had found a place in Northumberland, belonging to a Manchester cotton merchant, which they might have for three months in good order with housekeeper and servants—fairly cheap, too, though money was not one of their problems.

She felt the mild disapproval of the efficient woman who was waiting for her reply, but she could not force herself to do or say anything practical to-night.

"My husband writes," she said, knowing this well-worn formula would still cover much. "I expect that he would like to choose the rooms himself."

"Perhaps you'll look over them, ma'am, when you've had a cup of tea? There'll be time before dinner. I mean, I don't know where to make up the beds, or anything."

"Yes, we'll decide then. I really am rather tired."

"Tea is quite ready, ma'am."

Mrs. Fielding had her tea alone in the large drawing-room with the bow window, which was expensively furnished; she remembered something about "careful tenants, no children" in the advertisement that her husband had shown her. She tried to combat a sensation of loneliness, of strangeness, of dislike for another woman's possessions and atmosphere; to concentrate on the fact that Philip had surrendered to her passionate claims and come here with her, alone, far away from Angela Campion and her maddening influence. A triumph, and when she had been almost sure of defeat. But she could feel only lassitude; what an odd thing fatigue was, damping down the strongest passions, leaving only one desire, that for rest, rest, rest.

The journey had been comfortable, not too long. Of course it had not been the journey—it was that devastating struggle with her husband which had begun when she had discovered that he was in love with Angela.

She wondered now how she had had the tenacity to sustain such a conflict, in which she had, after all, played a poor part, humiliating, mean, ungenerous, unwise.

The housekeeper brought a message that "Mr. Fielding was seeing the luggage in" and that she "was not to wait."

"Yes, we have brought a good many things, books and pictures. Perhaps you will take my husband a cup of tea—wherever he is?"

The housekeeper lit the lamp and left the room. Mrs. Fielding had noted with some dismay that there was neither electricity nor gas in the house; she liked town life, she liked comfort, the very name Northumberland smacked, to her, of barbarism. She had had enough of rough ways when they had been poor; it seemed a shame now that they had the money—

She broke off her reflections, angry with herself—discontent was not for her, nor fatigue—and what weakness to think of victory as triumph—the hardest part lay before her—she had to consolidate her gains, to please, to propitiate, to be infinitely tactful. Philip might, even now, suddenly return to Angela— how could she, Grace, judge of the security of her tenure? His surrender had not been so warm or so eager as to make her feel safe for ever. He had seemed more to recognise the justice of her claims than to acknowledge the strength of his own affection or of her charm for him.

It was June, but she was glad of the wood fire. She had not realised how much later the seasons were in the North—as they

drove from the station (what a long way off the railway was) she
had noticed that many of the thick hawthorn trees had not yet
fully broken into bloom.

"I think, Grace, they want us to look over the house; are you
too tired?"

Her husband was speaking to her across the shadows; he
seemed very far away as he stood in the doorway. It would take
her, being used to a flat, some time to feel easy in these vast
rooms.

"No; I'm quite ready." It was difficult to be entirely gracious
without cringing, or seeming to cringe, for she was in the position of one receiving favours. She perceived that everything was
going to be difficult until she was quite sure that he was not re-
gretting Angela, not sacrificing himself to his duty, to his compassion.

"Do you like the place, Grace?"

"I think I do—very much. But I have really seen nothing of
it but this room."

"It's very curious. Unique, I should think. The last house in
England they tell me."

"The last house?—oh, Scotland, of course—but I didn't
know that we were so near the border."

"We aren't—the point is, that it's all heath, hills, open country—"

She followed him into the corridor, the housekeeper was in
front with a lamp. He still wore his heavy tweed overcoat and
looked, she thought, very tall and massive; he seemed quietly excited; at reunion with her in this solitude, or because of the crazy
old house? She knew that he was capricious, absorbed in violent
imaginations, full of an energy, a curiosity, that nothing could
exhaust or assuage—a brilliant mind, a wilful, impatient character, great gifts. She only half understood him, though she had

thought of little else but Philip Fielding since she had married him fifteen years ago.

"I must learn to like this house if it fascinates him," she thought. "I must get the history, the plan."

She tried to speak with animated intelligence—"What was the house, really—Medlar's Farm? But not in the least like a farm."

Mrs. Mace, the housekeeper, gave low-voiced information—no, not a farm, the dower-house of a big estate that had long since been sold out in parcels. The great mansion had been pulled down a hundred years ago—Vavasour, the name of the family, you could see their tombs in the old abbey, and that was only a ruin now—no, she could not tell how the name came, the land had been farmed for a generation, but she didn't know that the man's name was Medlar; she came from Newcastle, and had only been with the Holmes for two years—they were abroad, at least, Mrs. Holmes and the children were, Mr. Holmes was looking out for another house for them to return to in the autumn.

"Why?" asked Philip Fielding.

"Well, sir, the children aren't strong. It is rather a gloomy place for them, and there's very little company, and a great difficulty with maids, and Mr. Holmes thought he'd like to be nearer his place of business—it was only week-ends he could manage here, sir."

"I see. So the old place will be for sale?"

"I suppose so, sir."

"We might buy it, eh, Grace?"

"Yes—if we like it—"

They passed through a door that led to the head of a stairway. Mrs. Fielding immediately saw herself in a mirror that hung to her right hand, a mirror so dimmed that it might have been smoked. After all, she was glad of the lamplight, the shadows; she looked tired, middle-aged; she was glad, too, because of her good figure, her fine taste in clothes. Her graceful bearing, her costly, uncommon garments made her, she knew, attractive, even when dishevelled and fatigued—but why concern herself about her appearance? Philip was not looking at her; she tried to concentrate on the house.

They had passed into the Georgian wing; the unlit well of the stairs was hung with ugly, dark eighteenth-century portraits; on the landing where she stood were several mirrors, old Bible boxes, wig stands, uncomfortable chairs, wooden patterns, and warming-pans of tarnished brass.

"Junk," thought Grace Fielding as Mrs. Mace described how all these "antiques" had been found by Mrs. Holmes in the attics and barns.

"There is a lot more, ma'am, all manner of old stuff; a few years ago no one seemed to care about these things, and now everyone is after them."

"I suppose the Holmes bought the place furnished?"

"Yes, sir, all the furniture goes back to the Vavasour's day—except the room where Madam had her tea, the Tudor room they called it; Mrs. Holmes had that furnished to her own taste."

"And mine," thought Grace. "It is the only possible room that I've seen yet." She said aloud, "This part doesn't look as if it had been lived in for a long time."

"Well, no, ma'am; ever since I've been here it has been shut up—Mrs. Holmes preferred the older part, the Viking house, the children used to call it—that's why I was anxious to know if you wanted this opened—"

"Oh, we couldn't—use this wing, I mean—look at the state it is in—"

"It is quite clean, ma'am, the girls have so little to do, the house being empty, I keep it all ready—"

Philip Fielding, as if impatient of these feminine debates, went down the stairs into the dark, and the housekeeper hurried after him with the light.

The shadows fluttered down the stairs, pursuing the lamp. There was, for all the boast of Mrs. Mace, a smell of must, of damp. Mrs. Fielding wished that she were at home—no, home had been spoilt for her by the fearful scenes that had lately taken place there; they would move when they returned to London— wished, then, she was anywhere but here. It was no use, to-night she could not even enjoy the thought of her uninterrupted companionship with Philip. She was tired; now she was away from the fire the house felt cold.

She followed her husband and tried to take in something of the rooms that Mrs. Mace showed them; but the house remained a chaos—seemed to her to have no definite play; it had been so often rebuilt and added to; half the Georgian portion had been burnt down, the remaining rooms were too large for the proportions of the façade she had seen on driving up from the station. She counted dining-room, library, writing closet one side of the passage; two withdrawing rooms connected by folding doors and a lady's boudoir on the other; then kitchens, cellars, cupboards below in a dim subterranean region which she refused to inspect; and, above, four large bedrooms, a closet changed into a cheerless-looking bathroom, and, above again, attics. All the rooms were handsomely furnished with an uncomfortable confusion of objects. To Mrs. Fielding, used to a neat modernity, the whole place was like a museum; she was not insensible to the dignity and beauty of the various pieces of walnut and marquetry, the pictures, tapestries, candelabra, and vases that overcrowded these stately rooms, but she had no interest in the past.

"Do you like this better than the older part, Grace?"

Her husband's voice startled her into a sharp realisation of his presence; he had seemed merged into the shadows of the house; she had seen his figure looming ahead of her, lit by the dim lamplight, and scarcely known the tall man as Philip; she was fatigued to the point of hallucination.

"I saw nothing but—the Tudor room, don't they call it?"

"It is very queer, like a ship—slate floors, heavy timber."

"Ship's timber it is, sir, so they say."

"This part is more civilised. You don't like low ceilings, do you? Wouldn't you feel more at home in that big room up-stairs—with the chintz?" He looked at her kindly, she was sorry to need kindness.

"It seemed so cold—that big room—"

"It could soon have a fire, ma'am."

"Very well. Of course you are right, Philip."

His consideration for her increased.

"Wouldn't you like to go there—at once—as soon as they can get a fire? It isn't so frightfully cold. Mrs. Mace will send up some dinner."

Mrs. Fielding smiled. No use pretending, she was absurdly tired; the strangeness of the place was depressing, she had slept badly for so long now, and surely she was, for a while, safe. He would give her at least a few days; he would not abandon her cruelly . . . suddenly . . .

To distract herself she said, as she mounted the dark, dismal stairs:

"Naturally, the house is haunted?"

"They say so, ma'am, but I've never seen anything. There are old stories. I'm a stranger, as I said, and I don't encourage the girls to gossip. You can soon get a place a bad name."

"Especially a place like this," smiled Philip Fielding.

Grace Fielding was not frightened by ghosts; they belonged, in her opinion, to the dimmest realm of fairy-tale. She was not troubled by such remote terrors; she was completely absorbed in her own averted tragedy—was she quite sure that it was averted, or only held in abeyance?

*   *   *

She woke suddenly after deep draughts of sleep that she had snatched at greedily, and thought, at once, that it was strange that she should rouse herself in this complete silence, when she had been so utterly fatigued. It was alarming to realise that she was in such a state of nervous unrest that even exhaustion could not long hold her in blessed oblivion.

Another sleepless night; she lay resigned in the strange four-poster bed with the hanging of coarse twill embroidered by the hand of some dead Vavasour with indigo-blue flowers and red foxes. A night-light burnt on a side table and the embers on the wide hearth still glowed; through the half-drawn curtains showed a rift of ice-blue moonlight; the shapes of large pieces of dignified furniture were blurred by shadows. Mrs. Fielding felt her surroundings to be very stately and impressive after the impertinent prettiness of her London rooms; though this chamber was alien, it was soothing.

She tried to fix her thoughts on something agreeable: Philip's kindness last night—that now. He had been almost tender when he had said "good night"; he was asleep in the next room, a door half open between them, surely it rested with her to bring about a complete reconciliation—in this solitude.

But Mrs. Fielding could not, for long, keep her thoughts peaceful. What was the small kindness last night, a mere matter of courtesy perhaps, compared to the bitter brutality that had gone before? His strained voice, demanding his liberty, still echoed in her ears; he had pleaded with her, he had menaced her, he had reasoned with her—to set him free for Angela. She had, through all these storms, held firm.

"I can't prevent you leaving me—but I can prevent you marrying Angela. I won't divorce you. I won't give her everything. While I live you shall never marry her."

She was startled to find that she was sitting up in bed, saying, half aloud, these words that she had repeated, so often, with the dreadful tenacity of despair.

"But I was right," she muttered, casting herself back on the pillows. "I was right not to give way."

Angela played at virtue; that was what was intolerable. She wanted to be respectable, to have a good social position, to have the glory of being the wife of a famous man, to go everywhere with Philip, showing off her sham beauty, her odd gowns, her lisping wit; to share his fame, his popularity. On that dreadful day when she had come to see Mrs. Fielding she had as good as admitted this fearful greed.

"I inspire him; I'm really needful to his work; it's only right that it should be acknowledged. He'll go to pieces if you don't take care—it's a strain for him, you know. I wonder you don't see that you are being stupid."

"You're stupid too. Philip has only been famous, making money, for five years; for ten years I helped him, poverty, sickness, tempers, moods—he had all my money, that was useful too. You came along when he was rich, well-known, good-humoured with success. You can be his mistress if you like, but you'll never be his wife."

They had descended as low as that, quarrelling, bickering, over her husband; why must she remember it? Those ugly sentences would not be effaced from her mind, nor those flushed, distorted features, puckered with spite, of the other woman. How was it that Philip, so acute, so sensitive, could not see how trashy Angela really was? That she had nothing but her mediocre beauty, her quick cleverness, her eager self-confidence that seemed like talent. But how useless to speculate on what a man saw in another woman, Angela was young, seductive, shameless, full of vitality, an ardent flatterer; no doubt her lure was simple enough.

Mrs. Fielding flung herself out of bed: "This torturing restlessness! I hope that I'm not going to be ill—that would turn it all to ridicule. Philip, of all men, with a sick woman on his hands in this place."

The room was warm; she sat on the edge of the bed, trying to steady herself, and only fell into the last mistake of weakness, that of self-analysis.

Why had she clung so desperately to a man who did not want her? Because she loved him? Ah, no doubt she did, but she was long past knowing what love exactly meant, and there had been times, during the last months, when she had both hated and despised him.

Because she was afraid that, in losing him, she would lose everything that made life pleasant and exciting? She had passed her fortieth year; she had no talents; no one ever seemed to want her for herself, but as her husband's wife she was very welcome everywhere. Was she afraid of giving up her share in the fame she had helped him acquire—of falling into the background, of being merely a divorced woman whom people pitied?

She was flicked by imagined comments: "Poor thing! But one can hardly blame him, he must have felt her a drag, and then Angela Campion is so brilliant—and it isn't as if there were any children—and I believe that he has been very generous with the money—"

Her clamouring thoughts clotted and festered round the word "money." They had been poor so long; she had sold out her little capital to give him the leisure in which to write the things he wanted to write; she had rescued him from hack journalism; she had given up her own work on the stage to help him, to become his servant, his adviser, his clerk, his secretary, to be the butt, the shocker-absorber for all his moods, his despairs, his tempers. No children—her barrenness—that had seemed a virtue, a blessing then, now it was a vague reproach, a dim curse. Angela was smiling with an opulent promise of fecundity. No doubt Philip would be flattered by children in an expensive establishment with plenty of servants—but in the old days, in two rooms, in one room, children would have been the last touch of sordid horror—they would have made what was already bitterly difficult, simply impossible.

"Why am I going over this? I was trying to think why I won't let go—it is an obsession. There are other men in the world. I'm not a fool; surely I might find interests for myself—why do I cling?"

Because, perhaps, of sheer loathing for the other woman, that greedy, insolent, shameless thief, who had laughed in her face and just snatched Philip like someone might grab your bag in the street?

Perhaps.

She could not deny that to have foiled, to have humiliated Angela gave her a savage satisfaction; she liked to imagine that final interview in which he had said some equivalent to "goodbye."

But ignoble emotions can give, she thought, very little ease; the jealousy, the struggle was a torment, it hurt, sharply, to hate.

She left the bed, nearly stumbling over the unexpected old-fashioned bed-step, and put on her white wool dressing-gown; a bracelet of many-coloured gold winked on her wrist as she moved near the night-light; it caught her attention, for she was not yet used to costly objects. And her mind turned again to money. How suddenly it had come—a success in America, the play, a novel, lectures, films; there must be fifty thousand pounds behind them, and handsome contracts ahead.

It seemed incredible.

"Behind us? It is all his, really. I suppose, if we did separate, he would be generous. Angela has money. I should take all I could get. I have a right."

A right? Had she? Because she had shared his poor fortunes, toiled for him? He had *liked* doing that; the eager service, of the joyous hope of the future; his moods of passionate gratitude, his entrancing companionship, the fact that he always remained her constant lover, had made her happy—how mean to think of exacting payment for that—

She moved to the door of his room and listened; she could not even hear his breathing.

Why had he brought her here? She became suspicious— perhaps it was not, as he had seemed to promise, to affect a complete reconciliation, a renewal of their old relationship, but to persuade her, in this solitude, to let him go; to plead with her, to argue with her, to wait till she had, as he would think, recovered from the fatigue of the scenes in London, to shame her by all the forces of logic and all the strength of passion, into giving way.

"But I won't."

She took up the night-light and crept into his room. It was long since even this extent of intimacy had united them; since he had been sleeping in the "spare" bedroom at the flat she had never entered it; and he had been away so much, at his clubs, in the provinces, anywhere, any excuse.

Shading her small light she looked at herself in the mirror that hung inside the door before she looked at him, and her tired eyes were bright with self-defence.

"I am not dowdy, I am not old. I can hold my own with anyone. It's something, even nowadays, to be well-bred, decently educated, and Angela is common."

But Angela had hair like the floss newly unwrapped from the cocoon, and a gentle red mouth, lovely in shape, that required no lipstick, and a complexion that nothing seemed to ever fleck or flaw. The reflection at which Mrs. Fielding gazed so keenly was that of a dark woman, not ill-looking, graceful, with fine eyes and richly growing hair, but a woman who had lost all her lustre, all bloom, who looked, even in a half-light, burnt out.

She moved to the bed, another four-poster with stiff needle-work curtains and carved pillars, and stared down at Philip.

The obvious soundness of his sleep vexed her and made her envious. She thought that he, too, should have been tortured with insomnia. Was it not strange that he took the parting from Angela so lightly? And her suspicions returned. There was some trick in this abrupt, this almost careless, surrender.

She did not, in her own surprise, look at him with devouring affection, but with compassion, almost with contempt.

"Poor Philip."

He looked older than he was. He would soon be heavy, even stout; sagging lines showed round eyes and mouth, a fullness under the chin, his handsome hair was a little grey at the sides, a little sparse on top. When he was asleep all his attractiveness, his comeliness, seemed in eclipse.

Her gaze wandered to the unfamiliar pattern of his sleeping suit. She remembered, not so long ago, when she had known every stitch in every garment he possessed, so often did she wash and mend them. She glanced at his clothes, flung down untidily; at the little table on which were his watch, his pocket-book, his keys, a heap of coins. How soundly he slept, or how quiet she was! He did not stir as she picked up the pocket-book and peeped inside. Several of Angela's letters; she knew the thick, impetuous writing, the crisp peach-coloured paper. She might have guessed. She was afraid of the sharp crackle of the notepaper or she would have read these letters. They were addressed to his club.

A small dispatch case stood at the side of the little table; he had, she thought, placed it there carefully, well within reach.

It was locked, but it did not take Grace Fielding long to select the correct key from the cluster on the side table. She found within more letters, several photographs of Angela, a small bottle of colourless fluid, with a label on which was written in a strange hand "Headache Drops," together with some odd papers, pamphlets, and books.

Mrs. Fielding closed the case without interfering with anything. She had never, in any way, spied on him, read his letters, followed him, searched his pockets, yet it was not shame that made her pause now, but fear of his awakening.

"After all, there is nothing in it. He would be sure to keep her letters—her photograph. I'm as uncertain as before—it wouldn't help if I read what she has written. Will she write again—here? There's no telephone. And he can't go out casually to meet her. But I suppose she'd think nothing of coming to Newcastle or—what is the nearest town? What shall I do if business suddenly calls him to London? I must not keep turning all this over or I shall lose all control, go half crazy."

She retreated from the bed, taking the little light with her, shading it with her hand. Seen through the shadows, he looked grand, noble, in his sleep. How could she have despised him just now? Her mood was all tenderness; even his remembrances of her rival seemed merely pitiful, childish.

She passed on tiptoe to her own room, closing the door after her, thinking vaguely, dully, of the white swan she had seen from the train.

"If course I can't let it all go by default. He can't just drop into a quiet friendliness—shut me out, while he dreams of her. I must have an explanation." Like an echo came—"another scene."

The fire was very low in her room, it gave neither heat nor glow; the night-light was dying in her hand; the flood of moon-shine that slid between the curtain was a purple-green that startled the town-bred woman; it seemed odd that never before had she realised the colour, the strength of moonlight.

"Another scene? But I can't, I won't give way; I must find out why we came here—if he is genuine or only playing." She sat musing on the edge of the bed again, and her veering mood was once more tender.

"Poor fellow, he had been suffering too—those headache drops—he is generally so indifferent to those things, but he remembered to bring them." She smiled wistfully. "In the old, bad days, as he calls them now, he never had headaches."

*   *   *

They met at breakfast, which was set in the Tudor room. Mrs. Fielding had already been over what Mrs. Mace named the "Viking House," the old portion of Medlar's Farm, and hated it—dark, gloomy, every possible inconvenience, slate floors, heavy beams, little crooked stairs, little twisted rooms with small windows, a multitude of low doors, every bit of comfortable furniture looking sadly out of place. . . .

"Philip, that ancient part is out of the question, I simply can't be bothered with it—but we could be quite comfortable here. If you agree, we'll just shut that up and move everyone over here—"

"Did you tell the housekeeper that?"

"Yes, I did. She seemed very disappointed. I can't think why—that part must be very tiresome to run—the kitchen is appalling. No wonder there is a difficulty with servants."

"But you're safe there, Grace. I made sure of that before we came. There are two girls under Mrs. Mace—one is the wife of the chauffeur, Hicks, the other is his sister; they live in a cottage by the fruit garden. Then there is the gardener's wife to fall back on, in the next cottage—all these people are permanently engaged by the Holmes, at good wages, and would put up with anything to keep their places."

It was most unlike Philip to take any interest in domestic affairs, to be so exact over trifles.

"Funny for you to bother, dear. And why should they have to put up with anything? It seems to me that we shall give very little trouble."

Philip Fielding was silent; his wife was vexed by his musing air, his inattentive look, but she was careful not to show any impatience.

He was suddenly, eagerly speaking.

"Grace, there is something I ought to tell you."

She sat rigid—a confession—Angela—the real reason for their coming here. . . .

"I saw Holmes in London when he came up on business—"

"Mr. Holmes! What has he to do with it?"

"It is his house."

"Oh, you're talking of the house!" She was both relieved and disappointed.

"Of course. Holmes was quite frank about it. The place has a nasty reputation. He can't live in it—can't let or sell it—probably they'll put it down in the autumn—if I don't buy it—"

"Ghosts?"

"Yes. The very ancient part is all right, even the ghosts have died of old age, I suppose. It's this wing. You won't get Mrs. Mace to come here much—she sleeps in the cottage, you know, we are quite alone at night."

That pleased her, real solitude—and an excuse for her to demand that he never left her. . . .

"What attracted you about the idea, Philip? I didn't know that you were interested in ghosts!"

'Not put like that—just ghosts! But—the other side of things, atmosphere—suggestion—always! And I wanted to get away, really away. When I saw the place—"

"I didn't know you had been here before—"

"Yes, those few days I was in Birmingham—I just ran over. I was going to say that the very sight of it made me realise how disgustingly banal a rut we had got into—the sheer cheapness of one's own little moment, little interests, the chatter, the money grabbing. I want to do good work, Grace."

"Can you do it here?"

"Yes. It is a real get-away isn't it?"

"Oh, that, yes! I feel cut off—from everything."

"We are. Isn't it a relief?"

"Will the ghosts help you to write, Philip?"

"I dare say. I've got so many ideas in my head, poems, plays—I do want them unspoilt. I am really afraid, Grace, of writing for money. It's so insidious—a temptation—to please the American market, the managers, getting anxious—for fear you let them down. I wanted to get away."

"Well, here we are!" How long could he be so impersonal? Was there to be nothing to clarify their relationship, no promise, no pact? She must be patient.

He continued eagerly speaking, without conceit, with rather a touching lack of self-confidence, with a genuine humility, a real desire to avoid the false values that so speedily surrounded success. But she was weary of this delay in their complete understanding.

"Well, you need not worry about money, Philip. And if you like the place and feel you can work here—there is nothing against it, is there? Only," she rose, making a light question into a direct challenge, "What am I to do all day?"

"You always seem to find plenty of interests, Grace."

"In the old days when there was work for me, yes—and, in town—before we disagreed—yes; but here? With plenty of servants and no society—utter loneliness, isn't it? And I'm not a woman for long walks with dogs or helping in the garden—"

"I thought that you, too, wanted to get away—"

"From London? From Angela?"

"Among other things—"

"Is it that, Philip? Did you really bring me here—to make a clean break?"

"I thought you couldn't stand any more of it. You couldn't, you know."

"I can't stand it here, either, if I'm not sure."

She held on to the back of the oak chair, feeling that her pose was theatrical, her voice harsh, and not able to alter either.

"How sure do you want to be, Grace?"

"I thought I'd made that clear—we simply can't go over it again—as if I could! But just to come here—"

"Isn't it enough?"

"You know that depends on you."

She had always been thankful that he had never tried to fence with her, to use any verbal quips or evasions, those maddening confusions of words that torture like darts of wild fire and come to no conclusions.

He said now, simply: "Angela and I—we shan't see each other again. She is going to Africa, on a long tour." As his wife did not answer, he added anxiously, "That makes it all right, doesn't it?"

"Yes. Oh, I suppose, yes." She crossed to the fireplace, sat down on the padded fender, trembling; he came and stood over her.

"What is the matter, Grace?"

"I feel such a beast."

"We were all rather beastly."

"Even Angela?"

"Of course, Angela too. It wasn't the sort of thing that could happen without making everyone—beastly."

"I know." Tears lay in her eyes. "That is why you should never have begun it, Philip. We have always been rather lofty, you and I—and then—you did bring us down with a bang, didn't you? You made me show the very worst of myself." She smiled wistfully. "I don't believe I'll ever forgive you for that.

"It's so difficult to forget," he said quietly, as if he agreed with her self-contempt. She was deeply stung. It didn't need much for her smouldering wrath to flame, but she kept herself in hand.

"Of course we've discussed things that ought never to be mentioned—and lost self-respect, horribly. It was worse for me—I was so acutely humiliated—"

"Don't—"

"But I want to say that I wasn't really always in love with you, Philip. I quite despised you often—but I wanted the position, the money. And I—*disliked*—Angela, it was so obvious that she would make any man—a wretched wife."

It seemed to her that she had salved her tattered pride by these foolish words—which he did not even know the truth of it; he was looking at her, curiously.

"Well—that's reasonable. And now that Angela has cleared out—you'll be happy here?"

"No, Philip, it isn't reasonable. Nothing is reasonable." Tears of sheer weakness were running down her face. "And I can't be—happy—anywhere—till things were like they used to be—"

"You'll upset yourself again. Poor child, can't you stop crying?"

"Not easily—it was all such a ghastly shock."

"I've been punished too. I feel a fool, a prig—oh, I don't know—Grace," he took her arm abruptly. "I've got through it—we're here together, help me to get straight again—"

She stared at him, winking back her tears.

"Why do you look at me as if you don't believe me?" he demanded.

"You gave way so suddenly. Are you sure that Angela didn't get tired of waiting and sent you off."

"I don't think," he said sullenly, releasing her arm, "that we ought to talk of Angela."

"No? Why not? I suppose she—you—used to discuss me—oh, what am I doing? Our first morning and I am spoiling everything!" Her distress was so piteous that he said at once:

"Never mind, dear, we'll get along all right. You're overtired; you ought to rest for days and days. We'll go motoring a bit, the air is excellent and there are some wonderful places round here."

She should, she knew, have been satisfied with this poor substitute for the passionate lover's reconciliation that she desired; but she had not the strength to resist saying:

"You're kind. But if I was to say—after all—you can have your divorce—I suppose you'd wire Angela not to sail for Africa?"

She did not like the queer breathless tone in which he counter-questioned: "But you won't?"

"No, I won't."

*   *   *

Mrs. Fielding found that there was even less for her to do at Medlar Farm than she supposed—the house "ran" itself. Mrs. Mace organised everything, and there were really no neighbours. The nearest house was shut up; it belonged to wealthy people who were hardly ever there. The nearest village was merely a group of cottages, a church, a school. Medlar's Farm was far off the high road, and the village was well away from even the motor-coach route. Mrs. Mace mentioned that the only "good" doctor lived twelve miles away—not much for a car, of course, but, with no telephone, no wonder that Mrs. Holmes, burdened by young children, found Medlar's Farm too lonely.

Grace Fielding would have preferred to have lived in the cottages by the large walled fruit gardens; they were cosy and cheerful, with just the pleasant air she associated with the country. She liked Hicks and his wife, the pleasant young sister and the baby, the cat, dog, and poultry, everything there was sane and normal. In the big house it was not—the maladjustment between herself and Philip seemed to affect everything.

The entry of Mrs. Mace to end an already delayed breakfast had interrupted their conversation at a dangerous point:

"But you won't?"

"No, I won't."

He knew, at least, that she would not give way. He had made no further attempt at an elucidation of their position, nor had she; her fatigue was like a barrier between them. He said continually, kindly, that she must rest, and left her, under that excuse, much to herself until she wished that she had never confessed to fatigue.

Of course this could not go on for long, these lonely nights, these merely friendly days, but he continued to hold her at bay, and she was exhausted, content to drift awhile on the placid tide of this imitation happiness. She had, after all, some satisfactions—Angela did not write, for Mrs. Fielding saw all the post that came to Medlar's Farm. Perhaps Angela had already sailed for Africa. Why had Grace Fielding not felt a throb of triumphant joy at that news? Because she had not really believed it. This renunciation had seemed too sudden. She could not question the strength of his passion—and yet he had been able to re-linquish the object of it so suddenly.

She watched him suspiciously, knowing all the while what a foolish thing it was to do, but could not detect any uneasiness on his part. He appeared absorbed in his new book, and deeply interested in fitting up the old library as a work-room. In the brief evenings he would talk, brilliantly, enthusiastically, of his plans—poems, plays, novels, and she would listen intelligently; on the surface it was like the old days.

He recurred to the subject of the reputation of the house.

"Do you mind, Grace? I thought you wouldn't—"

"No, I don't; I wish I did. It would be rather an excitement. I'm sure there are ghosts, and sure that I shan't see them. The past is quite dead to me."

"Doesn't this house, the things in it, mean anything to you?"

"I feel that it is gloomy, rather sad, quite out-of-date—"

"You don't have any sense at all of the people who used to live here?"

"No—do you?"

"Not exactly—but I want to—"

"Why, Philip?"

"It's so tremendously interesting. There is a lot in that sort of thing, I'm sure, despite all the rubbish encrusted round it. I would like to—get in touch—"

His words were, to his wife, incongruous to his appearance, his character; he seemed, in everything, worldly, there was nothing of the effeminate dreamer about him, he had been a good soldier, was a good sportsman; perhaps it was foolish of her to connect poetic effeminacy with spiritual matters.

"Why did you want particularly to come here, Philip?"

"Well, for the solitude—and then, the story—one of the stories of the place—is exactly the same as one I've been wanting to write—when Holmes told me that, I felt I must come. Of course it is only an experiment—but it would be extraordinary if we could get through—really—take the stuff down as it were—direct from one of the real people."

"Which story is it, Philip? You've told me so many lately."

"Not this one. I can't yet. I don't know it myself. I have to wait till it comes, bit by bit—"

"But the facts? What Mr. Holmes told you?"

"Oh, just a rather ordinary murder."

"I see."

"Sure you don't mind?"

"No. I suppose there have been murders in most old houses—and worse horrors than murders. I'm not a sensitive person, as I keep reminding you. But I do think it rather odd that you—" She broke off abruptly; was it so odd? Perhaps this passionate throwing of himself into a new interest was not so odd, perhaps it was his way of trying to forget Angela. "What are these ghosts supposed to be?" she added, though she was not really concerned at all in that aspect of the affair.

"I won't bore you with them. They are rather a tangle too—so many and, I believe, quite usual. Mediums have been here and exorcists, all no use. Holmes admitted that he only advertised on a desperate chance—he wanted to keep the servants on till the autumn; they suit him, and so on. He put in 'no children,' you remember?"

"What did he see himself?"

"Nothing much. Rather a farrago. But it's got a nasty name. No doubt," he added with relish, "the worst haunted house in the North of England."

"The servants don't say anything."

"Honour bound, eh? And a bit scared too. I shouldn't question them."

"I don't." She thought stupidly: "But I shall have to question you, things can't go on like this."

*   *   *

A few timid walks, a few swift drives in the car, gave Mrs. Fielding an impression of a country that seemed to her far more alien than any foreign place that she had seen; hills, lakes, open plain, lonely roads, a few far-scattered farms, a few small villages, grey, sombre, without flowers or orchards, not in the least like the villages of the south. Stone walls instead of hedges; a wide, distant, tumbling horizon; a cold, thin air, and, the farther one turned north, an increasing bleakness of landscape, of weather. Grace Fielding had always had an aversion from chilly desolation, and this country seemed to her desolate indeed. Even the masses of June flowers could not, she thought, soften the grim outlines of the hills, the barren effect of the moors: the sweet flowering grasses, the lovely blossoms were so small, the landscape so large. She did not like to see the hawks hovering high in the cold-looking remote upper air, and every turn in her walks or drives would bring suddenly to her hostile gaze a vista of some unutterable melancholy, distant, other worldly, lit by some wild gleam or steady radiance that reminded her of the awful landscape of the Apocalypse.

Yet she preferred abroad to the house. Not that she had any sense of atmosphere or contacts with the dead, or with sinister spirits who had never been alive; not that she concerned herself with any of the stories of the place (being too self-absorbed to care), but the dark, rambling stairways, the unfamiliar rooms and old furniture, combined to depress her, and she was bored, too, by lack of any occupation. It was all very well to say "rest"; but idleness was not rest. While she lounged in an easy chair, her hands slack, her head sunk in cushions, she was thinking, furiously, her mind racing round the problem of herself, Angela, and Philip.

A problem that, she was sure, had not been solved by this exile in Medlar's Farm.

Philip was kind, but no more. He put up his work as a defense—that and her presumed fatigue. He behaved as if he had never loved Angela, but he also behaved as if he had never loved Grace.

He was not altogether reserved: she was allowed to help him by dealing with such of his official correspondence as his secretary forwarded from London; he continued to discuss his work, his plans—how desperately she wished that she did not feel that all this was part of a barricade against her, that she did not detect in all he did and said a certain hollowness, a bright falsity—"Or am I imagining that? Have I been so tormented that I can't become sane again?"

She gloomed and brooded, her passion turned inward by his withdrawal from that final reconciliation, that complete renewal of their love that alone could have assuaged her long bitter tumult of soul. In those moments (every day becoming rarer) in which she was able to see herself with a detached judgment, she feared that the well-spring of her life had been corrupted by the struggle with Angela, and that poison would flow for ever through all her being, even through her dreams, which were always seething with doubt, dread, and suspicion.

*　　*　　*

Mrs. Fielding came into her husband's study holding a glossy society weekly. He was surrounded by books, by maps, prints, drawings, and a confusion of small articles, pipes, a pair of mittens, a wig stand, some skates, an odd stirrup—all old, clumsy, tarnished.

He had, she noted, rearranged the books in the heavy oak cases; many of these were tumbled out on the floor—such large, heavy books on such ponderous, forgotten subjects. The summer landscape, a corner of the garden, the dipping, tremulous line of remote hills, that showed through the tall, uncurtained window, seemed to belong to another world from that of which the room was part.

"Seen any ghosts, Philip?"

"I wonder." He was good-humoured. "I'm getting it, anyhow, a suggestion here, a line there—all these things," he pointed to the objects on the large table, "belonged to *them*."

"To—*them*?"

"I see." She glanced at the shrunk mittens, the ugly spur. "A man and a woman."

"Well, yes—"

"Which was the victim?"

"I'm not going to tell you." He smiled. "When I've got the story clear, I want you to guess the end. Besides, I'm not quite sure myself."

"Neither am I, Philip. Sure of what?"

"Sure of the murderer—"

"It must be a queer sort of story if there is any doubt—"

"Is it—there are two stories, you see." He seemed really enthralled, delighted by his secret thoughts; common sense told her that he was not acting, yet she completely distrusted him. "I shall get them both, I feel certain—the stories, I mean, and the people as well—all here, telling me everything. It is the most fascinating pursuit in the world. If I could only get materialisation."

"You haven't—ever?"

He did not seem to notice the listlessness of her tone.

"Well, yesterday, nearly. I was reading of *them* lost on the mountain, in the mist, and I did feel my feet wet, dripping from the long grass, and then, suddenly, there was a portion of a bro-cade sleeve near my chair. I could see the pattern, the threads of the material, the outline of the figure was being built up—then, nothing!"

"I mustn't forget that you are a very accomplished writer of fiction, Philip. What is the theme of this complication?"

"Jealousy." He spoke with a maddening impersonality, as if he did not know the name of the passion gnawing at her, day and night. "Stupid," thought Grace Fielding, "or cruel?"

"I see." She placed on the table the magazine that she held. "I see, too, that Angela isn't going to Africa."

"Oh, I didn't know." He glanced down at the open page which showed Angela, cunningly photographed against a gauzy background, delicious in a wide hat and roses. The caption stat-ed that "this beautiful and accomplished actress" was shortly to appear in a West End production.

"It may not be true—and, Grace, do you much care if it is?"

He looked at her steadily; there was not much feeling in his question.

"I shouldn't care—other things being equal," she muttered. "But—"

"Tell me what is wrong—"

"This house, this country—"

"You aren't getting scared?"

"Oh, no! Ghosts, all that sort of thing doesn't exist for me—haven't I told you—often enough? But it's dull, gloomy, alien—and you so absorbed. Couldn't we go away. Italy? France?"

"We could. But not just yet. I want to get this work in hand. I'm sorry, but *I* like the place."

"How soon could we go away?"

He considered a second. "A month? Say, the middle of July? If there is anywhere one could go—quietly—in July—"

Instead of rejoicing at his speedy surrender to her whim (for so it must seem to him, she knew) her suspicions increased. Why did he give in, as if it was not worth while to dispute with her?

"A month is too long," she said sullenly.

"Well, sooner, then—give me a week or so. I can come back here in the autumn, if you hate the place—"

"Come back?"

"Yes, I've made up my mind to buy Medlar's Farm—it's a ridiculously low price. And I couldn't endure to think that it should be pulled down—why, that would be enough to make the ghosts haunt one indeed."

"I don't think, Philip, that it would matter if it was pulled down. It's strange that you like it. I can't understand how it can—soothe you. Don't you ever get headaches here? It's so aimless."

"You know that I've never had a headache in my life."

She thought of the small bottle with the label that she had seen in his dispatch case, and she smiled.

"I can't stand much more of Medlar's, Philip."

"Well, you go on somewhere, and I'll follow—"

She tried to thrust aside all the reserves, the shames, the doubts, that tried to strangle her love, to speak directly to the man whom he had been.

"Oh, Philip—let us go away—together. This place isn't right. Leave your work for a little—let us try—"

"A second honeymoon?"

These were the first words in bad taste that she had ever heard him say; he spoke tenderly, yet the short sentence made her see herself as a withered, middle-aged, greedy of affection, even—lustful.

She left him, the portrait of Angela by his hand, and he turned to his books as if the interruption had been of little moment.

*   *   *

At dinner that evening Philip Fielding spoke pleasantly to the housekeeper.

"Mrs. Fielding doesn't like Medlar's as much as I do, Mrs. Mace. One of these fine days she is going off—leaving us."

"I'm sorry to hear that sir. I hope that Madam hasn't seen anything. I always said—that Georgian wing—"

"No, no—nothing of that kind. She is simply bored, and I mean to send her off somewhere a bit brighter and follow on—I can't leave just yet. I suppose that you could look after me for a while, Mrs. Mace?"

"I'd try my best, sir."

"You do everything now," said Mrs. Fielding. "I dare say that is why I find it dull. But I don't suppose that I am likely to run away quite as soon as my husband seems to think—"

"Don't you listen to her, Mrs. Mace—I'm expecting her to fly off any day now—"

When the housekeeper had left the room Grace Fielding asked:

"Why did you tell her all that? Nothing is settled about my going away."

"But you might want to, suddenly—and there is no need to let her think that we have quarreled. Besides, I really wanted to know if she'd put up with me, alone."

"It's unlike you, Philip, to be subtle and far-seeing—"

"Is it? I'm only just the average fool always."

*   *   *

When Mrs. Fielding again visited the chauffeur's brick cottage she asked:

"What *is* the story of Medlar's Farm? I mean, the one that makes people refuse to live here? I hear that it must be pulled down if my husband doesn't buy it?"

"Well, ma'am," the young woman evaded, "it is a lonely, inconvenient sort of place—"

She was awkwardly embarrassed; plainly this was a forbidden topic.

"What does it matter now, Mrs. Hicks? So long ago! And I'm sure that you're not afraid of ghosts any more than I am?"

The other gave her a searching look.

"I don't know, I'm sure, ma'am. I always like to be indoors when it's dark—"

"Well, what is the story? Some murder?"

"Yes. A horrid murder—a man and his wife—he murdered her—"

"That's not so uncommon—"

"But they were gentry. I don't rightly know the tale, and I did promise I'd not speak of it. Mrs. Holmes said that one keeps these things alive by speaking of them—"

"I mustn't ask you, then. Poor woman! You might tell me her name, I suppose? Is she buried in that ruinous old abbey?"

"Susanna Vavasour her name was—and she's buried in Crompton Old Church—the one that'll be submerged when they finish with the lake for the waterworks. And that fits in with the old stories, too, for she said she'd never sleep till the Resurrection, and they are moving all the bodies before they drown the church."

*   *   *

Mrs. Fielding's habit of stealthy spying on her husband increased. She found little to reward her, but one day, creeping into his study, she found an interrupted letter on his desk—

Dear Angela,

Don't write again—not until I've done what I set my hand to—

So Angela wrote to him, though not to the house. Of course he was frequently out in the car and could easily pick up her letters at any village post office.

*   *   *

Mrs. Fielding's patience broke; under some trivial excuse she made a scene, as fierce, as pitiful as any she had made when he was at the height of his passion for Angela. At first he was soothing, compassionate, then stern and angry, finally goaded into retorts, but at last, in a hasty agony, he had resworn his old vows: he did love her and Angela was nothing: everything should be as it had once been: yes, they would leave Medlar's Farm: yes, they would go to Italy, in a few days, if she wished.

What more could even her greedy jealously wish?

When she dragged up to her room, he did not follow her but sent the housekeeper to look after her. Mrs. Fielding, really ill from emotion, lay broken in the Tudor bed, pleading a sudden nervous attack, thinking to herself:

"It is all false; he means nothing of what he says—he is too kind, he gives way all along the line, he is far more considerate than he used to be—why all this trouble? When one embrace, one kiss, would be enough—"

She took a sleeping draught as a desperate escape from her misery, and woke in the middle of the night. She was cold, bewildered, and felt, as she moved, sick.

More like a sensation than a thought there ran through her consciousness: "Something is wrong—with me—with the house; everything is worse than it was in London. Is it possible that these dead people are really impressing me, influencing me, filling me with—despair? For why should I despair? The situation belongs to me again, if only I could handle it. But I can't. Why do I disbelieve everything he says? Take no comfort from his promises, his kindness? He even asked Angela not to write again—until he had done what he had set his hand to. A reconciliation with me, he meant—a complete reconciliation."

She sat up in bed; the night was warm, there was no fire, no moonlight, the night lamp flickered heavily; the door between their room was closed.

Insomnia again; the sleeping draught had had little effect. How foolish to isolate oneself here—so far from a doctor or even a chemist.

Her nausea passed, leaving her charged with hectic energy. She sprang from bed, half dressed, took the lamp and went downstairs, indifferent to the darkness that her little flame only feebly scattered, with no aversion from the loneliness of the shut-in stairs with the bleak portraits.

She entered the study and began to turn over her husband's papers, searching for some letter to or from Angela, some clue to the labyrinth of his soul. There was nothing, neither letter, note, or diary. She wondered if she dare steal into his room and open the dispatch case again. And stood irresolute, staring at the piles of books, the pages of paper, covered with a fine, hurried handwriting.

She had never taken a keen personal interest in his work; her joy, her pride, her labour, had all been for the man, not for what he had accomplished. She would have rather, indeed, that he had expressed himself in action, for she had a faint touch of the primitive feminine contempt for the poet, the artist.

But then, as there was nothing else for her jealous scrutiny to feed on, she began to turn over the pages of notes for his new work—she did not know if it was to be poem, or play, or story.

The first sheet she took up was headed—*Susanna Vavasour,* and was covered with rough jottings.

"The crime was so exquisitely planned as to be impossible of detection. No one will ever be quite sure."

"Her ravaging jealousy might have driven a better man to a worse deed."

"He found the other woman a harassing difficulty—he had to rely so much on her patience and discretion; and every day he longed for her more and more. Yet the thought of his utter freedom—so soon to be achieved—kept him calm, even cheerful."

"A simple, tasteless, odourless, colourless liquid—cyanide of potassium. He had arranged, cunningly, about the servants. Nothing could be more lonely than their situation."

"Could she not have foreseen her danger? No, jealousy caused a kind of aberration in her usual acute brain—"

Mrs. Fielding put down the sheet of foolscap. A huge spider was running over the rubbed leather books shown in the circle of the night-light; she watched it, a speeding blot, hasten into the shadows that filled the entire room, leaving only herself, a few sheets of paper, a fountain-pen, and the murderer's iron spur visible in the wavering yellow glow.

*   *   *

Mrs. Fielding returned slowly to her room, holding on to the high, polished ramp with one hand, while the lamp shook in the other.

"If one believed in guardian angels—what instinct sent me down there?"

She was very cold, but neither frightened nor appalled. It was all so logical—no doubt it had been planned from the moment that Angela had given her that contemptuous warning—"If you don't take care, he will go to pieces."

An aberration indeed, but now it had gone; the congestion in her brain was relieved, she neither loved nor desired Philip, she was neither bewildered nor suspicious. She knew. It was all so logical, everything fitted in so exactly. She sat on the edge of the bed again, the light on the side table.

His sudden surrender, his attempts to soothe her, the choice of this desolate spot that no one wanted to live in, that he was going to buy—and shut up. "I might rot in one of those awful cellars for a hundred years and no one come near." All the domestic arrangements, the solitude at night, the difficulty of getting a doctor, the fact that no one locally knew her, no one would miss her, his preparation of Mrs. Mace for his wife's sudden disappearance, the headache drops, concealed in his case, the unfinished letter to Angela—"what I have set my hand to—"

What a fool she, stupid, jealous, loving Grace Fielding had been, to dream for a second that she could separate those two. She would not give way, so they had planned to destroy her. While her wretched body that he had once caressed lay corrupting in this cursed spot, Angela, sleekly triumphant, would become Philip's wife.

Like the last gleam of light in a stormy sky before the sun is finally obscured came the thought: "Of course this is all ghastly nonsense. I'm brain sick—Philip isn't a murderer! No, nor is Angela. This would never have occurred to me in London, the cheerful flat, the friends—the fame, the money—those were the real things—this is only the awful house and thinking of the story of Susanna Vavasour." But this gleam, which she clutched at as if it were the last spark of sanity in a world of madness, was soon spent; she remained, not only emotionally, but intellectually, convinced that Philip had brought her here to murder her; everything fitted into this belief.

Was he not violent, impulsive, abnormal, like all men with a touch of genius? Did not his work deal, however beautifully, with crimes, cruelties, and the darkest of border lands? Had she not herself often heard him excuse a murderer and declare that every human being was a potential criminal?

She had pressed him too far, and he had decided to be rid of her. Marriage was Angela's price, and he had resolved with all the fury of his passionate maturity to have Angela. It was all very simple. He had, no doubt, been searching for some lonely place when he had seen the advertisement of Medlar's Farm, and the coincidence of the old murder had fascinated him—also the utter security offered by a house in which no one would ever live—which he could buy cheaply and leave for ever deserted without exciting comment.

Ah, it was not all play-acting, his poring over the story of Susanna Vavasour. No doubt he was trying to cloak himself in the personality of the dead murderer, to learn from him how to be rid of a jealous wife.

A tasteless, odourless, white liquid—cyanide of potassium?—what was that?

Mrs. Fielding, very cool and deliberate in her actions, went to her medicine cupboard and took out from a corner a small empty bottle, which she carefully washed. She then shivered into her husband's room, unlocked and searched the dispatch case which he again had left close to his bed. The bottle labelled "Headache Drops" was still there; she opened this, and with great nicety poured the contents into her clean bottle, and filled the original bottle with water from the glass on the bed table.

After she had done this, she looked long at her unconscious husband, screening her night-light with a hand that was quite steady.

He was sleeping rather uneasily, turning from side to side, his face twitching. She noted on the side table a pile of papers and old books relating to the Vavasour case and the history of Medlar's Farm.

How clever he was, how cool. If it had not been for that odd intuition, like a whispered warning in her ear, that had sent her down into the library—he would have completely succeeded in his cunning plan.

But she, too, was clever and cool, and could be cunning. She stared at him without a spark of affection, even with a wonder at herself for all the pain she had undergone on his behalf. She viewed his dark, heavy features with distaste; an old tag jangled in her ears—"love to hatred turned"; what was it? "A woman scorned" . . . her memory halted.

She returned to her room, gripping the bottle with the liquid taken from her husband's case, and recalled another line of the hackneyed quotation: "Hell hath no fury—"

* * *

Mrs. Fielding's quiet, casual insistence had induced the housekeeper to speak of the ghosts of Medlar's Farm. She did so reluctantly, but not without a certain relish in the topic.

"You see, ma'am, it's the *influence,* that's what is so bad. That's why Mrs. Holmes took the children away—the medium they had down here said it was dreadful, pure evil, and that if anyone was a sensitive, as they call it, or ill, or in trouble, it would be very dangerous for them to come here—"

"You mean that the ghost would get hold of such a person, enter into him, as it were, to do a crime?"

"That was the idea, ma'am—nasty, I call it."

"No doubt, Mrs. Mace, it is very nasty. Have you ever heard of such a case among the people who have lived here?"

"Well, ma'am—there's talk, you know. Mostly suicide, as if the poor things were trying to escape—but, there, I mustn't chatter. While you're living here, you won't want to hear these old tales. And I dare say that it is all nonsense."

"But you wouldn't care to sleep here?"

Mrs. Mace smiled submissively: "I must say that I shouldn't, ma'am, not for *payment*. Though I must say I've never seen or heard anything."

"Neither have I. But all the same—"

*   *   *

Mrs. Fielding took a fair motor run to a distant town where she had seen *"analytical chemist"* on the bow window of an old-fashioned ship, and stood, formal, smiling, amid the delicate soaps, pleasant bottles of perfumes and lotions, the cases of pretty cosmetics, combs, and sponges.

The agreeable young man behind the decked counter leant forward, all civil attention as Mrs. Fielding approached with her question.

"Can you tell me, please, what cyanide of potassium is? Is it a poison?"

"Yes, indeed! A terrible poison." The young man's candid eyes stared from behind his thick glasses. "Prussic acid is another name for it—"

"Oh yes, I've heard of that. What is it like, please?"

"A tasteless, odourless liquid—or powder—a very little would kill anyone, instantly. It is the quickest poison.

"Thank you so much. I have a friend who said she had got some in Paris—she rather teased me about it—"

"Paris? Perhaps. You couldn't get it over here, not easily—"

"I must get it away from her. How could you use it?"

"It depends what form it is in," replied the young man doubtfully, wondering if he was doing right in giving any information. "I'm not an expert—you'd find it in some book on toxology, you know."

"If she was to pour a few drops into tea or coffee—or—" Mrs. Fielding's glance fell on the shining array of perfume atomisers—"spray it down the throat from one of those?"

"Yes; it could be used in a syringe, of course—"

"I dare say it is all a joke—I just wanted to know. I'll look it up—thank you so much—"

Mrs. Fielding had left the shop before the young man could pass round the counter and reach the door. She had seemed to him sane and honest, but her questions had slightly disturbed him. However, she was a stranger, a tourist no doubt, and it was not likely that he would ever see her again, and he thought, as he watched Mrs. Fielding's graceful figure disappear up the street, that if he had been indiscreet, no one would ever know it, if he himself was quiet about the dark, expensively dressed woman and her unusual questions.

*   *   *

Mrs. Fielding met her car at the public parking place. She did not wish Hicks to know that she had been to the chemist's shop. An old castle was her excuse for two visits to the distant town. She congratulated herself on the adroit quickness that she was acquiring.

On the long ride back she hugged and turned over her knowledge, as if it gave her an aching pleasure, like pressing a throbbing wound.

How did one get poison? She did not in the least know. She had heard of arsenic in rat-bait, sheep-dip, weed-killer, but this other, more deadly stuff, in a neat bottle? What did it matter? Philip knew everyone, went everywhere; no doubt he would find no difficulty. . . . She remembered an enthusiastic acquaintance with a man who specialized in poison mysteries.

*   *   *

Philip Fielding, after days of easy good-humour, fell into a peevish gloom; the weather was wild, dark, and rainy, his work had "stuck." He was not sure, after all, that he liked the atmosphere of the place—it *was* sinister and—rotten.

"Confound these Vavasours and their ghastly crimes—it's about got over me. Musty and stinking. I wish I had never begun. And such a puzzle too. All the crucial parts of the records seem to have been purposely defaced or destroyed."

"Going to give it up, Philip?"

"I think so. You're right—this place is no use. Let's get away—Italy?" He placed his hand on her and looked at her with what seem the most candid affection; she sat immobile—"He's jibbed it—or—remorse?—or—another plan?"

"What on earth are you staring at, Grace?"

"Oh—a great spider, passing along the wall just behind your head—I never saw such a large one—"

"I thought you'd seen one of those tiresome ghosts—at least!"

She laughed with that hearty loudness so uncommon in women of her type. Philip, continuing to press her hand, seemed pleased.

"You've got your spirits back, Grace, anyway, however much you dislike the place—"

That evening their reconciliation seemed more complete than it had been since Angela had enticed him away. But she had no pleasure in this; she judged him clumsy, tiresome, and viewed with malice all he did.

* * *

And in the morning, to her bitter, secret triumph, his mood was changed. He would not immediately leave Medlar's Farm; he had got over his disgust of the Vavasours and their crimes; the story was, after all, piecing itself together in his head. . . . To Mrs. Fielding this was the unmasking of a villain. She was savagely pleased by his exposure (as it was to her). After this, no doubt of his purpose entered her mind, which became focused in this central fact—that he had brought her here to murder her, calling in, with tricky cowardice, the aid of a long-dead murderer. Nothing fantastic in that, grotesque as it might seem. Even scientific researches admitted, as a commonplace, that awful and violent deeds left behind them a hideous force which haunted the scene of their unnatural actions, and which could seize on to a receptive person exposed to its influence.

Mrs. Fielding had no doubt whatever that her husband shut himself up in the library day after day, not to write his story, but to invoke the dead murderer, to summon him to his aid to commit a similar crime. She remembered how intensely interested in mediums Philip had been a few years ago, and that he had himself undergone some training in occultism.

Of course he had learnt a few tricks.

She felt no concern in the original story, only in its effect on Philip. She did not wish to fumble round the details of the ancient murder, to pore over old books and dingy pictures; she asked no more questions about the history of Medlar's Farm, either from the servants or from her husband, who must by now, be an expert on the subject. But she had the curiosity to visit Crompton Old Church, where Susanna Vavasour lay buried in a grave that would soon be disturbed.

*   *   *

The large lake, Crompton Old Water, was in the hands of the engineers; the head of it had been already devastated and disfigured by a colony of temporary iron dwellings for the workpeople. Mrs. Fielding passed a school, a club, a dance hall, rows of neat cottages, women and children going about their work and play. The church, she was told, was at the other end of the lake, a walk of two miles. That and the vicarage were already shut up, there was nothing much to see . . . but Mrs. Fielding set out along the lake side where the path soon became little more than a bridle track.

She found it astonishing to observe how soon the large activities of the engineers were left behind; after half a mile there was no sign that this, the wildest and most remote of the lakes, had ever been disturbed. To her left cascades of wild flowers and a few delicate trees bordered the water; to her right, beyond a belt of brambles and tall weeds, rose a sloping hill scattered with sheep. The loneliness was complete; there was not a boat nor a bird on the dark surface of the lake, and the hills beyond shut it into isolation.

Mrs. Fielding passed neither human being nor animal—a derelict farm gate in a sudden broken wall of stones was the only sign of human handiwork.

The day was fair, cloudy, with a faint milky vapour high in the heavens and a sunshine that seemed to fall through veils of mist from very far away. Wild thyme, mint, and heather gave a fragrant sharpness to the air; the towns-woman noted, even through her abstraction, the tall perfection of the unimpeded weeks with unblemished blooms of white, yellow, and red. She did not know the names of any of the flowers (save the butter-cups), and lovely as the strange blooms were, they added to the alien atmosphere of the grave landscape.

When she reached the abrupt turn of the lake, there was the church, hidden in yews, and, opposite, the vicarage with shut-tered windows in a neglected garden. Beyond, the path straggled into the wild hill-side and disappeared. It was impossible to pro-ceed any farther; the other side of the lake was inaccessible, for a thick growth of trees rose from the verge of the water.

Though she had taken the car as near as she dare to the lake head (for she was secretive about her wish to visit the church),

Mrs. Fielding was fatigued by her unwonted exercise. She sat down on the bank beneath the vicarage gate and ate some chocolate that she had brought with her. The loneliness penetrated deep into her being; shut-up church, the empty house— were far more emblematic of solitude than the lonely land and water. The people who had lived here, been buried here, had left behind them a heritage of utter desolation.

Here was not only the loneliness of nature's utter indifference to humanity, but the loneliness of humanity's own futility and frustration.

Mrs. Fielding's soul became stripped of all that was of little moment in her existence. She cared for nothing save for what was associated with her hatred of the two people who had robbed her and then planned to destroy her. She was no longer concerned, even with her own escape, which she could easily achieve by merely leaving her husband, but solely with the consideration as to how she could most injure them—Angela and Philip—

She could not think, even in her concentrated malice, of any better way than that she had already employed—of refusing to release Philip, of refusing to give to Angela the triumph of being his wife.

She would hardly be able to continue living with a man who was watching for a chance to murder her (yet she felt herself capable of thwarting him even in this), but she could, somewhere, *live,* and thus defeat them.

She rose, haggard, graceful in the expensive clothes for which Philip had paid, and passed into the churchyard. The gate in the brick wall was swinging on rusty hinges. When she had passed this she found herself in a tangle of shadow from the yew trees that crowded round the small, decayed church of native stone, and seemed to gather all the graves into their darkness as by an incantation; for in the little space where the sun shone no one was buried, but the evening meadowsweet grew waist high.

The church door, sunk in the low porch, was locked. Mrs. Fielding, in sullen vexation, shook the bolts; then turned away with a scowl on her face.

But perhaps Susanna Vavasour was not buried in the church, but somewhere in the blue-black shade of the yew trees.

So, stooping under the flat boughs, peering at crazy headstones, Mrs. Fielding searched the lonely churchyard. There were crosses, mouldering from damp, wooden boards rotted from the sunk supports, long mounds that sent the low lusty weeds that grew thereon higher than their fellows, and presently there was, to the north of the burial ground, an altar tomb, protected by an iron railing that, rusting into decay, had fallen this way and that.

Mrs. Fielding stood and stared at this tomb that stood almost out of the shade of the yews and the barrenness of the ground they grew upon. She could read a few half-defaced letters on the flat table-like stone that was cracked across in two places and bound by the hairy cords of a red-leaved ivy. Susanna Vavasour. Then some Latin that Mrs. Fielding could not understand, some hollows in the stone that still held last night's dew, then a few English words, broken and in an unfamiliar spelling. Mrs. Fielding made them out to read thus:

"For what I did I can answer . . ."

There seemed no sense in this sentence, but Mrs. Fielding was in no mood to cavil at that. She stood long, half in the misty sunshine, half flicked by the outflung boughs of the yew tree, thinking of Susanna Vavasour. And of the other woman in her story. Had he married her when his wife was—dead? Was he hanged for his crime? She wished now that she knew the details of the old tale.

Though all was so fair and still, her humour corrupted the

sweetness of the placid day. She felt the stench of rotting bones that must long since have become one with the mould, and sensed that somewhere near her feet crawled obscene insects, the horrid devourers of dead flesh.

She clung to the railings, and the rust came away in flakes on her gloves, the corroded spikes touched her cold face. She stared at the letters on the dark tombstone, which held, she believed, the secret of Susanna Vavasour.

A white butterfly, greenish yellow at the wing bases, fluttered on to the damp stone and then instantly away. Mrs. Fielding gazed after it and trembled to think of its destination.

The remote peace of the churchyard was to her heavy with menace; never had she been in a more awful place.

She thrust her hand through the crazy railing and beat her feeble fist on the rough stone.

"What happened? Why didn't you escape? Stupid—to allow him to kill you—and go to her."

She was not surprised at the sound of her own voice: for lately she had got into the habit of muttering to herself, and her words seemed to be at once caught up and involved into the silent threat of the stillness.

She tried to evoke an image of Susanna Vavasour from out the churchyard hush. Closing her eyes she forced her imagination and visualised at once a woman in a tight-fitting bodice of a green that seemed of the very darkness of the yew trees; her face was colourless, neat featured, and a small quantity of pale hair was drawn away from a high, smooth brow. "Of course," thought Grace Fielding, "that is a portrait I saw without noticing it closely—a print on Philip's desk." She opened her eyes and the vision remained; a picture, like a transparent palimpsest, over the still flat boughs of the funeral trees, over the still air.

The woman now appeared to be seated on the tombstone

and looking fixedly at Mrs. Fielding, with the almost painful intensity of one who wishes to convey an important message and may not speak.

She was leaning forward, and Mrs. Fielding marked the tarnished silver buttons of braid that fastened the lustreless taffeta across her narrow breast, and that her pale skin had a faintly wrinkled, perished quality.

"It is certainly the picture I saw—if one wishes one can really evoke a phantom—I wonder if it is Susanna Vavasour."

Her eyes were feeling the strain of this long stare at the creature of her own creation, she supposed, for the vision began to waver into ripples of light, like the emanations of intense heat, but, before it had entirely disappeared, Mrs. Fielding observed a large spider crossing the crumpled flesh of the bosom: "Why should that come into my mind now? The same insect that I saw crossing Philip's papers—the night that I found out—"

She moved away from the railings of the tomb; she felt suddenly listless and exhausted; the loneliness and the stillness of the place hung on her like a weight.

She thought of the water soon to be poured by the engineers into the lake, water that would rise, rise, until it was over the empty church, over the vicarage—what would they find when they opened the tomb of Susanna Vavasour? She would like to see that, a heap of dust, a few yellow fibrous bones. She put her hand on her own arm and thought of her own skeleton rotting in the cellars of Medlar's Farm, while far away Philip lay in the clasp of Angela.

She wandered over the open space beyond the graves and broke down the wild flowers as she went, a trail of destruction behind her.

Nothing more to be done here—nothing to be discovered or gained. Her sullen glance travelled over the church. She was close to a sunken doorway; in the keystone of the arch above it was a curious, clumsy carving that caught her attention. A grotesque fiend with medieval horns and tail was pursuing a thin creature in grave-clothes who turned at bay, and, with an expression of the utmost horror, cast a net over the enemy who writhed in astonished helplessness. Mrs. Fielding thought that the victim who suddenly became the aggressor had a look of Susanna Vavasour in the pinched features.

"Susanna Vavasour? But I've never seen her—yet that image of her was very strong. I suppose that is what Philip does—evokes people like that—"

She turned away, loathing the place, yet hating to leave it; she felt that she had been defeated in the attempt to surprise some secret.

"Now I must go home." Her whole being ached at the word. Home. Medlar's Farm, the alien rooms, the dark stairs, the shut cellars, the shut-up attics, and Philip, watching her, waiting for his opportunity.

As she turned away from the closed house from which the chimney smoke would never rise again, from the church where no more prayers would ever be said, she looked backwards continuously, and her fancy set Susanna Vavasour in her tight, green-black bodice, leaning over the gate of the churchyard, beckoning earnestly to her as if she wished to whisper to her some important secret.

*   *   *

When Mrs. Fielding, tired and moody, turned into the gate of Medlar's Farm, she saw, in the avenue of ancient pollarded limes, a slim, smart, glossy blue car; her muscles became taut—Angela! While she, Grace, had been day-dreaming in the old churchyard that would so soon be submerged beneath the lake, and therefore of no concern to anyone, Angela and Philip had been together.

Mrs. Fielding went directly to the library, and, a little breathless from haste, opened the door.

There was Angela, seated by the table on which was Philip's confusion of books, and there was Philip, standing in the window-place.

Angela had been crying; her hair was bright above her green leather motor coat, her hands, outstretched over the piles of paper, twisted the silk cap that she had snatched off. Almost suffocated by hatred, Mrs. Fielding leant inside the door.

"I thought you'd be back soon," said Philip, without moving. "Angela was in the neighbourhood and thought she'd look us up."

"Good morning," smiled Mrs. Fielding.

Angela gave a glance over her raised shoulder.

"Oh, don't pretend—you know I came to see if Philip could bear it."

"Do you think that he can?"

Angela stood up, and shook back her short hair with a movement that was none the less sincere because she had several times employed it on the stage. She was obviously ready with a flaming retort, but Philip came forward with authority.

"Look here, we can't wrangle over this. Angela was up in the lakes, and it was quite natural that she should think of coming over here—"

"Quite natural," said Mrs. Fielding.

"And she's going away, at once."

"Oh, you won't stay to luncheon, Angela?"

"Don't be a fool. As if I could take anything from you."

"Except my husband—"

"I gave you an opening there, didn't I?" replied Angela recklessly. "Well, haven't you thought better of it? This must be ghastly for you, too—this awful place—"

"Don't," put in Philip sharply. "I told you that it would be no good."

"I want to hear Grace herself—for the last time. Oh, you can't be so crazy! You'll give us—the divorce—"

Mrs. Fielding continued to lean inside the door. She thought: "I suppose this is my last chance, a kind of ultimatum. If I refuse, I pronounced my own death sentence."

She looked from one to the other, and it did not seem at all incredible to her that she looked at two people who had planned to murder her. . . . Of course, this visit had been to urge on Philip's flagging courage. . . . Perhaps Angela expected to find her ill, dying.

"It's nonsense for you to ask me," she said in a loud, harsh voice.

Then Angela spoke the words that had just been running though Mrs. Fielding's brain.

"It is your last chance."

"Of what?"

"Of behaving decently."

Mrs. Fielding shook her head. These evasions and double meanings rather confused her. She looked without pity at Angela's soft prettiness, flushed by a swift drive, by bitter tears—"I suppose she was crying because he hadn't got rid of me yet."

Aloud she said:

"I can't prevent you and Philp from going away together."

Her husband answered:

"You know that Angela won't have that, Grace. Isn't it a case for a little kindness? Angela, you'd better go."

"I've had no kindness," muttered Mrs. Fielding. She watched Angela pick up her motoring gloves and linger, slowly putting them on.

"She's asked me," thought Mrs. Fielding, "to be decent, to be kind—if I was either, I should leave them alone together. But I won't."

She followed them to the waiting car. She wondered if Angela was the same kind of woman as the rival of Susanna Vavasour. She saw her look at Philip, and his evasion of her glance.

"There is no need for speech, they understand each other perfectly."

"You'll be all right?" asked Philip, as Angela grasped the wheel. "It's a long drive—"

"Yes, thanks—all right."

And she was gone, with no more than that. Husband and wife watched the blue car glide through the open gates of Medlar's Farm.

When it had disappeared Mrs. Fielding said:

"I suppose that you hate me for sending her away?"

"You didn't send her away. She was just leaving when you came in—" In a tone that forbade her to pursue the subject he continued swiftly: "Where have you been all the morning? I thought you couldn't do these long walks?"

She re-entered the house; she was quite broken with weariness.

"I had a fancy to see Crompton Old Church—the one they are going to submerge. A curious carving there—a fiend chasing a soul who has turned round and netted him—"

"Haven't you seen that drawing of it in the library? It is quite famous—the local name is—'The Devil Snar'd.'"

*　　*　　*

They sat slackly either side of the deep wood fire that Mrs. Mace had carefully piled up: it was raining again and the June evenings were cold. It seemed, too, that even in midsummer these rooms would be damp and chill. The lamp cast a circle of light over the figure of the man, sunk in a deep chair with his book; over that of the woman, sunk in a deep chair with her idleness. Beyond all was shadow which obscured the pretty modern trifles with which Mrs. Holmes had tried to soften the gauntness of the Tudor room, as the ancient dining-room was vapidly named.

Philip Fielding did not like the room, nor, indeed, this part of the house. He had been impatient to return to the library, but soon, and with quite a good grace, had acceded to his wife's request for his company. She lay stretched almost at full length, her hands clasped behind her head, her long body relaxed. She could see little of her husband, for he held up the massive book like a shield before his face.

"Isn't that great tome heavy, Philip; doesn't it make your hands ached?"

"I hadn't noticed it—"

"No? Well, I wish that you would put it down and talk to me—"

The book was not lowered.

"What do you want to talk about, Grace?"

"We have enough subjects—haven't we?"

As he did not reply, she continued:

"Angela. Why was she up here? I thought she had had a new part in London—"

"I believe she is taking a rest first."

"A rest!" laughed Mrs. Fielding. "I should not have thought that she found it very restful to come up here to see you. I never saw her so upset."

The book, at that, was put down, and her husband's stern face looked at her out of the shadows.

"Look here, Grace, we simply can't discuss this. Angela has

gone. I didn't know that she was coming—"

"How can I tell that you are not lying?"

"I suppose you may infer so from the fact that I never lied to you before—"

"I wonder. You are so cool, so indifferent, Philip, and yet you ought to be in torture. I can't understand how you can give her up like that—"

"Can't you? Why?"

"People don't. And I never thought that you had much strength of character."

"I have nothing to say, Grace, and you will only make yourself ill if you keep on brooding over these things."

Completely changing her tone she cried, sitting up violently:

"I can't imagine *what* you can see in her. Look at her to-day—so ordinary, so cheap, just like any young woman tearing over the country in a vulgar-looking car. She walks badly too; that's always been against her on the stage—"

Her voice trailed away, extinguished by his silence. He had taken up the book again; she could no longer see his face.

She clasped her hands round her knees, steadying herself by the interlocking attitude:

"Are you reading about the Vavasours, Phil?"

He responded at once.

"Yes, there is a tract on the case, bound up here with some other pamphlets—"

"The case? Was there a trial? Was he hanged?"

"No. It seems never to have gone beyond gossip. There was an inquest, but no verdict. It all seems to have gone by default."

"I suppose that encourages you," smiled Mrs. Fielding.

He looked round the side of the book.

"Encourages me? What do you mean?"

"How near we are to it," she thought; "he almost sees that I know."

"I mean your story, of course, Phil."

"Well, I don't see that it is very encouraging to find all researches blocked—there's been a lot destroyed, purposely, of course. It is difficult, nowadays, to realise the power a family like the Vavasours had—they really could do almost what they liked."

"Convenient." Mrs. Fielding continued to fix her husband with an unwinking gaze from the dark eyes that had lately become so hollow and so shadowed by bistre stains.

"I had a queer experience in that old churchyard to-day—I found *her* tomb, and I tried to shut my eyes and force myself to see what she was like—"

"Did you get anything?" His voice sounded eager; he put the book aside and sat up. Her twitching smile broadened; there was a ghastly amusement in thus playing with him when she knew his secret.

"Yes, but it was just a replica of some print I've seen on your desk. Quite strong though. I seemed to still see her, even after I'd opened my eyes. She was seated on the edge of her own tomb, and trying, I thought, to tell me something."

"They always do—but it is so difficult. That is how it happens to me. I actually saw *him* the other evening. You know I told you, the patch of brocade—well that came again—then I built up the whole man—of course there are a hundred explanations."

"Do they matter?" Mrs. Fielding rose swiftly and stood before the fire which made a steady red light behind her thin figure. "What did he tell you, Phil? How he did it?"

"As if one ever got anything as concrete as that! Besides—I don't believe that he did do it." Philip Fielding seemed troubled. "I like him—if he was a murderer, I feel sure that he was justified."

"Justified!" echoed Mrs. Fielding. "So you think that murder can be justified?"

"I've always said so."

"That's bold, Philip." She shuddered, despite the heat flowing about her. The big man was looking at her with the blankness of utter malice, or so she interpreted his stare; she felt then very near her own death. "Perhaps to-night, perhaps any night, he will find that the poison has been changed, and take other means." For the first time since she had discovered his purpose she was afraid and melted by compassion for herself.

"Don't you feel well, Grace? I don't think we ought to talk about these things—"

"It was the fire—foolish to stand so near, the heat on my back—" She sat limply down on the end of the long chair. "Tell me some more—I'm not frightened—of *them*."

He did not appear to notice her emphasis. He sat forward, his elbows on his knees. The wavering shadows, the light from the burning wood, were kind to him and returned to him that physical magnificence she had once so adored, and which now, in the common day, was something blurred and marred. His hair fell finely over his square brow; the flaring lines of the nostrils, the curve of the full lips, the set of the chin, had the pristine purity of line. And in the sweep of his heavy shoulders, the modelling of his sensitive hands, was strength and power. Her heart cried out for her one-time lover that Angela had transformed into a monster. To cover her almost uncontrollable emotion she said:

"Read me what you have done of your story Philip; it is a long time since you have read me anything of yours."

He acceded at once, and pulled a few sheets of foolscap from the thick leaves of the *Miscellanea;* perhaps he also was eager to escape from the present moment.

*   *   *

"They first met at a ball given at a castle near Hexham. Castle, I say, but the older portion was in ruins and a Palladian mansion had lately been raised there by a nobleman, rich from the plumbago and coal mines of Newcastle. Vavasour was poor and a nobody, younger son of a younger son, seventh son of a seventh son, the old women said. He had been abroad—a traveller who had often been forced to beg his way. He had worked, too, and gained much experience. I do not know what whim had prompted this return to his ancient home, which then he had no prospects whatever of inheriting. He was staying at this house which we now know as Medlar's Farm—then it was called Vavasour Hall. Susanna was wealthy—an heiress in the old sense of the word—that is, she quartered her father's arms on a lozenge, and would bring honours as well as riches to her future husband. She had never left the north, and was ignorant of much, yet well versed in inherited traditions of womanliness. She had all the externals of feminine grace, and possessed all those small dainty virtues which can be openly extolled. She was then, as I suppose, twenty-two or three years of age, and people wondered why she had not married before.

"As she entered the ballroom, the walls of which were painted with a design of blue lattice through which hung trails of covolvulus, she immediately saw him. She whispered to her father, on whose arm she leant: 'I will marry that man and no other.'

"She had been told since she was a small child that she might make a choice of a lord and master, but so far no man had pleased her more than very briefly. He, Philip Vavasour, had that external splendour which is rare enough and never fails of powerful effect. Though often decried and denied by the envious and the jealous, yet physical beauty is one of the most powerful things in the world, and Philip Vavasour had it, and with it that air of negligence which refutes all possible charges of coxcombry. He wore that blue coat in which he has been most frequently seen since his death. It was heavily frogged with a fine, plaited bullion braid; there was no collar, and folds of fine muslin were swathed round his neck. The pocket holes were very low; he hung a slender sword which he had himself bought in Toledo.

"He was presented at once to Susanna Oldmixon and glanced at her with indifference. She was not unlovely; she had the frail, cold, and precise look, I think, of delicately blown glass or finely moulded china, but to him she was not beautiful nor desirable. He was kind to her because she was friendly and he had been long away from home.

"When they had danced together they stood awhile in the window-place which was hung with straw-coloured curtains to keep out the winter air and set with a painted table for cards. He kept his hand long in hers, for she had said that she could read the lines on his palm and must thus trace his destiny.

"With this pleasant excuse they stood together, and she said afterwards, and repeated with a strange persistency, that she could see behind him a rich background, very different from this familiar room. She could sense about him the sea, a very different ocean from that which beat gloomily on the shores of Northumberland or surged in the grey waves of the Solway. The sea was vivid and pure beneath an untainted sky, it lapped against flowerly shores, the vision of which filled her with an unbearable nostalgia. While she murmured some hocus-pocus about what she foresaw of his life from the reading in his palm she was imagining herself wandering with him on those untrodden islands where fronds of ferns and palms, green as the green of her grandmother's emeralds which she wore on Sundays to the grey church, hung motionless against a purple sea. She saw about him caskets of jewels and panniers of fruit, and tall white buildings green shuttered against the midday sun, and colonnades of clear marble where rainbow-coloured doves trailed their wings along a pavement where hard orange grains were scattered.

"She saw him moving, at once triumphant and indifferent, among all these bright and beautiful things, and she saw herself as his perpetual companion.

"After a while she dropped his hand, giving up her pretense at fortune-telling, and sat down by the card table and crossed her fingers on her stiff silk lap.

"'It is true,' she said, 'that I have some gift of second sight, yet I have read very little in your palm, but I feel about you many strange and lovely objects.'

"'I have travelled a good deal,' he said, without surprise. 'I have taken care to see what was worth seeing in every country to which I have been.'

"'Do you hate this place?' she asked earnestly. 'The north, I mean. I have always felt alien here.'

"He smiled, shaking his head, with a movement rather like that of a noble mastiff who flicks the water from his face."

* * *

Her husband was startled when Mrs. Fielding spoke, breaking his story into splinters like a hard blow cracks ice.

"I don't believe any of it," she interrupted. "It is all a fiction. You didn't get that, Philip, out of your old book."

"It doesn't interest you?" he asked drily.

"Oh, it interests me, but a great deal of it is absurd. It's none of it consistent. Why do you go into those details—the colour of his coat, the set of his pocket holes, and even what there was painted on the wall of the ballroom?"

"Because I've seen that. Some of it I can't see, but I can see that and I have put it in."

Mrs. Fielding waves aside this explanation.

"And then the names! I don't believe he, the murderer, was named Philip."

"I didn't say he was a murderer, Grace. And as for the name, I don't know—yes, I did alter that. I like to call him Philip."

"Aren't you rather betraying yourself?"

"In what way betraying myself, Grace? Everyone betrays himself in his work. You can't keep it out—yourself I mean— Of course, this is only the first rough draft of the story; I expect I shall alter it a good deal. But don't you like it?"

"Like it," she exclaimed. "Of course, it's all rubbish, and you could have said it in such a few words. He married a woman for her money."

"There's a lot more in it than that, Grace. I wish you hadn't interrupted me just as I got to Barbara."

"Is Barbara so important?"

"Why, yes, of course; she was the reason for it all, the whole tragedy."

Mrs. Fielding rose and put the back of her hand to her

mouth, a gesture as if she struck her lips. Why didn't he say Angela instead of Barbara? The whole device was so transparent. He must think her an utter fool. She looked down at him and spoke, her voice muffled against the back of her own hand.

"It's getting late. I think I'll go to bed."

"You don't want to hear any more, then?" he asked.

"Not to-night. I'm not sure, Philip, that it isn't all dangerous."

She did not know what made her say that; it seemed to her that she was speaking more to herself than to him. "I mean, we ought not to let these dead people get hold of us like this. There's peril in it, isn't there? We should never have come to this house. It might make one do things." She ventured a glance at hm.

He smiled, shook his head.

"Oh, I don't go so far as that—hypnotism, hallucination—all the hundred and one names there are for it. No, I don't believe that. Besides, what did they do? I can't find out."

She said, trying to probe not only him but herself: "Why are we interested? Why do we care? Why are we going over all this old ground? It must be that the atmosphere of the house has got hold of us, Philip, and we ought to get away."

"Get away to what?" he asked; and she winced before the bleakness in his voice. "We haven't got a home, you know. Only a flat in London, and I don't feel that I could take up the old life."

"Don't you, Philip?" Her words were broken with an infinite regret. "But what about the Italian trip? You said you'd take me away."

"So I will, but I don't know—Italy? We might meet him there—Vavasour, I mean. He was in Italy. I dare say that is where he learned how to—" Philip Fielding broke off his sentence so completely that it seemed to her as if he bit a word on his tongue.

"Learned to—what?" she challenged.

"Oh, I don't know. All his tricks."

"How to murder his wife," she suggested on a rising note.

"I don't say that." He fumbled with the manuscript, folded it into the heavy book with the rubbed leather binding. "I don't know that he did do that. Anyhow, he was never found out."

"Perhaps you'll find him out, Philip."

She moved slowly to the door. It suddenly seemed impossible for her to go up those dark stairs, lined with those heavy, blackened portraits in the tarnished frames; to pass down the ill-lit corridor and enter the bedroom—the bed with the needle-work curtains, with the small modern medicine chest in which she kept the liquid that she had taken from her husband's dispatch cast . . . prussic acid . . .

"Don't ever read me any more, Philip," she implored hurriedly. "I don't want to hear it. I'm afraid the story will begin to haunt me. Leave me alone. It's all nonsense, really. We don't even know that these people actually existed."

"But I thought you saw her tombstone to-day, Grace."

"That might have been another woman. I don't know—I don't want to think of it."

He rose, and again she stared at him. She had the impression that she had received so forcibly on the first night they had come to Medlar's Farm—that he was of gigantic stature and, moreover, entirely alien to herself.

"Possession, perhaps," she murmured, and he asked her what was the word that she had spoken so low, but she shook her head several times, as if weary of all subterfuge. She sank into her chair again.

"Read some more, Philip. I've changed my mind, I can't go to bed just yet." She dropped into her chair with a certain violence, as if she had been thrown; he was, half reluctantly, opening the book that contained his manuscript.

"What did they know of poisons in those days?" she asked, shading her eyes with the back of her thin hand.

"Oh, a great deal, I expect. It was so easy to get hold of, too—"

"You know a great deal, too, don't you, Philip? I remember you read it up once, with that man Bates—"

"Bates? Oh yes—he was very keen—about La Croix and La Voison and those people—"

"What did they use—cyanide of potassium?"

"I suppose so." He seemed surprised by her use of this word. "Prussic acid."

"Yes. It's marvellous what it will do, isn't it? Colourless, odourless, tasteless—I believe that you could use it in a syringe— a few puffs down your throat—"

"I never thought of it—I suppose you could. Pretty ghastly, eh? But Vavasour couldn't have used that way—they weren't known—sprays, I mean, then. I don't even know if he could have got hold of prussic acid—"

"Go on with the story—"

Philip Fielding began to read again.

*　　*　　*

"'I should not care to stay here,' he admitted. 'And there is little danger that I shall do so. I do not think that my uncle is very pleased to see me at Vavasour Hall.'

"'You will go away again?' and desolation, like a veil, fell over her small, fine features.

"He did not answer, but continued to smile as if he noticed neither her nor her distress.

"To describe him would be to give a false impression, I know, of his appearance. I have not yet completely seen him. His hair was reddish and grew strong and thickly, it was harsh in texture. His features, noble in themselves, seemed a mirror for gay, passionate, and strange thoughts which continually changed.

"That night there was a great snow-storm. All the north was muffled and white. There seemed no longer earth nor sky, flakes falling close and steady across the heavy grey buildings closed in the horizon so that one might not see much farther than one's own out-stretched hand and brought hallucinations to those who continued to gaze at them; a man lost on the moors that night saw about him the likenesses of friends dead forty years and more.

"The complete stillness, the old furniture and the old boards that gave creaks that could be distinctly heard. Neither Philip nor Susanna could return to their homes that night. They slept for the first time under the same roof. He was woven into all her dreams like a thread of gold and scarlet.

"They met again in the morning, when he showed her some of his treasures: a casket of shells, some branches of coral, which he declared he had snatched from the hands of the sirens themselves, a necklace of thin gold coins like the last leaves of autumn. A fan, painted with a blue landscape; all these things looked strange in the cold light reflected from the snow without.

"The young woman was enchanted.

"She had her way like those under a spell often do. When the storm abated and the roads were passable her father drove over in a coach and four to Vavasour Hall and put his case before Philip's uncle; in brief, he offered the hand of his delicate heiress, and all her plumbago and coal mines, to the penniless Philip.

"The old Vavasour, I think, mocked a little, talked of women and fools and caprice, and asked what they knew of Philip who had been abroad so long and was by some accounts no better than a rogue, yet he did not say from where had come these tales so disgraceful to his own blood, and in the end, yet not without a touch of malice, said: 'That if the lady would, she must . . . No doubt Philip, for all he was such a vagabond, would be willing to pouch the money and settle down, but they must remember that the young man had nothing.'

"That point was emphasised. He stood three or four away from the succession to the Vavasour estates. His little portion he had long since squandered. The devil alone knew how he lived—perhaps on charity—he was no lover of work.

"'I dare swear,' laughed old Vavasour, 'that when he gets in those strange foreign cities, he begs his way a little. He comes begging to me, at least, and a spendthrift he is beyond cavil. One who has never achieved anything, and has no ambition or endeavour in him, and has, too, if I know him, an obdurate, a savage heart—but if your daughter—"

"'My daughter thinks he has all the qualities she admires. I, at least, have enough land for both. He will not want, Vavasour, with what I can give him.'

"The other man was amazed to hear Oldmixon thus plead his daughter's cause.

"'You must,' he said good-humouredly, 'be bewitched to wish such a one for your son-in-law. But what is to be will be. It is a piece of good fortune—ridding me of the rogue. I'll tell him to get to work on his wooing.'

"So Philip Vavasour was told by his uncle of his great good fortune. How he might become master of the woman in the north, and of all her possessions, and how she was fair enough and young, and of good repute and, more important, weak and wilful, as her obstinate choosing of a scoundrel like himself showed, and therefore might, in the future, be easily overcome and managed. But Philip received this news sullenly; he was never one to care about money and possessions, nor to desire to stay long in one place. Besides, he had just seen Barbara."

*   *   *

Mrs. Fielding impatiently interrupted. Her silence and, apparently, her absorption in the story had been so complete that her sudden voice startled him, so that the manuscript slid from his hands.

"Don't you see," she said contemptuously, "that it is simply our own story you are dwelling on?"

He repeated stupidly: "Our own story?"

"Yes," she said, "that's why I stopped you when you came to Barbara. Angela, it should have been."

She left the room, fumbling out into the dark.

*   *   *

Philip Fielding followed his wife, and if he had been brought sharply back from his ghost world to a realisation of her distress.

"You must not think that for a moment, Grace. Why, the case is utterly different—his own experience is the last thing that a writer like myself draws on—"

He spoke gently, almost affectionately, to his wife as she paused by the newel post of the short, dark stairway.

"I'm going back into the library for a little. It isn't really late, and I want to see if I can get any more of the story. I'm beginning to think you're right. What I've written is rubbish, especially the snow-storm."

"No, that's quite true," she broke in quickly. "Can't you feel how cold the house is now—June, why, it's ridiculous, I'm sure the snow is thick outside."

He looked sharply at her, and the pity in his tone deepened as he laid his hand on her arm.

"You mustn't worry yourself about these things, Grace. I'm afraid it is bad for you—being here. I'd no idea you had so much imagination. You usually despise my poor fancies. Are you sure you don't mind going upstairs alone?" She shook her head, and he continued: "You know I'd never have asked you to stay if you hadn't been so sure you didn't mind."

The little flame of the night-lamp that she carried upstairs with her was between them. It clearly picked his features out from the surrounding dark; she moved it as if she did not wish to see his face just then, and slowly proceeded up the stairs.

He called after her: "In that dark green dress you make me think of Susanna Vavasour herself."

Mrs. Fielding asked, turning to glance down over her shoulder: "How do you know she wore a dark green dress?"

"Well, I don't, really. I may have made it up or read it somewhere. Why does it surprise you?"

"Well, because I thought so too." She went on quickly up the stairs without waiting for him to reply. When she reached the top, she peered down over the balusters and saw that the hall was empty. He had, then, returned to the library and shut himself in, with what he termed his "poor fancies."

How could he be so tactless or so cruel? He had denied that she was the prototype of the woman in the story, yet said that she reminded him of Susanna Vavasour.

His fancies, or those of another? Those, for instance, of the dead murderer? He held her lamp high, and glanced over the heavy portraits on the upper wall, pictures placed so high that all Mrs. Mace's housewifely care had not sufficed to keep them free of dust, even of cobwebs. Her light was reflected in the highly varnished surfaces of the dark canvases.

She noticed now what she had not observed before, that they were all of men. One of them, no doubt, was the creature whom her husband had named Philip Vavasour—the murderer, the justified murderer, who had disposed of the jealous woman who tormented him. Disposed of her, destroyed her, for the sake of Barbara.

Which was he, did anybody know?

Mrs. Fielding thought that all these masculine visages were repellent, that there was slight distortion over each crudely delineated face. But she was beginning to imagine a slight distortion over everything, as if all the objects in the world had been slightly shaken out of place.

One of these painted figures wore a curious sage-green cloak bound with black, and carried, thrust into the folds on the breast, a stiff posy of unnatural looking, dim white flowers stained by tarnished red. The features were of a livid paleness, and Mrs. Fielding pondered as to whether or no this was a living creature or a dead body painted in grave-clothes.

She turned into her own room and lit the larger lamp which stood ready on the table by the bed.

Not afraid, not afraid of anything. So she assured herself. Why, she had never been afraid of the house nor of any phantoms there might be in it, and now her mood of fear of her husband had changed. She no longer dreaded him. She thought she had a guide and comforter, the prim-faced woman in the dark green dress like her own.

She thoughtfully stood by one of the posts of the narrow bed. With an idle finger she traced the design of bursting fruit and folded flower on the harsh twill where the thread, flourished there long ago by dead hands, was beginning to wear away.

She was endeavouring, through the slight and not disagreeable confusion that had fallen on her senses, which was like the first stage of the inhalation of a powerful drug, to trace out, with cool logic, the most probable course that her husband would take.

Angela, no doubt, had come over in desperation, to urge on him some immediate action. When he discovered that the supposed poison was not efficacious—he might have discovered that already, for all she knew—very likely she had already drunk the water with which she had filled the bottle in his dispatch case.

When he had discovered that, what would he do? Procure some more prussic acid? How easy it would be for him to take her out one morning, driving the car himself. She saw it all, the car, a picnic basket behind, Mrs. Mace smiling farewell from the steps, asking them if they'd forgotten the thermos and rugs, telling them the beauty spots they were to be sure not to miss. . . . No, that would not do. It must not be a picnic. He would tell the housekeeper that his wife had suddenly decided to leave. Had he not prepared the way for such a statement? He would say he was driving her to the station. There were many most lonely places where he could quite easily murder her; he had had many opportunities, on his lonely walks, of finding such a spot.

He could sink her body in a lonely tarn, or bury it in the dark woods, or even, with safety, leave it to bleach on some cold hill-side.

Yet she did not think he would do any of these things. She thought he would bring her back to Medlar's Farm, conceal her somewhere in the car and wait till everything was quiet at night, and then take her out and bury her in one of the cellars; or perhaps that was all nonsense, not the sort of plan that a murderer would think out at all. Perhaps he meant to give her another poison, one that acted slowly, like arsenic; perhaps he had the courage to watch her agony, summon a strange doctor far away, see that she died before the doctor appeared. The whole done in order, an inquest perhaps, but no verdict, or an open verdict as in the case of Susanna Vavasour.

Well, it would not matter which way he chose, all of them would lead to freedom for him. Her anguish was due to that, not to the contemplation of her own tragedy, but to the prospects of his freedom.

That journey to Italy! He would go, no doubt, and Angela would be his companion.

She left the bed and walked around the room; then drew up suddenly before the small cupboard in which she had put the prussic acid. She did not know why she had not destroyed it. As she leant against the wall there she felt as if someone were soothing and comforting her, advising her. . . . She could not catch the sense of the counsel which was being given to her. Then she became incapable of clear reasoning, and odd, broken sentences fixed themselves stupidly in her mind.

That old tag—"Hell hath no fury—" Then, the sentence that her husband had spoken when she had told him about the queer sculpture which she had seen in Crompton Old Church: "The Devil Snar'd." There was some meaning there, and she was like one fumbling about in the dark to find the handle of a door. Then it seemed that she had discovered, grasped, and turned it, and light broke in on her slowly—a cold and awful light in which Hell stood clearly revealed.

She was so horrified by this lurid illumination which was worse than any darkness, that she tried, for the first time in her life, to pray, to honestly send up an appeal for help to some high and merciful Power. She could not do this, but she could check the horror which had been breaking on her—and she remained for a while mute and immobile, crouched below the corner in which was the small medicine cupboard.

She believed that she saw herself—or Susanna Vavasour, or her own evil angel—at least a creature in a dark green gown who seemed to hover, in the likeness of a cloud, a few feet above the floor—blot the ancient wall, and she held a muttered colloquy with this phantom.

"I ought to be sure that it is poison—first of all. I ought to be sure of that—"

"You are sure. Didn't you ask the chemist?"

"Yes, but I only described the stuff."

"You showed it to him, don't you remember? And he said that it was prussic acid—enough to kill three or four people."

"Did he? I forget. My mind has been so confused lately."

The shape, she thought, stooped down until it enveloped her like a miasma.

"You must not be confused about this. He brought that poison here to destroy you. Everything fits into that, doesn't it?"

"Yes."

"He has to wait an opportunity, and to get up his courage; that is why he is dwelling on that old story—just to find out how the other man did it—"

"Yes, yes, of course."

"But now the poison is in your possession—"

Mrs. Fielding made a violent move with her hands, and cast off the whispering shape that dissolved into silent shreds of darkness.

She remained seated on the floor in the corner. She heard her husband come up to his room and move about—to and fro, up and down. She crouched in stillness until there was silence from his chamber, and then she rose and stealthily bolted the door between their rooms—but not for fear of him.

*   *   *

Mrs. Fielding came down late the next morning.

Her husband asked her with anxious solicitude why she had not allowed him to send her breakfast up to her room. She replied that she had no appetite for any food. Then, seeing his concern at her distress, she made an effort to conceal this, and talked for a while of indifferent matters. But the pretense would not last. She rapidly said, with an uneven shrill note in her voice:

"I did not sleep well last night. Those draughts are no use any more. I must really have something stronger."

"I was reading too late; all that old stuff we were talking of down here," he replied with regret.

"No, no it as not that at all. That quite went out of my mind. It was something I was reading just before I went to sleep. About a man," she hurried on, "who was practising the power of the human eye, as they used to call it. He practised on toads. He used to kill them by staring at them. Just get them somewhere where they could not move and gaze at them until they died. Then one day he got a toad which he seemed to suspect his designs, for it made the most frantic efforts to escape. But at last, finding itself cornered, it turned and began to stare at him, and he found that he couldn't look away, that all his own power had gone. The toad, helpless, continued to stare at him. It was cornered, mind you, Philip, you mustn't forget that, and it kept on staring at him, and in the morning they found him dead on the floor of his laboratory. Don't you think that is a horrible story?"

"It is a ridiculous one," said Philip Fielding rather uneasily. "If the man was dead in the morning, how did anybody know that the toad had stared him to death?"

"It doesn't matter in the least," she muttered, "whether it's possible or not. It's the idea of the thing." Then suddenly throwing back her dark head, she asked him a question that utterly surprised him: "Where is Angela staying? I want to go to see her."

"Why, Grace, I think it would be the most absolute mistake."

"I must see her, Philip. I really must."

He hesitated before the insistency, almost the appeal, in her voice.

"Do you really feel you want to see Angela? Feel kindly enough towards her for that? No! Don't do it, Grace. Besides, I expect she's left the lakes."

"I'm not going to make a scene," said Mrs. Fielding quietly.

"She's not the least what you think she is."

"I don't want to quarrel with Angela. You must see that. I've avoided plenty of chances of doing that."

"That's true," he agreed.

"Perhaps," she hurried on, in a dull flat tone, "I've relented, I've seen what a monstrous, crazy, stupid thing I'm doing. Don't you think that might happen, Philip?"

"I don't know how to take you this morning, Grace."

"Don't fence with me. It's not like you to fence with me. You know perfectly well you don't care for me any more, but you're still longing for Angela. You know what she's feeling about it too. Well then, I don't say I am not going to set you free. There might be a chance if you let me go and see her."

The eager expectancy in his look was as unmistakable as it was hateful to Mrs. Fielding. She went on, talking rapidly without much sense of what she was saying, but merely to put a barrier of words between herself and the possibility of violent action.

"Don't you think that the moment has come to be sensible? Angela and I might understand each other, after all. Of course, I was very rude to her the other day. I don't want to leave it like that. It's childish, don't you see? Tell me where she is, Philip."

He was silent, with the air of one trying to carefully choose words in a moment of excitement. This gave her further courage.

"You can trust me not to make a scene, can't you? In a public place. I'm past all that, too exhausted."

"Yes, yes, Grace. I wasn't thinking of that, but whether it's wise, whether we ought not to put it out of our minds altogether."

"But you know that we haven't. You're always thinking of Angela, and so am I. She might really as well be here, living with us."

"You're wrong," he quickly replied, but it seemed to his wife without conviction. "I wished you could understand me, Grace. I hoped that you did. No doubt you think I am letting it all go by default. We discussed everything so frankly in London, and I felt I couldn't go over it any more. I hope everything will be all right without that."

To her these broken, rather stiff sentences were only so many evasions. She continued to deliberately deceive him, as she believed he was deliberately deceiving her.

"I'm trying to get it all on to a better level, don't you see? There are some things I'd like to talk over with Angela. One ought to respect Angela, after all, don't you think?"

It was very strange, she thought, that he could accept her strange grin as a smile. He appeared to do so, and even touched her arm affectionately.

"Yes, yes," he agreed earnestly. "I am so thankful to hear you say that. I expect Angela must seem to you just a greedy little hussy, mean and hateful. She is not, indeed she is not. I'd like you to know it. I'd even like Angela and you to be friends. It's possible, isn't it?"

She turned away to hide her face, for she knew by now that her grin must be frightful. She had heard before that men indulged in this most stupid of delusions—that of supposing that two jealous women could, under any circumstances, become friends or admire each other. How was it possible that he, Philip, supposed to be so subtle and sensitive, could be thus thick-witted? His incredible stupidity suited her purpose.

"Tell me where Angela is, and I will get Hicks to drive me over. I suppose one can get there and back quite easily in the afternoon?" I dare say we can find many points in common, and might clear some things up."

At that he took an old envelope from his pocket, and wrote on it an address, the name of a village and a hotel, near one of the lakes, not fifteen miles away.

"I don't know if she's still there," he said doubtfully. "If you like to try, if you think it's any use—"

She interpreted his keen and wistful looks as meaning: "Are you, after all, going to put us out of our misery? Are you going to give us our freedom?" But these were not the words he said. Taking hold of her wrist, he awkwardly got out:

"I wish you didn't think I was such a cad, Grace. I always feel you do, even when you are trying to be pleasant. I ought to explain, but aren't explanations—painful? It wasn't a question of leaving you for somebody else, or of preferring someone to you. I know that would be quite unforgivable. It was just a feeling that we—our connection, whatever it meant, was dead, dead to you as well as to me. And that we ought, each of us, to try and make something fresh. Don't you see, our marriage had gone quite decayed and corrupt about us, and was poisoning us. I felt we ought to get away, for your sake as well as mine. Angela was my way of escape."

"Do you still feel that?"

"No, no." He shook his head again, but his words brought no conviction to her. "I don't say I do. Everything's been different since we've been in this house. As I said before, that life in London was stifling. Just a dead weight and trivialities. But here I've found what really matters."

"Your story?" she asked. "The story of your murderer?"

He did not flinch, even at this, which should, she knew, have stabbed him on the raw. She quailed before his courage. Nervous and sensitive as he seemed, he must have the steel nerve, the unrelenting purpose, of the accomplished criminal.

"Poor Philip Vavasour," was all he said. "I've written some more of that tale. I'd like to read it to you when you come back. I'm trying to see that it was not all dun and horrible. The dark side of love, I thought it at first. But now I'm getting through. I can't say I see more, but there is a greater light. I think I can redeem them yet."

"What was Barbara like? Is there a picture of her anywhere?"

"No, I don't think so. I haven't bothered much about Barbara."

"Was she like Angela?" asked Mrs. Fielding.

He looked at her in what seemed genuine surprise.

"Angela and Barbara! Why, I never thought of them together. I told you so before—"

He looked at her in a peering sort of way.

"What have you got in your head, Grace? You seem to me to have been rather unlike yourself lately, as if you're feeling after something. What is it? You've told me again and again that the old house and the old story are not getting on your nerves."

"I don't know."

He took her by the arms and stared at her with considerable appeal. "I wish I could get you where I am, Grace. I wish we could see eye to eye. Just the same distance, as it were, and the same horizon."

"What do you want me to see?" she asked. She thought of her own future grave in the deserted cellars of Medlar's Farm. No doubt that was the focus of his intense vision.

"I wish we weren't all so afraid of words," he said, almost sullenly. "This terror of being emotional and melodramatic; and if one's a trained writer it's worse. One's terrified of falling into the tricks of the trade. Words have been used too often, haven't they? Clipped and defaced like a base coinage."

"Still," she urged, "you're usually glib enough, Philip. Tell me before I go to see Angela what it is you want me to see eye to eye with you. Look, I am perfectly calm."

"I suppose," replied Philip Fielding quietly, "that what I've realised and what I'd like you to realise, dear, is that when it's all gone beyond chance of recovery, all the dreams, the hopes, the expectations gone, there's still enough left to make it worth while going on."

"That sounds like a riddle to me. Unless you just mean that we're growing old." Her voice rose high and shrill on the last words. She steadied herself and added: "See Hicks for me, will you, and order the car."

*   *   *

Mrs. Fielding had always been afraid of nature. She relished a landscape in a picture or seen from a distance or through a window, but like so many town-bred people she had a terror of lonely fields, lonely roads, of solitary woods, she would not have gone on foot after dark two miles away from a human habitation. She had never tried to analyse these fears. She merely avoided what she rather vaguely called "the country." But as the car took her along the solitary by-ways which led to the village where Angela was now staying, all these old dreads and fears dating back to her early childhood returned to her, and she connected them with her present tragedy.

The road dipped past a lake, ran up a hill, skirted a belt of woods, showed glimpses here and there of distant vales and waters, and all was awful to Grace Fielding. She wondered how anyone could have thought of nature as benevolent or gracious, as the kindly mother. Nature seemed instead a frightful destructive force, against whom long years of civilisation had scarce the might to raise barriers.

Every building that man had erected, every road he had laid down, every field he had hedged, every tree he had felled, seemed to Mrs. Fielding's overwrought mind like another feeble effort to thrust back and to hold at bay this mighty and malevolent power that dwelt in all lonely places; the waters of the lake were dark with the blackness of corruption, there was a livid carrion look about the bare sides of the distant hills where the dead heather, the colour of old blood, clung like patches of decay; she hated the woods in which no pleasant green plant grew and where the light only fell in bleached sparkles between the close trunks, and yet she was almost impelled to stop the car and wander away into those lonesome depths.

In the stretch of dale land, where there was no habitation in sight, they came to a gate in a stone wall. A ragged boy opened it for them. She saw a shelter made of sacking, dry heather, and boughs against the wall. The boy seemed delighted with the silver she gave him, and explained that the gate was shut because of the sheep. She thought his withered face repellent, and the thought of his vigil there, in that great loneliness, made her shudder.

"He must be by himself for hours, for the sake of a few pence—for how often do cars pass here. And what use is money to him in such a wilderness?"

Then, as someone drowning rises for the last time, and glimpses in a swirl of radiance the final gleam of day, she thought: "It is all right, really. It is only I who am infected." But she could not throw off this infection. "There must be something most horribly amiss with me, that I see nothing lovely or pleasant anywhere." She looked down at her long hand in the lap of her green tweed dress, at the rings and bracelets that Philip had given her, that now seemed to hang so slackly on her lean flesh, and again she thought of her bones which might soon be rotting in the cellars of Medlar's Farm as the bones of Susanna Vavasour were rotting in Crompton Old Church.

Mrs. Fielding was very tired when she reached the quiet but fashionable hotel where Angela was staying. She felt her limbs stiff when she descended from the car, an odd lightness in her head. Perhaps she had undertaken more than she could do, but her spirit, roused at her need, made a strong clutch on her sick body, and sent her into the hall, asking for Angela.

The actress was still there, though she was leaving that afternoon. Mrs. Fielding sent up her name, and went into the parlour which was arranged with studied unsophistication. Blue china on racks, sepia water colours of the lakes, and old pieces of dark polished furniture, all very clean yet smelling faintly of decay.

Mrs. Fielding approached the large coal fire, surprised to discover how cold were her hands and feet.

Angela came down almost at once. Mrs. Fielding was encouraged by seeing that she had lost her air of maddening self-confidence, and appeared agitated, almost alarmed. But Mrs. Fielding was also exasperated by observing that her rival's beauty, which had been so in eclipse on the day of her visit to Medlar's Farm, was now vivid with a feverish brilliance, lips moist and red, her cheeks glowing as if she had been walking in the wind and rain, and her eyes shining with a lustre which did not seem to be all reflected light, but to come from some inner passion.

"Did you want to see me?"

Mrs. Fielding nodded. The two women sat down, on either side of the fire. Mrs. Fielding was facing the window, the light of which made an aureole of gleaming threads on Angela's untidy hair. In this window hung a wire basket full of fleshy, pink, hothouse flowers and moist trailing ferns. Beyond she could see a square of lawn sodden from the late rain. A gardener was placidly at work, snipping off the soaked, bruised heads of the dead roses.

"Angela, I'm glad you haven't gone. I wanted to see you."

The other woman turned, on the defensive. Mrs. Fielding noted the firm whiteness of her throat where the yellow woollen bodice was open, observed the rounded curves of her arms in the tight clinging sleeves as they rested on the leathern sides of the chair, and thought of Philip.

"I don't see what there can be to say," said Angela with her usual frankness, but not with her usual insolence. "I suppose you know that Philip sent me away?"

Mrs. Fielding felt no triumph at this, as she would have felt a few weeks ago. She believed it a deliberate lie, part of a deliberate scheme.

"Did he?" she said in a flat voice. "I don't see that that makes much difference; it's all got rather ridiculous. I thought that you and I—two women—might clear it up a little. Philip gets involved with words. We ought not to hate each other, you know, Angela."

"But we do," smiled the other woman. "Won't you have

some coffee? You looked fagged out. It's a lonely drive, I know; it gets on one's nerves. Of course, if you're going to be decent, I shall be awfully grateful."

"By decent, you mean, am I going to allow, after all, the divorce?"

"I suppose I do mean that," said Angela. Mrs. Fielding noticed that she was shivering.

"I wonder what you see in Philip?" asked Philip's wife.

"I wish I could tell you. It's not fun for me, I assure you. It's tragic. It's simply killing me, the whole affair. I couldn't tell you what it is, whether it's just the old stuff, love at first sight, soul-mate, and all the rest."

"Men's second wives, when they're successful, are nearly always their soul-mates, and they're nearly always twenty years younger and thirty years more beautiful than the first wife."

"Well, you can put it like that," said Angela. "If you haven't come to tell me you're setting him free, I don't know why you have come. It can't be very pleasant for you, seeing me."

Mrs. Fielding thought: "If she knew the real reason for my coming, she'd think I was mad. I dare say she'd have me locked up or, if she knows what he's going to do, she wouldn't think me mad, but she'd warn him. He would be very quick about it. It would happen, perhaps, as soon as I returned to Medlar's Farm."

She put her fingers to her throat, and began plucking at the flesh there, as if trying in advance what it would feel like to have the life strangled out of her.

Angela rang the bell and ordered coffee.

"I haven't got a private sitting-room, but we shall be absolutely quiet here. There's only one or two people staying in the hotel, and they've gone off on some expedition. I ought to tell you that Philip didn't really know I was coming up to that awful place where you've taken him."

"Where he's taken me."

"Well, anyhow, I suppose I ought to let you know that. He didn't. It was quite my own idea. I suppose you will think it was quite shameless of me, but if I hadn't come you would have thought I was a coward, wouldn't you?"

"No, Angela," smiled Mrs. Fielding, "I should never think you were a coward."

"Well, I've tried to be frank. I don't see that what I did was so dreadful. I've tried to understand your point of view too."

"Have you, Angela? I never thought of that."

"Oh, I have, indeed. One has to put up a sort of self-defence. One gets hard when one feels strongly, you know. It's all pretty sickening, and I'm sure you thought I was out just for money, and his position. But it wasn't that."

"I don't care what it was," said Mrs. Fielding. "I haven't come to talk about that, and I haven't got very much strength to talk about anything. I think they're coming with the coffee."

She leant back in her chair, and Angela relaxed her attitude into one of indifference. The maid brought in the coffee service.

When they were alone again both women drank eagerly.

Mrs. Fielding fastened her gaze on the basket of frail, pink, fleshy-looking flowers trembling in the window-place, and on the figure of the man beyond walking round the verge of the damp grass, snipping at the sodden roses.

"Tell me what it's all about," urged Angela. She turned her large, slightly protuberant, brilliant eyes towards Mrs. Fielding, and added: "You poor thing, you really do look worn out. Whatever made you go to that horrible place? It seemed like a charnel-house to me. I know you think I'm an utter beast, but I have been frank, haven't I? What is the use of you and Philip just dragging on? You are still young, and there are heaps of other men in the world. I dare say that sounds vulgar, but we ought to be past pretences."

Angela had never before spoken with so much kindness and good feeling towards her victim, but this increased Mrs. Fielding's suspicion.

Angela was, then, an accomplice. Her business was to soothe, to placate. No doubt Philip had told her she had made a mistake in coming to Medlar's Farm; no doubt, she was trying, by a submissive behaviour, to-day to gloss over that mistake.

Mrs. Fielding drank another cup of coffee, and steadied herself not to swerve from the resolution which had brought her on this journey. She saw just one chance, for herself, for Philip, and even for Angela.

"It's not all over," she said rapidly. "I suppose you know that? It may seem very smooth, on the surface, I mean, but when he and I went away—I suppose it stopped the scandal—but that's not everything."

"I suppose you mean that though he left me he hasn't come back to you, not really?"

Mrs. Fielding did not directly answer this. She drank some more coffee, and warmed her hands and stared again at the basket of wax-like flowers in the window, before she answered.

"I mean that what you did isn't over, it's—like throwing a stone in a pond—the ripples go out and on for quite a long time. If you really want to efface yourself out of Philip's life—"

"But I don't," interrupted Angela. "Why do you suppose I came over to Medlar's Farm the other day? I couldn't believe that you would still want to keep him."

"Don't let's go over that, please. I'm sure I read somewhere that women can discuss these things, nowadays, quite coolly. There's all sorts of ways, aren't there, of being matter-of-fact, on these matters?" She remembered her husband's words: "One must not be melodramatic or emotional." "And I believe if one is really clever and smart and up-to-date, like you are, Angela, one can talk about the changing about one's husband or one's lover without showing any feeling at all."

"I have never been able to do it," muttered Angela, "and I must say it isn't very easy now. What have you come for? If you're still standing firm—if you won't give him the divorce—"

"I won't," said Mrs. Fielding, "I won't, I won't."

She checked herself, feeling that the reiteration of that word would drive her out of her control and added hastily:

"I've come to appeal to you to let go. That's what I want, Angela. I want you to write to him and tell him that you really have done with him. I want you to go away on that tour to Africa, India, Canada, I don't care where. I want you to, if possible, marry someone else. To cut right out of his life." She added on a sunken note: "That's the only way to save us."

Without reflecting a second Angela said: "I won't do it."

"You're convinced then, he still cares for you?"

"Of course. Poor Philip, he's trying to do his duty by you. I dare say he's sorry for you, but you must see for yourself—"

"Never mind what I see for myself," interrupted Mrs. Fielding. "It doesn't do to talk too much of what I see for myself." Repeating this again, she added: "It's because of what I see for myself I'm here."

"You're not very coherent," said Angela. "If you've come to me asking for any sacrifice or renunciation, I simply can't give it. Philip left me of his own free will. He chose between us. That sounds silly and simple, doesn't it? But he chose you, and you've got him. You must make the best of it. If you're driving him crazy, or he's driving you crazy, that's no affair of mine. I'm not leaving England, and I'm not marrying anybody else. If he ever gets sick of you, I shall be there."

"That's a funny way to put it," sighed Mrs. Fielding, rising.

Angela thought she had never looked so tall. She had certainly grown very much thinner during her residence at Medlar's Farm. "I thought you didn't want him unless you could marry him."

"It depends," declared Angela, with her devastating frankness, "how long you can hang on. I might get tired. I might take him without marriage. I don't know! I'm still hoping you'll change your mind and give us the divorce."

There was a large tropical plant with a single crimson flower on the mantelpiece. Mrs. Fielding looked past this at her reflection in the mirror beyond, and saw the red bloom like a blot against her thin throat. Looking into her own eyes she said:

"Of course—there's just one other prospect. I might die, you know, and then you could marry him, couldn't you? Without any more trouble at all."

"I hadn't thought of that. One doesn't, somehow!"

Mrs. Fielding's lips formed the word "Liar." Aloud she said:

"Something horrible will happen if you don't do this, Angela. Something you've not thought of at all, but that I know of. Won't you change your mind? You've got Philip on a sort of chain. If you would just snap it—"

"I'm not going to. You're mad to ask it. Even if I were to make you a promise like that, I shouldn't keep it. You're the one who ought to give way, and you know it. Of course, something dreadful may happen if you go on living in that horrible place. One or both of you will go mad, I suppose that's what you mean. It's ghastly for Philip. A sacrifice to his duty. I don't know how you can do it."

Mrs. Fielding continued to stare at her livid reflection in the mirror.

"Put it, then, for Philip's sake," she said; "say, to save Philip, you give him up. If you were to make it quite definite that he's nothing whatever to hope from you, everything would be different. He'd leave Medlar's Farm and go away. Perhaps I'd let him go away alone. He'd forget all about it. Everything would be, in time, like it used to be."

Angela shook her tousled head.

"No, it wouldn't. We can't forget each other. You ought to understand that. It's no good saying it's for Philip's sake. It's just your own jealousy speaking. I'm jealous, too, but it isn't out of jealousy I'm acting. It's because I know it would be no use."

Mrs. Fielding moved from the mirror and picked up her handbag and her gloves from the pretty chintz-covered chair.

"That sounds final. Very well, Angela, I've made an appeal, and you've refused. You'll take the consequences. Perhaps they won't be quite what you think they will."

"That sounds like a threat."

Angela's voice was faint, as if the struggle had been too much for her. It was the first time that Mrs. Fielding had observed her display any signs of weakness.

"You can take it like a threat if you like. Remember, afterwards, that I did give you this chance."

"I don't know what you're talking about," said Angela rather wildly. "But you look really awful. I shall write to Philip and tell him that he ought to have you looked after. I don't think you're quite responsible for what you're saying or doing."

Mrs. Fielding recoiled.

"Oh, I give you that impression, do I?"

"You do, rather. I say, you are all right, aren't you?"

Mrs. Fielding did not answer. She was pulling on her gloves, slowly, finger by finger. As if in self-defence and with an effort to be generous, Angela continued:

"After all, you ought to have all the winning cards, you know. You've got him there, day and night. You ought to be able to stand up for yourself and get him back if it's possible at all. I won't come again. I'll promise you that. Of course, I shall write, but you could intercept the letters, couldn't you? You see, you've got all the chances I haven't. I wish you wouldn't look so ghastly. I wish we could settle it all in a decent manner."

"That's wishing we'd both been different sorts of women. I don't think it's the kind of thing you can settle in a decent manner. You'll soon know how it's going to be settled, and then perhaps you'll wish—"

She broke off and pulled open her handbag, and snatched out her handkerchief and passed it rapidly across her face.

Angela said:

"I don't want to be a brute. Won't you stay here and have some food? If you hate to be in the same place where I am, there's another hotel a little father up the village. Quite a decent place."

"How fond you are of that word decent," smiled Mrs. Fielding. "What quite does it mean, nowadays, I wonder?"

*   *   *

On the return journey Mrs. Fielding stopped the car at the edge of the wood that bordered the lake with a lonely island in the centre.

When she had passed that group of trees before they had repelled her—they repelled her still, but lured her, too; she was bound to enter and walk under the cold, dark shade.

The moment she left the car she felt that she had left a place of protection, was exposed to many hostile influences. She walked trembling over a carpet of ground ivy and small plants; the only ones which were known to her were daisies.

She saw the water twinkling cold in between the dark trunks; she believed that her companion was the shape of Susanna Vavasour. She no longer tried to make credible explanations to herself about her conviction that this dead woman who had never left the earth had become her guide ever since she had come to Medlar's Farm; in the same way as Philip Vavasour was the guide of her husband.

But the shade in the tight green dress which matched the colour of the foliage no longer turned to her with the look of one trying to say something to her; what Susanna Vavasour had to say, Mrs. Fielding now knew. . . .

She went to the edge of the lake, an irregular shaped piece of water which ran in and out the dark outlines of the hills. It was towards evening, the sky seemed both hollow and transparent, like a great glass bell, thought Mrs. Fielding.

She remembered a horrid experiment which she had once read of: a mouse and a scorpion were once set by some inquisitive man of science under a glass bell, where finally, after a dreadful duel, the timid beast killed the poisonous insect. The same story, of course, as that of the man and the toad. It was her story.

She looked at the island, on which grew three trees, and thought that if she could reach that she might find herself at peace and be able to die without doing that which she felt herself impelled to do.

But there was no boat. She wondered if anybody ever did go to the island. Salvation was always just out of reach.

She knew that it would be better for her if she could sink beneath the cold waters of the lake into an eternal oblivion. She could not choose.

A white shape floated in the shadow of the island, a solitary white swan. Everywhere she looked, every thought that came into her head held an omen. She touched the sedges that trembled in the water; an unutterable nostalgia and melancholy bowed her spirit and confused her mind in a rising miasma of horror.

"How odd," she said sullenly to herself, "that people should have thought that Susanna Vavasour was the victim. She must have been very clever—yet how did she contrive it, when he must have died first? Only I, who have known her since she was dead," added Mrs. Fielding, "really know her. To me she is not disguised."

She peered keenly round to see if she could discover the shape in the dark green dress passing between the close-set tree-trunks. She strained her ear to catch some whispered counsel or warning.

But the silence was as complete as it had been on the day of her visit to the churchyard by Crompton Old Water. Only a little, low wind whispered over the water and stirred the leaves of the quiet trees.

Mrs. Fielding returned slowly to the car. Hicks looked rather curiously at her; he said something about a chilly evening, and getting home before the rain came . . . those clouds in the west would move up very quickly, he was sure. Mrs. Fielding had not noticed the clouds, but she noticed the word home, which had become lately, when applied to Medlar's Farm, most horrible.

Philip was waiting for her on the front doorstep. It was a long time since he had done that, but then, it was a long time since she had been to see Angela.

He helped her from the car, hoped she was not cold or tired. Mrs. Mace had a fine fire in the Tudor room. Grace had just escaped the rain, which was beginning to fall in large drops. He had been lonely without her, and had not been able to get on with his work. She smiled at him in return for all this solicitude. Anyone might have thought that they were happy. As he took her coat from her on the threshold, she thought:

"It is not so difficult to act and lie. I thought Angela so clever to-day, but, after all, I can do it too."

When she was in the easy chair by the fire, she told him in what she was sure was a natural tone:

"Angela is quite a dear. You were right, Philip. She is going back to London to-day. She is writing to you. I don't see why it shouldn't be, some day, all right."

"I'm glad," he answered abruptly. "Awfully glad, Grace. I won't ask what you mean by all right."

"No, please, don't. One must have time."

She looked at him from eyes swollen with fatigue.

"You're a very patient man, Philip. I'm learning to be patient, too." And then, deliberately striking a false note, she added harshly: "What do they call it nowadays in the modern jargon? Sublimating the emotions, isn't it?"

But even at that he would not show vexation, and said nothing more about Angela. Of course there was only one explanation for his control . . . it would not have to last long.

Their meal was pleasant, Philip made himself agreeable on a dozen indifferent topics, and she was quite intelligent and charming about what she had seen on her journey to and from Angela's hotel. She said nothing, of course, of the woods where she had crossed the ground ivy and stood among the sedges, and the swan in the shadow; nor of the island with the three trees, or of her own sense of how much better it would have been for her to have slipped under the water of the lake—to have drowned herself as Susanna Vavasour's resting-place was to be drowned.

She wore her dark green dress which he had once said made her look like Susanna Vavasour, and afterwards they went into the library. He took up his manuscript and read her again more of the old story, prefacing it with this explanation, which he gave her hurriedly, as if he wished to avoid personal matters.

"Of course, Grace, all the old sayings are really most true. I mean, about love and hatred being so close together, repulsion and attraction, all the ebb and flow of the same emotion."

"I know, I know," she said impatiently.

"Well, I don't want to be banal, Grace, but it's so clearly marked in this story. I don't know what I read you before, I've forgotten."

"So have I," said Mrs. Fielding. "It doesn't matter. Anything you've got—well, read it—"

"She married him; by sheer feminine tenacity she married him."

"I suppose you mean," said Grace, learning towards the fire, "that he just wanted her money. That's the usual solution, isn't it?"

She was rather puzzled about this part of the story, for it did not fit in with her own. Philip had not married her for money; but—she remembered her own small capital, ridiculous of course, but it had helped him, and then what had she not done in sheer work and labour? Why, it would have cost him quite a lot of money for the services of housekeeper and secretary, a companion, a general slave. Well, if he hadn't married her for money he had married her for what he could get out of her, and he had had it out of her for years. . . .

"Isn't that it?" she repeated. "He just married her for that."

"I don't know. He was a wild, adventuring spirit; he'd been all over the world without a ha'penny in his pouch."

"And then he comes home and marries a woman he doesn't care about and settles down. I suppose," said Mrs. Fielding, "he intended from the very first to make an end of her and go off again with her fortune on any journey—eh?"

Philip Fielding shook his head.

"That's too brutal and cold-blooded. That's not really human. I can't follow that at all. He was quite an honourable sort of man, not a born criminal. I don't believe people plan crimes of violence years ahead. They have to be exasperated, cornered, like he was."

"Well, he married her. That's enough, isn't it? Go on."

"Yes, and they lived for a while outside Hexham."

Philip Fielding was turning over the papers laying within the radius of his reading lamp.

"I've got some pictures of the place here. They've all got that ghastly bleak look of early steel engravings. But, of course, it was a human dwelling. It must have had its pleasant aspects."

"I don't see much pleasant aspect about any of the tale, smiled Mrs. Fielding. Then again she urged hurriedly, "Go on."

"They lived there and her father paid for their maintenance, until he, by a most unexpected series of deaths, just like any old melodrama—I can't make out how all these men perished, but they did, about five of them—he came into the succession. His kingdom, this estate, Vavasour Hall as it then was, the very house where we sit now. He brought her home. Her fortune, then, was a matter of indifference to him. He had, on his own, all the money he wanted. There were, after three years of marriage, no children, and that was a source of deep vexation. In those days," added Philip Fielding, with was may have been studied carelessness, "of course, children were very important."

"I suppose they are, sometimes, now."

"Well, I suppose so, but I mean we don't lay all that stress on them people did then. It was a question of a man's name, almost of his honour. Philip Vavasour, lord of the Vavasour estates, was quite a different man from the vagabond who was wandering over Europe without a penny in his poke or a care in his mind."

Philip Fielding paused, laid down his unlit pipe, and folded over the pile of papers.

"But I don't know," he added thoughtfully, "when he began to hate her."

"I think I do," said Mrs. Fielding, clasping her long fingers round her long knees. "It was when he first saw Barbara."

"No, I think it was before that. It was when he began to feel himself tied. He and this woman shut in this house. It is, of course, a horrible thing to live with someone whom you dislike and whom you can't get rid of. Dislike turns to hatred and hatred to murder. It's quite simple, really. She was none of your placid victims. She was a woman of character, of determination. She was, I think, in every way, save that of physical beauty, the superior of Barbara, who was the daughter of a yeoman farmer hereabouts. They were all, as I see it, quite frank one with another. When she first discovered that he was in love with Barbara, she probed the matter to the bottom. She was frightfully jealous, but she was prepared to endure an intrigue. They were common enough in those days. Women had to put up with them, and she had strong common sense. She found that Barbara and he were really infatuated, then she became alarmed. She faced him. She told him what she thought. And he said that it was true, that he would like to get rid of her and marry Barbara."

Philip Fielding looked at his wife beyond the radiance of the hand lamp. She shrank back against her chair and thought: "How can he? How dare he tell me this story so like our own? Is it to warn me, to give me a chance of escape, or merely for the pleasure of tormenting me?"

Philip Fielding suddenly withdrew his glance, sighed, and dropped his head in his hands.

"I can't get any further than that," he said.

"It seems to me," muttered Mrs. Fielding, "far enough. He had no choice but to murder her. Have you described that?" she asked, "the murder? Have you found out how it was done? He must have been clever, since there was an inquest but no verdict. He got away with it, didn't he? He had her buried. I supposed he married Barbara. Have you got all that?"

"I've got some of it, Grace. Why are you so interested? I thought you didn't care two straws about the old stuff. I've been wondering myself if it's a good story—if there's anything in it. I don't know—it puzzles me and weighs on me. Of course there is not only something but everything in atmosphere. It's coming to a place like this and exposing oneself to these old influences. It was stupid to do it, but I had to have a distraction."

"On her tomb," shivered Mrs. Fielding, "she has—*What I have done, I shall answer for*—' or words to that effect. Does that give you any clue? Does that help?"

He shook his head.

"I went over to see that the other day, after what you told me. I couldn't decipher much, only those words and the names. I don't see anything in it. It may have been added later. The whole thing's a bundle of contradictions. What has she to answer for, poor soul? And yet I don't know. To provoke someone to murder you—I suppose it is pretty ghastly. Murdering a soul, isn't it? She got the martyr's crown and he hell fire, at least that would be the old belief. I think that that may have been it. She stayed here and provoked him to murder her, and when she was dead she knew what a ghastly thing she'd done. Of course he used to walk for years, be seen continually, he often had a night-cap on and a sage-green robe bound with black."

"That's the portrait on the stairs."

"Yes, I believe that's he, but there, again, one's baffled. I think the face has been repainted. That man has not red hair."

"Would his hair remain red when he was dead?"

Philip Fielding shook his head.

"I don't know. I haven't thought of it. Let me read you what I've written. If you're interested, I'd like to know what you think of it, if it sounds like sense."

*   *   *

"Philip Vavasour often used to meet Barbara by the tarn high up in the hills. It was covered with red lichen and supposed to be fathomless; leeches were to be found there, but no fish. Near by was a large boulder which was called the Wishing Stone. Philip and Barbara had often crossed hands over it according to the subscribed rites, and wished, but so far their desires had not come to fruition. There always seemed to be a little creeping wind in this spot, although it was shut in by the hills, being on a ledge between two heights. There were no trees about save one or two lone thorns which bore scant blossoms, few leaves, and no fruit. The ground was always wet and cold, for beneath the heather and moss ran untainted rivulets from the hilltop. To walk there was to have the feet wet and cold to the ankles, to kneel down there and press one's hand into the chill green was to have one's palm full of pure water.

"It was on an autumn day when the clouds were very low and dissolving now and then into mists which obscured all save the pool and the thorn trees that grew near it, and Barbara told Philip that her father was becoming discontented at her long visits to this lonely spot, and with her known infatuation for a man who could not marry her. She had spoken of this before, there never had been any subterfuge between them.

"This afternoon her tone was definite. She looked at him expectantly. He did not answer; he took off one of his heavy gauntlets with the long tassels and set his teeth in the palm. He was a very strong man and one on whom an inactive life was beginning to press hard. The tragedy of waste was beginning to master him, waste of strength, of time, of love, of life itself. She, looking enviously at his magnificence, thought of this, and her sharp regret was echoed in his mind. So it seemed to them that they felt time flowing away between them and taking with it all they valued, for they were neither of them of a character to relish the placid delights, if there be any, of old age.

"He said at length, looking down at the marks his white teeth had left in the coarse leather:

"'Susanna won't give way. I never begged for anything hard before, but I begged hard for this.'

"Barbara smiled at his simplicity.

"'The harder you beg the greater your offence.'

"'I know. But what was I to do? I've offered her back all her dowry. All her estate, every penny of it, and more besides, but still she just smiled and said: "No, no!"'

"The mist was closing up round them, moving in steady gusts down the hills, and Barbara pulled her grey woollen hood closer round her face.

"'I can wait no longer,' she said. 'I shall go away. I shall marry another man.'

"The nearest thorn tree made a dark, sharp, crooked line against the encroaching mist. They both looked at it. It was the only definite object in a world of water and vapour.

"'You must decide,' she said, and she sat down on the Wishing Stone and clasped her hands round her knees.

"He was very splendidly dressed, as one not afraid to flaunt his station, the highest in this wild country. He had lately taken a dislike to the red colour of his hair, and it was thickly pomaded in a fashion not common to the countryside, though necessary in town. This destroyed the natural hues of his face and gave his countenance a livid look. His strong tresses seemed to resist the flour and grease, and where the thick curls broke from the riband on to the blue coat Barbara could see the natural harsh auburn colour; his coat was galfooned with bullion and his laces were costly. He carried a small sword. There was broken moss and heather on his wet boots; he had no hat despite the dampness of the mist; there was thrown over his arm a long, dark, high-collared cloak, heavy with moisture. He stared into the vapours in a peering fashion, as if expecting somebody to step out of that approaching obscurity and challenge him.

"'She fell down a short flight of stairs the other day,' he said. 'The heel came off her shoe. I could not go forward to help her. I thought that would have been the best way for all of us.'

"Barbara indifferently replied.

"'I think she would be better dead. A sour, barren, jealous woman.'

"'She would be better at rest,' he answered. 'She is so restless, Barbara. Up and down the house all day. Even at night she rises, takes a taper in her hand, and passes up and down the stairs in and out of all the empty rooms. And when I ask here about it she has some shallow excuse—that she has remembered some disorder in the household linen, or is searching for a shift she has forgotten. Or wishes to see if the maids have properly performed their tasks.'

"'Rest, she would never rest,' said Barbara, 'even if she were dead.'

"'If she were dead I should not be afraid of her,' he smiled. 'I should marry you then, Barbara.'

"'And take me to her house, to listen to her walking up and down all day and all night?'

"'Those tales have no credit with me. I never could see that if you had sufficient courage to destroy what was in your way you should be afraid of it—afterwards.'

"This was too plain for the woman's liking. It must always be a grotesque matter for two people to discuss the destruction of a third, in particular when these two affect to love each other; how reconcile the dignity of mutual love, the pain of mutual passion, and the baseness of a plot to murder?

"'You must tell me no more,' she said, 'lest I misunderstand you. What weight do you think to put on my conscience?'

"But they understood each other very well. There was no need for her to say more than this:

"'Susanna is not a strong woman. She may get the ague again this winter, like she had last—do you remember how she shivered, even in church that time, all her ornaments rattling? I won't pretend that I should weep for her if she should go, Philip.'

"'There is no obligation on you nor I to wish Susanna to live.'

"The mist lifted. The ancient dark landscape was clear about them. A few sheep were cropping in the middle distance and crows flapped towards the far-off hills. There was no autumn red or gold up there. The winter came with a black decay.

"Each of them marvelled a little, as far as there was room in their hearts for marvel, how it was they had not noticed before the strangeness of the country in which they had both been brought up.

"He had travelled much, she had never left her native hills, yet to both of them came the conviction that this was an unearthly landscape.

"A shaft of sunshine like a sword struck a distant peak.

"The man looked at it and made an effort to escape his doom, though he knew that it was as vain for him to try to do this as for one chained and riveted to a rock to endeavour to twist his iron fetters from the implacable granite. He said, his voice low and muffled on the rising wind:

"'Why don't we go away, Barbara, you and I? I know so many places in far-off countries. We should be quite safe, Susanna could do nothing. We might even be married abroad by some monk, if that would satisfy you. I think of houses, white, with jasmine growing up the front, and little green balconies and two shutters, where you and I, Barbara—I can get the money, a mortgage on all the lands.'

"She said exactly the words that he was expecting.

"'I won't do it, Philip, and you know as much. It would be

shameful, a slight and a disgrace. No woman of my family has ever been degraded like that.' She added with sad disdain, both of herself and of him: 'Probably you would get tired of me, or I of you, and both of us of love itself so far away in the strangeness and the heat. Exiled.'

"'We might tire of each other, of love itself, here,' he replied. 'Do you think that you could be content in Vavasour Hall—afterwards?'

"'After what, Philip?'

"'After her death and our marriage.'

"She glanced down at her feet, the damp was penetrating her thick latchet shoes.

"'It is I who will catch an ague, Philip. I must go home, and I do not think that I will come here again. It is a melancholy, perhaps a blasted spot.'

"'I know none other so remote,' he replied, 'and I have always thought, Barbara, that the Wishing Stone would, in the end, bring us luck.'

"'What have you wished on it?' she asked curiously.

"'It's part of the spell, is it not, we may not tell one another? But you know, Barbara, what I have always wished.'

"'Yes, for us to live together always. We ought to if it was meant we should. But how? How stupid a barrier marriage can be, Philip! A few words and a ring and she is there, always.'

"'Until Death do us part,' he smiled, and he drew his handkerchief from his left pocket-hole and wiped from his face vapour drops which the mist had left behind. Then, with his forefinger he made as if he traced words on the moist air. "'Here lies Susanna, first wife of Philip Vavasour." Could you go past that, Barbara, every time you went to church?'

"'Why not, Philip? It would be very natural for you to marry again if you lost Susanna. Nobody could say anything; there would be no scandal or gossip.'

"'Everyone knows that we love each other now,' he said sullenly.

"'But once we were married they would forget that. And if they remembered I should not care.'

"'Then you, too, Barbara, think a good deal of those few words and that ring?'

"'I too, am a woman,' she replied, using an excuse so foolish and so pitiful that he could only smile and forbear to argue.

"They moved down the hillside together, following the course of a small waterbreak that rushed from level to level beside a rude path of stone, marked here and there by low cairns which had long ago been placed to mark the ascent to the summit of the hill.

"'We did not wish again,' he said.

"'You meant to, Philip?'

"'Yes, just once more.'

"'I think there is no need. Your destiny lies in your own hands, after all.'

"They passed no living creature in their slow descent over the west stones, the soaked heather, save the sheep with the wet glistening on the oily wool, that scarcely moved or ceased from their laborious cropping as these two passed along, the mist gathering again behind them almost as if it drove them forward.

"They came out, at length, on to lonely fields and a lonely road, there were low stone walls and ash trees heavy with brilliant scarlet fruit. He said:

"'She ought to realise how foolish she is to try and separate us.'

"Barbara did not answer. She had to pick her way carefully over boulders. It was necessary for them to cross the bed of a stream. The sound of falling waters was perpetually in their ears, now nearer, now farther, now almost imperceptible, then with a powerful rush that silenced their speech.

"At the end of the watercourse they had to part with each to return to that place they were forced to name home, but which they loathed. They did not dare touch each other more than the tips of their cold wet fingers.

"Barbara still said nothing. Her spirit moved in a lethargy, she thought that she would at once sleep when she returned home. She saw herself, even while she stood there, rigid, opposite her lover, sleeping in the big tester bed in her low-ceilinged chamber. She saw the curtain a little drawn from the latticed window, and the wet grey light of sunset streaming in over her own prone figure.

"He let her go and watched her; she was soon merged into the dead colours of the landscape. He knew that if he did not free himself from his wife he would lose Barbara.

"When he returned that evening to Vavasour Hall, Susanna was, as usual, waiting for him. She was aware that he had seen Barbara, and when she looked at his face, as he flung off from his arm the wet cloak he had not worn, she knew that her doom was decided."

* * *

Philip Fielding laid down the manuscript, and Mrs. Fielding, who had been sitting back in her chair with her eyes closed, sat up, shivering, with a startled look like one awakened from a trance.

"Were you listening or were you asleep?" he asked.

"I was listening. I don't know quite how you could write it, Philip."

This was no mere cry of anguish. She was really bewildered as to how he had had the cold-blooded courage to put down in the shape of fiction his own interview with Angela, when they had first decided upon his wife's destruction, only of course that had not been on a Northumberland hill-side, but probably in Angela's pretty little flat. . . .

"I don't know what you mean," said Philip Fielding wearily. "Why shouldn't I write it? It just came to me, there didn't seem to be any effort at all. Besides, I believe it to be true," he added with some petulance.

"I have no doubt it's true, Philip, and that's why I wonder how you can write it. Of course," she added listlessly, "it's you and Angela. You know you were never any good at love scenes, but I suppose you can make an effort to reproduce that one."

She had recently been amazed to admiration by his skill in deception. She peered at him now, as he sat in the radiance of the lamplight, and was more intensely surprised than she had yet been by the natural way in which he said:

"Whatever do you mean, Grace? Myself and Angela! What likeness can there be? Why, of course, all that's gone right out of my head—put away in a watertight compartment. I shouldn't be likely to draw on that for anything. I've told you so, again and again."

"The whole story is you and Angela and myself," said Mrs. Fielding contemptuously. "What else? How can you be so stupid, Philip, as to try and hoodwink me? A jealous wife who won't let go, and a woman who won't come except on the terms of marriage. Why, it's too obvious."

And he did seem discomposed, even startled.

"On my word, I never thought of it," he said. Then with an awkward if charming tenderness he added; "You see, Grace, I never thought of you as a jealous wife. You were Grace always. It didn't occur to me that this story was in any way like ours. I suppose that does seem ridiculous, but really it did not. Besides, that aspect of it, the love, I mean, between Philip and Barbara, the attraction or the passion or whatever word you give to it, was not my concern, it was the crime, and, you see, the crime—well, I mean that's ridiculous! It simply doesn't touch us anywhere."

"Trying to reassure me," thought Mrs. Fielding, crouching over the fire. "He's afraid he's gone a little too far, and he's trying to put me at my ease."

"Yes, of course, that part of it is absurd," she agreed, careful not to let him see her face. "The crime, how ridiculous indeed! People don't nowadays, do they? Or only people in the slums. But I still think the scene with you and Angela—"

"You're obsessed with Angela," he interrupted with a sigh and a frown. "I wrote that blessed thing to get away from Angela, but you keep bringing her in again."

Mrs. Fielding crossed her fingers like a lattice before her face. Her muffled voice came to him with all the expression blurred:

"Are you sorry for Susanna Vavasour, Philip? How does that part of your story go? Do you really think you can enter into the feelings of that woman, shut up with that man, knowing he was planning to murder her? You say she realised her doom when he came back that night. I suppose after that she went trying to find him out and find out how he was going to do it? Wasn't there something of a tasteless, odourless white liquid? Prussic acid? I dare say she came upon that. And he probably, once he decided, would be quite agreeable, wouldn't he?"

"I suppose he would make an effort. He'll have to be careful not to overdo that."

"Oh yes," agreed Mrs. Fielding, still talking through her fingers. "Of course he wouldn't be quite such a fool as to suddenly cover her with caresses, and pretend he'd given up Barbara. But I suppose he'd be civil and passive. In a way, contented. He wouldn't be so worried, so distraught. He'd know it was only a question of time."

"He must have been a cold-blooded devil," said Philip Fielding with a note of uneasiness in his voice. "I can't quite get into his skin even now."

"Can't you? That's a pity!" She threw back her head and laughed. "You ought to, you know, if you're to write of it in a convincing way. You ought to quite get into his skin. I suppose you've been trying to, haven't you, when you were shut up here in the library?"

"Well, yes, I have. As you know, I think I've seen him. Those descriptions of mine aren't faked. They're just like he looked to me. Even the red hair showing through the powder, and that extraordinary design of brocade on the blue coat, the seams of the sleeves and the cuffs. Wild strawberries, I think they were, and a fruit like pomegranate or a pineapple. He was larger than life, of course, they always are. It seemed to me he was about eight feet from the ground, but I couldn't get him from below the waist. He seemed to rise on a kind of vapour. Well, when I'd got as far as that, actually visualised him, I thought I'd get into his mind. It seemed to me that it would be quite simple to just, as it were, project myself into his mind. I heard myself saying to him, 'How did you do it?' I remember," continued Philip Fielding, with rising excitement, "that here, in the evening, I had my hand on his old iron stirrup, and I thought, How could you do it, day after day, with her shut up here, even if you hated her, why didn't you clear out? Take the other woman whether she would or no? Take the money and clear out? She'd have gone with you if she'd seen it was the only way. How could you go on loving the woman, the other woman, I mean, if you knew she wanted you to murder your wife? After all, that wretched creature had been fond of you; was fond of you still, I suppose. Weren't you sorry for her when you saw her moving about the house, doing her miserable little bits of work, trying to interest herself in stupid futilities? The only thing that women had then—not that many of them have much more now."

Philip Fielding began to walk up and down the room. His wife, still crouching by the fire, watched him. When he was in the shadows he was almost lost to her, when he came within the circle of the lamp she could see him clearly. It was obvious that he was greatly moved.

"His courage is failing him. He's shirking it," she thought. "He is sorry for me, and he's beginning to hate Angela. It's clear now that Angela knows. I wonder if he'll go on? Or if he'll repent, in time? O God, do let it be in time."

"I suppose," she said, "that's where you're stuck in your story. When it comes to getting into the murderer's mind and wondering how he could do it."

"Yes, Grace, that's it, I'm stuck there. You see, one mustn't be outside, one mustn't blame or condemn, or say how horrible, or how ghastly, or what an atrocious criminal—one has to be actually inside the man to see why he did it. There's a justification for everything, you know."

"I never heard that before. It seems to me an extraordinary thing to say. But never mind that. The question is, have you found any justification for Philip Vavasour?"

"I think I have, Grace." He paused and began turning over his papers and prints. "I think that if the woman wouldn't let go, she really deserved to die. To be destroyed, to be put out of the way."

Mrs. Fielding pushed her chair back so that she was out of the reach of the firelight and quite eclipsed in the shade.

"Oh, you do, do you?"

"Yes, I felt that I could get into the skin of the poor wretch. I felt that I could get his viewpoint, when he didn't feel that he was doing anything ill or horrible at all, only something necessary, like killing a noxious insect, a spider."

"Why do you say a spider, Philip?"

"Oh, I don't know, they're harmless really, aren't they, and even bring luck? But I saw one just now, running over the manuscript, and it put it in my mind."

Mrs. Fielding asked her husband if he would give her a glass of water or an orange, if he had either one or the other there. He kept both in a cupboard near the bookcase.

Neither spoke until he had poured out the water and peeled the fruit and given it to her. Then he said, as if he had himself under much better control:

"I don't think we ought to talk of it any more to-night, Grace. It's the sort of thing that does get on one's nerves a little. I really shall be glad when it's over. I mean, when I've got it all down and forgotten all about it."

"Will you forget all about it, Philip? How soon, I wonder?"

She drank her water and played nervously with her peeled orange. He made a pretence of gathering up his papers, but merely placed them, with nervous movements, in different untidy heaps.

"Philip Vavasour," he said suddenly, and held before her an old stained engraving.

"It's not like you," she answered. "It's a strange face, I've never seen it before."

"Good God, Grace, why should it be like me? And of course it was a strange face."

"You've seen it, then?"

He did not seem to wish to talk further on the subject. She took the engraving from him and looked at it. The unskilful hand of the engraver had reproduced handsome, heavy features, which were, to Mrs. Fielding, for all her passionate interest, expressionless. The dress was unusually rich, and the detail finished with meticulous care.

"It is the same man," she remarked, "as he who hangs on the stairs, is it not? The green robe with the black edging. Is he dead, that one? The faces are the same. Oh, I don't know, take it away, Philip." As she handed the engraving back to her husband she added: "There's Hugh Vavasour written underneath. Why did you change the name and give him your own?"

"I don't quite know. It's an idea that came to me. It seemed to bring us closer together."

She played a while with her peeled orange, then began to tear it apart.

"The actual murder," she asked, "have you found out how that was committed? How it was that he got away with it?"

"No, I can't find out. I've told you again and again it all seems purposely blotted out. He died quite soon afterwards himself. Poisoned himself, perhaps. Cut his throat. I don't know. It seemed clear he never married Barbara. It was quite a destruction of all three of them."

"Of all three of them?" Mrs. Fielding rose abruptly, her face was livid. "You mean to say that Barbara was destroyed too?"

"Of course, she was bound to be, wasn't she? How could she have gone on living after that? I mean, I think they knew that day by the tarn that it was for all of them. They talked, of course, of being married, even of being happy, but they must have known, if they'd any reason left, that that wasn't possible. He felt bound to destroy Susanna, and Barbara felt bound to stand by and allow him to do so. And I suppose they didn't see much further than that. But they must have known that it was doom and destruction."

"What happened to Barbara?" asked Mrs. Fielding, taut and rigid by the easy chair.

"I can't find out. I don't know where she's buried or where he's buried for that matter. I shall get it if I stay here long enough."

Mrs. Fielding leant against the high back of the worn, warm armchair.

"I think I could write that part of your story for you, Philip. Barbara may have gone down to a lake, put her feet into the ripples, it would be very cold, you know; she would hesitate a little before she slid underneath the water. She would fix her eyes upon an island on which grew two or three trees. She would feel that if she could reach the island it might be sanctuary, even salvation. But it was too far off and there was no boat. Nothing much grew under the trees, save a little ground ivy, which was an unpleasant red colour—the whole landscape is terrible. In between the dark trunks of the trees there just comes a little broken light, but nothing whatever living in sight. Yes, she would hesitate quite a long time, imagining the water rising up, chilling her to the heart. I believe she might die of cold before she was suffocated. But that, of course, was the end of her. Or the end of her body, for her spirit, I suppose—"

Mrs. Fielding's voice faded away.

"You're getting overwrought, Grace," said her husband uneasily. "We ought not really to be here talking like this. It was a fool's move to come here. The influence is too strong for both of us. Now we shan't be able to get away."

He seemed to speak with genuine rage and regret.

"No," said Mrs. Fielding. "I suppose we shan't get away, for quite a long time, even if we died here. One or both of us, we should still have to stay, like they did, Susanna and Philip."

She gave a quick twitching shudder, as if she shook something from her shoulders.

"Now, I'll go to bed," she said in her normal voice. "I'm tired, really, but quite all right. Don't worry about me, Philip."

She smiled at him and left the room.

*   *   *

Mrs. Fielding was much surprised to find Mrs. Mace in her room when she entered. She knew how much the housekeeper abhorred this portion of the house, and never before had she known her enter it save in broad daylight and for a brief period, just sufficient to direct the cleaning and adjustments of the chambers.

"Why, Mrs. Mace, you here! Were you wanting to speak to me? You should have come into the library. I was only just speaking with my husband over his new book."

Mrs. Fielding was really surprised to hear how ordinary her own voice sounded. She was learning from Philip how to act perfectly a horrible part.

Mrs. Mace rose from the small chintz-covered chair she had taken by the fire. She had some knitting in her hand, and a small book which Mrs. Fielding was surprised to observe was the Bible. An old-fashioned idea this, she thought, the Holy Book to keep away the evil spirits.

"I didn't like to disturb you, ma'am, but I did feel I ought to see you. I was talking to Mrs. Hicks about it, and Mary too, and we all said—"

The woman paused, Mrs. Fielding clutched the edge of the mantelpiece.

"Yes, Mrs. Mace, you all said—"

"We all said we didn't think you ought to stay here, ma'am. Neither you nor Mr. Fielding. Especially you."

"Why especially me, Mrs. Mace?"

"Well, ma'am, if you'll forgive me saying it, you don't look at all well, and haven't been these last few days, and it's only the same old story over again." The housekeeper, who was obviously making an effort over her courage, spoke more rapidly with a touch of incoherence: "It's just as we expected, ma'am. We said that Mrs. Holmes oughtn't to have let the house, and it wasn't what you might call fair, and yet we knew you'd had warnings, and you *would* have this wing. It seems really as if it's the sort of thing people can't escape. Yet we did agree, Mrs. Hicks and her husband, too, and I, that we oughtn't to stand by and see it done."

"See what done, Mrs. Mace?"

"See this house, I don't know how to put it, ma'am, see it get hold of you. It always does get hold of them, you know, one or the other. Why, there was the governess, Mrs. Holmes's governess; I didn't tell you that. I didn't dare tell anybody. We don't like to open our mouths, and this part of the house is horrible, ma'am, horrible."

"I don't feel it, Mrs. Mace."

"No, that's the nasty part of it. You don't feel it if it's got hold of you."

Mrs. Fielding smiled.

"It's very kind of you, Mrs. Mace, I do appreciate it, and I don't suppose we shall stay here much longer, either of us. I might go any day, so might my husband. But this old story has got hold of him. It *is* only an old story, you know, and I don't think there's much of it true. He can't find out very much, and as for the ghost and the hauntings, well, all old houses have that, and I'm not susceptible, as I told you at first. I'm not likely to see anything."

"Maybe, ma'am, you're not likely to see anything." The housekeeper seemed to search anxiously in her mind for some expression to explain her fears. "It gets hold of you," was all she could repeat.

"Yes, I see what you mean. You're afraid *for* me. Perhaps, if you were a little cleverer you'd be afraid *of* me."

"Afraid of you, ma'am?" There was a note of incredulity in the housekeeper's voice. She took two steps away from where Mrs. Fielding, a tall, dark figure in the dark green dress, leant against the mantelshelf.

"Don't you think it might get into me as well as into him?"

"I didn't say it had got into him, if you mean Mr. Fielding, ma'am."

"No, but that's what you thought—the murderer, you know. I know all the tales, all the explanations, the influence, the atmosphere, an evil spirit left behind finding another body to work out its purpose, its *thwarted* purpose, Mrs. Mace, don't forget that. This man Vavasour never did it."

"Never did what, ma'am?"

The housekeeper fell back another pace.

"Never did the murder—how stupid everybody is! It came to me quite a long time ago, or was it only yesterday? One doesn't count the days much in a place like this. Of course it was perfectly clear. He wanted to murder her, but she discovered it in time, and she murdered him!"

"Has Mr. Fielding found that out?" stammered the housekeeper. "Has he found that out, ma'am, among all them old papers?"

"No; he doesn't know, or pretends he doesn't know. I do, I am quite certain."

Mrs. Mace rubbed her hands nervously together and retreated still farther into the shadows by the great bed. Ever since the Fieldings had come to Medlar's Farm she had been prepared for something—outlandish—as she vaguely termed her dreadful fears; but when the terror came it was almost unendurable. Mrs. Fielding was smiling; she felt a certain exaltation, as if she had stepped beyond all human woes.

"Queer that I should be the first to find the truth about her, eh, Mrs. Mace? When Barbara came over that day she found him dying and Susanna had gone out to the lake—they thought he had drowned her first, then poisoned himself, but Barbara *knew*."

The housekeeper listened intently as Mrs. Fielding continued:

"Don't you see? I saw that statue, when she took me by the hand, showing me the devil pursuing a poor tormented wretch. He turned round suddenly and trapped his tormentor. So did she, this miserable Susanna. She wasn't going to be murdered, Mrs. Mace; she wasn't going to run away and let the other woman have him. She murdered him. She found that tasteless, odourless white essence that he'd prepared for her, that he was watching for an opportunity to give her, and she changed it, and she put it into some drink for him, and he died with that horrible swiftness that he had prepared for her. She had quite as much courage as he had, Mrs. Mace. Women have, you know. She could stand by and see him drop dead. It was better than letting him go to the other. Don't you think so too? Don't you think she was justified?"

"I never heard that part of the story," stammered the housekeeper, "but very likely it is so. I don't know. It's a long time ago, and one hears this and hears that. But all I do know, ma'am, is that you shouldn't be staying here; it's having a bad effect on you, and you're not the woman you were when you came here. It's not only I who say so—nobody can ever live in this wing of the house. You ought to come into the old Viking part. It may be rough and rude, but it's quite wholesome."

Mrs. Fielding shook her head.

"You're mistaken. I'm quite well."

"There are the cottages," urged the housekeeper, as if the other woman had not spoken. "I'm sure Mrs. Hicks would do her best to make you comfortable. They'd give you a nice bedroom, and everything clean and pleasant. The children about might take your mind off things."

"What makes you think my mind is on—*things?*"

"Anyone can see it, if you'll forgive me, ma'am. You're hardly eating, and I don't think you're sleeping; taking drugs at night. Mr. Fielding has said to me many a time that he's worried about you. I felt it was my duty to speak, knowing the house as I do."

"Oh, my husband has spoken to you about me, has he?"

"Yes, ma'am, he seemed anxious, sorry he brought you here. He told me you'd be going away, and I hoped you would. Every day I hoped you'd say so."

"Well, I shall be going quite soon, Mrs. Mace. Just give me a few more days. My husband wants to get some more of his story clear."

"I don't think that story will ever be written, ma'am, if you'll forgive me. Certainly it won't ever be made into a book for people to read. Besides, if he wants to go on with it, that's no reason for you to stay, is it?"

"I've got another reason, Mrs. Mace. I think, yes, I want to stay until they submerge the church—Crompton Old Church—you know, and bring up the body of Susanna Vavasour. She said she would not rest until the Resurrection, didn't she? I'd like to see what's left of her."

"I shouldn't do that if I was you, ma'am, I really shouldn't. There won't be anything there, nothing but a few bones, nothing to explain the mystery. I don't suppose they'd let anyone in. Anyhow, it's all going to be done private, and late at night."

"They couldn't keep me away," said Mrs. Fielding, "if I made up my mind to be there."

"Well, now, ma'am, don't those kind of wishes and fancies show you're not yourself? You've been used to a different life. London, and lots of people—going about. This is no place for you to come to."

"I wonder why you're so concerned about me, Mrs. Mace. Do you see me marked down as a kind of victim? Like those trees in the forest that have the cross on them? They're the ones that are going to get the axe, are they not?"

Mrs. Mace stood silent a second, thoughtfully and anxiously eyeing through her thick pebble glasses the other woman. When she spoke, it was in a changed tone.

"Well, I shouldn't think any more of it to-night, ma'am. I should go to bed if I was you, and let me bring you a nice cup of hot milk or tea or whatever you fancy, and you'd better take one of your sleeping draughts. You don't look to me as if you were going to get a wink."

"Very well, Mrs. Mace." Mrs. Fielding sank into the easy chair in which the housekeeper had kept her vigil. "I'll go to bed, and I'll try to go to sleep. There's to-morrow and the day after, and I dare say one or two days after that. It's not all quite clear to me yet," she added in a musing tone.

Mrs. Mace began to prepare the bed.

"She made an appeal to Barbara, of course. I can see her going over the mountains. Begged Barbara to do as she had threatened, marry another man and go right away. She thought to herself, 'If Barbara does that, of course he will not have any reason to destroy me. He won't do it, and we might, in time, come together again. The enchantment might be broken. But Barbara won't go away.'"

She turned and looked at the housekeeper over her shoulder.

"Don't you see, Mrs. Mace, that put all the responsibility on to Barbara? She would not go away, and Susanna Vavasour was cornered. Barbara would not go away, and he was just waiting for a chance to murder her, so she—why, it's like the toad, isn't it?"

"The toad, ma'am? There's no such things here, I assure you."

"The toad in the story; it was cornered and stared and stared at the man who was trying to gaze it to death, until the man died."

"That's a horrid fancy, ma'am, I must say," said the house-keeper in great uneasiness. "You've got your head all full of the wrong sort of tales. I dare say," she added in a non-committal tone, "it was Mrs. Vavasour who murdered her husband. I always heard they died, one after the other, here together. But where he's buried I never heard any say."

"Perhaps," smiled Mrs. Fielding, dropping her graceful head on her thin hands, "she contrived to make it look like suicide, and he was buried at the crossroads, with a stake through him? No, that wouldn't be right, because he walks, doesn't he, in a blue coat? And suicides never walk."

"I'm not so sure of that," replied Mrs. Mace, reluctantly fascinated by this forbidden topic, like one drawn against her will into a magic circle. "I think some do—you haven't *seen* anything, have you, ma'am?"

"No—I've just imagined things."

"I've heard other people who have been here say that, ma'am. I've often wondered what this imagining is—that poor young governess now—"

"Did she see anything? What happened to her?"

Mrs. Mace pursed her lips, afraid of having already said too much. She was being drawn into that dreadful discussion that she most desired to avoid. But the next question that Mrs. Fielding asked startled the housekeeper beyond discretion.

"Do you know if it is easy to get hold of cyanide of potassium, Mrs. Mace?"

"Whatever makes you ask that, ma'am? Why, that's the name the doctor said—" She checked herself too late.

"What doctor? When? Cyanide of potassium—who got some? It's instant death, you know."

"It was the governess, ma'am She did get some—she told the chemist that it was to destroy an old dog—"

"But she took it herself, I suppose, Mrs. Mace? Or did she give it to someone else?"

"Oh no, ma'am, nothing of the kind! Only it was found out that she had got it, I mean—and there was trouble."

"A likely story," smiled Mrs. Fielding indifferently.

The housekeeper resolved to say no more on the matter. She took a long time adjusting the bed, arranging the reading lamp, and placing the hot-water bottle between the sheets, and as she went about her tasks she glanced frequently and apprehensively at the woman drooping in the chair by the fire.

Mrs. Fielding spoke no more. When the housekeeper at length approached her and asked her if she should assist her to undress and get to bed, she found that the tall, dark, elegant woman was asleep, her head still clasped in her hands and her elbow on the chair. Mrs. Mace, her rather hard-featured face set in lines of agitated resolution, stared at the sleeping woman for a while. Mrs. Fielding stirred. Her elbow sunk from the chair, her hand fell and her head drooped forward. She muttered: "I'll do it to-morrow."

The housekeeper gently laid her back on the cushions, so that in that natural attitude she continued her slumber. Then, with a precise gesture, she placed the Bible on the sleeping woman's knees.

"Never say, 'I'll do it to-morrow' unless ye add 'if the Lord permits,'" she murmured. For she was a woman who had found religion a strong consolation in many troubles and bereavements, and texts were more often in her mind than on her tongue.

When she had assured herself that Mrs. Fielding was deep in her exhausted sleep, the housekeeper took up the small lamp from the table by the bed and began to very cautiously and systematically search the room, every corner of which was familiar to her. She did this in as noiseless a manner as possible, and continually paused to glance at the sleeping figure by the fire. Mrs. Fielding stirred, groaned, and once repeated she "would do it to-morrow," but remained unconscious of the activities of the housekeeper, which included a close inspection to the small medicine cupboard in the corner. She examined carefully every object that she found there. None of them was calculated to arouse suspicion, for they were all known to her, or else, by reason of their colour, substance, or smell, obviously not what she sought.

It did not occur to her to inspect the contents of the atomiser of pink glass painted with blue flowerets that stood on the top of the shelf.

She stood thoughtful, not wholly satisfied.

"They get so cunning. I ought to speak to her husband. I wonder why they came here? She seems to me the last sort of person—and what made her mention that horrid stuff?"

Mrs. Mace hesitated. She would have liked to put Mrs. Fielding to bed, but dared not rouse her from what seemed a deep sleep, likely to last till morning. And then, as she became aware of the steady silence and of where she was, a place she had avoided during the whole of her stay at Medlar's Farm, and avoided especially at this hour, there was something else that she dare not do, and that was remain any longer in this solitary chamber.

She made Mrs. Fielding as comfortable as possible in the easy chair, and then, with hesitation, as if she was doing a mean action, she took the Bible from the sleeping woman's knee. She had not the courage to traverse the Georgian wing of Medlar's Farm, at this hour of the night, without the Holy Book under her arm.

*   *   *

Mrs. Fielding woke suddenly, instantly alert, and instantly that this was the depth of the night in which she was sunk as one might be sunk in the depth of a lake—away from all humanity.

The fire had sunk to a heap of ash, the lamp was still burning. She took this up and went directly to the library with as little hesitation as if some potent presence beckoned her onwards.

Her husband's papers, books, prints, lay in disorder close to the reading lamp. She lit this and put her own smaller light beside it, so that the table, encumbered with odd objects, was fully illuminated. There was the rusty spur and the shrivelled mitten of tarnished thread side by side; there was the print of Hugh Vavasour in his elaborate brocade coat, and there were the old books, musty, worm-holed, foxed, with rubbed leather covers and long letters in sepia-coloured ink that held the obscure and incomplete records of his tragedy.

Mrs. Fielding seated herself in the large chair her husband used, and then paused in her movements in order to listen to the stillness that held the large dark crowded room like a spell.

Then she began turning over the books, the spent husks of dead thoughts, passions, and pleasures. She looked sullenly at the headpieces and finials, queer symbolic devices of monsters, masonic signs, the arcana of the Rosy Cross, and none of them meant anything to her save the repetition of the word *Finis*, which she came frequently upon when turning these dry pages and became multiplied before her eyes until it was written all over the dark air beyond the circle of the lamplight.

"There is no need for Philip to read me any more of his story, I know it quite well—I could write some of it myself—"

She drew a sheet of paper towards her, and began to write as if she was taking down a dictation.

*   *   *

"Barbara could wait no longer. He had so frequently given her to understand that it would be soon now—that they would be immediately free. Nothing had been put plainly in words between them, but he knew what she expected. The suspense was exhausting her; she frequently made herself possets of borage and hellebore to keep off melancholy and her sick looks were remarked by her father, who chid her harshly for her misplaced passion.

"So, this autumn day she came alone, on foot, to Vavasour Hall. She knew that he had had the poison long in the house. He had procured it from an apothecary in Newcastle. Why did he hesitate? She was in the mood to strangle the narrow-faced, railing wife with her own hands. It was a day of wind and of low clouds scudding before the wind; the sheep stood with their backs to it, and the long grey wool was blown over their imbecile faces. Barbara walked rapidly, brittle fragments of fern and heather clung to her skirt, and her flesh became cold from the bitter air. When she reached Vavasour Hall there was no one about. The gates stood wide; the gardener's tools lay on the lawn which was strewn with dead leaves like withered garlands, but there was no gardener. The bleak light that fitfully penetrated the quick-driven clouds lay along the avenue of elms that had been in shade a few days ago. But a great storm had stripped off the last of the harsh, crinkled yellow leaves, and the black twigs showed bare against the lurid, vaporous heavens. The doors and windows of Vavasour Hall all stood open, despite the wind; some of the curtains were blown out against the grey stonework. Barbara caught her cloak which, filled with wind, seemed to pull her back, and entered the open, vacant doorway.

"There was no one within. He had done it, then. Some calamity had struck the household into silence. No doubt in the large funeral chamber the women were already laying out their mistress in the state bed with the black plumes where none but the dead ever slept. The crimped cap would be drawn round the narrow chin, the greedy hands folded on the barren breast, and the shroud folded and tied over the despised body that had been violently destroyed.

"'It would be wiser for me to go,' thought Barbara, but she remained rigid in the empty hall, the wind, tearing up the bare avenue and in at the open door, disordering her hair and her garments.

"Here, to this house, she would come as a bride; in the nuptial chamber where he had so often slept with Susanna, she, the second wife, would take off her bridal garters in the dark and toss them, through the half-open door, to the waiting maids in the ante-room. Already, in secret, she had embroidered those garters, ribbons of yellow, violet, and blue. Here in this house she would wake, after her marriage night, and see her husband beside her, and they would look at each other in the horrid bleached light of dawn and wonder if they heard a foot without or a scratching on the panel. Or would they, that night, sleep at all? Would they not rather lie wakeful, cold, and apart?

"She faced the wind, turning to leave the silent house when she heard a cry falling down the dark stairs: 'Barbara!'

"She obeyed this summons and went upstairs, passing no one on her way; but every door and window was set wide as if something had rushed through the house, striving to escape by every opening.

"She heard her name again, nearer now; it was his voice, though much changed. She traced it to the great chamber that had been in her mind when she waited below; the sleeping chamber of the master of the house, where so many Vavasours had been born and had died. Barbara crept in, cold from the constant wind and her constant fear.

"He was on the floor beside the monstrous bed; he had dragged down the sheets and coverlets in some frantic clutch; his shirt was torn aside, his neck and chest bare as if for torture or decapitation, and his dark red hair hung loose like the untidy mane of a bull. Barbara, in an instant fury, began to mock at this overthrow; what was this man to her then but a weapon broken in the hand?

"'Oh, coward! Is this your strength of purpose? Do you want to betray us?'

"'Is that you, Barbara? I cannot see.'

"'It is I. Were you not calling on me?'

"'Maybe. I am in some pain and think on the cause of it.'

"His voice was thick and his great eyes were dull; like a powerful half-slaughtered animal he heaved his length by the bed and gnawed at his fingers. The rain broke suddenly from the clouds and hurled long spears of water into the room which was drenched in a pale storm light.

"'Is this remorse?' asked Barbara bitterly.

"He began to cry, like a child—yet his tears were the difficult tears of the dying.

"'She found the drug—and gave it to me—I waited too long.'

"'Ah! Where is she?'

"'Gone. Gone. Gone. To the lake—'"

*   *   *

Mrs. Fielding came downstairs very late the next morning; she was angry with herself for oversleeping, and confused as to what had happened the night before. She remembered falling asleep in the library, then waking just as it was beginning to get light, and going upstairs again with the little low-flickering lamp in her hand, then falling, dressed, on her bed, and sleeping—without a sedative that time. The oblivion at which she had snatched greedily had been delicious, but it was hideously vexatious that she should have been late, for as she crept into the Tudor room, walking very softly, she surprised her husband reading a letter from Angela. She saw at once on the notepaper the name of the hotel she had visited and Angela's contemptuously individual handwriting.

Philip Fielding started when he realised that his wife was standing beside him, and deliberately, with an almost childish movement, hid the letter. She had seen two words written in that large hand, one was her own name "Grace," and the other was "poison."

"You might let me read that, Philip."

"I can't. I didn't mean you to know it had come. Angela ought not to have written. She said she wouldn't. You mustn't think she means anything, Grace."

"Show it to me, then."

"I can't."

He folded the letter up and put it in an inner pocket of his coat.

"You'll have to trust me to that extent, Grace. Sit down and take your breakfast. Mrs. Mace is worried about you. Thinks you're not too well, that the house is really affecting you. I must arrange for you to go away."

She took her seat at the breakfast-table and eyed his breast where, under the tweed coat, lay Angela's letter, with the two words, her own name and "poison." Angela was being very daring. Wouldn't that letter be evidence—afterwards? But of course he would destroy it.

She made another effort to goad him, not because she hoped to see the letter, but because she wanted to inflict torture on him, as he had inflicted torture on her.

"Let me read it. Why shouldn't I? I told you Angela and I were quite frank one with another. There oughtn't to be any secrets now."

"Grace, this isn't what you think it is. It's something between Angela and myself. It's nothing to do with—with—any feeling we have one for another. But I can't let you read the letter. It's most unfortunate you should have seen it. I shall destroy it at once. Don't think it's the kind of letter one treasures."

"I suppose not," smiled Mrs. Fielding.

He abruptly left the breakfast-table. She remained in her place, but neither ate nor drank that morning. She thought:

"Angela is urging him to do something. But I suppose by now he's found out that the poison's no use. That must worry him. But, of course, the last thing he'd think of is that I'd changed it. I expect he believes that whoever gave him, fooled him. No doubt he's already decided on something else. A knife, or a rope? I expect he'll suggest taking me out—a long expedition, insist on telling Mrs. Mace that I'm going away soon."

She nodded across the breakfast-table. She thought that at the other side of the white cloth and the handsome, antique silver, there sat another woman in a dark green dress, with a handful of pale hair fine as floss silk, her companion and her guide, who looked at her, nodded and said, "Now."

She tried to remember what had happened last night, but she was no longer capable of a coherent thought. She frowned, trying to recall what the young man in the old-fashioned chemist's shop had said to her—"Cyanide of potassium—a deadly poison," and then he had handed back to her the little bottle that contained the liquid that she had afterwards transferred to the atomiser of pink glass.

Transferred with what intention?

If Philip had said that the damp had touched his throat—she might say—"This is a very good lotion I had made up in town, try it with the spray." Or was not that part of her dreams, that, on waking, she never could recapture?

Last night, surely, Susanna Vavasour had come to her and told her exactly how it was done. But that was part of what she could not remember.

She went into the library where her husband seemed to be clearing up the materials for his work.

"I wrote some of your story last night, Philip; did you find it?"

"I? No—nothing."

Distressed, she began to search among the papers.

"Oh, I am sure I wrote—pages. This house, standing empty,

and the wind blowing through—"

He took her hands to stay her restless searching.

"Grace, you are getting full of fancies, really. There was nothing here when I came down this morning, but a pile of blank paper, like I left last night—"

She averted her glance as she reflected, cunningly: "Of course he is still trying to deceive me. He must have been rather frightened when he read what I had written and realised that I *knew*, so he destroyed the sheets."

"Grace, I'm giving it up, and the house. It was all an awful mistake. It hasn't come out a bit like I thought it would."

"No?"

"No." He was still holding her hands. "There is no escape here. We must get away. I can't bear that you should feel that this horrible old story is like ours—"

"I suppose not."

"Of course—it couldn't be. I don't believe these Vavasours ever existed. They are phantoms. Monsters. They have nothing to do with us."

"I suppose not."

"Grace, you look so lifeless. What is it, dear?"

He put his arms round her and she lay against his breast thinking the while of Angela's letter in which was the word "poison" between her and his heart.

"We were happy once, weren't we? How could you let it happen?"

She began to weep in her utter woe. He comforted her in a low voice and she slipped away from him. She believed that she saw a restless shape that moved to and fro whispering the word "Now."

"I'll go upstairs, Philip, and lie down till luncheon."

*   *   *

When Mrs. Fielding went upstairs she cautiously entered her husband's room and looked into his dispatch case. The little bottle labelled "Headache Drops" that she had filled with water was gone.

Upon this discovery she went to the corner cupboard in her room and took down the pink glass atomiser. There was about an inch of liquid at the bottom. Would it be enough? Had she lost some in the transference from one vessel to another?

She found the original bottle she had used, and very carefully poured into this the contents of the atomiser. Enough, surely. But she wished that she could more clearly remember what the chemist had told her—that, like so much that lay stagnant in her mind, was hard to recall.

She put the bottle in her handbag. Cornered, like the toad, like the mouse, like Susanna Vavaour.

As she came listlessly down the stairs, with this in her handbag, her husband met her by the newel-post, and affectionately took her arm.

"Listen, Grace. I'm not going to have any more of this nonsense. Mrs. Mace is right. You don't look at all fit. I'm going to send you away. I've made all the arrangements. If you'd rather, I'll take you away, the day after to-morrow. Let's make it Italy, after all. You can be ready, can't you? Get all you want together in a little while?"

"All I want?" thought Mrs. Fielding. "What is he thinking of? A shroud, a spade, quicklime?"

She allowed him to take her into the Tudor room. The luncheon was ready. He was very agreeable during the meal, and watched her anxiously: "Wondering why I don't drop and die, wondering why he can't destroy me."

They quietly talked of their coming departure form Medlar's Farm and discussed where they should go in Italy.

Mrs. Mace brought in the coffee, and set it on a tray of pierced silver by a bowl of pretty pink, waxy flowers which had just been sent in from the greenhouses; they seemed to Mrs. Fielding to be the same kind of blooms as those she had seen hanging in the wire window basket while she talked with Angela; while she gave Angela her last chance.

"Philip and I have very few more words to say to one another, and I suppose those few will be absolutely trivial and futile. We got as near to the truth as we could, but now we seem to have receded again. There's nothing more to be said, only something to be done."

The kindness of his manner strengthened her purpose, for it confirmed her conviction of his callous cruelty. He was soothing her, luring her on. She began to turn over in her mind what the moment, which she intended to forestall, might be like? When would his manner change? Would he, still with a caress, leap on her? Would he, drawing her to him, as if to kiss her, close his fingers round her throat? She had often read, as a child, with horror of murders. Particularly murders in lonely places. She remembered an old cut of a gig blowing along a solitary road and one of the two occupants turning to shoot the other, and she had often thought, even then, "What was the last friendly word? Did one begin to look sullen, the other frightened, or was there just a laugh, and then a flash? There must have been one awful second when the victim saw the murderer drawing out his weapon, when he realised—'that moment is for me.'"

Philip Fielding's voice broke in on her thoughts.

"It's a glorious day, not a scrap of mist for once, nor a drop of rain. I think we might take a long drive this afternoon."

"So he can't wait any longer."

"I should like," he said, "a long drive—to get quite away—wouldn't you?"

"Oh, Philip, there's a large spider over there. Do move it."

While his back was turned, while he searched for the insect, she had taken the bottle out of her bag and emptied the contents into his cup of coffee.

Philip Fielding returned to her side.

"I didn't see any spider."

"Oh, I suppose it ran away. Your coffee is getting cold."

She watched him drink, which he did without comment.

*   *   *

As Mrs. Fielding passed down the road on her way to the lake she saw a gleaming blue sports car pass in between the stone piers of the gates to Medlar's Farm.

Angela, who could not keep away; Angela, who would now watch him die, as Susanna Vavasour had watched her lover die.

Mrs. Fielding nodded and smiled to the pale-haired woman in the dark green dress who was her constant companion, and walked on with more eager steps towards her inevitable destination.

*   *   *

When Mrs. Mace opened the door to Angela, she thought:

"So here you are again, my lady. You're the cause of all the trouble, I'll be bound."

"I'll just leave the car there. I shan't be a moment. Is Mrs. Fielding in the house?"

"I think so, ma'am. I believe she's upstairs in her room. I'll go and see. Mr. Fielding is in the library."

"I won't disturb him. It's Mrs. Fielding I want to see. If she's out I'll wait."

Angela's manner was downcast and troubled; Mrs. Mace's instinctive dislike of her was quietened.

"Will you come in, miss, and wait in the Tudor room? I think that's the most cheerful."

To this strange remark Angela replied:

"I think the whole house is horrible. I'd rather stay in the hall until you know if Mrs. Fielding is in or not." She added impulsively: "This is a ghastly place, so lonely. As I drove along I saw two or three hearses. You know, it seems like a nightmare, not real—hearses on that lonely road."

For a moment Mrs. Mace was herself startled, and then she smiled.

"Oh yes, it was to be to-day, of course, if they couldn't finish last night. Those aren't really what you can call hearses, miss."

"Oh, I'm sure they were."

"Well, they're going to take the bones out of Crompton Old Church. The church isn't going to be drowned for a few weeks yet, but they're beginning to take the bones away, to the big cemetery at Hexham, I think. They haven't been burying there for a long time, so it can only be people who've been dead for years."

"I suppose that does make it better. Still, it was a nasty sight."

As she spoke Philip Fielding came down the wide dark stairs. As soon as she saw him and before he could speak she cried out awkwardly and rapidly:

"Oh, Phil! I want to see Grace—rather badly."

"I think she's upstairs."

"I'm just going to see, sir." And Mrs. Mace left them together, not without a shrewd backward glance.

"Come into the library," said Philip Fielding, and Angela followed him with apprehension and reluctance in her look and movement.

As soon as the door had closed behind them she began at once:

"Look here, Phil, you'll think I'm a beast to be here again, but it really *is* to see Grace."

"Mrs. Mace has gone up to find her. I think she's in her room. But what do you want to see Grace for, Angela? She came over to see you the other day, didn't she?"

"Yes, she did. I don't suppose she told you what it was all about."

"No, she didn't. I guessed a little."

"Of course it's all getting hateful to you, as it is to me," said Angela rapidly, twisting her fingers together. "She came and asked me to give up, go right away, like I said I would before, and I just told her 'No!' said I couldn't, but I've been thinking it over, Phil, and I've decided that she's right."

"You are really going away, Angela?"

"Yes, I am. Far away. I can still get a tour, Canada, Africa; oh, I don't know where. I'll try to find another man too," she laughed defiantly. "There's no cure for one love affair but another, is there?"

He did not answer, but stood rigid before the pile of papers on which his finger-tips rested.

"You see," said Angela, "I stood firm while she was there, I didn't want to make any pretences. I was trying to be frank, but after she'd gone, I thought it over. She scared me, Phil, she really did. She said that if I didn't give up, something dreadful would happen, that it was the last chance. And, you know, I've been thinking it over, and it did seem to me that we were on the verge of something dreadful, and that it wasn't worth while."

"What wasn't worth while, Angela?"

"Well, you and I. I don't say I'm through with it—I care awfully, but somehow—"

"You've seen Grace's point of view?"

"Well, I always saw that—I don't know, I don't want to talk about it. Of course we made a mistake," with a certain violent contempt. "We ought to have had the usual sly intrigue. That was the old-fashioned way, and those people knew what they were doing. This being frank, telling the truth from the first, and talking about divorce, and being so candid and so respectable, you see what it ends in. I don't like the look of Grace," she repeated.

"You're right that she's not been well here. I ought to have noticed it. I came here on—I don't quite know what with—when we—when you gave me up—I thought I'd come here and throw myself into the history of the place—you know I've tried that trick before, evoking the past, and getting into the skins of dead people, and Grace was always the kind that didn't mind a bit—anything odd, or occult, I mean, and I really thought the peace and quiet would be good for her." He hurried on painfully with his explanations, not looking at Angela, who was leaning against one of the high book-cases. "She seemed all right at first, and I did get absorbed."

"Into forgetting me?" interrupted Angela.

"Well, even into that. Yes, I must say you got blotted out a little. The influence of the place," he glanced round the dark room, "is very powerful."

"I always thought it was pretty ghastly. I don't know how you could live here."

"I had to do something violent and unusual. I had to get right away and make a clean cut, or I couldn't have borne it. I believe I've done it—made the clean cut."

"You mean you believe you can manage without me?"

"I think so, Angela."

"You beast," she said on a sigh. "But it's better. I dare say I can do it too. One doesn't want to be utterly loathsome. You ought to feel very flattered. Of course you understand that isn't that Grace is so much—crazy about you. It's all you stood for—all she put into the concern as it were that you knocked sky-high."

"Yes, I understand. I dare say I can make it up to her. We shall get along somehow. And you're right to be scared. I'm going to take her away to Italy. I think that's best. Mrs. Mace, that's the housekeeper here, spoke to me this morning—said she was quite strange, poor Grace, last night. Perhaps the house is getting hold of her."

"Strange, in what way?" asked Angela sharply.

"Oh, I don't know, she was talking about the old story. She's been visiting the churchyard where the woman was buried who used to live here. It's an old murder tale, rather sickening, no doubt. A story of jealousy."

"How on earth could you bring Grace where there's a story of jealousy and murder?"

"I suppose I was a fool. You know, it never occurred to me till she spoke the other night. She said when I was reading out some of my stuff—'Why, that's our story!'"

Angela did not answer; her huddled attitude showed a weight of uneasiness.

"She's a long time coming down," said Philip Fielding with a touch of concern. "I suppose Mrs. Mace can't find her. We were warned not to go into that Georgian wing of the house, it's supposed to be haunted. It's nonsense, of course, in a way, yet I don't know. I thought of buying the place, of probing the whole thing to the bottom."

"I don't know anything about it, but it seems to me the kind of thing you can't probe to the bottom, that will get hold of you and do for you, but that you'll never understand. Cut free, Phil, leave it alone, clear out, don't buy it."

"I don't mean to, not now. What are you going to say to her, Angela? Do you really want to see her?"

"Did you show her my letter? You must have got it this morning."

"No, how could I? It had got that bit in it—about—that rubbish about the poison, you know. I couldn't show her that. You should have written more carefully—"

"I wasn't thinking of being careful. She frightened me. I thought, when I came to think it over, that she might mean to poison herself—"

"I don't know why—and you shouldn't have written it."

Angela Campion ignored this tone of irritated rebuke, though it came oddly from one who had hitherto always spoken to her with love and deference; she defended herself.

"I had to warn you."

"But I couldn't show her the letter, don't you see? And that hurt her—and I can't see what made you think of poison—she couldn't get any here."

"I thought of it because I nearly got to that point myself," said Angela sullenly. "I was looking round for something, after you'd said good-bye."

"I've not forgotten. But it was only a wild threat."

"You were scared, though, weren't you? Don't you remember that you took away that bottle of headache drops you found inside my cigarette-box?"

"Yes, I came upon them yesterday in my case and threw them away. What has that got to do with it?"

"Well, that stuff was harmless, just something for neuralgia—but I had something in the flat that wasn't—"

"What do you mean, Angela?"

"I got it in Paris. Quite easy. I didn't take it, I don't mean to—but I came near enough it to realise that Grace might—

that's why I wrote, that's why I'm over here to-day. She did threaten something dreadful."

The housekeeper entered after a knock that neither of them had heard.

"Mrs. Fielding doesn't seem to be in the house, sir. Hicks and Mrs. Hicks—Mary—they've none of them seen her in the garden or the grounds. She hasn't ordered the car. She must have gone for a walk."

"Well," said Philip Fielding, with something of an effort, "I suppose that's quite natural and reasonable, isn't it, Mrs. Mace?"

"The walk in itself's quite natural and reasonable, sir, but if I was you I'd be inclined to go after Mrs. Fielding, because I don't think she's in a very natural or reasonable humour."

Mrs. Mace repeated her account of the agitation and strange behaviour of Grace Fielding on the evening before; and she added some details which she had not thought necessary to give before, for she was alarmed by the appearance of Angela and by the disappearance of Mrs. Fielding.

"You see, sir, I've been there before. I didn't like the look of any of it, and I made a good search of the room before I left her."

"A search of the room? What were you looking for, Mrs. Mace.

"For a revolver, sir, or a knife, or anything that you might do a mischief with."

"You had the same thought that I had!" exclaimed Angela. "You see, Phil, I was right."

"Say exactly what you mean, Mrs. Mace."

"I thought she might do something horrid, sir. You'll take my meaning. I've been there before. It was one of the young governesses, and then a lady that stayed here. Only just in time we was then, and with Miss Gates—too late. You see, sir, it's the influence of the place. It gets hold of somebody; it doesn't seem to have got hold of you, but it's got hold of her."

"You didn't find anything?"

"No, sir." Mrs. Mace hesitated a moment; no doubt it was all nonsense and just her nervousness, and no need to make a fuss. So she said: "No, sir, nothing at all." Yet could not resist adding: "But I don't like the look of it. They get so clever. Poor Miss Bates, now, she had it hidden away. Cyanide of potassium the doctor said it was—"

"I'll go after her," interrupted Philip Fielding as if he had not heard this. "I'll find her at once."

"I wish you would, sir," said Mrs. Mace. "You see," she repeated again, "I've been there before."

"I'll come too," said Angela. "The Bluebird will take us anywhere in no time. But what direction did she go?"

"Hicks says, miss, that she might be going to that lake where she made the car stop the other day when she went to see you. He says he didn't like the look of the way she was standing there between the trees staring down at the water. She's been up to that old churchyard, you see, sir," added the housekeeper, "and seen the old carving what they call 'The Devil Snar'd,' and she talks of that too often for my liking. There's a lot of people tried to snare the devil in this house, but none of them done it nor ever will, as I can see."

"It's the devil in ourselves we've got to snare, it seems to me," said Angela bitterly.

"That's enough for most of us," agreed Mrs. Mace.

"Shall we try the lake?" asked Philip Fielding. "I don't like to think of it. Of course it's all right. She has just gone for a walk."

"Let's try it," said Angela. "She'll be all right—if I can just speak to her."

*   *   *

As the sports car sped along the lonely road Angela, rigid at the wheel and staring ahead of her, said:

"We'd better say good-bye now, Phil."

He muttered from behind his upturned collar:

"Suppose we don't find her."

"Then it will be more than ever good-bye, won't it?"

"You mean that I shall feel like a murderer?"

"O my God, Phil, don't use that word! I wish I had given way before."

He did not answer.

The clear poignant sunshine of the day was gathering into the light vapour of a fair afternoon as they reached the little wood where Mrs. Mace and Hicks, the chauffeur, had thought Mrs. Fielding might be. Beyond they could see the lake, the island, the swan.

One of the hearses going from Hexham to Crompton Old Church was standing at the verge of the close trees; the heavy black shape looked ugly in the pale glow of the pure air.

"Perhaps," murmured Philip Fielding, who could not clear his mind of phantoms, "they've got the bones of Susanna Vavasour in there."

"Who's she?" asked Angela in frightened anger. "I believe you're crazy too, Philip."

The men in charge of the hearse and two woodmen were standing at the edge of the trees. Angela stopped the blue car. She peered over the wheel.

"I think that there has been an accident. I feel sick. Go and see, Phil."

"I can't. What is it? Can't you see?"

"Two of them are wet. They've got something on the grass. The same colour—a dark green dress?"

"Oh no!" cried Philip Fielding violently. They looked at each other with bitter accusation. "You are a little beast, after all," he muttered. "Why didn't you come over sooner to tell her you were clearing out."

"You don't know what you're saying," she whimpered. "Get out and see what has happened—"

"I can't. I feel as if I'd got to the end of the world—"

One of the woodmen was coming towards the car. Angela sprang out and ran towards him; she was talking incoherently.

Grace Fielding had been in the lake half an hour. One of the woodmen had seen her slip in, but it had been a while before he could find a boat and fetch her. She had been held up by a patch of reeds and alder bushes. He had shouted for his mate and between them they had carried her to the edge of the wood. They had stopped the first vehicle that had passed—it was the hearse going to Crompton Old Church to fetch the bones of Susanna Vavasour that had been exhumed that morning.

Angela leant against one of the trees. A clean white handkerchief covered the face at her feet, which rested on trails of ground ivy. Hadn't she and Philip often wished that Grace were dead? Was that what had brought a curse on all of them?

There was no room for Mrs. Fielding in the sports car, so they laid her in the dark carriage intended for another who had tried to reach the island with the three trees.

Philip Fielding was persuaded to get out of the car and walk up and down, supported either side by the strange men. He seemed to have lost the use of his limbs, for he dragged in the friendly grip like a paralytic.

He did not know that Angela was there; she was entirely effaced from his consciousness.

His mind was focused on Medlar's Farm, where a jealous woman in a dark green dress was restlessly walking up and down, in and out, searching for another companion. He thought that he could now understand what Susanna Vavasour had done, but he fumbled round the question as to what means she had employed. When he at length said, with a chuckle at his own cleverness: "Of course, Vavasour wasn't a murderer, after all, I always knew that—it was she—it was she once he'd cornered her—what did Grace say about a toad?"—they thought that the shock had unsettled his mind.

A sharp, angry cry came from the fields the other side of the road. One of the woodmen said:

"It's that fool of a boy, hurt his fingers setting rabbit traps—"

Angela looked stupidly down at her bare hands as if she expected to see them bleed, while the man in worn black said to Philip Fielding:

"I suppose, sir, I'd better go to Medlar's Farm?"

*   *   *

"Our Phantasie . . . intrudes a thousand fears, suspicions, chimeras on us . . . so many things are offensive to us, not of themselves, but out of our corrupt judgment, jealousie, suspicion, and the like; we pull these mischiefs on our own heads."
      DEMOCRITUS JUNIOR: *The Anatomy of Melancholy.*

Part Three:
Selected Appreciations

"I tried to train my character and to accumulate knowledge."
—Marjorie Bowen

This selection of tributes and remembrances brings together Marjorie Bowen's contemporary friends and colleagues and latter-day associates and critics. Novelists Rebecca West, Graham Greene, and Sally Benson discuss, respectively, Bowen's private struggles, the influence of her novel *The Viper of Milan,* and her books written as "Joseph Shearing." Journalist Gertrude Mack pays a visit to Bowen at home. Lieutenant-General F. de Bas praises Bowen's scholarship as a military historian. Historian Michael Sadleir writes about Bowen's "tales of terror." Jessica Amanda Salmonson discusses Bowen's autobiography, *The Debate Continues.* Edward Wagenknecht remembers his association with Bowen as both friend and informal collaborator. And Hilary Long pays a loving tribute to his mother.

Rose Petals, Drops of Blood

Jessica Amanda Salmonson

"As fast as the Mirthless Cosmic Jester poured misery into her, she made ink of bile to fill pages with dark visions, calamitous adventure, and cynical romances . . ."

> In 1998 Jessica Amanda Salmonson edited a volume of short stories by Marjorie Bowen, *Twilight and Other Supernatural Romances,* for Ash-Tree Press. A follow-up volume of stories was anticipated, for which she wrote the following essay. Neither the book nor the essay was published. Ms. Salmonson graciously extends her permission for the essay's inclusion here. It combines a useful and insightful overview of Bowen's autobiography, *The Debate Continues,* with her own sympathetic insights into Bowen's life and work. She refers to Bowen by her birth name, Margaret Campbell.

Though her childhood and early teen years are reported in first-person as in most autobiographies, Margaret Campbell nevertheless resorts to third person for the bulk of the rest of [*The Debate Continues*]! It is as though she were writing about a stranger whose life she has researched in detail, but for whom she has no immediate attachment. This distancing and flatness of narrative has its own power of gloominess—a report sent to us from some nether-region of deadened pain. Simultaneously, she invites us always to regard her as no less weak and quite as capable of folly as anyone around her, except in the case of an idealized companionship with an elderly physician which she seems never to have confronted for what it was, a fundamentally manic episode of emotional (if not physical; that may never be known) infidelity. Never is she vindictive in her record of the poverty and stupidity that so often surrounded her; hers is an expression of clear-sightedness of a sort seldom committed to print. *The Debate Continues* strikes me ultimately as a record of chronic depression and an unenviable if heroic sense of Duty, this from a woman aware of an unfulfilled *capacity* for more than evanescent gaiety.

Born Gabrielle Margaret Vere Campbell, 1 November 1885, in the hour following All Souls Day, on Hayling Island, Hampshire, her troubled childhood included a schedule of punishments for minor, contrived, or imagined sins of which even the brightest child could make small sense. She was frequently told she should never have been born. She was often informed that she was too tall, too plain, and too gawky, and should expect to live out her life as an old maid. Her younger sister was better treated, praised for her beauty and charm. But it was hardly a rewarding life for either child and, of the two girls, Margaret proved to be, in the long run, the sole survivor.

An education clumsily orchestrated by her astute though unstable mother was supplemented by voracious reading and self-education, her Nana's fairy tales, transient and usually inept tutors, and occasional art or theater instructors whose own lives were marked by frustration and who were constitutionally incapable of perceiving any mere child as promising. She managed somehow to make herself expert in certain adored historical epochs that were to inform her pen throughout her writing life. She even taught herself rudimentary Latin.

Little Margaret was an introspective child for survival's sake. Her mother, Josephine Elisabeth Ellis (Bowen) Campbell, made it known that she considered her daughter very dull. Her father, Vere Douglas Campbell, initially the more loving parent, was severely alcoholic and soon abandoned the family, or was tossed out by his termagant wife. Despite efforts of his brother to assist him through endless crises, he died of drunkenness and self-neglect. Shortly after publication of his daughter's first novel, his body was found on a London street with the address of his estranged wife and daughters in his pocket. By then, to Margaret, he had seemed long dead already, and she scarcely grieved, though the tragedy provided her mother refreshed opportunity for extravagant expression of life's continuing sorrow and unfairness to herself and self alone.

She, her mother, her younger sister, and their faithful if incompetent housekeeper Nana lived in abysmal poverty in a series of poor lodgings. There was rarely more than potatoes for the children to eat; some days passed with just a slice of bread for sisters to share, although their mother managed always to afford cigarettes. One of Margaret's fondest memories during these horrible times was of a landlady giving her a cucumber sandwich, an unfathomable delight in an existence empty of expectation. . . .

The plethora of thrilling *femme fatales* in Margaret's stories must, in part, reflect her darkest personal emotions and passing fantasies of redress against mother and sister, as suggested by the weird tale of embattled sisters in "The Last Bouquet." But more than this, the sensuality and *appeal* of Margaret's *femme fatales*, as in so many of her mystery novels—e.g., *The Moss Rose* (1935), which has both a corrupted heroine and a maniacal mother; and such weird stories as "Madame Spitfire" in *The Last Bouquet: Some Twilight Tales* (1933) and *Julia Roseingrave* (1933), sharing the traits of twisted intellectuality and blithe self-justification—draw upon the character of her mother, and upon her own mingled emotions of love, fear, anger, and sorrow for the prototype of her stories' most dangerous women. By contrast, those stories of abjectly victimized women—as in "The Avenging of Ann

Leete," included in the Arkham House selection *Kecksies* (1976), "The Orford Mystery" in *Old Patch's Medley* (1928), and "The Lady Clodagh" in *The Last Bouquet*—were fostered by her hard-won sense of the world's wild injustices. . . .

Still in her teens, while at Slade Art School in London, Margaret began her first novel, completed in Paris a year or two later. This tale of sinister swashbuckling adventure was the emotive historical fantasia *The Viper of Milan*. It was not quickly published, being rejected by eleven publishers because, as Margaret was informed, it was the sort of thing girls should never write. Some of these rejections included assurances that she showed promise, and advocated domestic love stories or children's books as more appropriate to her sex. When her *Viper* obtained publication in 1906, the publisher intended to pay her nothing while promoting the book (effectively it turned out) as a work of a singular precocity. This is perhaps why, even at so young an age as twenty or twenty-one, she embraced the often reprinted lie that she was born in 1888 rather than 1885, a small fudging of the truth since she *was* a teenager when the book was written, and her publisher would have her remain so a while longer.

The public loved the idea of a serious, severe teenage writer. Newspapers and magazines harassed the shy young author for interviews. . . . Margaret was too shy to appreciate the attention, nor did she relish risking her mother's jealousy. It was a biting sting for the failed playwright to be told again and again of her child's cleverness. Despite opportunities of social life among authors and publishers, Margaret held herself forever apart, struggling for quietude in that House of Commotions, in order to write additional novels that were soon to become the family's only revenues.

Margaret's authorly income was banked in her mother's name. A sort of pretense rose up, that it really was her mother's money. It was insufficient to keep a family of four (including Nana) and was badly handled besides. Her mother at once re-tired from all pretense of attempting personally to support her children and proceeded to spend her daughter's earnings with neither care nor qualm. . . .

She seemed not to mind terribly that the world reposed on her slim shoulders, though she wished that someone might once in a while express gratitude rather than envy and hostility. She knew she could have arranged their finances better if she took the funds into her own hands. Despite a reliable influx of funds, they were not better off under her mother's reckless manage-ment. Certainly no one had become happier. But Margaret dared not broach the subject for terror of her mother. The house was in physical chaos as well, but that was Nana's province, and Margaret was afraid of the old woman's witch-like countenance whenever she was riled. Her one recourse was to write more madly than before, to try to catch up with finances, vicious though that circle became.

She made an attempt at liberty, returning to Paris to live in an apartment of her own, exploring the Left Bank for inspira-tion, and still sending the majority of her income home to moth-er. But her mother followed after, clinging more to control of the income than to the daughter. With guilt as a weapon, Elisa-beth raged and wept until she won the day and brought her daughter back into the disruptive fold.

When a handsome young Sicilian began to court her, this was cause of jealousy too, as well as fear of losing the golden goose. Through her mother's machinations, the marriage was delayed and delayed, but in 1912 Margaret finally became Mrs. Zefferino Emilio Costanza. It was not for love she married, but for the chance of freedom, to pursue her dream of a domestic situation over which she had sufficient control to achieve peace and order. Eventually she and Zefferino went to Italy in pursuit of his occupation. He was an employee in an engineering and mining company, poorly paid but (he deluded himself) with prospects, and it did not take much to live comfortably in Italy. She loved Tuscany best of all. But Sicily, when emergency made it necessary to be near his family, was oppressive.

A persistent theme in her autobiography is that she did not love Zefferino. Respected and appreciated him at times, admired his good looks, treasured to some extent his devotion to her . . . but of deep romantic love there was none, not even at the start when he tenderly wooed her. He had a taste for cars and especially for motorcycles, at the time a novelty in Italy, and this troubled her since luxuries were not within their means. It did mean they were occasionally able to travel about Italy, Margaret in a motorcycle sidecar, though once they were wrecked and Margaret was some while recovering from her injuries. Business kept her husband away for weeks at a time in Florence. She never suggests he had affairs but it would certainly have been an easy option for him, and perhaps *de rigueur* for a Sicilian; and his rank jealousy of Margaret proves *he* thought fidelity an unlikely enterprise.

Zefferino, not unlike Margaret's mother, was prone to rages, so that she despaired of ever experiencing a peaceable home-life. It was perhaps normal of Sicilians, but in Tuscany his explosive temper alarmed witnesses. Wild outbursts were followed by tearful suits for forgiveness.

Margaret continued throughout this time to publish a considerable amount. They were living, however, in the beginning of their marriage, chiefly on her husband's income. Her advances and royalties continued toward the support of her mother, sister, and Nana, though this endless assistance was sent from safer distances than formerly. On one trip to England, after a long absence, she saw everything with fresh insight. She finally understood how demented their lives had been. Nana's slovenliness had worsened, her mother's lazy self-absorption had become a mania, her sister's selfishness and inertia were unabating, and their utter reliance on Margaret was as unchecked and unappreciated as ever.

Zefferino was often sick. He had a slowly, steadily murderous strain of tuberculous which physicians hoped was chronic bronchitis that warmth and fresh air could fix. There were times he seemed almost well, but these moments decreased in frequency. He eventually lost his position. He and Margaret had thereafter nothing to live on but her earnings. These were insufficient when the lion's share must still be sent toward the support of her mother and sister. Somehow she managed everything; there was no one else to even try.

Finding his prospects evaporated, reliant on a wife's income, Zefferino's self-worth was sorely battered. Margaret feared he was beginning to hate her. The more her life changed, the more it failed to change.

Forced to his native Sicily during the early months of World War I, she was not receiving much from her publishers given the political climate and could never be certain new writings would reach English destinations. For a while she could write nothing at all, for there was no money for paper and ink. Her misery in the acutely male culture of Sicily was piercing. No one knew she was the breadwinner; her in-laws had no concept of permitting her peace and privacy to write. Relatives were allowed to believe Zefferino had made some sort of fortune in England. They were more than a little angry with him for not sharing his supposed wealth. In such a masculine culture it would be grotesque for the truth to be known, had they capacity to know it.

The whole of these women's housebound, circumscribed lives was founded on ghosts of possibilities Margaret could barely grasp. They would invade her apartment at random, as though it were their own living room, then chatter among themselves, benignantly ignoring her alien presence. Even Zefferino became barbarous in this environment, withdrawing into the shadowiness of the men's society.

Ignoring her concerns, Zefferino entrusted her during illness and pregnancy to superstitious women who disapproved of physicians. When the time came, a decrepit wise woman served as midwife, a hag devoid of hygienic principle. Her expertise included a fatalistic acceptance that mothers and/or newborns do not always survive. Paramount in her body of vaunted wisdom was a conviction that should a mother touch her face during parturition, this would cause disfiguring birthmarks to appear on the newborn's face, arranged like the mother's fingertips. When Margaret amidst birth pangs committed the ghastly crime of pressing palms to face, she was held down and bound limbs to bedposts. Her pleas were disregarded in deference to the old witch's commands. Margaret gave birth thus spraddle-arm and -leg, caught in nightmarish horror attended by careless foes. They nearly killed her and she did not soon recover.

Zefferino with clumsy loyalty wished to ease her unhappiness. He agreed to go with her to England as soon as passage could be arranged. This was not easy, for Germany and England were at war, with Italy's position undecided. After a few weeks of preparation, chance arose, and they made it to England, her husband in the meantime having contrived a plan to establish himself as a poultry farmer. She had not the heart to be truthful about this idiotic gambit, so permitted their finances to be drained for the sake of a Kent farmhouse overlooking the sea.

He strove relentlessly to succeed, daily rising early, in all inclement weather, preparing chicken mash for his flock. His desire to be a good husband and good provider, for all his limitations of temperament and ability, was pathetical and poignant. The chilly, windy outcropping on which the farm was situated hastened the deterioration of his health. They could never have guessed how cold it would be even in spring. His persistent cough was their world's primary song. And in that gloomy Kent home, their daughter, five months of age, somehow contracted meningitis and plunged swiftly from rosy good health into the depths of a grave. Margaret discovered that a life of depression and gloom was nothing compared to grief for the loss of a child; and her tale of a ghost-baby in "The Blue Glove" in *The Pleasant Husband and Other Stories* (1921) projects a self-portrait for what she knew would be a lifelong sorrow. Zefferino grieved most awfully as well. Amidst his gale of mournful tears he conceived an irrational plan to exhaust every possible resource for the sake of a stained glass window commissioned for a church, to stand as a lasting memorial to their daughter. When it dawned on him that this deranged scheme was unobtainable, he caved in to his illness, and the unhappy couple abandoned the farm.

If a wicked black comedy were contrived in which ill fortune and tragedy were heaped higher and higher, then wracking illness, aspirations proven ridiculous, and a dead baby for good measure might well come into the mix. Margaret's trials outpaced even absurdist imagination. As fast as the Mirthless Cosmic Jester poured misery into her, she made ink of bile to fill pages with dark visions, calamitous adventure, and cynical romances—tales populated by innocents and villains alike ill-fated—delightsome unpleasantries to mesmerize her faithful public.

Zefferino left for the heated climate of his own country, still hoping his lungs might repair. Margaret struggled on in England, alone or with Nana as companion. She had the good sense not to live with mother and sister, whose unrepentant jealousies extended to a vulgar satisfaction that her only child had died. Wartime payments for new writings had decreased, but at least her books were wanted, and she was able to support everyone, if barely. And she was, she discovered, pregnant with a second child. This sparked a considerable hope.

War still raged when news came of Zefferino's further decline. His relatives in Sicily, fearing him contagious, refused to care for him. He went to Tuscany and over-extended his wife's income to rent a costly, out-of-the-way villa. This debilitated him completely, and he wrote pleading for her to come. Her infant was scant weeks old and she hated to leave England, let alone entrust her new son to Nana. How could she, who did not love her husband, behave with greater empathy and devotion than his blood relatives, who turned him out to die alone? As she had built duty into a high ideal, it would suffice. She rushed to him across Europe, at not inconsiderable risk. The ship that left port beside hers was torpedoed. On the trains were many suspicious that a lone woman must be an English spy pretending to have a sick husband at journey's end. A stick-thin dying man greeted her coldly. He had wanted to see his son, not her. How dare she leave the boy behind? He was never told, nor could ever quite believe, he was dying.

Wild rumors surrounded the strange couple in their isolated villa. Zefferino was an outright pariah, as though he were indeed the Plague. Margaret was outcast by association. Zefferino in pain and fear became tyrannical. She did everything to ease his days and nights as life slipped out in rasping coughs. Once-princely good looks grew steadily more cadaverous. Over a decade before her autobiographical account of these last horrific months with Zefferino, she had already fictionalized the events. *Stinging Nettles* (1923) depicts an Italian husband as a diseased wastrel whose wife selflessly nurses him into the grave, though having for him little honest affection. Earlier still, she composed a superb tale of unjust revenge, physical horror, and revulsion; "Giuditta's Wedding Night" from *Shadows of Yesterday* and one of Sir Arthur Conan Doyle's favorite stories. It reflects an appalling sense of its protagonist as an enslaved Bride of Plague.

Toward the end of it, she undertook a dalliance with her husband's final physician, a father-figure nearly twice her age. Whether this dalliance was strictly of the heart or had a physical component is uncertain. Certainly her sons do not countenance the idea that it could have been more than emotional, but their opinion is protective and filial. In her fiction, at least, women in similar circumstance behave with extreme passion. But my libertine guesses can no more be proven than her children's conservative assumptions. What she confesses autobiographically is sufficiently surprising.

This physician was a man of courageous stature, gray whiskered, grave, kind, intelligent. On their first meeting, he took her measure, saw her desperation, held her face in gentle hands, and kissed her forehead. He told her, "You cannot go on this way. You will die." For the first and only time in her life, Margaret's heart was completely won. Her unhappiness had stemmed less from enslavement to a bitter mother, then a dying husband, than from their unutterable lack of tribute for what a spectacularly good slave she was willing to make of herself; for, as she confessed in her essay included in *Myself When Young*, "I had early resolved that self-abnegation was very desirable." Now someone recognized her excellence, and she fancied the heroic doctor a vastly more pleasing master than any she had previously encountered.

In an autobiography that in general avoids all tricks of an author's trade, her treatment of the physician relies utterly on fictional methods, perhaps, as I believe, because there was nothing very realistic about her confidence in him. His was a classic seduction. He admitted from the onset that he was too old for her, and laid a groundwork that would transform even his plan to disappoint into evidence of his personal gallantry. It usually dawns on women, months or years later, how stupidly duped we can be; but Margaret in her self-imposed emotional exile, naiveté, and willingness to be abused, had only the experience of books, dreams, and sorrows. She believed in the loving, godlike gentleman with a faith that only the most deprived pagan ever can sustain.

Though she candidly reports that this man was a lifelong expert at love, she never faces the simple fact of his tender roguery, even while describing it perfectly. He had probably convinced scores of women across his years, including many another "pending widow," that each had been his only *true* love, despite his footloose history. But now he was old, and Margaret was apt to be his last conquest. Last loves are frequently second only to first loves, so I can accept, at least, that affection was not one-sided, though there seems small likelihood it could have been as all-consuming for him as for her.

Confession of a history of carelessness makes such rogues all the dearer to dazzled maidens. Margaret persuaded herself that each was the other's greatest love, predestined, sacred. She had become desperate after months lying alongside Plague; for Zefferino could only be soothed when she lay embracing him at his most revolting while she displayed no revulsion. And this Plague that was her husband possessed an increasingly monstrous ego. He held a bell in one hand, a watch in the other, and sat in a window observing her in the garden below, timing her so as to permit no more than an agreed-upon fifteen minutes liberty before ringing the bell madly to call her back. Night or day she answered that bell; he deprived her of rest, so that she grew haggard. The grotesque thoroughness of her enslavement to the never-loved was in its eerie way heroic. But it left her emotionally vulnerable.

The physician, though still possessing soldierly bearing, was in the first stages of palsy and knew he would too soon be reduced to invalidism. He made it clear he would never stay with Margaret merely to be nursed into the grave, as Zefferino was then being nursed. But at the same time he constructed fantasies for her: *if* he had not been too old for her, *if* his health had not been at risk, they would find future happiness in his villa on Lake Como, where she would bear many of his children, and he would support her from his sufficient wealth. Since she did not agree he was too old, and could not see that he was ill, she heard these fantasies as actual plans.

As he set up the rules, she must, on the one hand, never expect anything permanent; on the other hand, nothing was beyond the possible, dreams were permitted. It was, at most, a fine affair; only, she forever after regarded it as much more. As an interlude in a nearly lifelong depression, this liaison became inexpressibly glorious. The illusion he created for her was to remain with her always. In a way, it was no different than the illusions they both permitted Zefferino—that the doctor was a genius who would cure him, that Margaret was a faithful and adoring wife—but if her account is as honest as it seems, as honest as she could make it, she evidently never perceived this parallel.

She would carry with her to the grave this absurd belief in having once possessed a soulmate. I admire this author so much that I wanted her, in her autobiography, to show perception even at this moment of bright blot. She might have said, "Some would call it stupid and immoral, but I needed this illusion; life is nothing without illusion." But she lacked sufficient insight for this one thing, and it made me wonder about other claims for herself—the perfect child who won only abuse; the willing sacrifices that never earned gratitude—for sometimes indeed the strangest demons are the quiet ones who wait and observe and are easily mistaken for angels, especially by themselves.

Yet I still believe in her abject goodness, however stifled her emotions or yet sinister the inward life that poured forth into sumptuous, frightening prose. It was just that she needed to believe in an ideal mate who belonged to her alone, to none other, a man who in every way measured up to an impractical ideal of masculinity as invented for so many of her historical tales. She preferred to write in historical settings because even villainy could be reshaped as something suave and wonderful, such as could never exist nearer to her in time. It is perhaps no coincidence that Death himself is called the Last Physician, and the Devil is in many places of Europe called Doctor. Had she and her grand physician lived together, he would have broken her heart, or else she would have written that she hadn't loved that one either. But as he remained behind, memories became fertilizer for an awesome personal myth.

I find myself able to pity the tyrannical Zefferino, who in his broken way adored this most adorable and self-effacing woman. A quiet demoness can be perceived in any way a sorcerer desires, and Zefferino desired her to be in love with him. To his final hour, he believed he might recover and be forever with the woman who forgave his rages and weaknesses and was intensely devoted to him. I pity, too, her second husband, Arthur L. Long, who was not permitted Zefferino's illusions. She met and married him even before the vaunted Physician died. The Physician was by then only an ongoing series of adoring letters sent from a sickbed in Italy, the last of them dictated because his hands shook too much to hold a pen.

Once again she was eager to marry without love—she had learned nothing really. One wonders if she checked the mailbox on the way to the wedding ceremony, so that she might have something precious up her sleeve as she intoned an insincere "I do." Most grotesquely, when she planned (with the Physician) to have more children (with whomever else; Arthur as it turned out), they were to be in spirit the children of her psychic paramour, and they were to be raised to be as bold and perfect as was He.

When Zefferino died appallingly in 1916, Margaret returned to England and to her infant son, who did not remember her. She brought with her the specious plan to wed, in one year's time, the Physician awaiting her in Italy. But he soon wrote to inform her this could never be, they must never meet again, for he wanted her to remember him in the twilight of his prime, rather than as a sick old man. This news was not to change her marriage schedule, for within a year she became, instead, Mrs. Arthur L. Long.

Arthur was from the start informed, so always knew, that he was one more ingredient in her discouraging life. He was resigned to acceptance of her imaginary true love, with whom he could never hope to compete. The marriage "took," I think on the basis of her sense of duty. She continued as ever to be the chief breadwinner, for Arthur was, by his youngest son's admission, "idle & incompetent," and her situation in many ways resembled what she had previously experienced. Either she chose badly, because hastily, a man of doubtful character; or his own bitterness in not being loved drew from him an evil temper. Her weird tale "Decay" in *Seeing Life!* (1923) is a cynical commentary on the merits of marriage. . . . It gives evidence of *why* she sought so often to imbed her brighter idealism in stories of historical eras, there being so little fineness in the here-and-now.

She seems never to have overcome a tendency "to judge myself as futile, of little importance on any count" . . . Yet she had the great reward of children who truly and completely fulfilled her life's desire to be loved, appreciated, and recognized for who she was. She added, "To be secure, to be able to devote oneself to a happy home of children, to have a large family growing up about one, still seems to me an ideal existence and worth the sacrifice of everything else in the world."

With one of two children surviving from her first marriage and two more sons from the second, her responsibilities were never to abate. Leisure remained alien to her experience, but having the boys meant all her industry had purpose. Her own mother died with unhappiness unhealed—depression is often inherited— and Margaret's sister simply went away, after which Margaret supported her immediate household without hangers-on.

She had always to rush to the next money-making project and hoped Arthur would prove himself capable of catching any glaring problems before a manuscript was shipped off. As her youngest son reported in a personal correspondence, "She knew that sometimes her sentencing could be a little involved, a similar adjective used too often in close juxtaposition, and so on. This was supposed to be my father's job but he was quite useless. Thus a number of 'unclarities' could slip through."

If there is one intentional dishonesty in her self-assessments, it is in her autobiography's highly synoptic closing portion, in which she implies a blissful family life with Arthur. It would hardly have been charitable, let alone safe or wise, to have described honestly who she intended, come what may, to stick it out with for life. And until her death, she worked nonstop, with only enforced Christmas days entirely away from her work. To the end, she never lost her extraordinary ability, and her last, posthumous novel *The Man with the Scales*, emulating E. T. A. Hoffmann, is as richly imaginative and sinister & gorgeous as her first.

Graham Greene

The Lost Childhood

Graham Greene

"[She set the pattern] of perfect evil walking the world where perfect good can never walk again."

In his essay "The Lost Childhood," Graham Greene writes movingly of his first formative experiences in reading at the age of fourteen: "Perhaps it is only in childhood that books have any deep influence on our lives . . . In childhood all books are books of divination, telling us about the future, and like the fortune teller who sees a long journey in the cards or death by water they influence the future." But not even the books of Anthony Hope and H. Rider Haggard afforded Greene his greatest pleasure. He reserved that enthusiasm for The *Viper of Milan*, by someone called Marjorie Bowen. Here he found what he called his "pattern" as a writer-to-be—the pattern he describes in his memorable words, "of perfect evil walking the world where perfect good can never walk again."

But when—perhaps I was fourteen by that time—I took Miss Marjorie Bowen's *The Viper of Milan* from the library shelf, the future for better or worse really struck. From that moment I began to write. All the other possible futures slid away: the potential civil servant, the don, the clerk had to look for other incarnations. Imitation after imitation of Miss Bowen's magnifi-

Excerpt from *The Lost Childhood and Other Essays*. New York: Viking Press, 1962.

cent novel went into exercise books—stories of sixteenth-century Italy or twelfth-century England marked with enormous brutality and a despairing romanticism. It was if I had been supplied once and for all with a subject.

Why? On the surface *The Viper of Milan* is only the story of a war between Gian Galeazzo Visconti, Duke of Milan, and Mastino della Scala, Duke of Verona, told with zest and cunning and an amazing pictorial sense. Why did it creep in and colour and explain the terrible living world of the stone stairs and the never quiet dormitory? It was no good in that real world to dream that one would ever be a Sir Henry Curtis, but della Scala who at last turned from an honesty that never paid and betrayed his friends and died dishonoured and a failure even at treachery—it was easier for a child to escape behind his mask. As for Visconti, with his beauty, his patience and his genius for evil, I had watched him pass by many a time in his black Sunday suit smelling of mothballs. His name was Carter. He exercised terror from a distance like a snowcloud over the young fields. Goodness has only once found a perfect incarnation in a human body and never will again, but evil can always find a home there. Human nature is not black and white but black and grey. I read all that in *The Viper of Milan* and I looked round and I saw that it was so.

There is another theme I found there. At the end of *The Viper of Milan*—you will remember if you have once read it— comes the great scene of complete success—della Scala is dead, Ferrara, Verona, Novara, Mantua have all fallen, the messengers pour in with news of fresh victories, the whole world outside is cracking up, and Visconti sits and jokes in the wine light. I was not on the classical side or I would have discovered, I suppose, in Greek literature instead of in Miss Bowen's novel the sense of doom that lies over success—the feeling that the pendulum is about to swing. That too made sense; one looked around and saw the doomed everywhere—the champion runner who one day would sag over the tape; the head of the school who would atone, poor devil, during forty dreary undistinguished years; the scholar . . . and when success began to touch oneself too, however mildly, one could only pray that failure would not be held off for too long.

One had lived for fourteen years in a wild jungle country without a map, but now the paths had been traced and naturally one had to follow them. But I think it was Miss Bowen's apparent zest that made me want to write. One could not read her without believing that to write was to live and to enjoy, and before one had discovered one's mistake it was too late—the first book one does enjoy. Anyway, she had given me my pattern—religion might later explain it to me in other terms, but the pattern was already there—perfect evil walking the world where perfect good can never walk again, and only the pendulum ensures that after all in the end justice is done. Man is never satisfied, and often I have wished that my hand had not moved further than *King Solomon's Mines,* and that the future I had taken down from the nursery shelf had been a district office in Sierra Leone and twelve tours of malarial duty and a finishing dose of blackwater fever when the danger of retirement approached. What is the good of wishing? The books are always there, the moment of crisis waits, and now our children in their turn are taking down the future and opening the pages.

Marjorie Bowen: A Triple Personality

Gertrude Mack

"A gentle-voiced woman, with a halo of copper bright hair, came in answer to my ring at her Hyde Park flat . . ."

This account of Marjorie Bowen at home was published in 1932, at the time that the pseudonyms "George Preedy" and "Robert Paye" were first attracting attention in the literary world. (Another pseudonym, "John Winch," was also being employed at this time with the historical novel, *Idler's Gate,* but there is no reference to it here.) Included are some interesting details of the author's education of her children, her methods of writing, and her negative opinions of modern "psychoanalytical" novels. This last is especially interesting, inasmuch as her series of "true-crime" psychological dramatizations under yet another the Shearing sobriquet, "Joseph Shearing," would soon debut with the novels *Moss Rose, Forget-Me-Not,* and *Album Leaf.*

Readers of romance will be familiar with the writings of Marjorie Bowen. It is a name which swung wide and high in publicity when she, as a girl of 16, wrote *The Viper of Milan.* She was living in Paris at the time, studying painting and subsisting on crusts and ambition.

For 20 years she wrote under the name of Marjorie Bowen. Her brain teemed with ideas, she was an intense student of history, and her pen covered a wide field—novels, histories, short

---

Sydney Morning Herald (27 August 1932): 5.

stories. She could scarcely write quickly enough to clear the extraordinary storehouse of her mind.

Then one day reviewers sat up and shouted (with their pens) paeans of praise over a brilliant new writer, George Preedy—"a writer of genius," they called him. His book, *General Crack,* set the literary world talking, speculating, and asking where the young man was to be seen. The powerful writing showed fresh vigour of young manhood. In its breadth of canvas and splendor of colouring *General Crack* was compared with *Jew Suss* but, said the critics, it is a finer work. The shouts of praise penetrated to America and reached the ear of John Barrymore. He read the book. "I must act that part," he decided; "it was made for me." So *General Crack* was dramatized into one shape and filmed into another (far removed from the original book), and still gossip writers could get no "pars" about "George Preedy." After *General Crack* came *The Rocklitz* by the same writer. "A book of unforgettable powers," wrote one; "a work of genius," declared another; reviewers were delighted with their "find." *Bagatelle* and *Captain Banner* followed, and George Preedy was established as a great historical novelist.

No contemporary writer has scored a more remarkable success. Not one penetrating eye of experienced critics discerned that it was the hand of Marjorie Bowen who held the pen for George Preedy. The gentle, modest woman (I would almost say shy) had gained what she set out for—to interest critics and readers in the quality of her writing rather than her name.

Quietly amused by the game of hide-and-seek, Marjorie Bowen enjoyed yet another triumph when, under the name of Robert Paye, *The Devil's Jig* was published. It brought forth spirited reviews on the exciting story of 18th century London, which was accounted uncommonly artistic for a first novel, in its simplicity of style and construction. Again, no one suspects the real creator of the book.

For two years the secret of "George Preedy" was kept. A delightful experience—to sit back and listen to the clamour of praise and speculation about a writer who is oneself! The disclosure came at a theatrical rehearsal of *The Rocklitz* (which had been dramatized from the novel). Some reporters were present, and they had sudden illumination about the author when they saw Marjorie Bowen in consultation with the producer. With a whoop (if a silent one), they pounced upon her and said, "You are George Preedy." She would not deny it, though preferring to remain incognito. But the reporters had made a coup—and so the truth came out. There is no vanity in the personality of Marjorie Bowen.

A gentle-voiced woman, with a halo of copper bright hair, came in answer to my ring at her Hyde Park flat, and Marjorie Bowen, George Preedy, and Robert Paye (all of whom for the moment were Mrs. Arthur Long) greeted me. Self-importance was far removed from this simple-mannered woman; so far removed, indeed, that here in England she answered her own door-bell. She had been busy on a large piece of embroidery. The work, carried out from a William Morris design, was exquisite. I remembered similar needlework at the Society of Women Artists' Exhibition, and to my question Mrs. Long admitted that the embroidery I had seen was her work.

Mrs. Long has three sons—one at St. Paul's, one at Westminster, and the youngest at Colet Court. He has lately begun his schooldays, she told me.

"They had lessons at home with me until eight years of age—I think eight years is young enough for a child to begin school life—"

"Do you mean that you, yourself, gave them daily lessons?"

"Yes," she said simply. "I was their morning governess—I taught them to read and write and to know something of history—"

"English history?" I asked.

"More of world history than English history."

Mrs. Long told me she had never been to school herself. An occasional governess strayed through her child days, but reading and story writing and battling with poverty had been her teachers. Before she was fourteen, she had written a full-sized novel.

"I had an unsettled childhood," she explained; "my mother was Moravian and something of a Bohemian. She liked to move from place to place—our world was of artists and writers and actors—an ever-shifting world. It was a feverish kind of life—I did not like it, and I want my children to enjoy a sense of stability in home life."

Her latest book, *Violante: Circe and Ermine* [as by George Preedy] is now in press. The story is set in Toulouse in the days of the Troubadours of the 17th century, and in the opinion of her publishers, it is the most fascinating book she has written.

Mrs. Long's method of working is interesting. She has an ediphone in the room where she works, and to it she tells her story aloud. The tale unfolds from her brain as steadily as though she were reading it from a written page. When the story is told, she transcribes it to paper, developing and colouring characters and scenes. She finds the ediphone an inspiring helper. Listening to music frees her mind, she says. It was while hearing Beethoven's *Lenore Overture* that George Preedy's powerful drama, *Captain Banner*, took form in her mind.

Modern novels of pseudo psycho-analysis do not attract her. "I don't like the cynicism, the sense of futility in living that some of our cleverest writers express—I find them depressing."

Letter to Marjorie Bowen upon the Publication of *The Debate Continues*, 1939

Rebecca West

"It is wonderful for you to have developed your art in such adverse circumstances."

There are several striking parallels in the life and work of Marjorie Bowen and Rebecca West (1892–1983)—an abusive childhood, conflicts between motherhood and career, interests in the interface of Christian and Eastern faiths, the interface of femininity and power, interests in the occult, and the adoption of pseudonyms ("Rebecca West" was the pseudonym of Cicily Isabel Fairfield). West herself acknowledges some of these parallels in the following letter, which address Bowen by her birth name. This letter has never before appeared in print.

Old Possingworth Manor
Sussex
1939
Dear Margaret Campbell,

I have always admired your work so greatly—I think "Love" one of the best stories ever written—that I ordered your autobiography with a great deal of excited interest.[1] I didn't expect to

---

1. Bowen's story "Love" is a nocturnal, rain-swept tale of seduction, betrayal, and murder (not necessarily in that order). It first appeared in *Curious Happenings* (1917) and was reprinted in *Fond Fancy & Other Stories* (1928). It contains these memorable words from the villainous

be so much moved. I don't mean only that it is wonderful for you to have developed your art in such adverse circumstances. I mean also that you have had the courage to admit that you have been unhappy and have been the victim of continuous misfortune. The world is more hostile to such admissions than to any confession of guilt. You have to pretend that you've never been unlucky and that people have not been cruel, for no other reason that that the world is too ungenerous to like feeling pity.

I confess with shame that I thought you must lead a sheltered life because you were able to get on with your work. I realize it was simply that you had more "character" than I had. I must explain that my early life was something like yours—my father did not drink but was a gambler and wanderer, my mother was a better manager than yours but was intensely neurotic, and my home was as unendingly restless and torturing to the nerves as yours. I had thrown in a rich aunt who was a monster of evil (a morphine maniac, it was afterward found out) and poisoned everybody's life with horrible suggestions. When at nineteen I realized I would go mad if I didn't get away, I went straight out of the frying-pan into the fire, for I was betrayed into a position which was absolutely alien for me by the wickedness of an older woman. Thereafter, I had a ghastly life which went on for years. I sympathized so much with your financial difficulties—when, in my twenties, I was making over a thousand a year, I had not money enough left over to buy a decent dress, and I never had a holiday till I was over thirty. But the worst of it was that one didn't dare tell anybody or complain, for if one did one was met by such an appalling lack of sympathy. I wonder if you ever read Collette's story of her early life—it has something of the same atmosphere.

Lord Mulgrave to the heroine: "A pity that you did not ruin yourself for a better man than my brother."

Rebecca West

I thought the writing of the chapters about the Villa where your husband died a marvellous feat of evocation. It is difficult to describe happiness, but you have given it real placid ecstasy.

I hope you don't think this an intrusive letter. I was really so moved by your book that I could not help writing some of the things that it brought to mind.

I am yours, Cicily Andrews (Rebecca West)

[P.S.] I also had a Nana! Scotch and a sentimental humbug. I had to send her to New Zealand to get rid of her.

Mystery and Crime

Sally Benson

". . . underneath the surface of this pool of prettiness lie the weeds rooted deep in the soft mud, while myrtle creeps along the banks."

Critic and screenwriter (*Shadow of a Doubt, Meet Me in St. Louis*) Sally Benson published this essay before the identity of "Joseph Shearing" was revealed to belong to Marjorie Bowen. That revelation would come only a few months later. It serves us as a canny introduction to the true-crime novels Bowen wrote under the Shearing name, many of which were yet to be published. Benson makes no mention of her film adaptation of the Rachel Field novel starring Bette Davis that had been released a few months before. Her comment that *The Golden Violet* had not been published in America was soon to be remedied, when it appeared two years later under the imprimatur of The Readers Club. Her general assessment of the Shearing novels is astute, i.e., that underneath their "voluptuously refined surfaces" we find "weeds rooted deep in the soft mud . . . with a strong, red thread of murder."

A few years ago, when a book called *All This, and Heaven Too,* by Rachel Field, was published, there was a threatening sound of off-stage noises made by a select group of extras, numbering perhaps about two thousand. Their complaint was that the story of the Duc de Praslin, who murdered his wife, had been done before, and done superbly, by an English writer who signed himself "Joseph Shearing." The book, published in this country in 1932 and titled *Lucile Cléry: A Woman of Intrigue,* had already made its debut in England under the title *Forget-Me-Not.* The comparatively few

---

New Yorker (10 May 1941): 86–92.

people who read it were incoherent in their praise of it, but it did not sell. Other Shearing books followed: *The Spider in the Cup* (in England called *Album Leaf*), a story based on an early-nineteenth-century crime; *Moss Rose,* a dainty title for a novel based on the Jack the Ripper murders; *The Angel of the Assassination,* the tragedy of Charlotte Corday; *The Lady and the Arsenic,* a scholarly and grimly told tale of the life and death of Marie Cappelle, Madame LaFarge; *The Golden Violet,* a charming story of a lady novelist of the nineteenth century who discovers that guns really go off when one presses that little trigger.

For some reason, the last two books were not published in the United States, and the small group of Shearing addicts had to wait until 1939, when his *Blanche Fury,* a novel of romance and murder, beautifully written and with a conclusion that is masterly, was published. *Aunt Beardie*, one of the weakest of the Shearing books, came next, and now *The Crime of Laura Sarelle* appears.

This book follows the Shearing pattern, a pattern worth following, and is based upon an actual eighteenth-century crime. Laura Sarelle and her brother, Sir Theodosius, inherit Leppard Hall, a gloomy old manor house, near which flows the river Avon. In the dining room of Leppard Hall hang two portraits, of a man and a woman. The woman, painted in a gown of primrose silk, holding in her hands a laurel spray, was another Laura Sarelle, who died in 1784; the man, whose name is unknown, died on the gallows. There was, young Laura Sarelle learns, some stupid story about them—a mistake with a sleeping draught, an inquest. The mists that envelop the Avon close down on young Laura Sarelle, and she is haunted by the sixty-year-old mystery. The evil of the past lives on in Leppard Hall and in the mind of Laura Sarelle. She discovers a closet off one of the finest rooms in the Hall. It has been arranged as a distillery, and Laura learns how to distill perfumes and essences of roses and carnations; she also learns to distill an essence from the leaves that grow on a graceful shrub known as the Poet's Laurel.

There is a mounting horror in this book of the romance of Laura Sarelle and Lucius Delaunay, a young man of a noble house and no money. There is tragedy in the lives of Harry Mostyn, Laura's fiancée; of Sir Theo, her brother, who is absorbed in his translations from the *Enchiridion Epictete* of Arrian; and of Mrs. Sylk, Laura's slavish and distracted companion.[1] There are many adjectives to describe this book, adjectives that apply to all of Mr. Shearing's books: evil, sinister, ghostly, strange, baleful, terrible, relentless, and malevolent. But these words seem pallid. Such experts in murder as Edmund Pearson and the former Scotch barrister William Roughead have declared openly that the Shearing novels are the best of their kind published today.

Mr. Shearing speaks of one of his novels as a biography in the form of a novelette, "such a tale as our grandparents might have read in the pages of *The Family Herald*." He adds, "When all of this vast amount of material is selected, sifted, arranged so as to form a coherent story, it shapes itself, fact as it is, into a *feuilleton* of the most lurid and tawdry description . . . You may not believe in these people, but you are forced to admit that once they existed; you may refuse to credit these events, but you must acknowledge that they once took place."

He seems fascinated by the nineteenth-century heroine, "a noble and innocent victim." He knows that she is a pathological liar, a dweller in fantasy, and that she has enormous erotic sensibility. He writes that the romantic ideal of that period was a lazy life, full of costly luxuries, deliciously agitated by love affairs, voluptuously refined, relieved by the violent drama of evil, jealously, quarrels, death, murder, adorned with poetry, music, and all that was soothing to the senses. At times the reader of his books is almost disconcerted by the pleasant chitchat of the dialogue, the bell ropes of lilac silk, the dresses of dark-and-light-blue striped taffeta, the little velvet jackets of prune color with fringes of the same hue, the hats, with their ribbons floating at the back, poised sideways on smooth brows. Yet underneath the surface of this pool of pret-

---

1. The *Enchiridion* or *Handbook of Epictetus* is a short manual of Stoic ethical advice compiled by Arrian, a second-century C.E. disciple of the Greek philosopher Epictetus.

tiness lie the weeds rooted deep in the soft mud, while myrtle creeps along the banks. Mr. Shearing is adept at stitching together his swooning heroines, his young baronets, his flickering candles in their tall sconces, his hothouse fruits in high silver-gilt epergnes with a strong, red thread of murder. Mr. Shearing is a painstaking researcher, a superb writer, a careful technician, and a master of horror. There is no one else quite like him.

Marjorie Bowen's
Historical Reconstructions

Lieutenant-General F. de Bas[1]

"She leads her sea-fights as an expert admiral; and her battles prove her to be a skillful general."

Although his name may not be as remembered today as the others in this section of Appreciations, Lt. General François de Bas (10 September 1840–22 February 1931) was a Dutch general and an esteemed military historian who founded the Military-History Section of the Dutch General Staff. Writing in his preface to a collection of excerpts from Marjorie Bowen's historical novels about military leaders and their battle campaigns—including William of Orange and the capture of Namur, Peter the Great's victory over Charles XII of Sweden, and Don Juan of Austria's victory over the Turks in the Gulf of Lepanto—de Bas admires Bowen's research skills and historical reconstructions and declares that she "leads her sea-fights as an expert admiral; and her battles prove her to be a skillful general." The novels discussed here were all written before Bowen had reached her thirty-fifth birthday and remind us of the celebrity she enjoyed in her time as a historical novelist.

---

1. From Marjorie Bowen, *Affairs of Men: Being Some Accounts and Impressions of the Endeavours of Great Men, the Results of Their Efforts and Their Destinies* (London: Heath Cranton, 1921). The novels discussed here are, in order, *A Knight of Spain* (1913), *Kings at Arms* (1918), *Prince and Heretic* (1914), *Defender of the Faith* (1911), *God and the King* (1911), *Quest for Glory* (1912), *The Governor of England* (1913).

According to legend lore, the spirits of the departed return to the earth on the Eve of All-Hallows, and for a short spell endow those born at the time with extraordinary talents and faculties.

"Marjorie Bowen," the gifted writer of these following scenes of history, born a Hallow-een child, certainly was heralded into this world by many great spirits of the past. The variety of her talents and capacities, and the results of her works, would suggest the presence of a few of the great forces of her art. The characters and scenes she so vividly depicts undoubtedly show some remarkable insight into the past, which seems almost inexplicable.

Her works glow with portraiture and fine detailed description of men and their actions, their manners and behavior, the scenes in which they played their part in the world's history. All this is rich in colour, as if painted by a master hand. Being an artist of no mean talent, as well as a born writer, together with the faculties of a soldier and tactician, she combines pen, brush and sword, which explains the secret of her magisterial literary creations. She leads her sea-fights as an expert admiral; and her battles prove her to be a skillful general.

The record of the sea-battle of Lepanto (Navpaktos) on the 7th of October, 1571, is particularly striking, being the last encounter on a large scale between great fleets of galleys—two hundred and seventy-seven Turkish, manned with one hundred and twenty thousand troops, against two hundred and eight Spanish-Italian galleys with one hundred and eighty thousand troops. The blow, given by Don Juan of Austria and the Italian Republics to the naval power of Pasha Ali and Mahomet Scirocco, successfully combined to avert the ruin of Christendom.

Solebay on the 7th of June, 1672, is remarkably described. The narrator seems to be standing near Admiral de Ruyter, or by the chair from which Ruard Cornelius de Witt directed the bloody fight: she records as an absolute eye-witness the fight between the Duke of York's Fleet and the three squadrons of the Dutch Armament.

At Mooker Heyde on the Maas in the Low Countries, 1574, where Don Sancho d'Avila fought against Count Louis of Nassau and his younger brother Henry, she proves her tactical value by giving a *"precis ordre de bataille"* of both forces.

At St. Denis, 14th of August, 1678, she gives yet another proof of strategic conception, describing amidst the smoke of cannon and musket the positions of Monsieur de Luxembourg and of the Dutch troops, following up the engagements even till dark, when the discouraged French withdrew, closely pursued by the allied troops under Prince William III. of Orange.

She depicts with exactness the capture of Namur in 1695 by the same Prince (since 1688 King of Great Britain), being leader of the allied armies against Louis XIV. of France, who had endeavoured to make impregnable the ancient hill of the citadel, once destroyed by Julius Caesar.

We witness Peter the Great's victory over Charles XII of Sweden at Poltava (June 27th, 1709) with keen interest and follow the campaign with eagerness.

With plastic realism the author describes during the wars of the Austrian succession in December, 1742, Marshall Belle-Isle's retreat from Prague in Bohemia to Eger in Silesia. *The Quest of Glory,* from which this is taken, is a book written with such intensity of feeling and such beauty of conception that it will prove to be one of England's classics.

Myself being a cavalry-officer seem to ride on the battlefields of Naseby and Preston, with Oliver Cromwell in command of his Ironsides, as prompt as King Gustavus Adolphus, as ardent as Condé, and as precise as Turenne. A great leader of horse, he shares with Frederick the Great the credit of having laid the foundations of modern cavalry tactics.

The description of Monongahela and the storming of Trenton in the United States of North America inspire us with equal interest and enthusiasm.

Never since Motley's *Rise of the Dutch Republic* has any author written about the Golden Age of the House of Orange-Nassau like "Marjorie Bowen." Her two volumes on William the Silent and the trilogy dealing with Prince William III. of Orange, King of Great Britain, have raised an enthusiastic admiration for the author throughout the whole of the Netherlands and its colonies. These works are of great educational value and are used in the various Dutch institutions and public schools.

Real beauty is inspiring, and these vivid descriptions of sea and land-fights are only part of "Marjorie Bowen's" remarkable books; but we wish to especially point them out as having inspired Holland's greatest modern painter of military subjects, Hoynck van Papendrecht, to illustrate them in his masterful way . . . I need hardly say how great is the measure of my own country's appreciation of this author's work, both dealing with our own history and that of the other nations of Europe.

The romances from her pen are of great beauty, and, in contrast to the historical works, are indeed remarkable.

England is favoured with so fine a writer and is fortunate to have such an adornment to its already splendid literature.

Bowen, Preedy, Shearing & Co.:
A Note in Memory

Edward Wagenknecht

"She poured [her stories] forth with such unceasing, apparently effortless prodigality that one always seemed in the presence of some great natural force that must continue to flow forever."

Edward Wagenknecht (1900–2004) has been described as the last surviving great scholar bookman to be born at the end of the Victorian era. Among his many enthusiasms was his lifelong interest in Marjorie Bowen, whose work he supported as a friend, critic, and sometime agent. In the following essay, written just a few years after Bowen's death, he savors her humanity ("She was so good a woman that to know her even slightly was to think better of human nature") and points up her enigmas ("I was never able to believe that she quite understood herself"). He refers to the author by her name from her second marriage, Gabrielle Long.[1]

Boston University Studies in English 3 (Autumn 1957): 181–89.

1. The interested reader is directed to several more of Wagenknecht's studies of Marjorie Bowen: "The Amazing Mrs. Long," *New York Times Book Review* (2 May 1943): 2, 22–23; "Hair-Raising Narrative Is Masterpiece," *New York Herald Tribune* (18 July 1948): n.p.; and the long essay included in his *Seven Masters of Supernatural Fiction* (Westport, CT: Greenwood Press, 1991), 150–81. See also his recollections of his association with Bowen that are included in his memoir, *As Far as Yesterday* (Norman: University of Oklahoma Press, 1968), 192–98. His correspondence with Bowen, 1938–52, is among the Edward Wagenknecht Papers, Gotlieb Center, Boston University.

The death in London, two days before Christmas in the year 1952, of the lady known to the census taker as Gabrielle Margaret Vere Campbell Long robbed the English-speaking world of one of the most gifted and amazingly fertile storytellers that our time has known. I suppose that when an author who has produced some 150 books dies at the age of sixty-seven one does not ordinarily make much or a point of the unwritten books that one has lost. But it was impossible for at least one of her readers to avoid this sense of deprivation, along with others, in connection with Marjorie Bowen (as I generally thought of her), for to me her novels were a source of exhaustless and unfailing delight, and she poured them forth with such unceasing, apparently effortless prodigality that one always seemed in the presence of some great natural force that must continue to flow forever.

I have never ceased to marvel at how little appreciated she has been. How can anyone who has written so much manage to escape the notice of so many people? In this country most readers seem to know only the crime stories which she published late in her career under the name of Joseph Shearing, and when I search for the seventeen or eighteen Marjorie Bowen novels which my own collection still lacks, I am unfailingly presented with *The Hotel* or *The Death of the Heart,* by the excellent Elizabeth Bowen, since surely *this* must be the writer I am looking for! Hugh Walpole called Marjorie Bowen the greatest historical novelist England had produced in a generation; she was praised enthusiastically by Walter de la Mare, Compton Mackenzie, William Roughead, and other good judges; she collected as a matter of course reviews for which any writer in his senses would give his eyeteeth. At the very beginning of her career, she got off to an excellent start in America under the warm sponsorship of no less a writer than Mark Twain, to whom, in gratitude, she dedicated her third novel, *The Master of Stair.* Of critical evaluation of her work as a whole there has, however, so far been much less than she deserves. The contemporary novel must indeed be rich in talent if we can afford to overlook such a writer as this. Only where, one wonders, is it keeping itself?

I have spoken of Mrs. Long as a storyteller, and I do not write disparagingly; neither do I offer the phrase as a comprehensive or all-inclusive designation of her work. She did not neglect characterization; the backgrounds in her historical novels are rich, accurate, and based on wide and scholarly knowledge; she knew too that a work of fiction is the expression of an author's and a civilization's sense of values. Few writers since Wilkie Collins have come within hailing distance of her as a creator of "atmospheres" in fiction, and this is often of a weird or sinister variety, for she was, among so many other things, one of our best writers of stories of the supernatural. In one special technical device I know no writer who has ever surpassed her: she knew how to embody the whole spirit of a story in an object or a symbol, which would thereupon proceed to brood over her terrain like a malevolent, implacable god. Essentially, however, she always remembered something which a great many of her contemporaries forgot—and their forgetting threatens the future of the novel itself—she always remembered that prose fiction is a branch of *narrative art,* and that if it fails as a story, it will fail as fiction, no matter how brilliantly it may succeed as sociology or psychography or something else. From the beginning of her career to the end, she was never ashamed to enthrall the reader's imagination or to supply him with "a tale that holdeth children from play or old men from the chimney corner."

Edward Wagenknecht

That, no doubt, is one reason why she is neglected. She was an abnormally sensitive woman who did not enjoy the times in which her lot was cast, though being also an abnormally strong one, she voluntarily took upon herself not only her own share of their burden but several times that share. As a writer, however, she had no desire to chronicle either the horrors or the infidelities of our days; instead, she preferred to use her tireless imagination to create a world that was more to her liking. There are no "trends" to be studied in her novels. Fiction to her was not sugar-coated sociology; it was an art. If you would read her, you must read her as an artist; the significance of her pages rests within themselves and not in any references they may contain to that which lies outside.

Her range as a writer was very wide. She experimented endlessly, writing, for example, every conceivable kind of historical novel that can be written. She was Marjorie Bowen; she was George R. Preedy; she was Joseph Shearing. And both Preedy and Shearing won their spurs unaided before anybody knew that either was to be identified with the other or with Marjorie Bowen.

She once wrote a fiercely honest autobiography called *The Debate Continues*. There are sensational things in this book, but when I call it a fiercely honest autobiography, I do not wish to imply that it was in the least like Isadora Duncan's autobiography, for such books are less honest than exhibitionistic. Isadora set a fashion for "true confessions" in modern autobiographical writing, but in reading the books which followed in her train we need to remember that hypocrites do not always try to make themselves seem better than they are; sometimes they take up currently-fashionable sins so that they may appear worse. You may be willing to confess sexual delinquencies which a Victorian could never have revealed, but are you willing to set down the humiliating account of the last time you made a fool of yourself? Of how somebody slighted you in a painful way? In the Isadora sense, Mrs. Long had nothing to reveal. But, as Middleton Murry once expressed it in another connection, she made a holocaust of her whole life and came as close as a human being can come to painting an unprejudiced picture of herself; this she did neither for self-aggrandizement nor for self-denigration but simply to enlarge the world's knowledge of human nature. And her over-all description of herself in this volume is "a woman who earned her living by writing fiction—with occasional essays in that kind of history deplored by historians . . ."

If you write to earn your living, you are not always at your best; Mrs. Long, accordingly, left it to the reader to do some of the sorting which more fastidious writers do for him. Her reputation has suffered on this account, much as Trollope's suffered long ago. Yet I must say that I did not always agree with her evaluations of her books; some of the "potboilers" that she disliked most seemed to me to have more of her essential quality in them than did some of the works with which she had taken more pains. Neither do I believe, as many do, that her work would have been better in quality if she had written less, for writers of her kind must create freely and easily or else they cannot create at all. It is astonishing that a human being who possessed such exhaustless patience in the business of living should have had so little patience as an artist. Mrs. Long was so good a woman that to know her even slightly was to think better of human nature. Her loyalties were absolute and unquestioning, her tolerant understanding vast and overwhelming. But her attitude toward art was very much like Sir Walter Scott's, and there is no denying that she was often unpardonably careless in matters of detail. It was the large design that interested her, the broad imaginative conception, the great sweep of the brush. She had no patience to search out the *mot juste;* indeed, she could hardly bear to read her proofs. I do not believe that such a book as Virginia Woolf's *To the Lighthouse* was at all beyond the range of her talents, but her temperament being what it was, she could not possibly have written it. She professed indeed to think meanly of her work, but though I know she was completely honest about this, I was never able to believe that she quite understood herself. She was much too earnest a woman to devote her life to something she did not seriously believe in, and had she not known the value of her work she could never have been so grateful for appreciation as she always was. The real difficulty, I believe, was that she had never been able to satisfy herself: there was always a gap between her glorious dream and the embodiment she had been able to achieve for it. Once her creative impulse had exhausted itself and the book was done, she had, therefore, very little interest in it.

There were other contradictions in Mrs. Long also. She had a wildly romantic temperament, but her principles and conduct might have been approved by the strictest classicist. Her spirit was deeply religious; her "views" were, in some aspects, "rationalistic." She was one of the kindest women who ever lived; yet much of her work bears a deceptively "hard" surface. There are some books in which she has hardly created a sympathetic character, and even some of the historical personages of whom she has written—Lady Hamilton, for example, Mary Queen of Scots, and even in a measure, John Wesley—have been most unsympathetically portrayed.

Here again, though I have not always agreed with her judgments in individual cases, I am confident that it would be a great mistake to attribute any of this to what we sometimes call "debunking" tendencies, to a desire to degrade human nature. Indeed, it was quite the opposite to this tendency that was in operation. Mrs. Long's vision of human nature was so high that when she wrote of a human being, it was impossible for her to do other than apply the highest possible standards to him and to report her findings without fear or favor if she believed that he fell short. To do less than this would have been to trifle with truth. As for her crime stories, though they often dealt with very sordid matters indeed, she never handled them in a sordid manner. It would be idle to pretend that her love of drama did not make this kind of literary material attractive to her, but her mysteries are not "whodunits"; neither did she ever exploit evil for evil's sake. Extreme situations bring out extreme tendencies in human nature, and it was here that her interest lay. And if she sometimes attacked, it must be remembered that she sometimes rehabilitated also. She rehabilitated Mrs. Maybrick, for example, in *Airing in a Closed Carriage*.[1] At the very end of her career, one of her very few attempts to handle an American theme, *To Bed at Noon*, deals with the old subject of the Kentucky Tragedy. I am proud to think that I am "the only begetter" of this book, for it was I who suggested the subject to Mrs. Long, and she did me the honor to dedicate the novel to me. In writing it, however, she completely transformed the sordid character and motives of the actual participants in this notorious murder case and conceived her personages on a scale and plane of being much more congenial to her own idealistic mind.

This paper is not a critical study of Mrs. Long's work (although such a study greatly needs to be made); it is simply a

---

1. *Airing in a Closed Carriage* (1943) was based on a much-debated murder trial in England in 1889. Florence Maybrick was accused of the arsenic poisoning of her husband James. She was tried and sentenced to death by a judge, who was later found to be insane. Her sentence was commuted and after ten years she was released, after which she disappeared.

frankly personal note printed by way of prelude to an item of bibliography. It is not necessary, therefore, that I should here discuss individual books by Mrs. Long. Her trilogy about William III—*I Will Maintain, God and the King,* and *Defender of the Faith*—has always been regarded as one of her most substantial achievements. Different aspects of the Renaissance are considered in the very dissimilar kind of trilogy which comprises *The Golden Roof, The Triumphant Beast,* and *Trumpets at Rome*; while *God and the Wedding Dress, Mr. Tyler's Saints,* and *The Circle in the Water* concern the religious life of seventeenth-century England. But if I go much beyond these, I merely list my personal preferences, and I lack the space to support such choices here.

Marjorie Bowen's Tales of Terror

Michael Sadleir

"Even in her most venomous conflicts between unforgiving jealousies or cheated ambitions, she seldom fails to sound a note of compassion."

The last published volume of Marjorie Bowen's short stories to appear in her lifetime under her name was *The Bishop of Hell,* in 1949. Writing in the foreword, Michael Sadleir locates Bowen's terrors not in the conventional ghosting of the M. R. James tradition, but in her "massing together of human wickedness and frailty." Sadleir (1888–1957) was an English literary man of letters who specialized in nineteenth-century English Gothic fiction and was president of the Bibliographical Society in 1944–46. His best-known novels, *Fanny by Gaslight* (1940) and *Forlorn Sunset* (1947), explored the Victorian London underworld. The circumstances under which he came to write the following introduction are unknown, and it was not reprinted in a 2006 paperback edition, for which Hilary Long wrote an introduction and biographical note.

It is a privilege, in a Foreword to this volume of selected short stories, to salute in Marjorie Bowen an outstanding writer of what—for want of a better term—may be called "Tales of Terror" . . . . Marjorie Bowen, artist in the macabre, has paid penalty—in terms of literary recognition—for having been driven to do too many other things too often.

Marjorie Bowen's mastery of the ghostly tale is best revealed in her collection The Last Bouquet (1933), *from which many stories were culled into later collections, such as* The Bishop of Hell.

The Bishop of Hell, *first edition cover illustration*

A further misfortune is that the comparatively small proportion of her output designed primarily for her private satisfaction rather than for the market should be of a kind which, having fallen into disuse, has also fallen out of fashion. Perhaps *The Bishop of Hell,* which represents her own choice of Bowen-for-Bowen's sake, may restore to favour the peculiar species of romantic horror which distinguishes the true Tale of Terror.

A century and a half ago the Tale of Terror was as popular a form of diversion reading as is the murder-book today. Admittedly, the great majority of "horrid" stories of the late eighteenth and early nineteenth centuries are, to modern taste, so exaggerated, so inept and so crude, as to be unreadable (and who shall say that a hundred years hence our contemporary crime-novels will fare better?). But even the most absurd of them put a distinctive interpretation on their job of making the flesh creep—an interpretation revived, at intervals during the last thirty years and in an up-to-date form, by Marjorie Bowen and by her alone.

A Tale of Terror is not a ghost story, although it may deal in the supernatural. It is not a crime story, although it may pivot on a crime. It is not "Grand Guignol," although more than one Bowen story has what James Agate admirably described as "panoplied stresses," as well as the final horrific twist which we associate with this peculiarly French interpretation of the harmless sounding "puppet show." It is a deliberate massing together of human wickedness and frailty, of forlorn landscape, of somber furnishings, of desolate weather or of the menace of storm, which devil's brew is then administered to the reader in such a way as to provoke a gasp of fascinated horror, as though for one moment he had peered over the edge of a sudden fissure in his path and looked down into Hell.

It will be said (and rightly) that other story-tellers besides Marjorie Bowen have employed more than one of these ingredients of terror to achieve their desired effects. What qualities are hers, which give to the tales in this book (and to a few others whose absence we regret) their especial flavour?

Foremost is her shattering realization of the degrees of hatred possible between human beings bound together by self-interest, by blood, or by dead love. Husband and wife, brother and sister, parent and child, friend and life-long friend . . . in all such relationships she is ruthlessly conscious of the bitterness, jealousy, and cruelty which intimacy, once gone awry, can so tragically arouse. In the *Fair Hair of Ambrosine* we have rivalry in love under a cloak of loyal friendship; in *The Housekeeper* and *Florence Flannery* the nagging misery of a threadbare marriage; in *John Proudie* and *Scoured Silk* the horrors of revenge, taken in jealousy or to punish an old sin. . . .

Further individual characteristics of this teller of tales are her awareness and use of period-trappings. These she employs quite differently from that master of the ghost story—M. R. James. He, with a scholar's knowledge of manners, superstitions, and relics of the past, sets a tale of modern haunting against a background of ancient violence or (as for example in "The Mezzotint" and "The Doll's House") shows a demoniac possession of long ago still active and able to reveal itself to incautious archaeologists of the present day. In Marjorie Bowen's stories—whether of the seventeenth, eighteenth or nineteenth centuries—the tragic dramas are played out in their proper settings. "Period" is integrated; and further, being more of a literary artist than James ever pretended to be, she seldom permits such relapse of tension and atmosphere as frequently occurs—even in the best "stories of an antiquary"—when the author interpolates commonplace modern conversation or introduces would-be humorous cockney or rustic dialect. Every Bowen interior is described in detail and correctly—the billowing curtains, the uneasy portraits on the wall, the costumes alike of men and women all have a share in the accumulating menace of the tale. Nor is nature excused from playing her part. Outside the weather rages in the streets; autumn dies in wind and rain across a haunted marsh; in the garden of a dilapidated house the laurels rattle and creak about a space of rank grass patched with nettles. Out of doors, therefore, no less than within, suspense crowds in on us, and excitement mounts.

This mastery of descriptive detail and sureness in period expression, combined with a curiously inexorable reading of human nature, give to Marjorie Bowen's best stories a sinister force both realistic and alarming. Yet beyond realism and the power to create fear they have something else. They are indeed, in the classic sense, Tales of Terror; but they possess a further element, to which the old-time Terror writer did not aspire. Under the bitter fascinated realization of love turned to loathing, under the relentless evocation of gloom, decay, and tarnished grandeur, Marjorie Bowen has a capacity for anguished pity. Even in her most venomous conflicts between unforgiving jealousies or cheated ambitions she seldom fails to sound a note of compassion; whereas, in such a tale as "Elsie's Lonely Afternoon," her sympathy with the helpless little victim of adult enmity and avarice can wring the heart. In the same way a deserted house, a clump of rotting trees, a once fine garden now a tangle of briars about a chain of weed-choked fish-ponds, move her to that profound melancholy which possesses every romantic confronted with a fragment of past dignity now forsaken and desolate.

She hears the phantom footsteps whisper along the corridors of the empty house, glimpses the shadowy figures flitting among the trees or down the overgrown terraces of the ruined garden. Here once were happiness, noise, and colour; here now are only silence and devastation.

Surely the perfect epigraph for these stories, if one were needed, comes from Verlaine's well-known poem, "Colloque Sentimental"—

> In the deserted park, silent and vast,
> Erewhile two shadowy glimmering figures passed.

> Their lips were colorless, and dead their eyes;
> Their words were scarce more audible than sighs.

> In the deserted park, silent and vast,
> Two spectres conjured up the buried past.

A Remembrance of Marjorie Bowen

Hilary Long

"To me, she was everything enchanting. I owe all I have to her and I like to feel she is as near to me now as she ever was."

Hilary Long (1921–2007) was the youngest of Marjorie Bowen's three sons. Like his siblings, Michael and Athelstan, he cherished a lifelong loyalty to his mother and, like them, endured hardships during his service in World War II as a Major in the British infantry unit, the Green Jackets, in the North Africa theater. His brothers were held as prisoners of war by the Japanese and the Germans. In 2002 Hilary placed his mother's papers in the Beinecke Library at Yale University. The following are excerpts from his "random recollections" appended to a collection of Marjorie Bowen's short stories edited by Jessica Amanda Salmonson, *Twilight and Other Supernatural Romances* (Ash-Tree Press, 1998).

I am a hard-headed, practical man—a man, as they say, of the world. All my experiences have made me a down to earth realist. I have served as a soldier and been a boxer. I have raced cars and motorcycles. I have climbed mountains and crossed deserts. I have worked as an engineer and been employed for years in a cut and thrust industry. I have traveled much—been places and seen things. Some would call me a hardened old sinner with no illusions left . . . . I am retired now . . .

Marjorie Bowen—George R. Preedy—Joseph Shearing—John Winch—was a distinguished writer, a delightful woman and, as a mother, superb. As skill with a pen is beyond me, I shall cling closely to facts and quotations to support my frail framework of words. . . .

She was a considerable scholar—a Fellow of the Royal Society of Literature and of the Royal Historical Society; a Diplomée and Honorary Fellow of kindred Societies in Utrecht, Leiden, and the Netherlands.

As a writer, she had a long reach. She wrote many different kinds of books and used a number of different styles. Perhaps this is the reason that she has not been as widely appreciated as she might have been. Yet she knew her limitations. In reply to a letter of August 1944 asking her to try her hand at writing a modern story under a man's name, she replied:

> I shall always write as a woman—not as a super feminine woman like Virginia Woolf or Elizabeth Bowen or Katherine Mansfield but as (I suppose) an all round woman. As for the proposed story— even if attempted—any critic would detect that a woman had written it. I could not write a modern story. I don't know enough about modern life. All my experiences seem detached from the world about me for they are instantly recreated in the imagination and blended with dreams and what I know of the past.

She was highly praised by many fine judges, among them Arthur Conan Doyle, Walter de la Mare, William Roughead, Gerald Gould, Phillis Bentley, James Agate, and Rebecca West. Hugh Walpole called her the greatest historical novelist England had produced in a generation and it was this field that formed the bulk of her work. Mark Twain . . . admired her first two books. In 1907 he visited London and arranged a meeting. Addressing her as "Miss Marjorie" ("the privilege of three score and eleven"), he wrote, "I shall be in London for ten days—June 18– 28—and I think you will have to do as the American girls do: waive youth, sex, and other conventions and call me. Yes—and telephone me when you are coming otherwise we shall fail to collide for I shall be a very busy person."

They "collided" over lunch at Brown's hotel. It must have been an interesting sight to see the venerable Mark Twain, with his wonderful head of white hair, and the timid young girl talking together as colleagues in literature.

Marjorie Bowen in the early 1930s

She did not like talking or writing about herself, but in the following two letters to me she mentioned the autobiography:

August 31, 1940: I wrote *The Debate Continues* when I was very unhappy, almost in despair when nothing seemed to matter very much. There were a few things I wanted to put on record. It had for obvious reasons to be toned down fifty per cent but even so it seems to impress people as "very sad"; it was not meant to be by any means. I never read it over. I think "polishing" destroys the sincerity of such a document—besides, I had not the courage to do so . . . Perhaps you will read it some day, I don't think there is anything in it to annoy anyone.

Again:

> *November 1943*: I wanted to tell you I wish I hadn't written *The Debate Continues*. I never revealed anything personal about myself until that time when I wanted to see if I could get things straight by writing them down and to get through to some degree of truth. I never read it over nor any review.

The Debate Continues gives as honest a picture as anyone can give of themselves. It is a strikingly honest book, but there are two points in it I must correct. First, she writes, "I had been warned by my mother that I had not a spark of attraction . . . all the other girls were prettier than myself." This is totally incorrect and I do not think she could ever have really believed it. She was in fact strikingly good looking (there are photographs that prove it) and she had great charm.

Secondly, she states, "I was most fortunate in my (second) husband [Arthur L. Long] whose loyalty was proof against any trial." This is typically generous and completely untrue. This man was my father. Where he should have been a willing support to my mother, he was an implacable burden. A quarrelsome and jealous man, he did no proper work and earned nothing to help our little establishment. Maybe he had some virtue buried deep, but, dig as I might, any evidence of it avoided me. I did not like him.

She was very brave. She spent almost the entire World War II alone in central London. To the air raids was added the triple torture of three sons abroad on active service. She never stopped working—she needed the income—and even under wartime conditions her output was unbroken.

I loved my mother. To me she was everything enchanting. I owe all I have to her and I like to feel she is as near to me now as she ever was.

Appendix A:
The Bowen–Wagenknecht–
Derleth Letters

Beinecke Library, Yale University
Gotlieb Center, Mugar Library, Boston University

> All mankind is one author, and is one volume; when one man dies,
> one chapter is not torn out of the book, but translated into a better
> language; and every chapter must be so translated . . . some pieces
> are translated by age, some by sickness, some by war, some by
> justice; but God's hand is in every translation, and his hand shall
> bind up all our scattered leaves again for that library where every
> book shall lie open to one another.
>
> John Donne, "Meditation 17"

British-born Marjorie Bowen never met her two most important
American literary partners and correspondents, scholar-bookman
Edward Wagenknecht (1900–2004) of Boston University and
writer-publisher August Derleth (1909–1971) of Sauk City,
Wisconsin. All three were among the most prolific, versatile, and
successful writers of the last century—Wagenknecht for his
scholarly literary studies, Derleth for his "Sac Prairie Saga" of the
great American Upper Middle West, and Bowen for her celebrated historical novels and stories of British and European history.

Despite their differences, it was their mutual passion for weird
fiction that brought them together as correspondents in the middle decades of the century. Wagenknecht admired Bowen's ghost

August Derleth, Majorie Bowen, and Edward Wagenknecht

stories and in the mid-1930s sought her out as a correspondent. He eventually became not only her loyal friend but served in the capacity as her unofficial American agent, soliciting stories for some of his anthologies and recommending her works to others. It is in the latter posture that in the 1940s he brought her to the attention of his friend, Derleth, whose Arkham House imprint was becoming America's premiere publisher of dark fantasy. Arkham House was originally devoted to bringing the works of H. P. Lovecraft to the popular public; however, at this time, Derleth was actively considering publishing the work of leading British writers, including William Hope Hodgson, Lord Dunsany, and John Metcalfe, and it was to be assumed that Bowen would be a likely addition.[1]

---

1. The two indispensable histories of Arkham House are Derleth's *Thirty Years of Arkham House, 1939–1969* (Sauk City, WI: 1970) and S. T. Joshi, *Sixty Years of Arkham House: A History and Biography* (Sauk City, WI: 1999; rev. ed. as *Eighty Years of Arkham House* [Seattle: Sarnath Press, 2019]). "There was never any question about the name of our publishing house," reports Derleth. "*Arkham House* suggested itself at once, since it was Lovecraft's own well-known, widely-used place-name for legend-haunted Salem, Massachusetts, in his remarkable fiction" (3). Upon Derleth's death in 1971, writes Joshi, a succession of managing editors followed, including Roderic Meng and James Turner.

What follows is a hitherto un-
documented story, a virtual "episto-
lary narrative," in which we may
glean personal and professional
glimpses into a significant chapter in
the lives of these three writers.[2] I
have culled the letters from the Marjorie Bowen Papers at the Beinecke
Library of Yale University, the Edward Wagenknecht Papers at the
Mugar Library, Boston University,
and the August Derleth Archives at
the Wisconsin Historical Society, in
Madison.

H. P. Lovecraft

The Bowen Correspondence at Yale

I have written in brief in *The Furies of Marjorie Bowen* (2019)
about a cache of Bowen's letters preserved at Yale that describe
her sojourn in wartime London. Many are written to her youngest son, Hilary, who, like his two brothers, Michael and Athelstan, is soldiering in parts unknown (Folder 235). The cramped,
handwritten, and irregular lines are frequently difficult to decipher. (That truly would require the services of one of the expert
cryptographers at Bletchley Park!) There are hundreds of them,
many separated only by a few days. They are very chatty and re-

Arkham House is now, however, largely moribund.

2. One finds no reference to this correspondence anywhere in Derleth.
Wagenknecht fails to mention it in his obituary of Bowen in 1958 and
in his memoir, *As Far as Yesterday* (1967). Bowen's own autobiography, *The Debate Continues,* appeared in 1939, prior to her contacts
with Wagenknecht, and there is no mention of Wagenknecht and Derleth in the private papers I have seen. Moreover, there is no reference
to this correspondence in *Sixty Years of Arkham House.*

late news of the air raids, blackouts, and rationing. Here are the daily routines of the Bowen household, the neighborhood gossip, the daily postings of newspapers and books, birthday notes, etc. Many raise concerns if her letters are reaching her sons.

The Bowen–Wagenknecht Correspondence at Boston University

Most of these topics are taken up in greater detail in the letters Marjorie Bowen wrote to Wagenknecht spanning the late 1930s to the early 1950s, almost fifty of which are now preserved in the Gotlieb Center, Mugar Library, Boston University (Wagenknecht Papers, Boxes 1 and 2). Taken together with a few of surviving Wagenknecht responses, we get a sense of both sides of the correspondence. Although there is a warm familiarity in the exchanges, Bowen always formally addresses Wagenknecht by his full name or "Professor Wagenknecht" and signs her letters with her married name, "Gabrielle Long."

Her first letter of which there is a record is dated 7 February 1938. Her address at the time was "Chalom House, Spring Terrace, Richmond, Surrey." For the first and only time she greets him with the formal "Dear Sir." She responds to a number of his questions about her work as an editor of two volumes of short horror stories (*Great Tales of Horror* and *More Great Tales of Horror*, 1932–33), her encounter with Mark Twain in London in 1907, and her recently published biography of Mary Wollstonecraft, *This Shining Woman*. Her letter is brisk and businesslike, and its relative formality will soon give way to a more familiar tone: "Thank you sincerely for what you say about my work; it is most encouraging . . . No, I did not write the stories marked 'Anon' in those anthologies. I wish I had! They came out of an American collection that I was asked to edit and add to for the British publication. I wrote to the editor of that collection but got no reply, merely an assurance from the American publisher that these tales were *not* copyrighted. They are very good, especially 'The Two Ladies of Cologne.' No, I never wrote anything about meeting Mark Twain. I was 16 years old at the time and don't remember much about it. And thank you for your generous and understanding review of Mary Godwin. I see you think that I was too kind to Gilbert Imlay [Wollstonecraft's lover in France]. One knows so little about him and of the terms on which Mary went to live with him. But I fear she was in love and made 'scenes' about it—[next page missing]."

Wartime News
A year later England is at war. Letters now issue from her home at 46 Markham Square, London. In an undated later from 1943, she explains that all three sons have been on active duty since 1939, in the Air Force, the Gunners, and the Eighth Army: "They were, as you say, 'caught up in the turmoil of the times as soon as war began.'" One of them, Captain Athelstan Long, the middle child, has been imprisoned in Burma in a Japanese P.O.W. camp. She sends his address to Wagenknecht, in care of the Mountain Regiment Indiana Army, Royal Artillery, in hopes he can assist her in communicating with him: "Now the Red Cross informs me that letters from the U.S.A. are more likely to get through than from here, either by means of the American Red Cross or by personal letter. So I venture to ask you if you would be so very kind as to send a line to my son telling him his family and friends are well and thinking of him constantly. I write every fortnight the 25 words I am allowed—I cannot send cable or parcels—and I have not yet had an answer. Needless to say how grateful I should be if you would do this." Wagenknecht does indeed do so; and on 21 July 1945 she reports: "Athelstan returned home about three weeks ago. He received one of your letters, for which I and he can never thank you enough. He tells

me it came 'at a dreadful moment and made a great difference' to him. He was working as a coolie on the Burma railway. . . . He won't say much of his experiences, but one knows they were terrible. He had to see nearly all his friends die by disease, murder, or torture. He had many severe illnesses himself but being very strong and in good condition he survived and does not appear to be much the worse; but his heart is strained and he has great fits of melancholy . . . These are men who have had six years taken out of their lives by futile soldiering and imprisonment."

Marjorie Bowen's sons (from left): Athelstan, Michael, Hilary

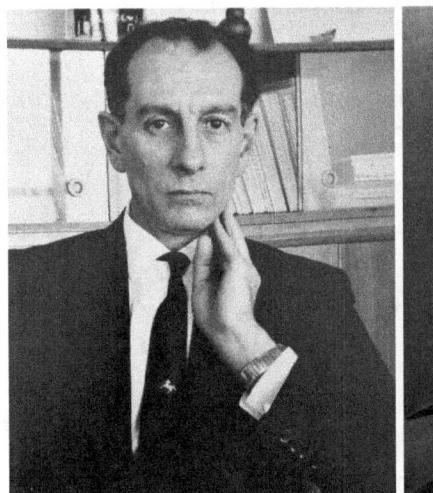 

Hilary, Michael, and Athelstan as adults

Regarding her oldest son, Michael, she reports good news on 9 April 1945: "He came home from Germany a few weeks ago—he was in an RAF camp and was subjected to brutal treatment, but after that had good treatment in hospital and is recovering. His character is not crushed. He has no bitterness. He is now in the country with his wife. I think he will soon be discharged, but he is not likely to fly as a pilot without long training, and he is needed in his former place in the Civil Service."

On 22 March 1948 she reports "Hilary had several false starts, motoring shutting down because of the stoppage of the 'basic' petrel and has now begun again in the film world. He did some 'documentaries' when he was in the Army and got in that way. He seems to like the work. It is the usual story here, the men who had six years of war don't find it easy to fit in to peacetime. Many are going to Canada. . . . My great personal excitement has been the marriage of Athelstan, the ex-P.O.W. Japan, to a Swedish girl. He is in the Colonial Service and goes to Nigeria on Saturday."

And, in turn, she asks questions about Wagenknecht's family and his homelife. Having learned from several letters from January and February that his son has been very ill, she replies on 7 August 1946, "I hope that your small son, David, has quite recovered from that worrying and undiagnosed infection that attacked him about Thanksgiving and Christmas and that your wife has got over the fright it gave her." Later, in an undated later from 1948: "I am so very happy to receive your letter with all your good news. It is indeed pleasant to know you have all this deserved recognition. Boston is the place in America I have always most wanted to see—such as my knowledge of America is of New England. Your description of your new home makes me envious."

Numerous letters reveal the difficult living conditions of wartime London during the Blitz and subsequent rocket attacks. On 9 April 1945 she writes about "the flying bombs and rockets that have ceased only the past ten days . . . We have had nine months of this horror and the damage has been heavy; one became used to the constant explosions, sometimes once an hour, several near here; and whenever they fell in London, one could hear them all over the city. They made, however, not the least difference to the war effort . . ." More news comes about the bombings on 21 May 1945: "The bombing has been intense until a month or so ago and mail may have been lost. It was nothing but the overwhelming state of the world and one's personal anxieties."

On 21 May 1945 she reports that London is "desperately overcrowded and not, to me, a happy place." Londoners are learning of the "appalling" atrocities in Germany: "We are exposed to the horrible publicity about the horrors in Germany . . . It was dreadful to see the crowds—including girls and children—waiting outside the cinema to see the 'atrocity' films. It was very wrong. Sensitive people were made ill, and others merely got a 'thrill.' Many already talk of the most appalling cruelties with the uttermost indifference. Much familiarity makes them callous . . . [but] it is so good to know that much of the slaughter and cruelty has stopped. Meanwhile, one makes garments and collects them [illegible] for 'liberated Europe.'"

Later, on 11 November 1946, she reports more disclosures about German atrocities: "We have had no pictures of the hanged Nazis in our papers. I believe there was one of the body of Goering, but I did not see it. Public opinion here was most certainly against the publication of these horrors and a suggestion that the film of the executions should be shown was rejected by the newsreel people. It also provoked a good many indignant letters to the papers. I never heard any discussions of the Nuremburg trials—indeed, one hardly heard them mentioned beyond the hope being expressed that they would soon be over. There was a high purpose behind the whole thing, but I fear there were too many difficulties in the carryout out."

Meanwhile, through it all, she's grateful for the presence of the American soldiers in the city. 30 March 1944: "There are large numbers of your countrymen—and a few country women—in Chelsea now; they are fine looking men, easy and pleasant and I admire their uniforms, dark olive tunic and [illegible] coloured trousers. I fear they must find it most dull here . . . One has not even any drinks to offer them . . . I wish I knew the different regiments as I do my own. I can only see different uniforms and badges without being able to discern the meanings . . . We shall miss the American soldiers soon to leave; everyone finds them—and the ladies—very courteous, easy, and practical." Despite the bombings, however, "I am really lucky in still having a home and ending the war in the same home where I began—at least in standing by my home I did keep it together to welcome two sons home."

On 18 December 1945 conditions in postwar London have worsened: "The shortage of everything is more acute now than during the war—transport, clothing, homekeeping are all in a wretched state and I think that everyone is very tired. The sheer act of living is such an effort . . . I don't feel much energy to face all the difficulties of mere existence . . . Since there is nothing here for Athelstan, he expects to return to India in the autumn in the Indian Political Service . . . There is nothing here for men who had their education ended by the war. Later, on 31 March 1946, she reports: "Athelstan is very pleased to have secured his appointment. There are only a few vacancies and many applicants . . . He has high ideals and I like to think he will go to help the British leave India with dignity after being there so many years."

The bedroom, living room, and dining room in the Bowen home in
Markham Square, London

It comes as a surprise to learn in her letter of 14 October 1949 of her involvement in a British-Soviet Union organization: "I belong to a Society for Cultural Relations with the Soviet Union.[3] I have seen some beautiful films shown by them and heard some very good literary talks, never a word of politics. I was on a public 'brain trust' for this Society and one of the authors who sent questions to the Soviet authors. I have met many of them at the Soviet embassy. I think our campaign against Russia most misguided. Some of the colour cartoon films for children are very beautiful, of course, no one will show them so they put them on at their own theatre. I belong to the Polish Society and am deeply sympathetic with General Anders and his men. It doesn't seem as if the best kind of human being could go into politics because whichever 'side' you are 'on' you have to condone appalling things. Does not the Chaplin centenary strike a sad note? If that man were to return he would not find any of his hopes for his country realized."

Painfully aware of food shortages, Wagenknecht offers to send food parcels. In an undated letter in 1948, she replies: "It is very good of you to suggest sending me something, but I have no excuse to ask. I even manage to send a small parcel to Germany every month. One is now allowed to send *rationed food*. I don't eat meat and I don't like tea, so I give away my share of that."

Mutual Literary Matters
Bowen and Wagenknecht share news and questions about their literary endeavors. In an undated letter from 1943 we find her

---

3. The Society for Cultural Relations was a Soviet-instigated British organization designed to influence British cultural figures' perceptions of the USSR's policies and actions and win sympathy based upon misunderstandings of the USSR's real nature. Details are scant about how many Brits were taken in by it, but it was probably a significant number.

reactions to Wagenknecht's appreciative article about her work, "The Extraordinary Mrs. Long."[4] She replies: "Thank you very much for your letter of May 7th and the article that you enclosed. I hardly know what to say about this. My writing has been since the war so utterly in the background that it is quite surprising to learn that anyone is interested in it . . . Life in London, where I have been during the war, has not been conducive to fostering the arts or taking any interest in one's own efforts; but I have, however, found some relief and pleasure in working at my books and trying to make them as good as I can. It is an added pleasure when one's attempts are recognized by anyone like yourself. I am most grateful to you for the generous remarks you make about my work, and these I certainly found stimulating . . . It is more than good of you to express your opinion of [my] books . . . and your opinion, needless to say, I value very highly. If one dislikes publicity, especially personal publicity, one is very thankful for such knowledgeable appreciation of one's endeavours, especially when one suffers, as I have, from a swarm of imitators who seem in every case to be far more successful than I am myself." And on 21 October 1949 she is grateful for his offers to write about her novels: "Yes, I would be very flattered if you were to write an article on my *The Fourth Chamber* [1944], which is based on Charles Reade's *Griffith Gaunt* [1866]. My novel follows the original case *very* closely. It took place in Derry, France, about 1696. The French punishment for bigamy was then— death. The man was tried by some French [tribunal] . . . He finally became a customs officer and was killed in some trouble with smugglers. His widow lived a long time together with the priest . . . I am so sorry I don't keep notes. I write from memory. I had a report of the trial, together with an editor's

---

4. *New York Times Book Review* (2 May 1943).

comments. I worked entirely from that, of course, and *not* by re-reading *Griffith Gaunt*. I always thought it a very fine novel and I wonder why it has not been reprinted. But when I read what was obviously the *original* case that Reade must have known, I felt that the *true* story was stronger, stranger and more exciting than Reade's story." Moreover, "I am glad indeed of your valuable assistance in drawing attention to my book about Mrs. Maybrick [*Airing in a Closed Carriage*, 1943] for I have to consider the commercial side . . . I am so encouraged and stimulated during this dreary time by your interest and owe you much for your two books that have been a much needed distraction during the last dreary and exhausting months."

It is apparently Wagenknecht's idea that she write a book about a true crime case in colonial Kentucky that she describes as "The Kentucky Tragedy." This excites a lengthy series of letters in the late 1940s. The book, initially to be titled *Beauchamp*, will eventually appear in 1952 under the title *To Bed at Noon* and will be dedicated to him. She demurs at his offer to assist her with background research. "I want to ask you *not* to take any trouble for me. You are too good-natured . . . It is true I feel alien in America and I have suffered from your nation's critics, but this I think I could do. There are a large number of books to be had here about Kentucky . . . If my version [of the original account] is ever published, may I just put a note stating that you told me of it?"

21 May 1945: "I have just finished the life of 'Gustavus III' [*Nightcap and Plume*], to be dedicated to all prisoners of war and the Swedish Red Cross. It has some 'propaganda' value, as it is the life of an idealist and pacifist, who was murdered for his beliefs . . . It will be published—at the earliest—in the autumn." At the same time, however, she questions her career trajectory: "I intend to drop 'M. B.' [Marjorie Bowen] and the purely historical

novels. The historical novel has been *overdone,* so cheapened and exploited that I do not feel I can do anything worthwhile in that line—or that it would be noticed if I did. The whole business is a 'racket' . . . I want to get with publishers for new work."

31 March 1946: "I have had no secretarial help at all since the war, when I had a full-time secretary and a typist. Now it is a question of doing it all myself. Between the constant shifting of papers and a fire, everything has become 'muddled' besides much being put away in a shed in the country. Naturally, I am fairly tidy and dislike disorder, but these circumstances have been rather overwhelming. Even now there is no prospect of help—and I have as much work to do as ever before."

On 22 March 1948 she chafes at the delays of a projected volume of short stories with a preface by Michael Sadleir [which was released by John Lane a year later under the title, *The Bishop of Hell*]. A month later she declares, "The delays in publication are almost incredible. Shortage of glue is one of the latest difficulties."

In April 1948 we find her dissatisfied with her publisher, with whom her pseudonym of "Marjorie Bowen" is "under contract": "I dislike Heinemann, their methods, production, etc. So much so that I don't want to write for them. I am trying to get released from this contract, but they won't let go. Until they do, I may keep on with the other two names ["George Preedy" and "Joseph Shearing"]."

Always concerned at her lack of formal education, and with disarming frankness, she admits to uncertainties about the lack of "correctness" in her writing style. 15 August 1950: "Your criticism and corrections are gratefully accepted . . . It seems to me unbearably tedious to read over one's own materials, looking for clerical errors. I do it, but errors slip through and then, if I employ anyone at a high price to proof-read the typescript, the result seems the same. I have, as far as punctuation goes, really given it up. There are so many disputes on the matter, the rules are constantly changing. The 'comma splice' seems to me to give rapidity to the sentence, 'semicolons' some say are out of date, yet now and then one wants them! The same with 'as' and 'like.' Some authorities declare 'like' should never be used. I shall keep your paper and use your corrections for the English edition— thank you so much. I suffer basic ignorance; when one is self-taught, one finds it hard to remember all the rules, especially as they change so much and seem so often in dispute."

In turn, we find her recommending for American publication several literary works. Undated letter from 1948: "Did I ask you if you knew *Confessions of a Fanatic* [1859] by James Hogg? I always thought it a wonderful story and never could find anyone who had read it. Now I see it is to be reprinted in a special edition with a preface by Andre Gide. Hogg wrote some other marvelous stories that I could never get anyone to take any interest in, but now I suppose they will be 'discovered.'" And there are inquiries about J. Sheridan Le Fanu. "Do you know of a novel by Sheridan Le Fanu with the title of *A Lost Name* [1868]. I bought some numbers of *Temple Bar* and this novel was in them as a serial. It is first-class material. Would it not do for a reprint for you? I might be able to get the other numbers of *Temple Bar* from the London Library. Or, perhaps you have them in one of your libraries."

Wagenknecht sends her several projects, current and in progress; and in the course of several letters, she responds with comments. Regarding his new anthology, *Six Novels of the Supernatural* (1944): "I much enjoyed your supernatural book, [whose contents are] all new to me, save [Walter de la Mare's] *The Return* . . . I was fascinated by *Sweet Rocket* and I have read it three times." She compliments his anthology *When I Was a Child* (1946) and an anthology on Jesus (*The Story of Jesus in the*

World's Literature, 1946).[5] She admits that after reading his *Abraham Lincoln, His Life, Work, and Character* and *Joan of Arc: An Anthology* (1946) she might overturn her aversion to both: "I don't like Joan of Arc, either. I couldn't say why. I think it was a most ghastly tragedy, but I remain quite cold towards the unfortunate creature. I know I am in a very small minority, but there it is." One of the books, *Murder by Gaslight* [1949], "is certainly an exciting collection" and it elicits an interesting comment on Wagenknecht's references to *Lady Audley's Secret,* by the British Victorian novelist Mary Elizabeth Braddon. We may readily see how her sympathetic description of the murderess "Lady Audley" strikes a sympathetic chord with Bowen and is reflected in many of her female protagonists: "The play taken from the novel is now running at the Bedford Camden Town and I shall try to go to see it when I return to London, tho' I fear they have 'gayed' it and that won't do, as the emotions dealt with by M. E. Braddon are too fundamental for parody. All the old melodramas are too strong for burlesque. I remember the enormous fame of M. E. Braddon and my mother's contempt for her. I think part of the story's success was due to being able to [attract] the audiences who would have found the other Victorian novelists too highbrow. She was read both by 'the idle rich' and the 'servant's hall.' And I suppose that is where the copies went, reread until hopelessly tattered . . . Anyway, I felt sorry for 'Lady Audley'—rather a Mary Queen of Scots character forced into violence in self defense; and the whole book reads rather now like society's revenge on the uncommonly beautiful and gifted."

And she responds to requests from him about her own writing and reading experiences.

---

5. Wagenknecht included an excerpt from Bowen's *The Debate Continues* (1939) in his memoir, *When I Was a Child.*

... for the assumption of a sane
or ought to tackle himself.
I don't want to read any of
the fiction on this subject, but I
shall ask M. Purnell, the librarian
of the London Library, if he can
get the items of your mention.
I doubt if he can, I mean
if the American authorities would
let the books out of the
country. I would like the photostats
if I can't get the books — but
there are two difficulties. Thus,
I don't want to bother you and
I am not sure if I should
be allowed to send the money
— everything is difficult now. I keep
these "confessions". I think the
attendant chaplains wrote them
for the most part. I feel sure
of this in the Scottish cases, there
would be such work over a
last dying speech and confession, etc.
There are some remarkable specimens
of these "confessions" given by

Two pages from a hand-written letter
from Marjorie Bowen to Edward Wagenknecht,
Courtesy of Mugar Library, Boston University

William Roughead. I, writing of
conscious, simply don't believe in
the ? conscious of the major
Weir or Madame de Brinvilliers.
I don't think such careers of
crime were possible and these
people were hysterical, neurotic
and worked on by pastors or
priests. In the Beauchamp story
I feel there is much that could
redeem it from
her heights out to many
squalor. There are far too many
"horror" stories appearing fast now,
don't you think? European as
well as American. Horror for the
sake of horror, with no more
than real interest that the "Haap
romances" of the 18ᵗ century. Some
of the French libros shown here
are tainted with this, in my
opinion. Le Secret de Mayerling
Stanning, Jean Travair, is simply
not fit to see. I had no idea
what it was like before?

There is this short autobiographical note in a letter of 9 October 1949: "I had no chance of reading fiction when I was young, there were always books in the different room I was installed in, but never novels. Always 'church' books, save, once, The Old Curiosity Shop. I read Dickens alone for a long time. When I went to Paris [as an adolescent] I read the Russian and French classics and Henri Beyle [Stendhal]. Soon after, I returned to England, I married and went to Italy where I could not get any books at all. Came the First World War and I was middle-aged before I got on to the Great English and American classics. I never belonged to any library save the London Library. I began as a child with Jane Eyre and my mother took it away from me. I had read nothing of Le Fanu and nothing of W[ilkie] Collins or Charles Reade. This must seem hard to believe, because now it seems to me as if my work was a follow, or copy of theirs, but it is not so. It was only after people said the stuff was like Wilkie Collins, Le Fanu, etc, that I began to read these writers."

Films and Filming in Post-War London

She obliges Wagenknecht's requests for information about post-war British films and her own involvement in the industry. "It is a great pleasure to me to send you some of our film magazines, also very easy as my youngest son [Hilary] is in the film business, on the technical side, as editor and commentator. We have only *two* serious film magazines here, *Sight and Sound* and *Sequence,* the rest are utter trash. British films are getting better, but I would not say I had seen even one quite in the first class. The best are known as 'documentaries.' [Alexander] Korda's long-awaited *Bonnie Prince Charlie* [1948] was such an utter failure that he plastered London with apologies and defiances. A very great deal of time and money was spent on what should have been a 'national epic' I doubt if this gets to America. There is so much in our history that would make splendid films, but no ever takes advantage of this wealth of material. I fear I don't know of any other serious British films."

Then, this surprise. 14 October 1949: "I did a great deal of work on [Hitchcock's] *Under Capricorn* [1948], for which I was well paid. I did not like the way the thing was shaping and it seemed the usual mess. They got a [illegible] in to rewrite it and I got my name taken off. It has had a very bad press, indeed, but I have not seen it and I don't know what materials of mine they may have used. It is not a good novel and Ingrid Bergman seems wasted on the part of a drunken slut—just as Vivien Leigh seems wasted in just such another part in [the stage play version of] *A Streetcar Named Desire* [1949–51]. I don't want to see this play. The critics seem daunted by it."[6]

Movie poster for Under Capricorn

She reports on 7 August 1946 that *Blanche Fury* and *Moss Rose* are being filmed: "The film rights are changing hands at high prices and there is much excitement about it in the film world." On 11 November 1946 she confirms that *Blanche Fury*

---

6. There are no references to Bowen's work on *Under Capricorn* in extant biographies of Alfred Hitchcock, save for this brief comment by biographer Donald Spoto: "Until the end of June Hitchcock worked at various times with Peter Ustinov and Marjorie Bowen on the problems of developing a coherent narrative out of the novel and the play" (Spoto, *Hitchcock: The Dark Side of Genius* 309).

is being filmed at Denham Studios with Valorie [*sic*] Hobson in the lead. On 21 October 1949, she talks about her aversion to certain films, including a few adaptations of her own books: "Surely the taste for pictures of the utmost degradation . . . is abnormal? You may think I'm a bad one to complain, considering some of the novels I write, but I have *never* dealt on squalor, torture, sex aberrations, or anything disgusting; and I *do* always keep the *basic values* in view. In all the film versions of my novels, 'horrors' are put in by script writers. In *Moss Rose* they kept nothing but the title. *Airing in a Closed Carriage* was a vindication of the [accused murderess] Florence Maybrick, after my careful reading of millions of words about her case. I thought she was innocent and deeply wronged. The film from this book, *The Mark of Cain* was an utter travesty and a complete failure. . . . There is a public for the heroic, the grand, the good, the beautiful, but there are far too many people whom one can only name parasites and panderers, trying to make money by appealing to the basest of human appetites. Sometimes I find it frightening."

Wagenknecht as Literary Agent

He requests she send him those novels that he thinks he can place with August Derleth of Arkham House. 21 July 1945: "I looked for a copy of *Black Magic* for you—of course, it had been 'borrowed,' but I am on the track of it and hope to send it in the next few days. I am sending you the Dr. Dee book [*I Dwelt in High Places*] and *The Haunted Vintage,* both suitable, I think, for Arkham House. I can also send other supernatural short stories and *The Devil Snar'd,* which is a long short, that appeared here once only in paperback." As of 13 September 1946 the prospects look good: "Mr. Derleth wrote that his letter about *Black Magic* would constitute a contract." At Wagenknecht's urging, she will send short stories to Derleth for a proposed volume of stories [which did not appear in her lifetime, but in 1976 under the title of *Kecksies*]: "My best stories in this line are "The Avenging of Ann Leete," "The Crown Derby Plate," "The Fair Hair of Ambrosine," at least according to good critics who rate them highly. They are suitable for anthologies." And later on 11 November 1946 she confirms she is sending more ghost stories to Derleth: "They were written a long time ago and were never published in America." However, on 22 March 1948 she observes that there has been no further communication with him. On the other hand, there is to be a proposed volume of short stories.

Decline and Death

An ominous notes creeps into her last letters in the Mugar Library Collection. Their inside address indicates a residence move to 34 Holland Park, London. On 24 July 1950 she cryptically refers to "bad family troubles, nothing to do with me, but all falling on me, not fantasies—but genuine heartbreaks. Though I tell no one, I feel my health to suffer—a perpetual fatigue." She concludes: "I have always felt, *most* strongly, even as a child, that if one could suffer *with* the person suffering most, one would be at peace. But there seems no way of doing that." Then, in a note dated 2 August 1952, she complains of recent discomforts. "I had a stupid accident in the half-light and, thinking of other things, I entangled the fringe on my bedcover with my slippers and did not observe what I had done . . . When I tried to rise, I was thrown against the half-open door and broke my arm in two places as well as opening the old crack in the rib; I was sent to hospital where it was impossible to write, and now I have to go every morning for treatment. Opinions are divided as to how 'bad' the injury is. I have to wait until I see the Surgeon again." She concludes: "I am acutely conscious how trivial I and all my

efforts are in the face of what is happening in the world just
how, but I have just to keep to my small routine." Two weeks
later, on 16 August, more news: "The Surgeon thinks the injury
is going on all right but that it will be weeks yet before it is
healed. Yes, it is the left arm and I was alone in the flat at the
time. In every way it is has been a sickening bother. In her last letter, dated 29 November 1952, she again refers to her "shattered
arm," although it doesn't give her much trouble. She promises to
send her recent book, *Mary Queen of Scots*: "I shall send you a
copy—with much diffidence. Yours gratefully, Gabrielle Long."

A month later, on 22 December, she suffers a serious con-
cussion from a fall in her home at 34 Holland Park. She later
dies in the hospital.

The Bowen–Wagenknecht–Derleth Correspondence
at the Wisconsin Historical Society

Details of the Arkham House project are fleshed out in a cache
of correspondence among Wagenknecht, Derleth, and Bowen
housed among the August Derleth Papers at the Wisconsin Historical Society. The letters range from 4 September 1945 to 20
April 1971, three months before Derleth's death on 4 July 1971.
Beyond shared confidences between Derleth and Wagenknecht
about family matters, shop talk about their current literary endeavors, and occasional political disputes, our concern here is their
mutual interest in bringing Marjorie Bowen's novels to American
readers via the publishing imprint of Arkham House. Bowen herself occasionally weighs in on the project. It is to be regretted that
it eventually came to naught, as we shall see. It remains one of the
great "might-have-beens" of modern fantasy publishing.

At the outset it is clear that Derleth and Wagenknecht enjoy
a warm personal and professional relationship. On 3 April 1952
Derleth expresses his admiration for Wagenknecht, with whom
he has enjoyed many years of correspondence and friendship: "I

value your friendship as that of a man of great personal integrity as well as of a scholar with more than average vision and scope of mind." And on 14 July 1965 he writes: "I marvel anew at your skill and creative ability; it is far more than competence, and there is no slacking off at any point in your range. . . . There simply are not many people writing in English either here or abroad who can hold a candle to you, either for volume or for consistence in the really engrossing way in which you present your material and interpret your people."

Moreover, it is also abundantly clear that both men share a warm regard for Marjorie Bowen. As her unofficial American agent, Wagenknecht is most persistent that Derleth consider her a publishing prospect. His earliest extant letter on the subject is dated 13 June 1945. (In this and other letters, I preserve the use of underlined and bold-face book titles.) He relays to Derleth Bowen's Markham Square London address and informs him of a number of her books that might constitute projects for Arkham House: "I had a long letter from her yesterday, and you will be glad to hear that she is sending me a copy of *Black Magic*. I will let you read it, and then if you decided you want to reprint it, I will give you the book to use for 'copy.' I have taken the liberty of telling her about you and about your interest in her work." He goes on to describe Bowen's circumstances in wartime London and her anxieties about the whereabouts of three soldier sons. Moreover, "her husband, who was badly crippled in the last war, has been travelling up and down England, working for the Minister of Supply, and was under fire from bombing again and again; and she herself was on a train which was both bombed and machine-gunned. She says all this would not matter 'if one could feel that all the nations were really working together for peace.'"

EDWARD WAGENKNECHT
233 OTIS STREET
WEST NEWTON 65, MASS.

January 13, 1953

Dear August,

Thanks for your letter.

Since you do not mention it, I assume you do not know that Marjorie Bowen died on December 23. I did not learn the fact until yesterday when the Publishers' Weekly came; if it was reported in the American press, I missed it. It is a great shock to me.

Her last letter to me was dated November 29 and was largely devoted to expressing her delight in Cavalcade of the American Novel. I am trying to find out whether her death had any connection with the bad time she has been going through with her broken arm.

I forget whether (if I ever knew), you have given up your plan to publish that collection of her short stories. I think you did tell me you had given up Black Magic. I happen to know that some time ago she made up a collection of her Joseph Shearing short stories -- those originally published in Orange Blossoms plus some others. Orange Blossoms never appeared in an American edition. Harpers did not take this item up; should you ever be intereste in it, I am sure you could obtain it through her agent, who is Harold Ober.

Yours,

Letter from Edward Wagenknecht to August Derleth noting Marjorie Bowen's death on 23 December 1952 (Wisconsin Historical Society)

AUGUST DERLETH

BAUK CITY, WISCONSIN

31 December 1948

Dear Edward,

I'll get around to writing Mrs. Long directly after the holidays.
I hope to do her short story collection early in 1950, but unless
printing costs drop materially, it will be economically unsound to
publish BLACK MAGIC. I am some $16,000 in the red now, and, while
my inventory is very high, it is still not a condition that should be
augmented. .... Anent the reviews -- perhaps you could review the
Dunsany, Smith, Quinn, and Derleth (which went out yesterday) all in
one review for the Sampler?   ... I enclose my most recent venture
into the comics, or evidence of it, in clipping. I plan to publish
this book late in 1949. I am still hard at work collecting data for
my comprehensive study of the comics, but I cannot afford to get at
it until I am economically free. And that is not yet. .... The Mc-
Cutcheon book was good, yes, but I had much the same reaction as you
manifestly did. I missed many things, but then, a good many more
were there. .... The expense and cost of this book offer an adequate
index to costs these days. Our ROADS cost us 67¢ a copy to manufac-
ture; NOT LONG FOR THIS WORLD cost $1.10 a copy to make. One cannot
go on publishing at that rate, clearly. My entire 1949 list will be
deferred until October, when we will begin the 1949 season.

All the best to you always for 1949 et seq. (NB: Yes, it is good
to know that de la Mare liked "The Turtle". I wish he could be persuaded to do me a short story the length of ROADS for a special Xmas
illustrated edition. Weird, of course.)

Letter from August Derleth to Edward Wagenknecht about proposal to
publish Marjorie Bowen's stories, 31 December 1948
(Wisconsin Historical Society)

Two months later, 31 August, Wagenknecht sends Derleth
several of Bowen's novels, including the fantasies *The Haunted
Vintage* and *I Dwelt in High Places*. Another novel, *Black Magic*, is
in transit. Bowen herself has suggested that her best supernatural
stories can be found in *The Last Bouquet*. To which Wagenknecht appends this tantalizing note: "She did make an inci-
dental remark, in her letter to me, which excited me a good deal.
She said that her husband, who keeps much better tab on her
stuff than she does, says that there are about fifty supernatural
stories of hers which have never been reprinted from the period-
icals in which they appeared in England."

Wagenknecht further notes, in a letter of 3 January 1946,

that Bowen herself is gathering together a collection of her stories in hopes for American publication: "I had a letter yesterday
in which she says that she is gathering together as many as possible of the ghost stories which have never been published in this
country, and which have had only serial publication in England.
She wants to know whether she should send them to me or to
you directly, and I have been selfish enough to ask her to send
them to me because I want very much to read them. With her
customary depreciation of her own work, she adds that the stories are not what she would write today but are not 'too bad.' So
I am hoping to see something that we shall both be very much
interested in and that you will very much want to publish."

On 12 February 1946 he sends Derleth a long letter enumer-
ating a list of Bowen's books and stories, many from *The Last
Bouquet*. "They vary in quality," he begins, "but I think the best
are very good indeed. I hope you will like them . . . These
books appeared only in England and have long been out of print
. . . All the stories, according to Mrs. Long, are her own copy-
right." He advises Derleth to communicate directly with Bowen.
But, as the following letters indicate, locating Bowen's novels
and stories during wartime paper shortages proves to be difficult. Derleth to Wagenknecht, 4 September 1945: "I am sorry
not to have BLACK MAGIC to read, but I assume it has simply
not come in, and that is all there is to it. Of course, I have THE
LAST BOUQUET, but I am, as you are, especially interested in
those 50 stories which her husband says have not been published
in book form. I have not myself had any word from Mrs. Long."

Later, on 4 October, Derleth repeats, "Nothing new on the
Bowen front, no. I have not had time to read her books, which
you so kindly sent, nor have I written to her. She has not thus far
written to me, though I continue keenly interested in those uncol-
lected uncanny tales of which you wrote me some weeks ago."

On 6 January 1946 we find Derleth's initial intention to publish a volume of her short stories, although he relies on Wagenknecht's advice. He admits he's still not heard from her—"but I shall certainly look forward to seeing her supernatural tales, and hope you'll read them at once when they come, and send them on to me so that I can make plans for the publication of a collection of them."

A month later, 14 February 1946, Derleth acknowledges he has received *The Last Bouquet* and several more stories she has sent him: "I do feel quite safe and sure in saying that we will certainly want to do a book, but whether we shall want to include all the tales she sent, I am not so certain." He goes on with enthusiasm about "The Crown Derby Plate" and "The Avenging of Ann Leete" ("certainly good stories, beyond question").

Bowen's letter of 22 February 1946 to Derleth acknowledges his receipt of *The Last Bouquet* and adds that she has also sent him *The Pleasant Husband* and *Curious Happenings*: "[They contain] ghost stories, none of which have been published in America. I am quite agreeable to the terms you offer and will you please take this letter as an acceptance of them? Moreover, I am pleased for you to have any of the stories for your anthology [*The Night Side*] on the terms you mention." She adds, regarding a proposed collection of stories, "I am glad to write a foreword for you if you wish. As for the title, could not one of the titles of the stories be used? Thank you very much for liking my work." Two titles are considered: *The Hidden Ape* and *Kecksies*. On 10 March that year she suggests, "I think *The Hidden Ape* is the best of the titles you suggest, but I don't mind which you choose.

Five days later Derleth writes Wagenknecht that he has offered "Mrs. Long" $50 to publish her story "Nightmare" in *The Night Side,* which appears a year later. He regrets he did not have time to publish "Scoured Silk" in his anthology *Sleep No More.*

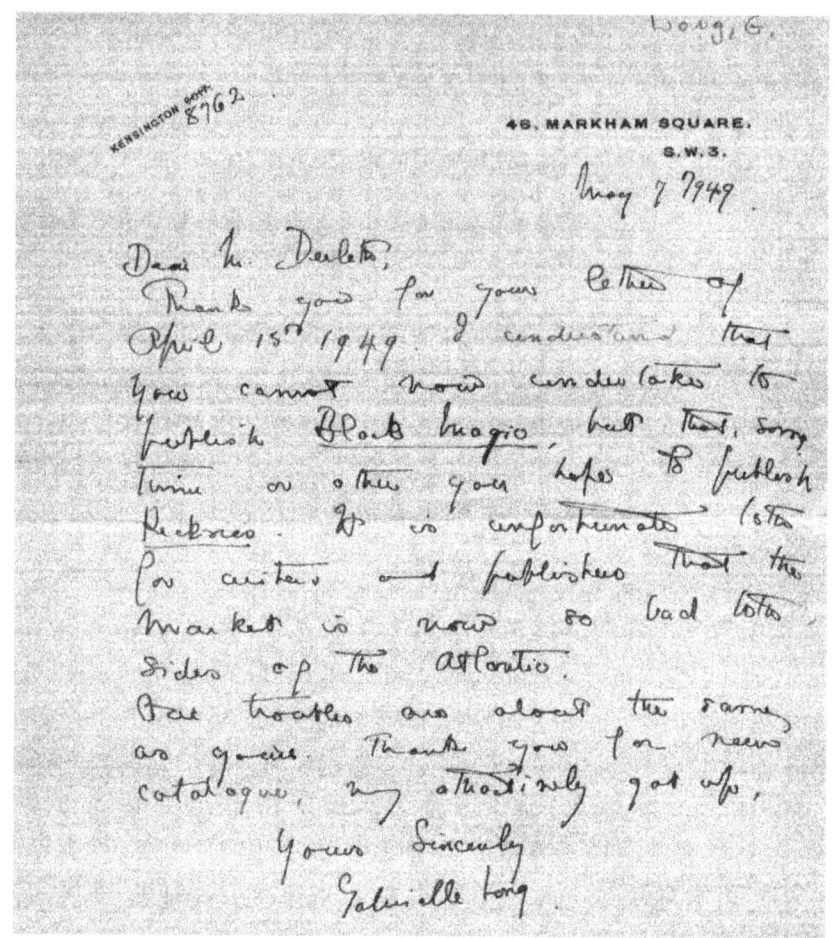

Letter from Marjorie Bowen to August Derleth acknowledging Derleth's
decision not to publish Black Magic, *7 May 1949*
(Wisconsin Historical Society)

By 5 March 1946 Derleth assures Wagenknecht about *Black Magic:* "The probability is very strong, however, that we will publish it."

To which Wagenknecht wonders, on 2 May, if Derleth would like to receive Bowen's story collection, *Seeing Life and Other Stories* for more story possibilities.

Later, on 21 August, Wagenknecht persists, "Have you contracted to publish [*Black Magic*]? When is *Kecksies* coming? And do you still have the other two Bowen books of which I forwarded you copies—*The Haunted Vintage* and *I Dwelt in High Places*? Have you either accepted or rejected them?"

Bowen weighs in about these various projects on 13 September 1946 to Derleth: "I have heard from Professor Wagenknecht that you are expecting contracts for your edition of BLACK MAGIC and GHOST STORIES. I am so sorry, but I understood that you considered an exchange of letters sufficient. Please send a contract and I will sign it with pleasure and return it at once. I wrote you last month asking when you like the preface for the Ghost collection; I think you had decided either HIDDEN APE or KECKSIES AND OTHER TWILIGHT TALES for the title." She goes on to acknowledge Derleth would not find suitable her novels, *The Haunted Vintage* and *I Dwelt in High Places*. Later, on 11 March 1946, Bowen writes that she has sent him "three more stories I thought you might care to have for the "Kecksies" volume." Finally, on 7 May 1949, she acknowledges that Derleth has decided not to publish *Black Magic:* "I understand that you cannot now undertake to publish *Black Magic* but that some time or other you hope to publish *Kecksies*. It is unfortunate both for writers and publishers that the market is now so bad both sides of the Atlantic."

On 1 July 1947 Derleth asks Wagenknecht, "I wonder if she would authorize me to sell for magazine publication some of the hitherto unpublished stories in our projected collection [*Kecksies*]. There are advantages to Arkham House for this. I am particularly interested in a project of this sort because our London agent has a good deal of money which he owes us and can't send out of the country; thus, selling stories for an English author will enable us to have our agent transfer our funds over there to the author, and allows us to get our money."

On 28 December 1948 we find a frustrated Wagenknecht still nudging Derleth about delays in publishing Bowen's works. "Mrs. Long seems somewhat concerned about when—or even whether—you are planning to bring out those books of hers. I think it might be a good idea to drop her a line about the matter."

Derleth replies three days later that he has decided to proceed with *Kecksies* but not to publish *Black Magic:* "I'll get around to writing Mrs. Long directly after the holidays. I hope to do her short story collection early in 1950, but unless printing costs drop materially, it will be economically unsound to publish BLACK MAGIC. I am some $16,000 in the red now, and, while my inventory is very high, it is still not a condition that should be augmented."

Derleth's letter of 6 January 1949 responds to Wagenknecht's urging him to proceed with publishing the short stories. He cautions: "I appreciate the suggestion about Mrs. Long, but it has been our unfortunate and costly experience that the best books by the best British authors do not sell as well as the poorest books by the poorest pulp magazine authors in the fantasy field. A regrettable fact, but true."

On 7 April 1947 Wagenknecht notes that novels by "Joseph Shearing" are attracting the movies: "By the way, Shearing is booming: four films in production—*Moss Rose, Airing in a Closed Carriage, Blanche Fury,* and the new one, which is *For Her to Keep* in England . . . It's the first real money she's had."

On 29 November 1949 Wagenknecht acknowledges to Derleth his role in Bowen's latest novel, *To Bed at Noon,* initially titled *Beauchamp:* "Joseph Shearing [sic] is working on a novel about the Beauchamp murder case, the Kentucky tragedy, to which I introduced her. So I shall have the pleasure of being the 'only begetter' of one of her books. She has been laid up with neuritis, which is all the more terrible for her because she is one of these people who cannot use drugs as pain-killers. Even the smell of alcohol makes her deathly ill."

Derleth reiterates on 24 March 1952 his interest in *Kecksies*. "We still hope to do KECKSIES, but just when I can't say. The fact is that our books by British authors have not done well."

Then, on 13 January 1953, Wagenknecht has sad news for Derleth: "Since you do not mention it, I assume you do not know that Marjorie Bowen died on December 23. I did not learn the fact until yesterday when the *Publishers' Weekly* came; if it was reported in the American press, I missed it. Her last letter to me was dated November 19 . . . I am trying to find out whether her death had any connection with the bad time she has been going through with her broken arm."

In the same letter, Wagenknecht suggests to Derleth yet another short-story project for Arkham House: "I happen to know that some time ago she made up a collection of her Joseph Shearing short stories—those originally published in *Orange Blossoms*—plus some others. *Orange Blossoms* never appeared in an American edition. Harpers did not take this item up; should you ever be interested in it, I am sure you could obtain it through her agent, who is Harold Ober."

Derleth acknowledges Bowen's death in his letter three days later and praises her work: "Yes, I knew Marjorie Bowen had died. It slipped my mind when I wrote to you, and I imagined it had slipped yours, too, when you wrote previously, since her death. It was itemed in *Time,* and the news service carried dispatches of it on the day of her death. Like yourself, I was very much shocked. I did not know she had broken her arm, but the news dispatches did not mention this fact, nor the cause of her death . . . There are too few writers of her caliber for us to lose any one of them, unfortunately. Certainly I can think of none other who had her creative capacity, and her high level of craftsmanship which was so remarkably consistent."

On 16 January 1953 we find Derleth still musing over what to do with Bowen's stories. "Yes, we gave up the idea of BLACK MAGIC, but I've not yet given up hope of doing KECKSIES. But conditions will simply have to improve before we can hope to go on with such publications. Our British authors have done badly for us."

Finally, on 16 May 1958, Derleth replies to Wagenknecht's note of 13 May and seems to reject finally plans to publish *Kecksies*. "I'm afraid the Bowen will not be done, much as I would like to do it. Our British authors, for all their superiority, simply do not sell well enough for us. . . . I can't go on sinking money into books when I can't get the money out eventually, for I have a family to think of now, and I must consider them."

Kecksies at Last

The short story collection known as *Kecksies* had to wait almost twenty years to see publication from Arkham House. At that time Arkham House was under the leadership of James Turner. It contains a cover illustration by Stephen E. Fabian and twelve stories, all of which are derived from Bowen's previous short-story collections. It is copyrighted by Bowen's son, Hilary Long, and preserves the preface originally written at Derleth's behest in the late 1940s.

Kecksies and Other Twilight Tales, *first edition cover*

Appendix B:
"The Music at Midnight":
The Female Gothic of
Mary Shelley and Marjorie Bowen

John C. Tibbetts
University of Kansas

I begin with two quotations:

> I was thrown entirely upon my own resources, and I enjoyed what I may almost call unnatural pleasures, for they were dreams and not realities. The earth was to me a magic lantern and I a gazer.[1]

> Take care—lest behind all the mummery you find the inexplicable— that dark tangle that lies behind all religion, all philosophy, all faith, all scoffing—that invisible world into which all, however scornful of what they term magic, who wish to explore the recesses of our humanity, must sometimes endeavor to visit.[2]

The first is by Mary Shelley. The second is by Marjorie Bowen. I would argue that their commonality borders on identity. Mary Shelley we know; she was born in 1797 and died in 1851. But who was Marjorie Bowen? That name is a pseudonym of the

---

Presented at "The Gothic, the Abject, and the Supernatural: 200 Years of Mary Shelley's *Frankenstein*," Carleton University, 2019.

1. Mary Shelley, "Mathilda," in *Mathilda and Other Stories* (London: Wordsworth Classics, 2013), 67.

2. George R. Preedy [Marjorie Bowen], *The Courtly Charlatan* (London: Herbert Jenkins, 1942), 76.

British writer Gabrielle Margaret Vere Campbell, who lived and died roughly a century later, from 1883 to 1952. You might wonder if mentioning this obscure writer in the same company as Mary Shelley, whose name recognition far exceeds hers, seems a dubious if not presumptuous undertaking.

Yet here I am, with no apologies, presuming to yoke their names and their work together as citizens in the sisterhood of the Gothic narrative.

I might note at the outset that both women were self-starters who rose above the limitations they faced in their upbringing, education, and professional opportunities. "I believe we are sent here to educate ourselves," Mary Shelley wrote, obeying the mandate of her mother, Mary Wollstonecraft, that women should cultivate reason through education, "and that self-denial, and disappointment, and self-control, are a part of our education" (Journal, October 1838; Sampson 235). Compare this with these words Bowen wrote about her own "education" as an artist and a woman: "I resolved to form my own education . . . I was resigned, without bitterness, to the obvious fact that no one would be able to do anything for me" (*Myself When Young* 52–54).

More precisely, Bowen seems to have felt a commonality of artistry and purpose not just with Mary Shelley but with her mother, Mary Wollstonecraft. Although Bowen never wrote a biography of Mary Shelley, she did write a biography of Wollstonecraft, *This Shining Woman,* in which the then Mary Godwin makes a brief appearance. It's a fine scene, limned in a romantic glow: Summer 1814, in the graveyard of Old St. Pancras Church. The tomb of Mary Wollstonecraft Godwin glimmers in the willow shade. Young Mary is "a slight, sensitive creature in mended gown and worn slippers" who hovers over the gravestone, "where passion lay buried." Described as the daughter of a cold philosopher and a heart-broken woman, "The second Mary knew as much about poverty, the shifts and intrigues of genteel insolvency, the harshness of creditors, the difficulty of raising loans as ever her mother had experienced at her age" (297–98).

Both mother and daughter, as we shall see, may be regarded together as a portrait of Bowen herself.

While both Mary Shelley and Marjorie Bowen garnered considerable fame during their lifetimes, only Mary Shelley has seen her reputation grow apace. While her most famous novel *Frankenstein* continues to attract new generations of scholars and enthusiasts, Marjorie Bowen and her numerous novels, stories, and historical romances have suffered an unmerited obscurity since her death. In my recent book, *The Furies of Marjorie Bowen,* I have attempted to play a small part in rectifying that.

If we struggle to understand the crises of identity and the transgressive impulses that fueled the writings of the outwardly respectable Victorian Mary Shelley, we are likewise confounded by Marjorie Bowen. How and why did this modest, self-effacing, and—like Shelley in her later years—outwardly conventional wife and mother of three children, who survived a wretched, lonely childhood, lacked a formal education, lived through two world wars, endured two troubled marriages, and was perpetually burdened as the principal supporter of house and home, manage such a prodigious output of works, frequently describing them, as did Mary Shelley in her 1831 edition of *Frankenstein,* as "my hideous progeny"?

On one level, the answer is simple enough. Assailed by more than her share of misfortunes, she wrote, like Shelley, out of necessity: "I found myself harnessed to a career of hard work, and I had to earn all I possibly could, to chase every odd five-pound note in order to keep with expenses" (*Debate* 95). On the other hand, again like Shelley, she obeyed the more imaginative dictates of the born storyteller: "I had an inexhaustible fund of invention, a fluent and easy style, a certain gift for colour and drama, and such a passionate interest in certain periods of history that I was bound, in reproducing them, to give them a certain life" (*Debate* 92). And finally, there is a third motivation, more mysterious than the above, and again one sympathetic with Shelley: Bowen's penchant for the dark and infernal. As Jessica Amanda Salmonson, observes: "As fast as the Mirthless Cosmic Jester poured misery into her, [Marjorie Bowen] made ink of bile to fill pages with dark visions, calamitous adventure, and cynical romances—tales populated by innocents and villains alike ill-fated—delightsome unpleasantries to mesmerize her faithful public" ("Rose Petals, Drops of Blood"). Bowen herself declared, "Few or none of these tales I had in my head were pleasant—magnanimous, heroic, lofty, but not pleasant, often full of dark and sinister shades . . . I found that, by writing of dark and gloomy subjects, I rid my mind of them" (*Debate* 84–85). And yet, at the same time, just as Shelley drew upon her inner self, Bowen confesses to a profound *empathy* for her subjects. We find one of her characters voicing her own credo: "As an artist, human material must interest me. I might have to draw a murderer or his victim. I must assimilate their characters" (*For Her to Keep* 91).

Thus, as I will argue, Marjorie Bowen may lay claim to be the literary "heir" of Mary Shelley. Almost a century apart, both women packed into the first twenty-five years of their lives more turmoil, heartache, and literary accomplishment than most writers do in a lifetime. Both grew up, neglected, marginalized, and forced into their own modes of self-education and self-actualization. Moreover, both were especially attuned to "The Music at Midnight," a darkling sympathy for the beauty of terror. More on that in a moment.

MARY SHELLEY (1797–1851) AND MARJORIE BOWEN (1885–1952)

I. OUTLINE OF PARALLEL LIVES:

A. Both endure troubled childhoods and are raised in a dysfunctional home.

B. Both have little formal education and are, to a degree, self-taught—Shelley from reading the works of her father and her late mother; Bowen from visits to museums and libraries. As a result, both miss the feminizing social life normally afforded to young women and as a result undergo an essentially interior adolescence.

C. Both inaugurate their writing careers while in their teens with their most famous novels, *Frankenstein* and *The Viper of Milan*. Both are essentially *Doppelgänger* stories. Both novels trace the fate of two contending characters yoked to a common fate—Shelley's Victor Frankenstein and his creature; and Bowen's Gian Maria Visconti (the Duke of Milan) and Mastino della Scala (the Duke of Verona). While critics were incredulous at the precocity of their female authorship, each gained the praise and support of a famous writer—*Frankenstein* by Lord Byron and *Viper of Milan* by Mark Twain (to whom her second book, *The Master of Stair,* was dedicated). The popularity of both books hamper, to an extent, public recognition of their later works.

D. Both are married to men who are eccentric and, at times, unstable—Mary with Percy Bysshe Shelley and Bowen with Zefferino Emilio Costanza. Both couples leave England to live in Italy. Both women continue to write during difficult circumstances while on the road. Life with the emotionally remote Percy Shelley leaves Mary struggling to write her second novel,

Valperga, a badly needed source of revenue; and in the un-published *Mathilda* a form of emotional therapy.

In her semi-autobiographical novel *Stinging Nettles,* Bowen describes her attempts to write while living with a sickly, demanding husband:

> Your work, your individuality, your chances went by the board, you were swept into another life . . . And with this heavy blight over you, you must work—you'd been fool enough to marry a penniless, sickly man . . . Fool, no doubt—but you thought you loved him, you wanted so desperately to be loved, you dreamed you could make it wonderful. (33)

E. Both lose their first-born within weeks after their births, Shelley's baby girl in 1815 and Bowen's daughter Giuseppina in 1915. Shelley is devoted to her one remaining son, Percy Florence, and will take great care in his raising and education. He stays with her until her death and afterward takes on the role of protecting and promoting her work. Bowen will have three more children, all boys, who survive her. One of the boys, Hilary, will likewise work to protect his mother's work, and just before his death he installs her papers at the Bowen Archive at Yale University. "To be secure, to be able to devote oneself to a happy home of children," Bowen wrote in 1938, looking back on her youth, "to have a large family growing up about one, still seems to me an ideal existence and worth the sacrifice of everything else in the world" (*Myself When Young* 60).

F. Both are widowed in their twenties. Percy Shelley dies of drowning; Zefferino of tuberculosis. Both women, now alone, transform their grief and loss into semi-autographical novels—Shelley's *Falkner* and *Lodore* and Bowen's *Stinging Nettles*.

G. Both return to England where they live out the rest of their lives.

H. Both spend the rest of their lives as the sole support of their families. They work as literary freelancers for a growing market of magazines. Mary Shelley ceases to write anything of substance after 1844. Marjorie Bowen continues to write industriously to the day of her death, in 1952. "I am still absorbed in my own world of make-believe," she wrote a dozen years before her death. "I shall never tell all the tales, describe all the scenes and fantasies that possess me. I sometimes wonder how many will be untold when I am dead" (*Myself When Young* 63).

II. OUTLINE OF PARALLEL WORKS

Mary Shelley and Marjorie Bowen alike secure their popular reputation as writers of a remarkable range of stories, including historical novels, contemporary novels of manners, anecdotal *contes cruels,* biographical portraits, and Gothic thrillers (ghost stories, *Doppelgänger* tales, apocalyptic visions, stories of reincarnation). Taken together, they reveal two writers who revel in a rich, descriptive prose that attends to details of place and scene. I submit that in these works we find elements of autobiography. I unabashedly subscribe to the words of Walter Benjamin. I put them in italics: *"The traces of the Storyteller cling to the story the way the handprints of the potter cling to the clay vessel"* (91–92).

A. Both frequently write about magic and alchemy. Mary was familiar with her father William Godwin's novel *St. Leon,* about a French aristocrat who possesses the secrets of the philosopher's stone and the elixir of life; and her novel *Frankenstein* and short story "The Mortal Immortal" allude to the practices of Paracelsus and Cornelius Agrippa. In a twist, the immortality achieved by the narrator in "The Mortal Immortal" is a "burdensome weight of never-ending time" that forces him to observe the deterioration and death of his wife while he remains healthy. And so he lives on, "alone, and weary of myself—desirous of death, yet never dying—a mortal immortal" (*Mathilda* 306).

Bowen's short stories and novels likewise frequently allude to alchemy and magic. For example, there is the great cycle of related tales, *The Seven Deadly Sins,* which are comic *guignols* in the manner of folk tales; and the short story "—He made a woman" retells the Celtic myth of Gwydion, who conjures the beautiful sorceress Blodeuwedd from twigs and leaves. In addition, two of Bowen's historical novels, *I Dwelt in High Places* and *The Courtly Charlatan,* chronicle the adventures of alchemists and magicians. The former is about John Dee, astrologer to Queen Elizabeth, and his infamous alchemist, Edward Kelley; the latter, about the Comte de St. Germain, magician to the court of Louis XV.

B. Both writers feature characters who are alienated from their times and circumstances. Shelley's *Frankenstein* and the short novel *Mathilda* are prime examples of protagonists destined to die isolated and emotionally stunted. In addition to the well-known plight of Frankenstein's creature, we consider the fate of Shelley's eponymous Mathilda, an outcast:

> Almost from infancy I was deprived of all the testimonies of affection which children generally receive; I was thrown entirely upon my own resources, and I enjoyed what I may almost call unnatural pleasures, for they were dreams and not realities. The earth was to me a magic lantern and I a gazer, and a listener but no actor. (*Mathilda* 67)

From an early age Bowen felt estranged from her overbearing mother and frequently absent father. Scattered throughout her memoir, *Myself When Young,* can be found references that profess to identity and gender confusion—such as: "I did not belong among the people with whom I was forced to mix"; and there is this heartbreaking admission: "When I grew older I realized with great regret, that I was a girl and should be, for the rest of my life, a woman. I regretted this miserable fact because it brought with it a sense of deep inferiority, and all whom I admired and on whom I had tried to mould myself were men" (56). Her most deeply felt novel of alienation is *No Way Home,* published under the pseudonym George R. Preedy. Significantly, this sprawling portrait of post–French Revolution exiles wandering across Europe was written during the years immediately after World War II. Everyone is in ghostly exile from a world that is no longer recognizable. She had kept the home fires burning in London under the shadow of the Blitz, uncertain of the fate of her three sons away at war in Japan, Germany, and North Africa. It was a time when "Home," for all of them, was nowhere to be found. Time seems at a standstill, "neither past nor future existed . . . the present was dim" (70).

C. Both write ghost stories derived somewhat from the model of Ann Radcliffe, the reality of whose apparitions is carefully couched in ambiguity. We are haunted by ghosts of our own making. Shelley's "Invisible Girl" is an effectively atmospheric example about a woman "haunting" a lighthouse. The very reality of her substance is confounded by the illusion which frightens her witnesses. Bowen wrote several hundred short stories, many of which are ghostly in nature, upon which her reputation today chiefly rests, including classics such as "Florence Flannery," "The Crown Derby Plate," and "Dark Ann." Her ghostly novels include *The Devil Snar'd,* about a writer haunted by a book, and *Laura Sarelle,* about an ancestral possession.

D. Both entertain with a certain relish and detail visions of Apocalypse. Shelley's novel *The Last Man* is about a global pandemic, and Bowen's *God and the Wedding Dress* is an historical novel about the plague that ravaged England in the mid-seventeenth century. Two of Bowen's most spectacular fictional apocalypses are *The Haunted Vintage,* in which pagan gods usurp a monastery, and *Black Magic,* about nothing less than the rise of the Antichrist.

E. Both pursue the Gothic trope of the *Doppelgänger*. In addition to the aforementioned famous duality of Frankenstein and his creature, Shelley's most famous example is "Transformation," in which a handsome young reprobate magically exchanges shapes with a grotesque dwarf. He is terrified at his grotesque results and reacts with words that echo those of Frankenstein's creature: "I turned my face to the sun, that I might not see my shadow" (*Mathilda* 206). In a confrontation between the two selves, the grotesque creature is defeated and the handsome man restored to his normal appearance. Bowen's stories are replete with split personalities and alternate selves. Her novel *The Fourth Chamber* features a protagonist dogged by the unpleasant and inconvenient appearances of his double. *The Veil'd Delight* is about a man in love with a woman whose double appears to him in a mirror. And in *"Five Winds"* a man finds himself in love with a woman who herself is a duality of the angelic and the demonic.

F. Both regard themselves as serious biographers of historical British, French, and Spanish figures, with a propensity for fifteenth- and sixteenth-century settings and characters. Shelley is the only female to contribute dozens of essays to several volumes of the *Cabinet Cyclopaedia* in the 1830s. She took biography seriously, drawing upon memoir, anecdote, secondary sources, and her own personal interpretations. A prime responsibility of the biographer, she says, is to indulge in "an exploration of character" (Sampson 233). Similarly, Marjorie Bowen's "straight," stand-alone biographies—including those of William of Orange, William Hogarth, John Wesley, and Mary Wollstonecraft—reveal the imagination of the novelist at work and allow her the latitude of personal opinion and interpretation. For example, among the

Bowen Papers at Yale we find this defense of romantic license in the writing of historical fiction: "There are so many tempting realms of history that have not been exploited, so many themes ready to the hand of the imaginative and romantic writer that lie in the endless records of the past" (Yale, Box 22).

G. Both exemplify the Female Gothic as famously defined by Ellen Moers as a construction wherein women are "examined with a woman's eye, woman as girl, as sister, as mother, as self" (quoted in Heiland 87–88). This is an examination conducted by women themselves—an exploration nothing less than a communion with the self. The words of Katherine Mansfield come to mind: "Come, my unseen, my unknown, let us talk together."[3] In her essay "Women and Fiction" (1929), Virginia Woolf demands we understand these women:

> It is only when we know what were the conditions of the average woman's life—the number of her children, whether she had money of her own, if she had a room to herself, whether she had help in bringing up her family, if she had servants, whether part of the housework was her task—it is only when we can measure the way of life and the experience of life made possible to the ordinary woman that we can account for the success or failure of the extraordinary woman as a writer. (77)

The books that result, however, continues Woolf, inevitably reflect

> women are beginning to explore their own sex, to write of women as women have never been written of before; for of course, until very lately, women in literature were the creation of men . . . If, then, one should try to sum up the character of women's fiction at the present moment, one would say that it is courageous; it is sincere; it keeps closely to what women feel. It is not bitter. It does not insist upon its femininity. But at the same time, a woman's

---

3. Katherine Mansfield, journal entry for 13 November 1921. In *Journal of Katherine Mansfield* (London: Constable & Co. Ltd., 1927), 195.

book is not written as a man would write it . . . The change which has turned the English woman from a nondescript influence, fluctuating and vague, to a voter, a wage-earner, a responsible citizen, has given her both in her life and in her art a turn toward the impersonal. Her relations now are not only emotional; they are intellectual, they are political. The old system which condemned her to squint askance at things through the eyes or through the interests of husband or brother, has given place to the direct and practical interests of one who must act for herself. (81–83)

In sum, both in life and in art the values of a woman are not the values of a man. "Thus, when a woman comes to write a novel, she will find that she is perpetually wishing to alter the established values—to make serious what appears insignificant to a man, and trivial what is to him important. And for that, of course, she will be criticized; for the critic of the opposite sex will be genuinely puzzled and surprised by an attempt to alter the current scale of values" (81).

The immediate strategy of the Female Gothic, concludes Moers, is one in which women impart a feminine perspective on patriarchal societies that thrive on the marginalization and outright repression of women (in Heiland 58–59).

Biology plays a crucial part in these agendas. Many of the narratives of Mary Shelley and Marjorie Bowen are "birth narratives," or "Mother's Stories," derived from their experiences and traumas with the birth and death of children. This sets them apart from other female architects of the Female Gothic—Jane Austen, Emily and Charlotte Brontë, George Eliot—who did not have children. We remember that Mary Wollstonecraft died giving birth to Mary Godwin, that Mary Godwin herself suffered several miscarriages and premature births occurring before and during her writing of *Frankenstein*, and that the mother of the eponymous Mathilda in Shelley's autobiographical novella dies shortly after giving birth. So much ink has been spilled regarding these circumstances that we can hardly add anything here. Such a strenuous study is demanded, however, in the case of Marjorie Bowen, whose fictions reflect her own trauma at the premature death of her own first child, as reported in excruciating detail in numerous stories, her autobiography *The Debate Continues,* and the autobiographical novel *Stinging Nettles.* For both Shelley and Bowen, birth and death, creation and destruction, are everywhere conjoined in their works. "So are monsters born," writes Moers (79).

H. Both offer commentaries and critiques of the status of women in society. The great example of such critiques were Mary Wollstonecraft's *Vindication of the Rights of Women* and her incomplete novel *Maria, or the Wrongs of Women.*

As Donna Heiland points out, [Mary Wollstonecraft "critiques British society with the aim of elucidating and suggesting correctives for women's place within it" (91). As a kind of companion or fictional sequel to *Vindication, Maria* is a highly melodramatic story of a woman falsely imprisoned in an insane asylum by a husband who has brutalized her and taken away their child. In her biography of Wollstonecraft, Bowen described *Maria* as a "medley of unhappy marriages, drunkenness, squalor, poverty, childbirth, the tyranny of the brutal male over the helpless female, the degradation of the very poor, defiance of convention." Wollstonecraft lacked the power, however, continues Bowen, to "enliven" the "gloomy history of the wronged Maria, and there is no attempt at 'atmosphere' save in a very occasional line." Nonetheless, "many years were to elapse before a woman wrote so frankly of sex" (313).

Bowen was right, of course. Despite a lifestyle among her fellow Romantics that is branded as "scandalous," Mary Shelley was relatively ambivalent toward her mother's inflammatory positions on women's rights, the double standard, and the marriage contract. Unlike her, she never wrote any political tracts on the subject. Regarding the "cause of the advancement of freedom and knowledge, of the rights of women," she writes, "I have not argumentative powers: I see things pretty clearly but cannot demonstrate them. Besides, I feel the counter-arguments too strongly" (in Sampson 231).

Moreover, her refusal to grant husband Percy's wish to novelize his play *The Cenci*—a horrific *guignol* of incest and rape, wherein a woman is executed for the murder of her tyrannical father—indicates a timidity toward the violence and tone of such subject matter. Instead, her stories about love and marriage are of a far more genteel nature, like the fantasy of love-fulfilled in "The Dream"; the satiric examinations of fidelity in "The False Rhyme"; and the witty dissections of marriage in "The Mortal Immortal" and the satire on patriarchal culture in *Lodore*. It is only in her novella, *Mathilda,* about a young woman who flees her father because of his incestuous feelings—"I believed myself to be polluted by the unnatural love I had inspired" (*Mathilda* 63)—that she feels free to unburden herself with a more emotionally candid and emotional view of illicit love.

It might be expected that a century later we would find Marjorie Bowen more solidly encamped in Mary Wollstonecraft's example. Indeed, among dozens of handwritten, unpublished essays in her papers at Yale, we find her industriously researching topics like "Efficient Women," "Educated Girls and Marriages," "Is Home Life Monstrous?," "The Modern Mother, "Women in Modern Fiction," and so on. Thus, in her published works dealing with women's issues she indicts social injustice on both sides of the gender divide. For example, in *Stinging Nettles,* which directly addresses feminist activity in the London of the 1920s, she is scornful about certain aspects of feminist thought and behavior, e.g., "women acquiring masculine qualities," and men who "ape the feminine to please the women." The reality is that there are men "really hating the women because they were so unwomanly" and "women really despising the men who were giving in to them." As a result, "all the broad outlines of sex difference are lost, obscured, denied, yet every one, in one way or another secretly centred round sex" (80).

Moreover, like a latter-day August Strindberg, Bowen finds in love and marriage materials for a series of savage attacks on hypocrisy and injustice. It is an extraordinary barrage of stories, *conte cruels* that dissect marriages gone wrong and husbands and wives behaving badly. They are by turns sometimes comic, sometimes farcical, sometimes downright horrific; no one escapes censure (although the women usually gain the upper hand). Her short story "Decay" says it all:

> [Their marriage] was all dead, love, ambition, kindness, the souls themselves, shut in, stagnant; he sold for money, his comforts; she sold for her satisfied lusts, each exacting the price . . . each *hating* the other—no children, nothing let in, nothing going on—putrid, rotten . . . each caged and caught by the other—stinking themselves to Hell. (*Twilight and Other Supernatural Romances* 74)

Victims and victimizers are locked in a deadly symbiosis.

Bowen is just getting started. Writing under the pseudonym "Joseph Shearing," she portrays a series of Victorian women who, upon facing the consequences of patriarchal oppression, limitations on employment, and the rigid requirements of social standing, lash out against their circumstances with the tools of blackmail and murder (including a wide range of deadly poisons). For example, as Bowen observes in *The Lady and the Arsenic,* these women "achieve a double life with the ease of natural duplicity and that elegant feminine dexterity for which hypocrisy is too coarse a word." In the face of criminal behavior, "not even the shrewdest, best-trained legal brains of the day could cope with the fearful complications created by the perverse egotism of the hysteric female desperately anxious to be the center of some powerful drama" (25–27). Bowen's gallery of poisoners, blackmailers, and seducers include Olivia Sacret, Belle Adair, May Tyler, Laura Sarelle, Blanche Fury, Angelica Cowley, Lucile Cléry, Lavinia Pierrepont, and Challis Allen—who all owe their duplicity, their fantasies, and their self-delusions to the figure whom she regards as the definitive example of the notorious and complicated female poisoner of the nineteenth century—Marie Cappelle Lafarge (1816–1852). Ultimately, these emerge as studies in psychopathology and identity confusion:

> Was Marie Cappelle a pathological liar, a fantasy-dweller, one of those criminals who are able to convince others of their innocence because they believe in it themselves? Or was she merely a woman so highly-strung, nervous and excitable as to be almost a dual personality . . . given her pathological state, Marie Cappelle might easily have persuaded herself of her entire innocence. (*The Lady and the Arsenic* 267–69)

But it is important to note that there is a sense of compassion, even empathy, that Bowen infuses into these stories. Significantly, she refuses to condemn her heroines explicitly. Thus, in *Lucile Cléry* we have the title character defending her life of blackmail and extortion with this justification: "Good God! Have I not been trained to be an adventuress? If there is no place for me in society, must I not make one? . . . I have had nothing out of life, nothing at all, my duty to myself is to get all I can" (82).

I. Both women cite among thematic materials the deadly agency of the Furies.

The theme of women who turn the tables against their male oppressors finds their source in the Oresteia trilogy of Aeschylus, wherein the Greek goddesses the Eumenides, or Furies, wreak bloody vengeance against men. Significantly, both Mary Shelley and Marjorie Bowen allude to the Eumenides in their stories. As Shelley's Mathilda begins her story, she advises the reader that this world is "the wood of the Eumenides [where] none but the dying may enter" (*Mathilda* 3); and in "The Invisible Girl," the protagonist is assailed by the Eumenides, "who tormented the souls of men given up to their torturings" (*Mathilda* 261).

Bowen also acknowledged as her muses the Furies of Greek and Roman mythology. Her female characters are rarely helpless. Inspired by the Furies, they give as good as they get. They are creatures of *agency*. More often monstrous aggressors than helpless victims, their murderous intensity and poisonous practices inspire, as already noted, dozens of novels. Thus Bowen, while happily not a poisoner herself—but perhaps under a "chthonian cloud" of her own at times—may be regarded as herself an agent of the Furies.

As both women eschew religious orthodoxy in favor of a personalized Romanticism that deconstructs and materializes divine creation and celebrates the world as a pantheistic confusion and transience, what prevails is the philosophy of Lucretius rather than dogmas of Christianity. Damnation and salvation, evil and grace, death and life all prevail, neither triumphant, neither defeated, but together, ongoing. "To examine the causes of life, we must first have recourse to death," declares Victor Frankenstein. Mary Shelley is the daughter of an atheist, the wife of an atheist, the inheritor of Enlightenment thinkers such as Denis Diderot and the pagan philosophy of the Roman Lucretius. And in her satiric story "Valerius, the Reanimated Roman," we find an outright attack on Christianity. Valerius awakes to a nineteenth-century Rome whose pagan glories have been usurped and "degraded" by a "Catholic superstition" that brought a "change so great, so intolerable, that that one circumstance destroyed all that had arisen of love and pleasure in his heart." He prefers to visit a Pagan temple, "when one feels the existence of that Pantheic Love" which "is the only feeling which animates the soul" (*Frankenstein and Others* 219–20).

Likewise, Bowen writes with an undeniable relish many stories about the pagan usurpation of Christian churches. "They say Pan has left his ruined temple to enter Christian churches and laugh in the face of the marble Christ" (*Black Magic* 273). And she writes with an equally vehement fury the reverse: Her *Carnival of Florence* is a savage indictment of Savonarola's Christian defilement of the glories of the pagan Rome of the Medicis in late fifteenth-century Florence: "'O Florence! O Rome! O Italy!' [proclaims Savonarola], 'the time for singing and dancing is over! . . . Rome shall perish in her wickedness, and in her own abomination shall she stifle!'" (160). Fundamentalist religion is a frequent target. Monasteries, churches, and clergyman are everywhere under siege, as in one of her most powerful novels, *The Abode of Love:*

> "It is the feebleminded who make all religions possible—it is such an old story. Mankind hasn't much power of invention, always the same rubbish—sacrifices, giving God his share of your meal, or cutting God up to eat so that his power passes into you, or turning your natural feelings from another human being towards some image or statue and writing love poems to that instead of to your mate, and going crazy and ill with the strain, always lamb and stars, and prophets and wise men and sacred virgins . . ." (153).

This is matched by her non-fiction critique of orthodox Christianity in her extended essay, *The Church and Social Progress:* "Turn where we will in history, we find that there is no Christian Church and no Christian sect with a record that gives it any right whatsoever to interfere in the affairs of, or to dictate to, the conscience of mankind" (23). Bowen finds a counterbalance, inspiration, and consolation in the once-notorious philosophy of the pre-Christian Roman Lucretius and his *De Rerum Natura*

(On the Nature of Things). Life is accepted for what it is, devoid of illusion, and the world is made more beautiful by its transience, erotic energy, and ceaseless change. In her beautiful story "A Trip to Verona," she cites Lucretius's parable of the "starry veil," wherein a character lost in religious fantasy is urged to throw aside his delusions and confront the material world: "You, signor, have contrived to draw the starry veil, the rosy canopy, so completely over your own existence that your life is entirely artificial, would you not sometimes care to see things in the common light of truth?" (*Bagatelle* 282).

And what about Death; what might lie beyond? Although Shelley's last years display a sturdy Christian example, we find in her stories a profound departure. The eponymous heroine in Shelley's *Mathilda* describes her own impending death as a pantheistic reunion of the corporal body with nature: "The turf will soon be green on my grave; and the violets will bloom on it. *There* is my hope and my expectation" (69). And in "Roger Dodsworth: The Reanimated Englishman," Lucretius is invoked in its rejection of a Christian afterlife: "Change, but not annihilation, removes from our sight the corporeal atoma; the earth receives sustenance from them, the air is fed by them, each element takes its own, thus seizing forcible repayment of what it had lent" (*Frankenstein and Others* 224).

And Bowen? Well, as with Mary Shelley, the precise nature of her spiritual and material self—Apollonian and Dionysian by turns—may never be precisely understood, least of all by her. "Rationalism attracted and convinced her mind," she once wrote, referring to herself in the third person, "but the heart has reasons that the mind knows not of, and she delighted in the mystics, and even at times could believe herself one with the harmony that runs through everything" (*The Debate Continues* 293). Her great friend and champion, Edward Wagenknecht, echoes this ambivalence: "[She] has, indeed, the mind of a skeptic, but she has the heart of a poet and the soul of a saint. Mysticism holds her, even though she cannot quite believe in it." She admits that "it gives me no pain to relinquish the hope of a personal immortality, for I am not fond of my own individuality, and I feel that the best in me is already one with the best in the universe" (297).

In her play *Homage to the Unknown,* a character in the Harlequinade breaks the fourth wall and steps forward to address the audience:

> We return to the earth like blooms nipped by a late frost; fall and are trampled into the field to rise again; and we have been a thousand fanciful shapes, you and I—and shall be another thousand yet. I have embraced you in the mountains of the moon, in the grottoes under the sea, on the clouds beyond the sunset, in twilight groves of Hades, on sweet violet paths of Parnassus—all the Muses assisted at our union, and Apollo played our marriage ode . . . (Bagatelle 186)

I conclude with words that I suggest apply to both Mary Shelley and Marjorie Bowen. Both writers attend to what the poet-cleric George Herbert once called "The Music at Midnight." "I interpret those words," said Bowen in her autobiography, "as the courage to find beauty in dark places" (298).

Works Cited

Benjamin, Walter, "The Storyteller." In *Illuminations.* Tr. Harry Zohn. Ed. Hannah Arendt. New York: Harcourt, Brace & World, 1968. 83–109.

Bowen, Marjorie. *The Abode of Love.* London: Hutchinson, 1944.

———. *Bagatelle.* New York: Dodd, Mead, 1931.

———. *Black Magic.* 1909. London: Sphere, 1974.

———. *The Carnival of Florence.* London: Methuen, 1915.

———. *The Church and Social Progress.* London: Watts, 1945.

———. *The Debate Continues*. As by "Margaret Campbell." London: William Heinemann, 1939.

———. *For Her to Keep*. London: Hutchinson, 1947.

———. *The Lady and the Arsenic*. 1937. New York: A. S. Barnes, 1944.

———. *Lucile Cléry*. 1932. London: Endeavour Press, 2015.

———. *Myself When Young*. As by "Margaret Campbell." London: Frederick Muller, 1938.

———. *Stinging Nettles*. London: Ward, Lock, 1923.

———. *This Shining Woman: Mary Wollstonecraft Godwin*. As by "George R. Preedy." New York: D. Appleton-Century Company, 1937).

Heiland, Donna. *Gothic and Gender*. London: Blackwell, 2004.

Moers, Ellen. "Female Gothic." 1974. In George Levine and U. C. Knoepflmacher, ed. *The Endurance of Frankenstein: Essays on Mary Shelley's Novel*. Berkeley: University of California Press, 1979. 77–87.

Sampson, Fiona. *In Search of Mary Shelley*. New York: Pegasus Books 2018.

Shelley, Mary. *Frankenstein and Others: The Complete Weird Fiction of Mary Shelley*. Ed. S. T. Joshi. New York: Hippocampus Press, 2018.

———. *Mathilda and Other Stories*. London: Wordsworth Classics, 2013.

Tibbetts, John C. *The Furies of Marjorie Bowen*. Jefferson, NC: McFarland, 2019.

Wagenknecht, Edward. *Seven Masters of Supernatural Fiction*. Westport, CT: Greenwood Press, 1991.

Woolf, Virginia, "Women and Fiction." In *Gravity and Rainbow: Essays*. New York: Harcourt Brace Jovanovich, 1958. 76–84.

Appendix C:
A Bibliographical Checklist

Prepared by Edward Wagenknecht, Boston University

[NOTE: This appeared in Professor Wagenknecht's article "Bowen, Preedy, Shearing & Co.: A Note in Memory," *Boston University Studies in English* 3 (Autumn 1957): 181–89. See the complete text in the "Appreciations" section.]

In the appended list, books published by Marjorie Bowen were not marked in any way; books by George R. Preedy are marked "GRP"; books by Joseph Shearing are marked "JS"; other pseudonyms are given in full. When the work listed is not fiction, its character is, I think, made clear by its title.

The original English publisher is given first, the original American publisher (if any), second. No notice is taken of reprints or of Canadian, Australian, etc. editions. Publishers repeatedly referred to are indicated by the symbols listed below.

A	Appleton and Appleton-Century	HS	Hodder & Stoughton
Bl	Basil Blackwood	Hu	Hutchinson
Ca	Cassell	JL	John Lane, The Bodley Head
Co	Collins	McC	McClure, Phillips
DM	Dodd, Mead	Me	Methuen
Du	Dutton	Od	Odhams
Ha	Harpers	R	Alston Rivers
HB	Hurst & Blackett	SB	Selwyn & Blount
He	Heinemann	SD	Smith & Durrell
HH	Harrison-Hilton Books	SH	Harrison Smith & Robert Haas
HJ	Herbert Jenkins	WL	Ward, Lock

This list is as complete and as accurate as I have been able to make. I have worked from the best and completest bibliographical sources available.

The Abode of Love. JS Hu, 1944.
Affairs of Men.[1] Heath Cranton, 1922.
Airing in a Closed Carriage. JS Hu, Ha, 1943.
Album Leaf. JS He, 1933; SH, 1934.
The Angel of the Assassination: Marie-Charlotte de Corday d' Armont, Jean-Paul Marat, Jean-Adam Lux. A Study of Three Disciples of Jean-Jacques Rousseau. JS He, SH, 1935.
Aunt Beardie. JS He, HH, 1940.
The Autobiography of Cornelis Blake, 1773–1810, of Ditton. Se, Cambridgeshire (Sometime Bunker of the Netherlands and Naples)[2] GRP Ca, 1934.

Bagatelle and Some Other Diversions. GRP JL, 1930; DM, 1931.
"Because of These Things . . ." ME, 1915.
Beneath the Passion Flower. GRP American title of *Passion Flower,* which see.
The Bishop of Hell and Other Stories, with an introduction by Michael Sadleir.[3] JL, 1949.
Black Magic. R, 1909.
Black Man, White Maiden. GRP HS, 1942.
Blanche Fury; or, Fury's Ape. JS He, HH, 1939.
Brave Employments. Co, 1931.
Boundless Water. WL, 1926.
The Burning Glass. Co, 1918; Du, 1920.

Captain Banner: A Drama in Three Acts. GRP JL, 1930.
The Carnival of Florence. Me, Du, 1915.
The Cheats. Co, 1920.

---

1. Selections from the author's historical novels, chosen by herself.

2. This work, despite its title, is a novel.

3. Tales of the supernatural, reprinted from earlier collections.

Child of Chequer'd Fortune: The Life, Loves and Battles of Maurice de Saxe, Maréchal de France, Born 1696, Died 1750. GRP HI, 1939.

The Church and Social Progress: An Exposition of Rationalism and Reaction. Watts & Co., 1943.

The Circle in the Water. Hu, 1928.

The Courtly Charlatan: The Enigmatic Comte de St. Germain. GRP HJ, 1942.

The Crime of Laura Sarelle. JS American title of *Laura Sarelle,* which see.

Crimes of Old London.[4] Od, 1919.

Crowns and Sceptres: The Romance and Pagentry of Coronations. John Long. LTD., 1937.

Curious Happenings. Mills & Boon, 1917.

Dark Ann and Other Stories. JL, 1927.

Dark Rosaleen. Co, 1932; Houghton Mifflin, 1933.

The Debate Continues, by Margaret Campbell, Being the Autobiography of Marjorie Bowen. He, 1939.

Defender of the Faith. ME, Du, 1911.

The Devil's Jig. By Robert Paye JL, 1931.

Dickon. HS, 1929.

Double Dallilay. GRP Ca, 1933; A. H. King, 1934.

Dove in the Mulberry Tree. GRP HJ, 1939.

Dr. Chaos; and The Devil Snar'd. GRP CA, 1933.

The English Paragon. HS, 1930.

Ethics in Modern Art. Watts & Co., 1939.

Exchange Royal. Hu, 1940.

Exits and Farewells: Being Some Account of the Last Days of Certain Historical Characters Well-Known in Their Own Times.[5] SB, 1928.

The Fair Young Widow. GRP HJ, 1939.

A Family Comedy (1840): A Comedy in One Act. Samuel French, 1930.

The Fetch. JS Hu, SD, 1941.

Findernes' Flowers. GRP HS 1941.

---

4. Includes "The Seven Deadly Sins."

5. Reprints material from *God's Playthings.*

Five People. WI, 1925.
"Five Winds." HS, 1927.
Fond Fancy. SB, 1932.
Forget-Me-Not. JS He, Ha, 1932.
For Her to See. HJ Hu, Ha, 1947.
The Fourth Chamber. GRP HS, 1944.

General Crack. GRP JL, DM, 1928.
A Giant in Chains. HU, 1938.
The Glen o' Weeping. R, McC, 1907.
God and the King. Me, 1911; Du, 1912.
God in the Wedding Dress. Hu, 1938.
God's Playthings. Smith, Elder, 1912; Du, 1913.
The Golden Roof. HS, 1928.
The Golden Violet. JS He, SD, 1936.
The Gorgeous Lovers. JL, 1929.
The Governor of England. Me, 1913; Du, 1914.
Grace Latouche and the Warringtons: Some Nineteenth Century Pieces (Mostly Victorian). SB, 1931.
Great Tales of Horror, edited by Marjorie Bowen. JL, 1933.

The Haunted Vintage. Od, 1921.
Holland: Being a Survey of the Netherlands Commonly Called Holland. Harrap; Doubleday, Doran, 1929.

I Dwelt in High Places. Co, 1933.
I Will Maintain. Me, Du, 1910
Idler's Gate (La Porte des Faincéants), by John Winch. Co, Morrow, 1932.
In the Steps of Mary Queen of Scots. Rich & Cowan, 1952.

The Jest. Od, 1922.
Julia Ballantyne. GRP HS, 1952.
Julia Roseingrave, by Robert Paye. Been, 1933.

King-at-Arms. Me, 1918; Du, 1919.
A Knight of Spain. Me, 1913.
The Knot Garden: Same Old Fancies Reset. GRP JL, 1933.

The Lady and the Arsenic: The Life and Death of a Romantic, Marie Cappelle, Madame Lafarge, 1816–1852. JS He, 1937; A. S. Barnes, 1944.

Lady in a Veil. GRP HS, 1943.

The Lady's Prisoner, The (juvenile).[6] Bl, 1929.

The Last Bouquet: Some Twilight Tales. JL, 1933.

Laura Sarelle. JS Hu, SD, 1941.

Laurell'd Captains. GRP Hu, 1936.

The Leopard and the Lily. Me, 1920; McC, 1907.

The Life of John Knox. GRP HJ, 1940.

Life of Rear-Admiral John Paul Jones . . . GRP HJ, 1940.

Lovers' Knots. Everett, 1912.

The Love Thief. Od, 1922.

Lucile Cléry, a Woman of Intrigue. JS First American title of *Forget-Me-Not,* which see.

"Luctor et Emergo"; Being an Historical Essay on the State of England at the Peace of Ryswyck, 1697. Northumberland Press, 1925.

Lindley Waters. GRP HS, 1942.

Mademoiselle Maria Gloria (juvenile).[7] BI, 1929.

The Man with the Scales. Hu, 1954.

Mary Queen of Scots, Daughter of Debate. JL, Putnam, 1934.

The Master of Stair. American title of *The Glen o' Weeping,* which see.

Mignonette. JS He, Ha, 1942.

More Great Tales of Horror, edited by Marjorie Bowen. JL, 1935.

Moss Rose. JS He, SH, 1935.

Mr. Misfortune. Co, 1919.

Mr. Tyler's Saints. Hu, 1939.

Mr. Washington. Me, 1915; A, 1912.

My Tattered Loving (The Overbury Mystery). GRP Hj, 1937.

Nell Gwyn: A Decoration. HS, A, 1926.

The Netherlands Display'd; or The Delights of the Low Countries. JL, DM, 1926.

---

6. In the same volume: *The Story of Mr. Bell,* by Geoffrey Boumphrey.

7. In the same volume: *The Saving of Castle Malcolm,* by Madeleine Nightingale.

Nightcap and Plume. GRP HS, 1945.
No Way Home. GRP HS, 1947.

Old Patch's Medley, or a London Miscellany, Being Some Adventures of the Old Gentleman in London City Some Two Hundred Years Ago or So Here Recorded. SB, 1928.
Orange Blossoms. JS He, 1938.

The Pagoda (La Pagode de Chanteloup). HS, 1927.
Painted Angel: A Mystery of the Napoleonic Wars. GRP HJ, 1938.
Passion Flower. Co, McBride, 1932.
Patriotic Lady: Emma, Lady Hamilton, the Neapolitan Revolution of 1799, and Horatio, Lord Nelson. JL, A, 1936.
The Pavilion of Honor. GRP JL, 1932.
Peter Porcupine: A Study of William Cobbett, 1762–1835. Longmans, 1936.
The Pleasant Husband. HB, 1921.
The Poisoners. GRP Hu, 1936.
The Presence and the Power: A Story or Three Generations. WL., 1924.
Primula. GRP HS, 1940.
Prince and Heretic. Me, 1914; Du, 1915.
The Prince's Darling. GRP; American title of *The Rocklitz,* which see.

Queen's Caprice. GRP; American title of *Double Dallilay,* which see.
The Question: A Play in One Act. Samuel French, 1931.
The Quest of Glory. Me, Du, 1912.

The Rake's Progress. Rider, 1912.
The Rocklitz. GRP JL, DM, 1930.
Rococo. Od, 1921.

The Sacked City. GRP HS, 1949.
The Scandal of Sophie Daws (biography). JL, 1934; A, 1935.
Seeing Life! and Other Stories. HB, 1923.
"Set with Green Herbs." Benn, 1933.
The Shadow on Mockways. Co, 1932.
Shadows of Yesterday: Stories from an Old Catalogue. Smith, Elder; Du, 1916.

Sheep's Head & Babylon and Other Stories of Yesterday and Today. JL, 1929.

So Evil My Love. JS; American title of *For Her to See.* which see.

The Soldier from Virginia. American title of *Mr. Washington,* which see.

Some Famous Love Letters, edited by Marjorie Bowen. HJ, 1937.

The Spectral Bride. JS; American title of *The Fetch.* which see.

The Spider in the Cup. JS; American title of *Album Leaf.* which see.

Stinging Nettles. WI, Small Maynard, 1923.

The Stolen Bride. Dickson, 1933.

The Story of the Temple and Its Associations. Griffin Press, 1928.

The Strange Case of Lucile Cléry. JS; later American title of *Forget-Me-Not,* which see.

Strangers to Freedom. Dent, 1940.

Sundry Great Gentlemen: Some Essays in Historical Biography. JL, DM, 1928.

The Sword Decides. R, McC, 1908.

The Third Estate. Me, 1917; Du, 1918.

The Third Mary Stuart: Mary of York, Orange, and England, Being a Character Study, with Memoirs and Letters of Queen Mary II of England, 1662–1694. JL, 1929.

This Shining Woman: Mary Wollstonecraft Godwin, 1759–1797. GRP Co, A, 1937.

To Bed at Noon. JS He, 1951.

Today Is Mine: The Story of a Gamble. Hu, 1941.

The Triumphant Beast: A Tribute, a Confession, an Apology. JL, 1934.

Trumpets at Rome. Hu, 1936.

Tumult in the North. GRP JL, DM, 1931.

The Two Carnations. Ca, P. P. Reynolds, 1913.

The Veil'd Delight (The Rainbow in the Mirror). Od, 1933.

Violante (Circe and the Ermine). GRP Ca, 1932.

The Viper of Milan. R, McC, 1906.

"William, By the Grace of God." Me, Du, 1917.

William Hogarth, the Cockney's Mirror. Me, A, 1936.

William, Prince of Orange (Afterwards King of England): Being an Account of His Early Life Up to His Twenty-Fourth. Year JL, DM, 1928.

The Winged Trees (juvenile). Bl, 1928.

Withering Fires. Co, 1931.

Within the Bubble. JS He, 1950.

World's Wonder and Other Essays. Hu, 1938.

Wrestling Jacob: A Study of the Life of John Wesley and Some Members of the Family. He, 1937.